THE VALE
OF
SILENCE

R. A. FINLEY

This is a work of fiction. All of the characters, organizations, places, and events portrayed are either products of the author's imagination or are used fictitiously. Any resemblance to actual persons, living or dead, is entirely coincidental.

ISBN: 0-9893157-4-6
ISBN-13: 978-0-9893157-4-6
eBook ISBN: 978-0-9893157-5-3

Published by Hickory Tree Publishing

Book Design by R. A. Finley
Cover Design & Artwork by R. A. Finley

10 9 8 7 6 5 4 3 2 1

First Hickory Tree Publishing Edition

THE WHEEL OF THE YEAR

To my mom

And to persistence.

THE VALE OF SILENCE

Thia McDaniel

The recent heir to Eclectica, her great-aunt's store in Granite Springs, and the inadvertent inheritor of the powers of an ancient Celtic goddess.* A novice when it comes to magic (and running a store), she faces a steep learning curve and dangerous road ahead.

Cormac

The son of Idris Cathmor and a *leanan sidhe*. He possesses a dark past, rather questionable morals, and considerable magical ability.

The Society of Brigantium

A powerful London-based secret society dedicated to the study of the occult. Having lately endured infiltration by followers of Idris Cathmor,* the organization is undergoing many changes. Some resent this new order. Others see opportunity.

Arthur Barnstable (*Director*)
Beatrice Meriwether (*Assistant Director*)
Quentin Reynolds (*Agent in Charge: London*)
Edith Wilkinson (*Field Agent*)

Abigail Collins

Eclectica's manager. She has become Thia's close friend and, as a practicing Wiccan with some magical talent, she has been helping her to navigate her new life.

Declan Murphy

An international businessman with dark powers and a mercenary reputation (along with a team of actual mercenaries). He owns the Landmark Hotel and several other local properties.

Kendra Ross

Director of operations at the Landmark Hotel and a member of Murphy's off-the-books team. Good friends with Abby and lately Thia, she helps with Thia's defensive training.

Cassandra Swinton

A disgraced Brigantium agent, she is in their custody for conspiring with her father Idris Cathmor* and for crimes later committed in Granite Springs.**

Skati

The leader of the Rekkrs, a violent motorcycle gang with ties to the criminal underworld. He has mysterious abilities and a grand plan.

Book One: The Stone of Shadows   **Book Two: The Darkest Midnight*

If you play a game of chance, know before you begin

If you are benevolent, you will never win.

William Blake

PROLOGUE

Pine Meadow
Near Granite Springs, Oregon
04 February

Sunset should have blazed over the meadow in brilliant, fiery hues. Reds, oranges, golds. Colors as spectacular as the woman herself had been. That would have been no less than she deserved—which was nothing of this. She should be here; but then none of them would be in this particular location, now, if she were. Thia was aware that this made little sense. So little did, lately.

The time had been chosen to coincide with the setting sun, but unlike some people (one, specifically, had come to mind), no one involved in the planning could do anything about the thick canopy of cloud.

Ladened with threat of yet more snow, it hung low over the long meadow to turn winter's early sunset into an even earlier dusk. There would be no full dark, not with so much reflective white on the ground and surrounding woods. A mix of pines and firs, that was, all of them motionless for the absence of wind. Their needled branches were bowed, burdened by days of excessive, late season storm. Thia felt a sympathetic ache as she studied them with distracted concern. She knew what it meant to carry such a cold, relentless weight; to have more and more piled on until one either bent with it or broke.

Taking a slow, difficult breath, she stepped from the woods to make her way to the gathering set in the meadow's approximate center. Preparations had finished while she'd held back. She hadn't meant to be the last to arrive; she just hadn't been ready. She still wasn't. She kept her eyes downcast, watching her booted feet along the path. Mason jars lined both sides. The candle flames within danced, shining on the clear glass and sparkling on the snow. Snow that muffled and absorbed sound. She heard only the soft, frozen crunch of her steps. The soft rasp of her breath through her scarf. The soft thrum of her blood behind her ears, of her heart in her chest.

Heavy with sorrow, raw with grief. Clichés, but no less accurate. That was how the aftermath of this loss felt, as if the usual buffers from the world's full impact—its overwhelming complexity and fragile impermanence—had been torn away, leaving Thia exposed to a pressure so immense that simply putting one foot before the other felt like an almost impossible slog.

At her approach, the circle of mourners shifted, opening a place between her friend Abby and a man she recognized as a Landmark parking attendant. She stepped in, murmured a greeting. Now that she stood closer, most faces were familiar, with one notable absence. Given the family's opinion of him, though, it was understandable.

Abby, with her gaze fixed on what lay at the circle's heart, reached out her hand. Gloved though it was, this was nonetheless a speaking gesture for someone who, as a rule, shied away from contact. Thia clasped it. Her mitten made the grip awkward.

Instead of the expected withdrawal, Abby kept hold. "This is so hard," she said in the way of a plea, although there was nothing Thia could do. Nothing anyone could do.

Or say.

She gave Abby's hand a gentle squeeze. This *was* hard—yet how much harder for a *best* friend. Abby's eyes, red-rimmed and haunted, were dry. That was a result of effort, Thia knew, because she was making the same. So many tears had already been shed. So many more were to come.

It was time.

A single, solemn ring of a bell had her turn to face forward, into the circle. She could no longer avoid what had brought them all here: The timber and brushwood pyre and what had been laid so carefully upon it. Even now her mind balked and her eyes wanted to rebel. But looking away would not change what had happened. As impossible as it continued to seem, this was reality. Unacceptable yet undeniable.

The body had been wrapped in undyed silk and laid upon cedar branches.

Thia's gaze went unerringly to the top, where the familiar face would be and she braced herself, afraid of both what she would see and of her response . . . but nothing was visible beneath the shroud.

That made for a different kind of trauma and, irrational as she knew it to be, she couldn't help worrying that not enough air could pass through the cloth, that the artfully bound strips were too tight. Stifling. But of course none of that mattered.

What lay there so impossibly still did not breathe, did not feel. It was merely what remained.

Five days earlier...

CHAPTER 1

As the lone occupant of the pub's front corner table, Cormac had a wall at his back and a clear view of the door. The Cobbler's Findings was that sort of establishment—the sort where such precaution was advisable. And because his was that sort of life, potential exit routes had been scouted before his first trip to the carved, oaken bar. By the time his pint had been pulled, those routes plus two more had been assessed for convenience and likelihood of success. Ranked thusly, they sat in the back of his mind much in the way he sat now, waiting for the action to start.

Patience had been a painful lesson of his youth. Well over two centuries later, it remained more a matter of determination than inclination. An inherently impatient man playing a role.

He allowed himself an inward smile. Technically, he played the role of a man as well, since his blood and talents contained a vital inheritance from his Otherworldly mother. Man and *leanan sidhe*, he was. Both yet neither. It made him adept at pretense—and at identifying the like in others.

Good thing, considering why he had come all this way to County Kerry.

His timing could have been better. Torrential rain and gale force winds had battered the whole of the western coast for two days.

Through the bank of mullioned windows on his right, he kept an eye on the flooding street and beyond, where Dingle's mid-sized harbor was crowded with trawlers of all sizes and conditions, all bobbing wildly on the bay's dark, choppy water. Even the most intrepid fishermen had been forced ashore, for which the pub could credit the brisk mid-afternoon business along with the pervading odors.

The front door opened on a rush of sound, letting in such a force of cold, briny air that empty packets of crisps blew off the nearest tables. Three more fishermen—large ones— stomped inside. Water cascaded down their yellow slickers as if they had come from the sea itself.

They fought the wind to get the door shut. It took all three together along with a stream of profane bickering. Croatian, Cormac thought it was. Afterwards they laughed, wide smiles splitting the wet shag of their beards. The brawniest took a good-natured punch to the shoulder and then, intent on the bar, they began to wend their way between overfilled tables. The noise level, having dropped when wary interest shifted to their arrival, rose again.

Tension remained high.

With deliberate unconcern, Cormac returned his outward gaze to the newspaper crossword on his table and penned an answer. He kept his inward gaze—his Sight, it was called— directed at his surroundings.

Where the winter storm took away opportunity in the form of fishing, it put in place another that was potentially more lucrative: Smuggling.

He had spent countless hours in places nearly identical to this. He knew there were three types of players present. The first and largest in number were fishermen who could be had if the money was right—and it almost always was. With the climate's future proving to be inescapably volatile for north Atlantic fisheries, the numbers of ships-for-hire had swelled exponentially.

Next were the thrill seekers, those who thrived on danger. Maybe they had started out with good intentions; maybe a criminal record made finding other work too difficult. Maybe they had learned the trade when The Troubles were at their peak and this was how they kept their glory days alive.

Cormac knew how potent a drug danger could be. Raised to be of service to Idris Cathmor, when he had come of age, he had been put toward "acquisitions." Objects, information, people—all by any means necessary. He had spent the greater part of his Otherworldly-extended life being both thief and confidence artist, in and out of some level of danger on the regular.

It was who and what he was.

He had, in the shock and lengthy aftermath of Idris's death, lost sight of that. He was returned to it now, like slipping back into a familiar autumn coat after a long, bewildering summer.

The third type, present here as surely as one or two had been present in the other places visited in his search, were not like him. They were worse.

He lifted the pint to his lips, used the act as another chance to survey the room. The winter ale—this was his third—was surprisingly pleasant. Smooth with a complex finish.

The back of his neck prickled.

Idly, he set down the glass and, angling his head, met the bartender's dark-eyed stare. The latter wiped hands the size of hams on the apron tied around his barrel of a middle and turned away to pull more ales for the Croatians. But Cormac did not miss the subtle tip of the chin given to another dark-eyed watcher across the room. This one was seated much as he was: back to a wall; half-finished glass and newspaper on his table.

The prickling of Cormac's neck became a buzz. Full alert. He eased his grip on the glass and, with deceptive calm, took up his pen to resume working the puzzle. The man across the room pulled out a smartphone. One touch of the screen and a call was placed.

It did not last long. A few words spoken with lips too stiff to be read. Another touch of the screen and the mobile was set down beside the folded paper. The bulge in the latter could have been anything: a pack of cigarettes; a gun.

Cormac, having left off using any glamours or other means of disguise, had no doubt that he'd been recognized—either from prior awareness or a database accessed from that very phone. In these modern times with CCTV and widespread addiction to posting on social media, he continued to do his best to limit exposure. Likely, few images of his true appearance existed, despite his recent lapses. But exist they did and he used that deliberately here.

He lifted his head, met the other man's stare full on. Amber flickered in it, a show of power too quick to be a threat. More like an acknowledgment. Cormac didn't bother with a show of his own; the man was a gatekeeper only. Outside, as framed by the windows, a sleek luxury sedan pulled to a halt.

The arrival did not go unnoticed throughout the pub. Talk dropped to a low, nervous hush or ceased altogether. No one looked directly at the door, yet all waited for it to open.

It did, easily despite the storm, and was then just as easily closed. The small man it had admitted wore no raincoat, but not so much as a drop had touched his crimson pinstriped suit.

His diminutive stature and bright red hair in combination with the golden buckles on his heeled leather shoes left no question as to his identity. More gold gleamed on the buttons of his coat and, given how it acted in the light, in the fabric itself.

Cormac had expected someone higher up to be called, but

not *this* high. It was both intriguing and troubling.

The room was stillness itself while the O'Shannon wended his way to the bar. Once there, he greeted the bartender with simple familiarity.

"Rory." His high-pitched voice fit his size—five feet at the most—but was nevertheless discordant given the amount of power he carried.

"O'Shannon." The bartender turned to his left and, from a special shelf, took down a bottle of whiskey and a cut crystal tumbler. He set them on the bar, pushed them to the front edge. The O'Shannon took both—the gold of multiple rings glinting on his blunt-tipped fingers—and with a quick pivot, headed directly for Cormac.

Bright green eyes sparkled beneath bushy, ginger brows as, above the Donegal-style beard, a smile began to creep its way into being.

"My, my," came that treble, sing-song voice and a chill skittered down Cormac's spine. To cover for it, he used his foot to push out the table's other chair, opposite. His hands remained as they had been since the O'Shannon had entered: flat on the table in the accepted gesture of "no threat intended." When lethal magic could be called to one's hands in an instant, it certainly wouldn't do to raise them.

The O'Shannon nimbly sat. His smile widened to reveal a shiny gold tooth. "You're looking quite . . . *yourself* on this fine afternoon, Idris Cathmor's son."

Cormac's jaw clenched on a flare of resentment. Ever in his father's shadow. Ever his instrument.

The O'Shannon chortled, having so easily won a reaction. Nudging aside Cormac's newspaper and pen, he put his glass down to then deftly unscrew cap from bottle. "I'd offer condolences on your loss," he said, pouring himself two generous fingers of whiskey. "But as I'm thinking you found it no loss at all, I'll save the breath." He recapped the bottle, set it aside.

Then, with a pointed glance at Cormac's hands, he raised the glass in toast. "*Sláinte.*"

Taking that as a grant of permission, Cormac took up his pint for a welcome swallow.

"Well, now." The O'Shannon set his glass beside the bottle. Crossing his arms, he leaned forward. No fewer than seven gold buttons ornamented each cuff. "Never did I think you'd be sitting plain as day here in my own place of business. So when word of that very thing reached me, I said to meself—O'Shannon, I said, there's bound to be good reason, for the boy isn't stupid—not like your cousin Diarmuid or the *eejit* your sister married. No, I said, Idris Cathmor's *Cormac* wants something, he does, and you'd best get down there to find out what that is."

The joviality was a mask, Cormac well knew. Everyone did, which was why the tone of conversation in the pub remained hushed if not outright cowed.

Slowly, Cormac withdrew a leather pouch from his jacket, draped over the arm of his chair. He held his hand out, over the table, and let the pouch drop. It hit the table with a thud. The metal within clinked faintly.

The O'Shannon swept it up with the speed of a dibstones champion. He gave it a little shake, his head cocked. "Brass?"

"Naturally."

The flash of the O'Shannon's grin revealed two more of his infamous gold teeth. With quick, avaricious tugs, he loosened the drawstring, then shook the pouch over his cupped hand. Several of the twelve dozen cobbler's nails dropped out. He made a hum of appreciation. "You have more of these?"

"I do."

"Ah. Well, then." With a wave of one hand above the other, nails and pouch vanished. "Let's step into my office, shall we?" Giving no time for objection, he rapped two knuckles on the tabletop.

Everything around Cormac and the O'Shannon froze like a paused television program. People were caught mid-gesture, some with pint glasses tipped to their mouths, the beer they had intended to drink no longer flowing. On the hearth, the flames stood as if sculpted. Outside, raindrops hung like beads on invisible threads. Not a single ship moved in the harbor. The waves, the storm, all of it suspended. All of it, silent.

The O'Shannon's office, as it were. Not so much a where as a when. A place outside of time.

When one was caught up in this particular Otherworldly trick, the hardest adjustment to make was not to the disconcerting visuals and absence of sound outside the—well, it was referred to as a "fairy circle," but that was a bit of a misnomer; for one, it was spherical, surrounding its occupants in every extent.

It took away the *feel* of all that lay beyond. *That* was what made adjustment difficult—the absence, and the conflicting sensations which resulted: One of the world closing in; the other of being entirely adrift.

The O'Shannon took up the whiskey bottle. The scrape of the metal cap seemed overly loud. The clink of glass against glass. The splash of liquid.

"I hope you won't be wanting another just yet," he said with a nod toward Cormac's nearly finished pint.

It wasn't that Cormac couldn't pick it up and drink—he was as free to move as the O'Shannon—but he could not leave the circle. There would be no refill.

"I'm fine."

That got a merry laugh. "If you were fine, boy, you'd not be calling out the likes of me. You aren't usually so obvious." A greedy light entered his eyes. "You must want whatever it is very much indeed."

Usually these things were an intricate dance of allusion and subterfuge. But, as had just been observed, Cormac had been unusually obvious. Might as well keep to it.

"The Achill Bell."

Smile gone, the O'Shannon tipped back in his chair.

"For a start," Cormac added, and then finished his ale. It did nothing for the dryness of his throat. His hand was steady, at least. He schooled his expression to one of amusement. The bitter kind. "I assume you've heard about Idris's collection."

"About it not being where it ought? Mm." The O'Shannon's fingers drummed the table. "To hear it told, all of Fiend's Fell sits empty." He referred to Idris's mountain stronghold, used for centuries to house the man himself and the main of his unnaturally extended (and abruptly ended) life's work. Relics, grimoires—any and everything that might be of use in ritual magics.

It had been Cormac's life's work as well. Work he had been raised to do. *Made* to do, with the expectation of inheritance serving as the only light in times of extreme dark.

Earned through his labors and his blood, the collection was rightfully his.

"'Tis the general notion that you're behind the clearance," the O'Shannon said, offhand. "After all, you killed the man."

Cormac jerked hard on the reins of his temper. He would not give the O'Shannon the satisfaction of having provoked another response. Strictly speaking, Cormac had not been in control of the power that had flowed through him as he and Idris fought. The Society of Brigantium had. They had used him as a conduit.

Yet the O'Shannon was technically correct, and in Cormac's line of work, to be seen as capable of patricide was a plus.

"For myself," the O'Shannon offered into the stillness, "I'd wondered what took you so long."

"Risk assessment."

"Sure, fair enough." A twinkle in his eyes, he swigged his whiskey. "Did you really call down a storm—and on *Insi Orc,* no less?"

"On Samhain?" Cormac scoffed. "That would be a foolish thing to do." And just as foolish to admit to it.

"Indeed." Grinning, the O'Shannon steepled his beringed hands. "Ah, but I do enjoy dealing with you, Cormac son of Idris. Should anyone hear of such doings that night, it won't have come from me." He winked. "Not for a time, yet. Longer, if you make it worth my while."

Information with a side of blackmail.

"The Achill Bell," Cormac insisted. "Whatever you have on it. Then we can discuss compensation. For the *assistance*." To suggest payment was for anything else would be tantamount to an admission—as the O'Shannon had intended.

Never trust a leprechaun.

"I'd be wanting it in the form of a good turn," the latter said. "Your skills in . . . *procurement,* shall we say."

Never trust a leprechaun and—above all—never owe one a good turn. Unless the alternative was worse.

"All right—*if,*" Cormac emphasized, "your information is of equal value."

Glee immediately suffused the O'Shannon's face. "Oh, 'tis grand! Absolutely grand." Clapping, he bounced on his seat. "What I can offer holds great value. A great deal, indeed."

Dread was a warning Cormac had no choice but to disregard; he was here because he was running out of options and time, both. He needed the Achill Bell to fulfill a bargain made weeks ago. A bargain made upon pain of death.

He arched a brow.

So it was done. The O'Shannon lifted one hand. A slim red book materialized in his grasp. He set it on the table and with one ringed finger, slid it forward.

Cormac picked it up. The weight of the good turn owed was made manifest, borne on sheets of vellum bound in crimson leather.

A great deal, indeed.

Pub sounds flooded in. Conversation. Thuds of glass upon wood. The outside roar of the storm. Cormac looked up from the book. All around, activity had resumed.

The O'Shannon stood, and the tumbler and whiskey bottle vanished from the table. A glance showed them to be back on their special shelf.

"It has been a pleasure, Idris's *Cormac*," the O'Shannon said, again putting malicious stress on the name. With a laugh, he spun on the heels of his fancy shoes and headed for the door.

Across the room, the man who had been watching rushed to get there first. He held it open.

"I'll be in touch," the O'Shannon said over his shoulder, and left. His lackey followed.

With door's closing, the atmosphere lightened. The book in Cormac's hand did not. It remained damnably, menacingly heavy. He laid it on the table.

Only after the O'Shannon's car drove away did he open to the first page of barely legible scribbles. As if Gaelic was not challenging enough in written form, the dialect was Munster Irish. An intentional choice, no doubt, to make things more difficult.

Leprechauns.

Cormac wanted another pint.

CHAPTER 2

"**I** have no idea what I'm doing," Thia said when she and Abby entered Eclectica's upstairs café. That was a phrase she had been using with distressing frequency of late, either out loud or repetitively to herself. Usually it related to spell-casting or otherwise wielding the dangerous magical power she had not asked for and could not reliably control.

Today, however, in what could be considered a refreshing change, it related to the running of the popular retail business she had never expected to inherit from her great-aunt Lettie.

Specifically, she and Abby were to hold interviews for the combined positions of café manager and baker. The post had been vacant since shortly after the previous holder had been used as leverage in an extreme act of revenge. (The same act which had culminated at the city's winter parade and severely damaged a lengthy stretch of Main Street.) Zoe's need to start a new life in Portland was understandable—had, in fact, been encouraged—but the timing added to what was already an intensely stressful situation.

Stressful situation. Also known as Thia's New Normal.

"Comfy chairs or table?" she asked Abby. With the morning beverage rush over, they had their pick of the whole café.

Longer than it was wide in order to accommodate kitchen, restroom, and storage areas, the space could be described as *intimate.* Less favorable would be to call it *small.*

Two pairs of comfy chairs bracketed a single row of bistro tables along the exterior, exposed-brick wall while a second row ran through the room's center. Parallel to that and before the kitchen divide was a lit refrigerated case and short counter with four padded stools. A few larger tables had been placed outside all of this in what was a sort of vestibule between the café, the Rowan Space (where classes, psychic readings and other special events were held), and the dog-legged staircase to the retail floor below.

"Table," Abby decided, moving past. Her usual riot of black curls had been pulled into a bun at her nape. The impression was business-like and surprisingly intimidating. She set her plaid work tote on the middle table, directly across from the counter, then began rearranging chairs. Two on one side, to face the entrance from the back patio, and a third—culled from a neighboring table—on the other. Its occupant would have a clear view of the empty bakery case and "please ring for service" sign and bell.

Other than three predictable times each day, café business had become so sparse that to staff it full time was a waste. It was a temporary problem, with two of the probable factors to resolve soon. The area's reconstruction hassles were far less than they had been, and reports were that almost all major repairs were on track to finish by the middle of February— believe it or not—only a couple of weeks away. Tourist season would begin a few weeks later, after the Shakespeare Festival opened its new run of shows. The third factor was the most obvious, and the most under their control: the lack of Zoe's baked goods. With the other resolutions on the horizon, it was time to fill the open position.

Unfortunately, qualified bakers were thin on the ground, and there hadn't been much out-of-area interest so far. Spooked, maybe, by the recent attack. Today's interviews would be the first.

While Abby took the left chair for herself and removed a legal pad and pen from her tote, Thia's insecurity increased. Three interviews had been scheduled. Why hadn't it occurred to her to take notes? She had nothing at all. And what if she got thirsty?

The glossy, cherry red espresso machine beckoned from its showcase position behind the counter.

"I could use a mocha," she said, heading over. "Can I make you anything?"

"Actually, I thought we could have the candidates prepare drinks from the menu. If things are going well." Abby pulled a typed page from within the legal pad. "And I wrote up some questions."

"Oh. Perfect." Thia wasn't sure whether to be grateful for her friend's managerial skills or embarrassed by the obvious lack of her own. But Abby *was* a manager; Thia's background was in graphic design and website creation. She had always been a job interview-*ee,* not an -*er.* She reversed course.

"I have an extra pen." Abby volunteered, and bent to dig into her tote on the floor beside her chair.

"That's great. Thanks." Thia sat beside her and angled the list so she could read. "You should probably take the lead on this first one, right, so I can get a feel for—"

The door opened. Silhouetted against the morning bright-ness was a giant with a mass of writhing tentacles in place of a head.

At Thia's shocked gasp Abby jerked upright, gripping a ball-point pen like a weapon. "What?" She didn't sound nearly as alarmed as she ought. "What is it?"

Thia didn't know. She had only recently begun her folklore studies. Getting control of the relatively new-to-her magical powers before she injured herself and those around her had taken priority. She might guess this was a gorgon—familiar only because one was depicted on the protective pendant she wore—if what she had initially identified as tentacles were in fact snakes.

Maybe there was no danger, no matter what this was. Her pendant remained dormant against her skin. Had it sensed a threat, it would have heated. Then again, it could not detect every possibility, and there were so many.

Followers of the sorcerer Idris Cathmor saw Thia as instrumental in his death and the collapse of a scheme to take over the Society of Brigantium. His daughter Cassie hated her for that plus killing Cassie's twin brother (never mind that they had been trying to ritually sacrifice Thia or that he had been the one who had decided to tackle her while she held a knife). Cassie was behind December's parade attack, and had promised to try that sort of thing again.

Or this strange being could be from the Otherworld. He could have heard that Thia possessed some of the Cailleach's power, and he had come to take it.

"If we run, will it chase us?" she whispered to Abby, who frowned in obvious confusion.

"What are you talking about?"

The answer was self-evident, or should have been. Was it visible only to Thia? She was about to point when the figure took two steps inside, allowing the door to close and shut out the backlighting sun.

Not tentacles or snakes but dreadlocks. The white-blond, fuzzed-out tubes were of immense size and disarrayed scope with tips dyed Cookie Monster blue. Astonishing, sure, but dangerous?

Probably not.

They belonged to a young man, twenty-five, twenty-eight at the most. He blinked a few times. "Oh, hey."

He must have needed to adjust to the change in lighting,

too. The interior, to use the same kindness as with its size, was "comfortably shadowed." In other words, it could be hard to see when coming in from a sunny day.

"Hello," Thia greeted with outsized enthusiasm. Relief was causing her to overdo it, and Abby gave her another frown. "Are you Leo? Leo Deakins?"

"Yeah, that's me." His approach set the tubes of hair into a wild motion that persisted several seconds after he stood at the table. His face had the look typical of local snowboarders: Ruddy cheeks above a scruffy beard and a pale, goggle-shaped band of skin across the whole of his eye and brow area. "Are you who I'm meeting?"

Blended scents of tobacco and a formerly illegal substance tickled Thia's nose. She glanced at Abby, whose face was now carefully blank.

Thia extended her hand. "I'm Thia McDaniel. Nice to meet you."

"Hey."

She endured an awkward clasp: more fingers than palm and too much grip. Oily, but that could have to do with baking, she supposed. When it was over, she lowered her hand beneath the table, casually rubbed it on the dun-colored wool of her pants.

"Shall we?" Abby gestured for him to sit as planned across the table. "I'm Abigail Collins. I manage the retail space." She did not offer her hand. She never did with strangers.

Leo spun the wooden chair around, straddled it, and then proceeded to unwind miles of macramé scarf from around his neck. The activity set his hair into renewed motion. Up close, it revealed itself to be a mix of cords and mats. He dropped the scarf to the ground, unbuttoned his patchwork coat.

"This is the whole deal, huh?" His red-rimmed gaze flicked from one side of the narrow room to the other. He did not seem to approve.

Nor, it seemed, did Abby. Her response was clipped. "Yes. Kitchen and storage, there." She pointed her pen at the pass-through window in the wall behind the counter. "Eclectica takes up the rest of this floor and all of the main."

"Oh, right." Leo's attention had traveled the counter and was somewhere near the espresso machine. "Gene said this was part of a toy store."

"Toys?" Thia cleared her throat, got her voice back down to its usual alto. "There are specific things for kids, sure, and others they might like but, no, we're not a toy store. Mystical, New Age, folklore-themed products, seasonal gifts." Not to mention occult supplies, potions, herbs. She figured he'd get the wrong idea about the herbs.

"Who's Gene?" asked Abby, and Leo's attention drifted to her.

"He's, um. He's a dude from . . . uh." Eye contact made, he fell into a curious, unblinking silence.

"A dude from . . . ?" Abby prompted, holding his gaze. In the café's low lighting, her eyes appeared violet. That might be enough to stun him into silence, Thia supposed. It was such a rare color.

"He comes into Total Basic a lot. Told me you guys—sorry, you gals had an opening."

"Total Basic?" Thia tried to recall what he'd written on his application. She should have reread it before his arrival. She would do that with the others, after this finished. Abby probably had them in her tote. "That's the restaurant where you work now?"

He blinked. "Yeah. It's a—"

"How did Gene know Eclectica had an opening?" Abby was oddly intense.

"Um." Leo's shrug set his hair briefly bobbing. A fresh waft of scent tickled Thia's nose. "I guess he heard about it."

"What's his last name?"

"Gene's?" He shrugged again. "No idea."

"And he, what, just offered this information to you? Out of the blue?"

"About the job? Uh . . . maybe? No, wait. I might've said something about wanting to branch out." The poor guy had broken out in a sweat.

Abby was turning the interview into an interrogation, but why? They had advertised the job opening. It wasn't a secret.

Thia took pity on him. "Total Basic is that raw food and juice bar near the university?" At his nod, she went on. "I can imagine that would feel a bit limiting."

"Yeah, I guess."

Abby tapped her pen. "So you mentioned to Gene No Last Name that you wanted to leave, and he told you Eclectica had an opening that might suit?"

"Um." Leo swiped at a dreadlock that had dropped in front of one eye. "It's not totally that I want to leave. I mean, like, there's a simplicity there—you know, *basic*—that's cool. But, yeah, he told me about this place and I thought, 'Wow, a café in a toy store. That'd be a trip.' And to be a manager would be a good career move, right? So I had to check it out."

"And now that you have?"

"And learned that Eclectica is not a toy store?" Thia added gently.

"Yeah, uh . . . ." He took another visual tour. Lace curtains over high windows; well-loved vintage furniture that served as condiment and utensil stations; local art on the walls. This month's installation—panels of crewelwork depicting Pacific Northwest wildflowers—had been stitched by one of Abby's fellow coven members. The work was exquisite. Leo finished his perusal. "It's kinda small."

"Thanks for coming in," Thia said. She'd told Abby to take the lead, but enough was enough. "We'll be in touch."

"Oh. That was quick." His smile was toothy. He leaned over

to retrieve his scarf. "Cool."

Leo Deakins wasn't right for the job. Anyone could see that. Except him, which was part of the problem.

"Thanks again," Thia said as he got to his feet.

"Sure, yeah. Good talk." He rewound the scarf around his neck. "Oh, hey—I remember now. Gene said he heard about the opening from a girl he's been seeing. She works here, I guess."

"You guess?" Abby asked.

He nodded, dreadlocks springing. "Yeah. I've seen her with him a few times. About this tall"—he indicated a height of about six feet—"with a ton of different colors in her hair. And it was, like, piled up with fancy sticks poking out."

"Samantha," Thia said. One of the part time clerks. Such a hairstyle wasn't uncommon in Granite Springs, but the height made the identification more likely.

"Cool," Leo said. "She'd probably know his last name."

"Yes, probably," she managed with a straight face. After he left, she turned to Abby. "What was that all about? It was like good cop, bad cop."

"I'm sorry." Abby set down her pen. "I got a weird feeling after he said the name Gene, so I thought maybe that was someone we should be concerned about. I don't know." She shook her head. "It was an overreaction."

"No," Thia said, remembering her own. Besides, Abby had a history of being right. "What kind of weird feeling?"

"A murky one." Abby sighed. "Murkier than usual."

She denied having psychic abilities, but she had *something*. The way she described it, a vague premonition might come out of nowhere, or she might pick up on someone's emotions or a single, stray thought. A kind of talent, she called it, but not one she could use well.

"A feeling like something bad might be coming or is already here," she continued. "That someone is working against . . .

I don't know. Us? The store? Or it could have nothing to do with us, just a chance feeling. Gene could be about to break up with Samantha," she said lightly—only to become serious again. "We might want to see if we can strengthen Eclectica's wards tonight. And on your house, too. Just in case."

● ○ ●

An Daingean, Ireland

With the little red book secure in a zippered jacket pocket, Cormac pushed out into the storm. The storm pushed back with fierce, rain-laden wind straight off the Atlantic. Not two steps from the pub and he was drenched. That and the biting cold justified a quick pace. He wouldn't want anyone to think he hurried for another reason.

Muttering profanely, he zig-zagged over to the car park.

He'd had enough of being watched. And, after weeks spent traversing it, enough of Ireland. He had not slept under his own roof in . . . months? It spoke volumes that he could not immediately recall.

His mutters and the splashing slaps of his half-boots were lost in the combined noise of wind and wave. The sea itself had forced its white-capped way through the harbor's mouth to beat against the docks and cause even the largest trawlers to strain against their moorings. Metal clanged and creaked— and crashed when a dumpster slammed, windblown, into the side of an equipment shed.

By the time he was wrestling the key to the rental Peugeot from his trousers, the latter had soaked up three times their weight in water, adhering to him like a second, ice-cold skin. He used the fob to unlock the driver's side door as he neared. The reflections of the overhead lights danced on the rushing wet of the tarmac.

With the back of his hand, he swiped at the rivulets running down his face, a move that allowed for a more thorough scan of the area. A confirmation, specifically, of what had caught his eye upon leaving the pub: Near the harbourmaster's office at the far end of the car park was the same Range Rover that had dogged his travels since Killarney.

He could use a spell to open the Peugeot's door, have it ready for him to slide inside without pause. Had he been alone, he would have done. Since he wasn't, he used the handle. Much could be revealed by one's use of magic and he wasn't about to offer that sort of opportunity.

The wind caught the door and, after Cormac flung himself into the seat, made the closing of it a wrestling match.

Rain sheeted down the windows, blurring the Rover's image in the rear mirror. Model and color were common enough. If the men inside had bothered to change the number plate, the vehicle would have been unremarkable. Either they were incompetent or they wanted to be noticed—presumably as a method of intimidation.

Their identities weren't needed in order to surmise intent. As word continued to spread about Idris's missing collection, Cormac could consider them the tip of an iceberg.

After his Sight assured him that the protections around the Peugeot remained strong, he shut his eyes. Concentrated.

"*Ádrúwe.*"

The water evaporated from his skin and clothes while the pool that had formed at his feet shrank rapidly, soon to be as if none of it had ever been. He opened his eyes, put his hair to rights with a quick drag of his hand. Then he took out his smartphone.

Face ID unlocked the home screen; a single touch opened the app for Holpnick's leyline charts. It wanted permission to use location data. He granted it, then watched the map zoom in on the Dingle Peninsula. Two blinking red pins marked the nearest portals. Only one of those could be ridden eastward. It was a direct line—one entry, one exit.

His destination would be obvious, and he could no longer

afford company. The time had come to make a statement.

He shut the app, pocketed the phone. As it happened, he knew just the place.

He stuck the key in the ignition, turned it over. Heat began to rush from the vents as the engine purred. He watched in the mirror while he turned on the headlamps, flicked on the back window's wiper, and released the handbrake.

The Rover remained dark.

He put the Peugeot in gear, drove out of the car park and past the pub. The latter's windows showed a clear view of the table where he had been seated, now occupied by the Croatian fishermen.

At the edge of town, he eased the car through the flooded roundabout and onto the regional—not the national—road. Both ultimately led to the same destination, but the regional did it via Connor Pass. Treacherous in the best of conditions, in these it could be deadly.

Would be.

The mirrors picked up a pair of lights. The Rover, trailing at considerable distance.

Outside town, along a stretch of outlying farms, it dropped back further, visible only in the straightaways between more and more frequent sequences of curves.

The incline increased as the road narrowed. To the left was sheer rock, the exposed face of a mountain that bisected the peninsula. To the right was an aged wall of stacked stones, fragments of that same mountain, carved off to allow for the road and then arranged to give an impression of safety. Sure, it might save a pedestrian or cyclist from going over, but a car? Cormac's jaw set as he accelerated around a sharp bend.

While he had never driven this stretch, he had flown over it some years ago. He knew the layout well enough, and exactly what he wanted.

Pinpoint flashes gave the Rover's location. Five, maybe six

minutes behind at current speeds.

This high on the pass, snow mixed with the rain and the wind had gained the force of a gale. The Peugeot shimmied, its tires fighting to grip the slick tarmac despite the traction charm he had crafted earlier.

By day this was one of Ireland's most scenic drives, offering expansive views of rolling hills and lakes far below, all the way to where sea met sky at the horizon. Tonight, with the storm to block out the moon and stars, nothing existed beyond the reach of the car's beams.

The road widened to form one of its rare pull-outs. The last one before the peak.

A few feet beyond, he stomped on the brake, wrenched the wheel so the Peugeot's front end came to rest a scant inch from the rock wall. It would appear as if he'd lost control. What he'd do next would indicate why.

Crafting the desired image in his mind, he drew upon the power carried in his bones, his blood. The power of the Other. He let it gather around the image and, when it was enough, he set it loose.

Like an aimed arrow from a bow, the power sought—and struck—its target. The right rear wheel deflated. The Peugeot tilted.

He turned the engine off but left the electrics on. Then he set the handbrake and craned to look out the back window. Tied to the wiper's motion, the view alternated between the red of the taillights smeared across the rain-drenched glass and, when cleared, the black of the road behind.

A gust rocked the car.

He barely noticed. Power coursed through him, close to the surface. Ready.

Twin points of white appeared in the distance. The Rover, rounding a curve less than a mile away.

Cormac got out. The cold was fierce. A stinging mix of rain, sleet, and snow struck his exposed skin while the wind cut through his jacket and again-sodden trousers. His feet sought purchase—not always successful—as he made his way to the car's boot to stage the rest of the scene.

The jack, placed near the punctured tire. A hazard flare, set alight and tossed into the road so there would be no choice but to stop. Tire iron, held casually alongside his leg.

The approaching Rover slowed.

Cormac made a practiced show of surprise quickly followed by hope. He waved his left hand—the one not holding the iron—and smiled as the Rover eased to a stop in the pull-out. Squinting, he used his left arm to shield his eyes against the full beams. They promptly dimmed.

He lowered his arm.

Both of the Rover's front doors opened to let out two wary young men. Mid-twenties. Old enough to know the risks. Old enough to know what they were stepping into with him, here, this night.

Without question, they were physically fit for a challenge, but the way they flaunted power meant they weren't anywhere near his level. The more power one had, the more one worked to conceal it.

"Gentlemen," he greeted with warmth as the storm battered them all. He took a subtle step forward. With his right arm loose at his side, his grip tightened on the iron. "Perhaps you can help."

In their moment of indecision, when the two men looked to one another, it was all over but for the doing.

The ball of lethal *wælfýr* formed at Cormac's left hand. He sent it flying toward the more distant man and, with tire iron swinging in a low arc, lunged for the nearer. There was a burst of light as the *wælfýr* struck its target full in the chest—*one down*—while the tire iron caught the other man at the knees, sweeping his legs out from under. He toppled backward, arms flailing, eyes wide. He hit the ground, opened his mouth as if to shout but Cormac was already moving in, the iron raised high.

One to go.

CHAPTER 3

"I'm to be off site," Declan announced, striding past the reception desk. The woman on duty was one of Kendra Ross's new hires. His mind already well ahead, her smile went unnoticed. "Emergency only," he said over his shoulder as he reached into the satin-lined pocket of his overcoat to switch his phone to silent.

"Yes, sir."

He nodded at several guests on his way through the lobby—they might post reviews; it paid to make an effort—and held the door open for two more before he was able to step outside.

Construction noise, no longer subject to the hotel's layered dampening spells, spiked.

The sharp pops of a nail gun one block over. The whine of compressors. The shrieking grind of a distant wood chipper.

Declan grimaced. Today, despite significant citizen protest, three grand trees at the Plaza were to be brought down. He set off in the opposite direction, Eclectica being his destination. A gust of wind lifted the ends of his loosely draped scarf and drove a chill past his overcoat's unbuttoned front.

The *nafásach* plan the city council had green-lit went so far beyond repairing the damage from December's violence that it amounted to a complete redesign.

To be sure, the entire Plaza area suffered from longstanding issues with flow and visibility. But the plan which had been pushed through failed to address anything so useful. Window dressing only, the changes were to be—and as such, the city was on a fast track to turning a quaint, old-fashioned square into a modernistic swath of uniformly-gray pavers edged with cement planters.

In an even worse affront to Declan's aesthetics, a proposal to dress the planters in a discordant mosaic of abstract shapes and murky colors had received unanimous approval. It made one wonder about the state of the mayor and council, it did.

If this was the result of an influence scheme, it was a piss-poor one for its complete unanimity. Such an occurrence was rare on any council, but in Granite Springs? Unheard of and thus highly suspect. Better to allow for a few opposing votes.

No, the more Declan worked the whole thing over, running the variables and considering the particulars of each council member, the more bizarre this all became. It was more like the mayor and entire council had lost their minds, each and every one.

At the curb, he waited for a dump truck to finish its turn off Main onto First Street. Ice and slush lingered in the shaded gutter. The truck exhaust lingered as well, clashing with the sweeter scent of freshly chipped tree. Both of them, products of progress born of opportunity.

Mindful of his patent leather boots, he set out across the street.

Was this the right progress? The right opportunity?

His own plans were, to be sure. Not the Plaza nonsense—he wanted fuck-all to do with that—but his plans to modify and expand what was his. If Declan Murphy could be said to love one thing, it was opportunity. And he excelled at identifying and seizing it.

The violence done to Main Street had been an affront and a tragedy for which he never would have wished, but it had left glorious possibilities in its wake. Already he had purchased two buildings from owners wanting to cut their losses, and he had placed offers on two more. A tidal wave of opportunity, this was, and he was prepared to ride.

As of today, he owned three of the four corner properties on this intersection. The Landmark—called the Anthony and Cleopatra at the time— had been first, his introduction to the region. The tallest building for miles and an Art Deco beauty, it would always be the crown jewel of his Oregon holdings. Soon after, he had acquired the building directly across it on First Street—the one he was currently walking alongside. It now held the hotel's spa and some rented shops and offices.

The building across from the Landmark on Main was his latest. The former home of the Ice Cream Shoppe, its front had been blown away at the start of the parade attack. Subsequent explosions had made it an easy acquisition. Plans had already been drawn up and there was a crew on standby. The concept would be much the same—artisan ice cream, gelato, frozen yogurt—while adding a menu of quick, light lunches to appeal to tourists and locals alike. Despite some unexpected issues with the Planning Department, he was banking on a late spring reopening.

His steps slowed, stopped altogether as he considered the missing piece of the four-corner set: Founders Hall.

Like the Landmark, it was a registered historic building and an impressive example of early Twentieth Century architecture. As far as anyone could tell, the Hall was wasting away. Four floors of prime location and all they were used for was rented storage space on the upper levels and, on the ground, an ever-changing assortment of struggling shops. The potential had been pricking at him for months.

The Landmark ran at capacity all summer along with most

holidays and festivals. Founders Hall would be ideal as a sister hotel. Give it more of a European flare and an accompanying restaurant and bar. It would be a brilliant transformation.

As his mind's eye presented a slideshow of possibilities, he stroked the neatly trimmed hair at his chin. Emblematic of his own transformation, that was. Mustache and goatee. Back in fashion of late, not that he cared. Did Abigail?

Jaysus. With a start, he resumed walking.

Which was worse, that he had been standing with his guard down on a public street or that his thinking had gone in such a direction? His brothers would turn in their graves.

Wherever those might be.

The sight of Kendra Ross strolling with her arm about none other than Neil Amundsen kept his thoughts from straying a second time—and a much darker path that would have been. He might be grateful for it if he weren't so surprised. He was not one for surprises.

She was smiling over at Amundsen—his arm was about her in return, very cozy—as if he had said something to amuse. That was yet another surprise, as Declan hadn't credited him with having a sense of humor. Nor had he considered him to be Kendra's type.

Not that Declan had given much consideration to what her type might be. He didn't mix business with pleasure, as a rule, and Kendra Ross was too valuable, first as a lieutenant and more recently as hotel director. Not to mention that she was good friends with Abigail Collins.

He trusted her with the Landmark and to have his back in a fight, just as he'd have hers. On her own time, she was her own woman.

Still, he had eyes in his head and a brain behind them, didn't he? Kendra Ross was a fiery beauty in possession of a mind as sharp as an obsidian blade and could be nothing short of glorious in battle; Neil Amundsen was a drab, watered-down bureaucrat, unexceptional in every way. Average build, with vaguely Nordic features. Hair a diluted yellow ochre. Eyes, an unmemorable, washed out blue.

On looks alone, Kendra Ross could do better. Then there was the fact that Neil Amundsen was an unmitigated ass.

He also happened be the city manager.

"Ross," Declan said when they met up. "Amundsen."

The man's arm tightened on Kendra's waist and drew her closer to his side. "Murphy."

Declan let one eyebrow arch and watched tension increase in Kendra's frame. Annoyed by the patriarchal display, he had no doubt. And not comfortable with her boss knowing her personal business. Fair enough. He didn't publicize his, either.

Even were he so inclined, Abigail would likely murder him in his sleep. Try to, that was. The woman was both infuriating and—

And there Declan's thinking was straying again, this time in company. Never mind his brothers, he would turn in his own grave—the one he had been bound for all those years ago. To be sure, he'd get back to it sooner rather than later if he kept this up.

"I'm headed back to work," Kendra said, likely mistaking his distracted silence for disapproval. "We ran into each other on my break. Neil and I."

To put her at ease, Declan shrugged. Employee breaks were none of his concern. Besides, was he not himself taking time away from his desk so as to do a thing in person he could have done by telephone? "I'll see you there in a few, then," he said, and prepared to move on.

Amundsen stopped him with a deceptively mild, "I understand you're waiting on some permits."

"That I am. To do with the former Ice Cream Shoppe."

"Yes. Such a shame when projects get bogged down in red tape."

Ah. Declan's senses sharpened. "Isn't it just."

The red tape Amundsen referred to was exaction; the bog, Declan's continued refusal to acquiesce to a hike in the Planning Department's under-the-table "fee." It was a matter of principle. Their mutually beneficial arrangement was of long standing: Irrevocable and, more to the point, nonnegotiable. So, while he contemplated the most effective way to make that clear to them, wheels which would have otherwise been greased had become stuck.

Curious that Amundsen knew of it.

Declan's easy smile came from long practice. "I'm sure that will sort itself out." The handy thing about corrupt officials was that they *were* corrupt. That made them vulnerable.

"Of course," Amundsen said. "One way or another."

Kendra, adept at navigating undercurrents, made an abrupt and cheerful change of subject. "I hear you've set something up with Fiona this evening," she said to Declan. "To do with Eclectica?"

No choice but to admit it. "I have. I'm after making the rest of the arrangements now." Discomfort let slip more Irish into his speech than usual. "If the ladies are willing."

"They ought to be. Fiona would be an excellent get for the café." Mischief danced in the spring green of Kendra's eyes. "I didn't know she had any interest in leaving us, but I suppose I might have missed that . . . while she and I renegotiated her contract only last week."

Damn. She had sussed that he was orchestrating the whole thing. But that didn't mean he'd cop to it. "Right. Well. We can't know everything about our employees."

"Oh, sure, yes," she agreed dryly. "Good thing she kept you informed, though, so you could broker this for her."

"Indeed."

Rather than take the warning in his tone, Kendra grinned. He nearly laughed despite himself. Contrary woman.

Amundsen checked the ostentatious Tag Heuer around his wrist. The move pulled her closer still. "I need to be getting back to City Hall, I'm sorry to say. If you'll excuse us?"

Surprisingly, Kendra allowed herself to be herded. But she sent Declan a teasing, "Say hi to Abby for me, would you?"

"And Ms. McDaniel, of course," he said, refusing to take the bait—if mere bait it was.

"Of course." With a laugh that sounded far too knowing, she returned her focus to her companion, saying something apologetic about the time before they were out of earshot.

Declan resumed his walk but considered a complete change of plan. Somehow Kendra had picked up on something. From him? From Abigail? He should have kept to his office, done this over the phone. Better yet, he should scrap the whole deal. Declan Murphy, going out of his way to solve someone else's business problem? It was so blatantly out of character that he might as well have painted a sign.

No more, he decided. He'd see this through, because it had already been set in motion, but that would be the end of it. He couldn't afford the distraction.

● ○ ●

Landmark Hotel

Kendra loved every part of the hotel, but she loved the lobby best. Loved the rich cream of the walls and the gleam of the brass fixtures and how the light—no matter the time of day or weather—played across the floor's polished granite. Loved to see guests make use of the seating areas, whether for drinks and conversation or for the simple pleasure of being there.

The window views were not what they once were, but soon that would become a good thing: how the people of Granite Springs turned a painful negative into a positive. After all the construction and landscaping work finished, the Landmark's views—and the city itself—would be better than ever.

Murphy had promoted her from Front of House to Director

of Operations back in October, but she still felt the need to pinch herself. She enjoyed shouldering the responsibility for the running of the Landmark and its people so much—that at times it felt like a dream.

Maybe not so much this morning, she amended to herself as both the head chef and the events coordinator converged on her in front of Reception. They spoke at once, an insensible barrage of agitation.

Nina Allegretti, brought in from one of Murphy's international holdings for her decades of experience with everything from celebrity weddings to major spiritual conventions, was showing the wide eyes and overwrought gestures of a person pushed close to breaking.

Chef Pasquale, famous for his composure, was doing a fine impression of a volcano about to blow. His formerly tall toque was crushed in one of the fists he waved while his face turned lava red.

"Hey, hey, hey," Kendra soothed, holding up two placating hands even as her own stress level ratcheted up. "It can't be as bad as that."

It was, they insisted, talking over one another—Nina with the speed and ferocity of a machine gun; Pasquale in a mix of English and French. Gradually, Kendra put together what had happened and, unfortunately, they were right; it was as bad as that. With only two day's notice, their catering contract for Mayor Pallister's party had been canceled.

Hours and hours of planning, wasted. Extra staff had been hired. Supplies had been purchased.

"What reason did he give?" Keeping her voice low, Kendra guided them toward her office, away from guests and other employees. News was already spreading, she had no doubt. She needed to get the situation under control, then mitigate the damage. She might be able to get the mayor to un-cancel.

"He did. It was his assistant who called," Nina said. "Seems that *Himself*"—she spat the word—"couldn't be bothered to do his own dirty work."

"Lack of the balls," Pasquale said.

Kendra opened her office door and gestured them in. Each picked a chair, and they arranged them as if around a campfire. Everyone on staff knew she preferred to avoid the distant formality of her desk when emotions ran hot and nerves were fraying.

As they sat, Kendra looked to Nina. The older woman was actually wringing her hands. "Tell me exactly what was said."

A little over an hour later, plans had been made to deal with the purchased food; Nina and Pasquale—prides soothed and anxieties eased—had gone to put them in motion.

Kendra's job was less about the hotel itself and more about the people within it. Knowing the strengths and, yes, weaknesses of everyone on the team, and working with those. She enjoyed smoothing things over for both the guests and the staff. Life in general could be tough. To be able to make it less so through efficiency, logic, and basic situational awareness was a thrill she had never expected to find for herself.

What made her truly love her job, though, was that for as much as she enjoyed smoothing things over, she also understood there were times when it was necessary to rough them up. And she enjoyed that, too.

Comfortably settled behind her desk, she put in a call to the mayor's assistant. Her blunt-nailed finger tapped on a copy of the catering contract while the line rang. Once. Twice.

Picked up.

"What's the deal, Jeff?" she asked by way of greeting.

"Kendra?" The young man's voice went up an octave. There was the sound of something dropping. "Shit. Oh, shit. Hold please, I just knocked over—" Recorded music began to play.

Leaning back in her chair, she idly swiveled it to and fro, a pendulum ticking off the seconds of her impatience.

The line clicked and Jeff came back on. "Sorry about that. I knocked over my mug. Okay. Hi. So I, uh, suppose you heard about the party."

"I did," Kendra said. "And I have to say I'm surprised. His Honor does understand that he's liable for half the remaining money due and that there will be no refund of his deposit."

Those were not questions. Mayor Pallister might lack fortitude but not intelligence. He wouldn't have signed a contract he hadn't read—not with his own money at stake. This was his event, not the city's.

Last-minute cancellation came with a hefty cost. It had to or the Landmark could be at enormous risk with every event. Last August's multi-day Lughnasadh celebration, put on for a global consortium of Druids, had come in somewhere around half a million.

"Yes," Jeff said with a sigh. "He knows."

"So the party is just, what—off?"

"No, no, it's still on," came his puzzling reply. "He's hired Ledberg Events instead."

"Who's that?" The name was entirely unfamiliar. "Are they from Portland? Seattle?"

"No idea. All Mayor Pallister told me was the name."

An unknown competitor snatching clients out from under contract? Murphy would hate this.

"Any idea what the reason is?" she asked. None of this made sense. "Better rates, better food? Anything?"

"Rates, I wouldn't know, but food? Come on, right? Yours is the best there is." The sound of shuffling papers came over the line. "I have no idea why he canceled. Honestly. But he does this. Changes his mind like a switch gets flipped. You're lucky it's not the day of. That thing with the library tree? That was him, going back on agreements."

Last summer, the city had been set to remove a century-old cedar by the public library. Something to do with it being root bound or pushing up the sidewalk or both. Weeks of citizen protests ensued, including the installation of a camping platform high in the branches. After that appeared to succeed—tree saved, sorry to upset everyone, no need for concern—the town woke to find it gone. A removal crew had come at the crack of dawn, ousted the sleepers from their platform, and had the tree down in an hour.

"He gave no reason at all for dropping us for this Ledberg group?"

"I'm just his assistant. He never explains anything to me." Jeff sighed. "He came out of this morning's meeting, told me to cancel things with you guys, and if Ledberg Events called I was to put them straight through. That's it."

"Who did he meet with this morning?" Kendra asked, but then realized she knew. Neil had mentioned it.

Which meant the meeting was unconnected. The party was the mayor's personal event. And, if Neil had known about the change of plans, he would have said something to her.

"Okay, well, let me know if you hear more, please." Kendra ended the call. Murphy could hash things out with the mayor if he chose. She had a waiting list of things to do and thanks to this, she was—she checked her watch—fully fifty minutes off schedule. She pulled over her work laptop.

The screen woke to the internet browser, open to what she had been doing all morning: Property record searches on the county's website. If she knew what Murphy's plans were for certain projects, she might feel more invested in the research, she thought as she typed in the address of—

Frowning, she double-checked the numbers on the list she'd been given. No, she'd read them right. They were the address of the building next to Eclectica. Had she been wrong about Murphy's reasons for going there this morning? She'd thought it had to do with some kind of thing between him and Abby, but he might've gone to check out the building and nothing more.

Still, she couldn't be entirely wrong about her boss and her friend. The former would not have arranged to lose such a talented baker to the latter, otherwise.

She mentally filed that away to think about later—or better yet, would ask Abby directly.

With a click of the mouse, she opened the property details on-screen. The present owners were Sam Wiggins and James MacGonigal. She set the page to print.

Reading the next address on Murphy's list, she let out a low whistle.

Founders Hall.

If he got that, he'd own the entire intersection and nearly half of the block the Hall sat on. Its parcel included the adjacent land, currently functioning as two parking lots.

An annex, maybe? The Landmark could definitely use more space. She ran the search. And felt a jolt at the result.

The Carl Verner Family Trust.

Not noteworthy on its own, but that same name had come up in December when she'd pulled the record for The Valhalla in preparation for sneaking inside with Murphy and Cormac.

Founders Hall and that disturbing dump of a roadside bar—known hangout of the Rekkrs, the biker gang responsible for so much of the Main Street damage—had the same owner. One who had so far proved impossible to track.

She picked up her cellphone, scrolled her contacts for the Brigantium agent stationed in town.

The call went straight to messaging.

"Hey, Edith. It's Kendra," she said after the tone. "Have you made any progress tracing that Carl Verner Trust? I've found it on another property record. Call me back when you can."

There was a knock on her door.

She disconnected the call. "Yes?"

Penny, a front desk clerk, opened the door just enough to

poke her head into the room. "Sorry to interrupt, but Sixteen is saying they requested a set of willow wood runes when they made their reservation, but we have no record of it."

Already guessing what had gone awry, Kendra pushed her chair back and stood. "Did they place the reservation with us directly?"

"No. They used Big Deal."

"Of course." That discount site was forever losing special requests. "I'll talk to the guests. We have a set in oak. Hopefully they'll be all right with that."

Never a dull moment. Tucking her phone into her pocket, she left her office.

● ○ ●

Eclectica

Because Thia was working the back door like a fan to clear the remaining *eau du* Leo, she had a perfect view when Declan Murphy entered from the stairs. The model of a tall, dark, and handsome Irishman, he was also the epitome of confidence and athleticism. And style. His black-coffee hair was expertly trimmed, as was his relatively recent goatee; his clothes, from his charcoal wool coat to the three piece suit beneath were designer, tailored to a millimeter, and undoubtedly cost more than Thia could estimate even if she tripled her wildest guess.

The Landmark had two restaurants along with full beverage service. The man who owned all that wasn't seeking them out for espresso. Had he learned of something—a threat against her, or them? The store? He didn't look worried, though.

Not that he ever had, that she'd seen.

Abby's back was to his approach. With how the two of them could be, that wasn't ideal. Thia tried to get her attention.

"Hm?" She looked up from the next applicant's résumé. "Are they here already?" Off Thia's gesture, she craned in her seat. Her expression soured. "What do you want?" she called, then promptly returned her attention to the application papers.

Inwardly, Thia cringed. Bickering made her uncomfortable, but also, Murphy was an influential businessman on a grand scale. He also had a mysterious background and some sort of paramilitary force.

A number of them had come to her rescue in Orkney. He had wielded a magically-charged battle axe.

He was not someone to risk provoking by being rude, yet Abby frequently did just that. Their clashes were legendary.

"I might have someone for your café," Murphy said, moving into Abby's line of sight but speaking to Thia. As the fabric of his coat settled, he adjusted the lay of his Burberry scarf. "If you come to the Landmark this evening, both of you"—a quick glance at Abby—"you can meet with her. Sample some of her wares."

When he leaned casually against the counter, Abby's eyes narrowed to hostile slits. "And if we already hired someone?"

One of Murphy's brows lifted. "Have you?"

"No," Thia answered, but she might as well have been on the moon. She watched as a kind of staring contest ensued.

Then, surprisingly, Abby began to look like she was fighting a smile.

More surprisingly, so did Murphy.

Thia had a light bulb moment. Of course. Oh, of *course*. She should have noticed the signs before this.

"Six o'clock?" Murphy offered, straightening away from the counter. "Up in the restaurant. You'll be expected."

With that, he strode past Thia and out the open door to the patio and Blooms Alley. She let it close. "Did we say we would go?"

"Infuriating man," Abby said, but she didn't seem infuriated to Thia. On the contrary, she seemed rather pleased.

Quite a change from a month ago.

After Abby had been struck unconscious at the mountain lodge, Murphy had been the one to carry her to safety. He had seen to it that she was taken to The Retreat for immediate care. He had shown concern in the days after, too, while she regained her strength.

Prior to that, Thia had never known him to patronize Eclectica, but he had since become a frequent visitor. Picking up an item for a hotel guest; inquiring about the state of business during the Main Street construction work while on his way to or from some meeting or other; browsing the weekly new arrivals display.

Not very subtle, in retrospect.

"Abby," she asked carefully, "am I going to be a third wheel?"

"What? What are you talking—No." Shock and innocence, well feigned. "Tonight? It's business. You know how he likes to be involved in every damn thing. He's a megalomaniac."

"Yes, of course. He's infuriating, and totally not interested in you."

"There's nothing going on." She sounded so adamant. Was that because it was the truth or could someone who was so adept at reading other people be blind to herself?

Maybe she was fully aware—and didn't want those feelings, or anything that might come of them.

Thia retook her seat for the next interview. "Would it be a bad thing? If there *is* something between the two of you, would that be—"

"He's complicated, Thia. Extremely complicated." Not *it's,* but *he's.* Not the situation but the man. Abby let out a breath. "I don't know that I can handle complicated right now."

Thia knew the feeling.

Oh, did she ever.

CHAPTER 4

Cormac chose to exit the line at the Hyde Park portal, a full two miles from the Brigantium's headquarters off Pall Mall. He couldn't risk another tail even if it proved to be as poor as the last, and he needed some time in a natural setting. Leyline travel came with aftereffects, no matter the journey's length.

He landed in a crouch, surrounded by shrubbery in a raised garden bed. The storm that was raging over Ireland had yet to cross the sea, so while London's air was damply cold, the evening sky was clear.

The paved walks on either side of him were crowded with pedestrians; the street behind, with cars. That was the trouble with city portals: Potential witnesses.

Thankfully, most Londoners didn't rate the sight of a man emerging from park-side shrubbery as worthy of note. The concentration of bars and pubs plus a general lack of public toilets might account for that. He fed into the impression, staggering a bit on the way to a row of benches before sitting clumsily on the nearest. He didn't earn so much as a glance. The prevalence of smartphones helped, too. People who were not part of a chatty group were involved instead with calls, texts, music or whatever else connectivity had to offer.

In addition to the portal, this northeast section was home to a major Underground station; several bus stops and taxi stands; and Speakers' Corner. An area historically designated for free speech and debate, it had also been the home of the Tyburn gallows until the government decided to hold public executions at Newgate instead.

The last hanging here had been in 1783. Idris had brought Cormac to one a few years prior. James Hackman's, if memory served. A clergyman. Idris had judged it not to be missed.

Well into his fourth decade, Cormac had believed himself inured to such things, but he had not been prepared for the spectacle that had been made of the death or for the crowd's ravenousness. In more ways than his father had intended, it had proved a valuable lesson.

To his right, a double-decker bus dislodged its riders onto the pavement, and he smoothly tagged along with those going into the park. Yet again, no one paid him any mind, not even when he drifted away, cutting across a short strip of grass to a border of towering linden trees.

He stopped, leaned against a trunk. He used to carry cigarettes for cover but now his mobile phone did the trick. He pretended to check messages while he scanned the area both visually and with his Sight. The park's crisscrossed network of paths were well lit and this stretch didn't offer much low-lying cover.

In summer, there would be groups picnicking and playing sports on the lawn. All around, the trees would be leafed out, offering shade and a soothing, breezy rustle. Tonight, amidst winter-bare branches and hoarfrost, there were only people wanting to get elsewhere. Cormac detected a few who carried unconcealed power, but nothing comparable to his.

A domestic hobgoblin, grocery bags in hand, gave a passing nod as he hurried past. Cormac nodded in return.

After another minute of waiting, he put away his phone.

"Thank you," he told the tree, and laid a hand on the rough bark. From the *Sidhe*, he'd inherited an ability to draw energy from the natural world. This linden tree had given generously despite its seasonal slumber, and Cormac had been able to replenish what the leyline had taken.

He stepped sideways along the trunk until he was in deep shadow. Then he set about glamouring himself an appropriate disguise for the dinner-hour environs of St James.

Knee-length coat—iron gray, he decided. Trousers and suit jacket in a lighter shade, with a white shirt and burgundy Half Windsor tie. Black scarf looped about his neck. Black leather shoes, not too polished. Raven-black hair (his own little joke). The cut was longer than he preferred, and uninspired. Bland facial features, neither ugly nor handsome. Ordinary. Boring.

He left the trees to rejoin the path and its constant pedestrian stream. He kept his steps quick—Londoners were brisk walkers—but took care not to convey a sense of purpose.

Purpose drew the eye. Purpose sparked curiosity.

He might be acting with an overabundance of caution, but he'd never met anyone who regretted doing the same. He had met plenty who would come to regret not acting with enough.

On his smartphone were photos of two such men—the ones from the Range Rover—and of their passports and what he had found in their wallets before he'd put it all back. Nothing had revealed their affiliation, but he had his suspicions and little remorse. They had known who and what he was. They had known what he could do, and now they would serve as a reminder, and a renewed warning. He had been more lenient of late, but he had not "lost his edge," as rumor had begun to have it.

To local police, however, their deaths would look accidental. A winter storm, a foolish choice of road, a loss of control, and over the edge they'd gone. Cormac had staged the scene with care wrought by experience.

Exiting by way of the park's southeastern gate, he proceeded through one of the city's most convoluted intersections. He chose to cross over to a memorial-strewn island, then over to walk along Constitution Hill. The ten foot wall of razor-wired brick on his right was the northwestern border of the Palace Garden. The perimeter of Green Park was across the road on his left.

He had counted fifty CCTV cameras since he had dropped out of the line. Twenty had been within the last five minutes.

When Idris had first sent him out, the only cameras were the "pinhole" kind: Camera obscura, by which images were projected onto a surface but not captured—not unless they were then traced in ink. There had been no such thing yet as film. No such thing as automated permanence. He had been able to go about Idris's business without being recorded and stalked by any number of the technologies which pervaded the modern world.

Having reached the wall's end, he continued to skirt Green Park. He kept pace with the most populous string of walkers, staying to the main walk by the road instead of cutting across on one of the smaller. His nerves prickled, a warning that he was being watched, but his Sight revealed nothing of significance and he was not too concerned. This close to a royal residence, everyone was watched.

The King's security might detect Cormac's use of a glamour, but that in and of itself shouldn't raise alarm. Any number of people who could craft such spells did. To hide a perceived flaw, to appear younger, thinner, fitter. It saved the bother of cosmetics. His reasons were not as innocent, but they weren't *nefarious*. His relationship with various government agencies was less than amicable, that's all. Anonymity was preferable to heightened scrutiny—or, should the old warrants still exist, arrest.

Too, he had a reputation to protect. If it got around that

he was on speaking terms with the Brigantium, he would find himself no longer on speaking terms with a whole host of his usual contacts. And as for his rivals . . . well. No need to spend time thinking about that.

He continued to follow the pavement as it angled past the palace front and equally imposing Queen Victoria memorial. A complicated woman, she had been—and likely the Society of Brigantium owed much to that.

The loose clusters of people he had been walking with had gradually moved ahead. New ones had taken their place, only to move on as well. His pace had slowed, testament to a reluctance he preferred not to acknowledge.

Instead of Hyde Park's larger portal, he could have used the access point within Green Park. He could have taken time among *those* trees to settle himself and craft his glamour. Yes, he'd wanted the distance in order to ascertain if he was being followed, but this was a less populous area. A follower would be easier to spot.

He turned left, ascended the steps to Waterloo Place. The base of the column erected so the Duke of York's effigy could literally lord over the area would provide Cormac cover while he studied his destination, ahead.

A grand white Palladian in a neighborhood of grand white Palladians, what set it apart were the armed guards on the roof.

Parked cars lined the horseshoe-shaped street. The traffic within moved steadily, all of it comprised of drivers in search of an available spot. When none was found, they rounded the Duke's column to try in another block. Pedestrians walked without pause. Cormac was the only lingerer.

With a sigh, he stepped away from the column.

He felt the guards' attention immediately and took care that his pace and posture were relaxed, his power entirely cloaked. They would sense the glamour, but he had called ahead, told the old woman to expect him. Presumably, she would have communicated his impending arrival to security—but no one knew his present disguise, and he couldn't drop it until he was in the building, away from outside observation.

The entrance was a portico supported by four sets of paired columns. By the time he arrived at the top of the steps, two men in typical doorman's garb had come forward to block his way.

"Sorry," said the bald one, not sorry at all. "This is a private club."

The other watched with narrowed eyes and a tense, locked jaw. His hair was done in a military buzz cut, and his hand stayed close enough to his coat front to suggest a weapon was holstered within.

Cormac held himself motionless, his hands palm forward—*nothing to see here*—at his sides. "I have an appointment," he said in distinctly plummy tones. The dialect of the aspiring elite, to correspond with his appearance.

The bald man didn't budge. "Name?"

Cormac quoted the phrase given over the phone: "*Nebula pervenit sicut parum cattus pedes.*"

The fog comes on little cat feet. At least one person in the Brigantium's security force had a sense of humor.

It was not Baldy, here, unfortunately. "You aren't like your photo."

"Not at the moment, no. May I?" Cormac slowly lifted his hand to indicate that he wanted to reach into his coat. "My passport."

Baldy exchanged a look with Buzz-cut before nodding.

With extreme caution, Cormac took the passport book—newly covered in royal, post-Brexit blue—from his inner coat pocket and held it out for inspection.

"You could have stolen that."

"And stolen the pass-phrase as well?" Cormac resisted a roll of his eyes.

Jaw muscles bulged as Baldy clenched his teeth.

"The longer we stand here," Cormac pointed out, "the more interest we'll draw."

The Brigantium presented itself as an elite, scholarly club. Guards on the roof could be attributed to the value of what was inside. That the Society collected antiquities, rare books, and the like was well-known among the general public. Moreover, it took the effort of looking up to notice the guards, and most people tended to focus on what was at eye level. The well-lit portico, however, might as well have been a stage.

Baldy glowered. "I'll take him to the front office," he told his partner and moved to allow Cormac to go ahead. "They can sort it out."

● ○ ●

Brigantium Headquarters (Inside)

A poor, chemical facsimile of jasmine scent began to fill the air of the ritual room, and Beatrice's nose twitched along with her temper. These were not the right candles, and she made a mental note to track down whoever had made the error so the expense could be deducted from their stipend. The odor, in this instance, would not affect the divination, but it was intolerably bourgeois and the guidelines were clear: Candles were to be unscented unless otherwise specified.

She became aware of a faint gritting sound in the relative silence. Her teeth, grinding. She forced her jaw to relax.

Really, how difficult was it to simply do one's job? She took a deep breath, recentering herself, and let her gaze go soft. The trio of fat, white candles and their agitated flames seemed to merge with their reflections on the lacquered table.

As per protocol, the flames were the room's only source of illumination. They didn't cast far, scarcely reaching beyond the table's circular edge to the eight participants seated there. Their white, silver-shot robes glinted, but the shadows within the hoods were deep, revealing only the vaguest hint of the wearers' features.

Fabric rustled to her right.

Damian, with a faint clearing of his throat, began. "Imbolc draws nigh."

Hearing a satisfactory measure of pomp, Beatrice relaxed slightly. She had considered taking the lead tonight, but this was an elementary ritual and she was coming to understand the importance of not giving the impression that she needed to do everything.

"Imbolc draws nigh," he repeated, "and so begins the transformation from winter to spring, from slumber to waking. 'Tis a time of planning, a time of preparation, and so in this spirit we humbly beseech thee, O magnificent Cerridwen, to—"

A mobile phone loosed a sequence of grunting vibrations. Beatrice's mouth pinched. *Silenced* was not the same as *off*.

"—guide us," Damian continued. "Reveal to us what may lie ahead in the coming days and weeks and months—"

The phone vibrated again.

"Oh for Brigid's sake." Tracking the sound, Beatrice glared across the table. The offending device was brought out.

It *would* be his, of course. He would be the only one who would dare. Quentin Sigmund Aloysius Reynolds, source of almost perpetual aggravation.

The screen lit his unrepentant face as he held it to his ear. He was *taking* the call. She was going to crack a molar.

"Ah," he said after a moment. "Certainly." His gaze met hers before the screen went out and his hood shadowed him once more. "Your visitor is downstairs."

Her ire immediately changed targets. Given the priority of what this concerned, she could no longer fault Quentin for having brought a live phone into a ritual. She could, however, resent Cormac for his timing.

"That man," she said, as good as a curse. With a clap of her hands, she triggered the overhead lighting. "I'm afraid we'll have to postpone," she told Damian, and flung back her hood.

"What has happened?" enquired a thin, quavering voice.

Beatrice managed to bite back a sharp remark.

Leslie Mullen, positioned between Quentin and Eben, was not cut out for ritual work—nor for much work at all beyond the cataloging of pillywiggins. Yet, in one of life's jests, she was a powerful medium. Simply having her in the room exponentially increased the chance of success.

Beatrice stood. "Quentin and I have business," she told the silly woman.

Two stations over, Arthur Barnstable leaned back, crossed his arms across his chest. His hood had wreaked havoc with his snow white hair despite whatever he had used earlier to slick it down. "Am I meant to be included in whatever this is?"

He sounded unusually testy.

"Of course," she assured him. As their Society's director, it was his right to be apprised of every situation. However, he was not adapting well to the ongoing crisis and she, as assistant director, had found it expedient to not bother him with matters of a certain complexity.

This was the first instance he not only seemed to notice but to mind.

"There wasn't time before," she said.

Although he harrumphed, this appeared to mollify him. He pushed back from the table, clearly set on including himself.

Quentin gave her a look she knew well. They had been over this. He felt she was acting beyond her scope—becoming a tyrant, to use his exact words.

Having replaced his leather glove, removed to take the call, he reached for his cane.

She averted her gaze. His opinion of her had formed in his youth and he had yet to examine it under the wiser lens of an adult. She always had his best interests at heart. Same as she had now with the Society of Brigantium and the various organizations it served.

"I will send out a text," she announced, "when we get this rescheduled. Thank you."

At the door, she glanced back. Damian and Eben had extinguished the candles and were beginning to pack up the implements that would have come into later use.

She cleared her throat to get their attention. "Please inform whoever is responsible for the jasmine that I'll have a word with them tomorrow." She unlocked the door, pulled it open as Arthur neared.

"I'll catch up," Quentin called from the table.

"Very well." From anyone else, she would have objected. But she disliked watching him walk. He had been such an athletic boy.

She supposed he held that against her as well.

"We put too much on the boy," Arthur said when they were out of earshot. They traversed side by side along the upper floor's west corridor, their steps muffled by a series of antique Persian runners. "The strain is beginning to show."

"Quentin? He can bear it," she said, although she had begun to wonder.

But he had been raised for this work. She might not have prepared him for the present crisis—an organization riddled with traitors and nearly undone—but none of them had been prepared for that. They would all do what they must.

The corridor terminated at the wide landing of the central staircase. No rugs here; it would be a sacrilege to cover the intricate parquetry.

"What is it that we're doing, Bea?" Arthur inquired as they started down.

No matter how many times she made this descent, it never failed to inspire. First was the view, the overlook of the entry hall and its magnificent display of class, wealth, and history.

Next was the act itself, the immersion into all that grandeur, that importance, to become part of it. More than part of it, she thought with pride.

She had attained authority over it.

Full authority lay on the shoulders of the man at her side, at the moment, but in all the ways that counted, the Society—and the privilege of responsibility—was hers.

"We received a call earlier," she informed Arthur now, as she should have done at the time. "Cormac claims to have vital knowledge regarding his father's collection. He requested a meeting."

"Requested, was it?"

Her hand tightened briefly on the banister. "Insisted."

"You believe that should be tolerated?"

"In this instance."

His mouth flattened. Not a good sign. "And you presumed I would not?" He navigated the final step to the marble floor.

Their destination was to the right of the main doors. They cut a diagonal track across the mostly deserted hall.

"I was concerned you wouldn't approve, yes," she admitted. "Should I apologize?"

"Would you mean it?"

"I might."

Their strides, shorter than when they had begun their work together, matched with learned companionability. The clicks of her mid-heel loafers and the muffled taps of his Oxfords synchronized on the black and white tiles. Quite possibly, she knew him better than she knew herself.

He had begun to suspect she was more suited to what his role had become than he was. He would soon resent her for it, if he did not already.

"I can't say I approve of this," he said. "Opening our doors to that trickster-thief. He has been a thorn in the Society's side since the founding. How many times has he prevented the acquisition of a valuable artifact? Relics. Grimoires. Snatched up and put entirely out of reach."

"Exactly," she said. When under strain, he tended toward short-sightedness. That was another reason she took so much upon herself.

They were nearly at the security office. She touched his arm, halting their progress. "Information, Arthur," she said. "He holds a wealth of information with regard to those same artifacts. What he did with them—whether he delivered them to his father or kept them for himself or sold them on the black market. Then, beyond those, beyond what we know about, he is familiar with the entirety of Idris Cathmor's collection. A collection which he is in the process of locating."

"I'm aware of all that," Arthur argued. "But he is the half-*Sidhe* issue of the strongest sorcerer we've had the misfortune to encounter. He trained in the darkest of arts and holds an unknown amount of power that he can put to foul use. He cannot be trusted, Bea. If you let a scorpion onto your back, expect to be stung."

"Ah, but his stinger has been removed, my dear. Or at the very least, fettered."

Arthur stared.

"By *love,* my dear." Beatrice laughed. "Hadn't you picked up on that? He is besotted with Miss McDaniel. As long as Thia benefits from our protection and training, Cormac won't do a thing against us."

"Poor bugger." He walked on. "If that's true."

She caught up in four strides. "Sorry?"

"A difficult business, love."

She endeavored to gauge his mood, but he was keeping his face forward, leaving her only a side view of one eye and half his mouth.

"Is that why Miss McDaniel's pendant remains unfortified?"

he asked. "You're holding that out like a prize, are you? One more reason for her to enter the fold? That too is a dangerous game to play, Bea. What if something happens to her in the meantime, when a fully warded pendant might have kept her safe?"

She made no response; they were within the hearing of the two security agents outside the closed office.

"Sir. Madam," said the senior of the two, a man with buzzed wheat-blond hair and a perpetual scowl. Harry Jones. He had been promoted immediately following the Inverness attack. Meant to be temporary, that would in all likelihood be made permanent. Nearly thirteen weeks later, and his predecessor remained in coma.

Yet another tragedy wrought by Idris Cathmor, that attack. The lives lost. The injuries. Cassandra was to blame as well, Beatrice allowed. Evidence at the time had pointed so conclusively to Cormac that it was difficult to amend her thinking.

To blame him and his father was easier than to admit that the Society had in some way allowed that to happen by way of misplaced trust and, worse, inattention.

"He is inside?" Arthur asked Jones unnecessarily. That was why the men stood there, after all. The skin around his eyes and mouth was drawn, Beatrice noted; a sure sign of either anxiety or frustration. In this case, she presumed both.

Jones stepped aside, giving access. "I should mention that he didn't look like himself. When he walked up. Made things trickier than they needed to be."

Arthur paused in turning the knob. "Not like himself?"

"Like a different person," Jones said. The other agent, a bald man by the name of Taylor, held out an image printed from security footage.

Beatrice stepped forward to take it and, indeed, the subject was nothing like Cormac as they knew him. She passed the printout to Arthur and asked Jones, "A glamour?"

He nodded. "Readings confirmed it."

"You'll append this to his file, I trust." Arthur returned the page to the other agent.

"Of course, sir," Jones said. "Thin as it is."

Cormac was very good at what he did, which meant there was little known about either him or his centuries of activity. Since October's events, other agencies and organizations had been queried. So far, none had much to add.

"Thank you." Arthur pushed open the door.

"Remain here," Beatrice told the agents and then followed Arthur into the cramped, spartan room. Its beige walls were devoid of artwork or window; its furnishings, a purely functional table and chairs.

Cormac sat at the far side, facing the door, with the whole of the table between him and whoever might enter.

Nothing about his appearance connected him with the man in the printout she had just seen. Not the waxed canvas field jacket he now wore nor the black jumper beneath. Not the brown hair, stylishly cut. Not the whole of his preternaturally attractive face.

He resembled himself—or, more accurately, the self that he most often presented to them, which in by its very nature was damned deceptive.

For one thing, despite his presumed age, he appeared to be in his thirties. For another, he was not physically imposing. With his average height and build, he could easily be underestimated in terms of threat. Beatrice, however, had seen him in action.

Cormac's interest skipped over Arthur to fix on her. "Is this how you treat your friends?" he asked, his voice a mild, lightly accented baritone.

The accent itself was difficult to pin down. English, yes, as if trained for the stage but with overtones of the North and also, perhaps, a different era.

Arthur sputtered. "Now see here—"

She silenced him with a firm hand on his shoulder and then moved to sit across from Cormac. "Is that what we are now? Friends?"

"Would you prefer the alternative?" Mischief glinted in eyes the color of a tempestuous sea.

"Your appearance caused unnecessary trouble."

"One never knows who might be watching."

Arthur noisily pulled out a chair. "What is it that you want?"

"Arthur Norbert Barnstable, I presume," Cormac said with a smile that boded ill—for her as it turned out, when he asked with feigned innocence, "Did she not tell you?"

Beside her, Arthur paused in the act of seating himself.

"I see that she hadn't." Cormac's smile widened. "I want to meet with Cassandra Swinton. Alone."

"No."

Beatrice and Arthur had spoken simultaneously. She qualified it with, "Not alone."

That earned her one of Arthur's warning looks. "Bea."

She knew what she was doing. "Quentin will be present in the room." She did not mention that she would observe and record the entire encounter.

"Bea," Arthur repeated. He had yet to sit.

She would have to lay this out for him, when as the director he ought to have understood immediately. She asked Cormac, "This concerns Idris Cathmor's missing collection?"

"It does."

"If that collection fell into the wrong hands"—here she sent Arthur a look of her own—"how dangerous might that be?"

Cormac merely lifted a brow. Annoying creature.

But Arthur had taken her point. "You will wear a blindfold to and from the meeting," he said brusquely. "You are not a member."

Cormac's response was a languid shrug.

Beatrice felt a momentary concern. Doubtless he possessed an excellent sense of direction, given his raven abilities. She would arrange to have him taken on as convoluted a route as possible.

After a perfunctory knock, the door opened and Quentin strode in. He used his cane but lightly. She eyed him critically, found his stance too easy, his expression too bright.

"What did I miss?" he asked, far too cheerful.

Drunk, damn him. Or worse.

CHAPTER 5

The crisp late-winter light brought out a wealth of detail in the mountains across the valley while, above, the cloudless midday sky was a deep, rich blue. The construction sounds were quieter than usual, coming only from down at the Plaza.

Halfway down First Street, between the Landmark and the Post Office, Kendra left the sidewalk for the alley that served as access to two parking lots and the back of the long block of buildings on Main. Typical of alleys, passageways, and paths in Granite Springs, it had a name: Founders Way.

There were any number of things she could be doing with the end of her lunch break, yet here she was, using it to walk to Founders Hall. As for her intent, she supposed she would know when she got there. Call it intuition, instinct, or a waste of time, but the issue of the property's ownership had been nagging at her since morning.

Founders Hall was in the exact middle of its block and equidistant from the Landmark and Eclectica. It had the same registered owner as the biker bar associated with the Rekkrs. That bar held the residual feel of a terrible event—or events, plural; she hadn't been able to tell.

That had been nagging at her, too, that feeling.

Her talents were physical. Hand-to-hand combat. Weapons made of solid matter, whether infused with magic or not. She held power, yes, but could only make use of it through action. It made her faster, stronger, more alert, but it was not for her to wield in its own right. Not like how Murphy could shape and launch *fýr,* or even a basic use like lighting a candle with a finger-snap.

Nor was she psychic—hell, she had barely any skill with the Sight, and that was low-level basic. So it had been surprising to step inside the Valhalla in December and feel horror. It had been as if, along with cooking grease, cigarette smoke, and spilled beer, the place was coated with the worst emotions. Hatred, rage—everything awful. Weeks later, the memory of that remained horribly present.

Unlike the Valhalla, Founders Hall seemed unobjectionable. A squarish, four-story building that only gave the impression of enormity because, with the exception of the Landmark one block away, no others approached it in size. The side which faced First Street lacked windows, as if designed in expectation of future construction—or, she supposed, it could have been the other way around; something that had once been next to it had been removed. Presently, mounted on the plain brick surface was the ruined framework for a reindeer-pulled sleigh done in string lights. A limp piece of exploded balloon-float hung from a bent antler.

During the parade attack, she and her team had scaled the brick exterior in order to take a position on the roof. She had wondered then about the absence of outer security measures, but had been too thankful for it to give it much thought. The interior protections were rumored to be top-notch. Maybe that was enough. Yet she couldn't imagine anyone in the business of renting storage space would believe there could be *too much* security. Even assuming the idea was to avoid attracting attention—having a lot of elaborate measures could suggest that whatever was inside was *worth* all the fuss—that there wasn't so much as a single one outside *was* odd.

She chafed her hands. Within the shade of the building, the temperature dropped sharply. She should have worn gloves— and not just for warmth: It seemed that fate was presenting her with a chance to go inside, and gloves would have guaranteed that she wouldn't leave prints.

The rear entry was deeply recessed. An alcove, she thought that sort of thing might be called, with the door installed on the right side—perpendicular to, not facing, the Way. There was a single step up from ground level to cement. From any angle other than straight on, it would be difficult to see.

The door itself, metal and rather thick, had been propped open with a dented coffee can. Closer inspection showed it to be filled with sand and cigarette butts.

She searched for signs of surveillance, video or otherwise.

From what she understood, shops that leased space in the front had no access to other parts of the building or even a pass-through to the alley for trash pickup or parking. An odd arrangement, but that was often the norm with older buildings, whether by original design or changes over the years.

Case in point, the second recessed doorway further down. Framed by once-glossy tiles, it was a remnant of the building's years as a lodge—Elks or something. A neon arrow mounted above continued to receive electricity, humming and glowing at all hours. Within the former entrance, however, there was no door, only scarred cement and plaster where one had been permanently sealed and covered over.

She reached beneath her coat and into her trouser pocket for her cellphone. Edith had shared an app for ward detection. Before it, Kendra had used a dowsing rod—not exactly inconspicuous. Now she looked perfectly normal, a woman come to a standstill to respond to a text or an email or check the stock market or Instagram a photo or make a TikTok or whatever else people were doing on social media this season.

She touched the app's icon, then made sure it loaded before she locked the screen and dropped the phone into her coat's outer pocket. A signal would be broadcast, or it would look for them . . . Edith had explained about Bluetooth and Wifi and a database of known patterns of resonance, but most of it had gone over Kendra's head. The only thing she figured she needed to know was that the app could detect energy-based spellwork from a distance of ten to fifteen feet.

Without hesitation she walked to the open door and crossed the threshold. Behave as if you belong, she had been taught, and most people would assume you did. Anyone who might have observed her out their office window or as they walked or drove by would think nothing of her later.

The air was redolent of old building. Dust and must and pine-scented cleaner. No warning signal yet from her phone.

She stood not in a room but a vestibule. Straight ahead was a set of upward leading stairs; adjacent was another door left ajar, revealing a narrow set of downward stairs. Light penetrated only a few feet.

Staring into the darkness, she shivered. The air from below was colder than that of the alley. Damper, too. She backed away, turned her attention to the stairs going up. The floor's checkerboard pattern of beige and black linoleum continued up the treads like something out of an M. C. Escher print.

Floorboards creaked overhead and she froze.

Somewhere distant, on an upper story, a door clicked shut. She waited a solid minute before determining that the threat had passed. She cautiously started up.

At the level of a typical floor was a cramped landing. Boxes of various sizes, messily stacked, lined both sides. The smell of chemical cleaning agents grew stronger, and Kendra began to breathe quietly through her mouth to lessen the chance of a sneeze. Her nose was tickling.

She was on the final leg of stairs, her head not yet level with the next floor, when the squeal of stubborn hinges had her freeze a second time. Twenty, maybe twenty-five yards ahead by the sound, a door closed. Keys jingled and a lock turned. She continued to hold herself still, gambling that whoever was there would go deeper into the building instead of straight toward her.

"Please," came a familiar voice. "You don't understand the cost." Alma Robinson was the leader of The Retreat, a spiritual center located in the mountains northeast of town.

What was she doing here? The Retreat had multiple buildings on acres of land. It wouldn't need rented storage space, nor would Alma, personally. And why should she should sound so frightened?

Her voice—and two sets of footsteps—came closer; Kendra rapidly calculated options and risks. To leave would be noisy and she doubted there was time. Thinking to take cover, she looked to the boxes.

Restaurant supplies, according to the labels. Wine glasses by the gross. Serving trays. Cocktail napkins. The stacks were tight and too precariously tall to risk forcing herself between them, let alone behind. She felt like she was on the verge of a terrible mistake.

"It's no cost to me. Only profit. Always profit."

She startled at that second voice, familiar yet not. She had never heard such coldness in him. Such darkness. Her foot came down wrong on an uneven stair tread and she lost her balance. She caught herself on a stack, her fingers brushing across cardboard, and a sharp pain shot up her arm. Her ears rang as if her head were a struck bell, her brain the clapper.

She shook her hand, her head, and kept moving—clumsy, disoriented—down the stairs. Her phone was vibrating madly in her coat pocket.

The ward alarm.

"Wait here," she heard Neil instruct Alma, and she could

tell he knew. That was another shock. She had taken him for a skeptic, not a practitioner.

He had been pretending with her. Lying.

She gave up any remaining hope of stealth and ran down the stairs. Feet pounding, heart thumping. Her breathing was rough. Panicked. She never panicked. Never.

Her vision swam—No, not her vision. The stair treads were moving, the checker-patterned staircase pulling into itself.

What *was* this place?

She leapt the final distance, aiming for the open door and the ground outside as the floor's linoleum folded like origami paper to expose a dark, yawning hole. She landed shy of the threshold but momentum carried her forward. She stumbled past the open door and almost tripped over the coffee can. It went over, scattering sand and cigarette butts and as she set off in a flat-out run across the parking lot.

Get away. Take cover. Her goal was a dense planting of native shrubs and grasses, an experiment in drought-tolerant landscaping let run wild. She dove the final distance.

She thought she made it in time. Neil had not yet reached the top of the stairs when she had made her leap over the hole. To follow her, he first would have to put the staircase and floor back in order, wouldn't he?

She waited, her gaze fixed on the building. She couldn't see the door within its alcove, but she would see if someone came out, into Founders Way. She forced calm into her breathing. Her pulse continued to race.

Why had Neil been there? And what the hell kind of magic had that been? The moving stairs and floor, the pitch-black hole—bottomless for all she knew—were the stuff of nightmares. She stifled a shudder, and only then realized that her right hand was moving, rubbing her left—the one that had triggered the wards. Those fingers had gone somewhat numb.

She risked a glance away from the Hall.

The tips were cobalt blue, as if she had dipped them in ink. Marked.

● ○ ●

Founders Hall

Upon his return, the man Kendra and most of Granite Springs knew as Neil Amundsen found Alma exactly where he'd left her. He walked past. "I'll have someone show you out."

"What's happening?" the *blakkr-skinn* woman asked.

As if he would answer to her.

Her next question followed him down the corridor and held an amusing note of desperation. "You can't just—I have not agreed to anything."

He paused to look back. Such a proud thing she was, with her chin jutted boldly forward and her spine ramrod straight. What a pleasure it was to put her in her place. "Haven't you?"

"No." She dared to hold his gaze. "What you ask—the intent of it. The darkness will come back on us all, threefold."

"On *you* it will, yes. On *your* people." Not him. Never him. He watched the realization dawn.

The horror on her face delighted, and he smiled. "Hey," he said smoothly, "it's nothing to me if you won't do it. I'll file the paperwork on another tree removal this afternoon." He turned away, walked out of sight around the corner.

One . . . two . . . three.

"Skati," she called after him, using his honorific. At last.

With the right pressure on the right spot, anyone could be bent to his will.

"We'll do it. Do you hear me?" She was pleading. Fear bled through every word. "I said we'll do it!"

The rush of victorious pleasure was intense. "Excellent."

Although he had spoken softly, the acoustics were such that it would carry. She had heard. He had no doubt.

When he reached the inner offices, he saw that his staff had anticipated his need: His scrying mirror awaited on his desk. He sat. "Have my guest escorted out. Through the tunnel."

The staircase had performed adequately but the outer door had taken precious seconds to close after the ward had been tripped, and that was unacceptable.

It should not have been open in the first place.

"Where is Kjeld?" he asked casually, and drew the mirror close before sparing a glance at the five men present.

Pale faces, all. Silent confirmation.

"I believe I was perfectly clear." He began circling his hand over the mirror's polished obsidian face. "No use of the street level door. Not even for fucking Starbucks."

The mirror activated, momentarily sparing the men. It was their fault the intruder had gotten as far as he had. Security from the offices to the outer door had been deactivated so that Kjeld could bring in overpriced, over-sweetened treats.

How fortunate, then, that Skati didn't trust his own people not to steal, so he had personally placed additional measures on the boxes. That was what the intruder had triggered—and why he would be easy to track: He had been tagged.

Or rather, *she,* Skati amended as the mirror's presentation of fragmented shapes and colors coalesced to show a troubling complication.

He rubbed a hand across his mouth. Fury and reason warred. Hot against cold.

Cold won.

Eventually.

"Have my guest brought back to me," he ordered, referring to Alma. His men snapped into action.

His voice had been tense. He worked on that while he made a call on his mobile. He wanted the number to be recognized.

In the mirror's show, Kendra Ross took out her smartphone and stared at the screen. She had left her hiding place in the ugly experimental "garden" and was stopped halfway across

Main Street—undoubtedly headed for the Landmark and its protections.

Little good would they do her.

Carried within the blue stain, working its way deeper and deeper into her skin, was a compulsion spell. One of Skati's best. Drawing on it, he prompted her to take his call.

Bewilderment and terror mingled in her expression as she touched the screen, lifted the phone to her ear.

Her reluctance suggested the worst-case scenario: She had heard him with Alma. What and how much were irrelevant; she could connect him—as Neil Amundsen—to the building. That could lead to other connections.

Too, whether or not she understood their significance, she had seen the boxes of supplies.

"Kendra, love," he began, then looked up from the scrying vision. His men had returned with Alma. He gestured for her to approach and his men to stay out. They closed the door as she crossed to his desk.

"I've someone here who needs to speak with you," he told Kendra while he held Alma's wary gaze. "It's a matter of some urgency, I'm afraid. Do you have a moment?"

He tugged on the compulsion spell's marks. In the middle of the street, Kendra came to a dead stop.

Temporarily muting the phone, he told Alma, "My friend needs to forget the past, oh"—he had to think something had drawn her to come inside, some curiosity or suspicion, and when she might have picked that up—"let's make it from this morning on. Consider it proof of efficacy."

Alma shook her ornately braided head. "Without the herbal components, it won't be nearly as—"

He waved that away. "I won't hold that against you. A few hours should do it." He could put everything in place by then.

Alma stood close enough to be able to see into the mirror. She stiffened, ready to retreat. "You won't harm her."

Stubborn. And, it would seem, forgetful.

He could lie, he supposed. He simply directed her attention to a set of paperwork next to the mirror. An arborist's report, bought and paid for, and the Tree Commission's recommendation, obtained by other means.

Bribery and influence. He hadn't had to do much, considering. It was a lucky coincidence for him that the commission was oblivious to the very things under their jurisdiction—the *vordtré* and their role in maintaining the area's unique ethos.

"You won't harm her," Alma repeated with less confidence.

He put the mobile on speaker and set it between them on the desk. He had her. He returned his attention to the mirror.

Kendra had not moved. She was still in the street, her head bowed, hiding her terrified face from any view but his. The mirror's vision allowed him any angle, any distance. He went in close. Such lovely eyes she had—made more so by the fear currently filling them. A shame he wouldn't be able to enjoy that more thoroughly.

"Still with me, my sweet?" He pitched his voice toward the phone.

She shuddered. Part of her wanted to fight the compulsion, but it was too strong.

"Wonderful," he said, and with the lift of his hand, he got ready to cue Alma. "Here's someone for you. Do listen closely, all right? There's a good girl."

CHAPTER 6

Brigantium Annex
Whitehall, London
30 January

Sound and atmosphere and an excellent, inherent sense of direction could communicate much about a place, which meant that the hexed blindfold Cormac had been made to wear was more nuisance than hindrance. Beatrice Meriwether had required that he be taken on a ridiculous route but should have saved them all the trouble. He had flown over London countless times in raven form.

He knew well its distances, its magnetic fields.

"They're less than five minutes out." Her voice placed her ahead of him by roughly seven feet. A metallic rasp and snap of a door latch preceded a change in air pressure. Her heeled shoes clicked on cement as she walked on. Stopped. "Nine steps forward."

Acoustics suggested she stood in a small, enclosed space.

The hands that had gripped his arms for the whole of this process pulled away. The two escorting agents had used more force than mere guidance necessitated, all so he wouldn't rip off the blindfold, presumably, and learn exactly where he was.

Two steps took him through a doorway, and Beatrice came to stand behind. He continued forward. Six more steps.

The door closed.

She had told him to take nine but he didn't feel the need. He stopped. Braced himself.

The Brigantium would be foolish to try something against him while he was technically (albeit temporarily) not a threat, but old habits—especially within a bureaucratic organization such as this—died hard. Only a few months ago they would have considered him quite a prize.

If he were to disappear, no one would know where to look.

Who would even know to try? Or care? He always worked alone. He spent most of that time in disguise or otherwise attempting to avoid notice. He had no friendships to speak of—or, he hadn't until a few months ago.

While his eyes had nothing but black fabric to see, it was an opportunity his memory couldn't resist. Thia McDaniel. Her smile. The weight and depth of expression in her hazel eyes. The light, floral scent of whatever soaps she favored. The soft warmth of her skin. He had been doing such a good job of not thinking about her at all.

Yes, she might wonder if she never heard from him. But she would likely assume it was an absence from her life, particularly, and by choice. After all, he hadn't kept in contact with her these past weeks, since leaving Granite Springs. Leaving her.

Assuming she *did* become concerned, where would she turn for assistance but to the Brigantium? Beatrice would feed her a concocted story, and that would be the end of it.

Declan Murphy, though. Thia might turn to him, and when Cormac missed the deadline for getting him the Achill Bell, Murphy would have no choice but to mount a search. How ironic that a bargain made upon pain of death might be what kept Cormac from suffering the same incarcerated fate as the woman he had come here to see.

He stayed braced, but the door remained unlocked and only

Beatrice had entered the room with him. He could hear her, standing a safe distance to his left. Her breaths came calmly. Evenly. She believed she was in control.

"May I?" Not waiting, Cormac removed the blindfold from around his head. There was no need for his eyes to adjust—the room's only light came through a pane of glass which ran the length of the north wall. A one-way mirror. The room beyond that was brightly lit, the better for the mirror to work, by a pair of harsh overhead fluorescents.

He wadded the blindfold in his fist. The hex on the fabric had prevented him from using his Sight.

No matter.

"Whitehall." He pointed above Beatrice's head. Her mouth pinched in dismay and no small amount of anger, he was sure. Stairs, elevators, straightaways, turns. Down, up, up, down, around and around. He had told them what a waste of time it was, but his escorts had persisted.

Enjoying himself, he pivoted forty-five degrees clockwise to point again. "Whitehall Place." Another pivot, another point. "Court." Another. "Horseguards."

Full circle, he smiled and, opening his fist, let the strip of fabric drop to the floor.

"Do you have permission from the new owner"—an upward tip of his chin indicated the structure above—"or do they not know this is down here?"

By his calculation, they stood beneath the western portion of what had once housed the massive War Office. The building had been bought by an international conglomerate with plans to transform it into apartments and a luxury hotel.

"They are unaware." Her expression was murderous. "And so they shall remain."

"Of course." Much as he might relish making trouble for her and her Society, he lacked the time.

He went to the one-way mirror. The room on the other side

was equally compact and equipped with a metal table and two chairs. All were bolted to the floor. A floor, as he could sense, that had been lined with lead. So had the walls and ceiling.

On a hunch, he touched a finger to the glass, found that leaded as well. Rather old fashioned and not entirely magic-proof, but there were additional measures in place. It was not lead that restricted his Sight.

He took a slow, measured breath. His unease annoyed him. His half-sister's powers had been bound to a crystal sphere. She was disarmed, physically and magically—and no match for him regardless.

"This will be recorded?" he asked Beatrice, more as a way to pass the time. Of course it would be recorded.

"Yes. There are cameras in all of our secured areas. They record constantly."

Inside, outside. The modern world: Cameras everywhere— mounted and handheld—filming everything and nothing.

"If you attempt to do her harm," she threatened, "you will be stopped. We do not condone torture, not even for vital information."

"It has its uses," he said with a casualness he did not feel. "But as a way of obtaining information? Not effective." He'd seen enough of it to know.

"Good," she said, as if he had assured her of something.

People tended to hear what they wanted.

Footsteps in the corridor heralded Cassandra's arrival. On the other side of the glass, the door opened. Quentin entered and positioned himself in the near, facing corner. Two guards followed. She was between them, much as Cormac had been. She wore a typical prison jumpsuit, this one the sallow green of a bowl of mushy peas. Her hands were cuffed behind her back.

"Give them a moment to secure her in place," Beatrice said when Cormac moved.

Ignoring this, he walked out. The interview room's door was open. The guards were placing Cassandra in the nearest chair, the one which put her back to the entrance—and to him. Had she been told whom she was to meet? Was she expecting him?

The guards uncuffed her wrists only to lock them into metal bands welded to the tabletop. Then they left, stepping past Cormac to station themselves outside.

That was his half-sister, sitting there. She had tried to kill him. Twice, at least. Their father had adored her and her twin brother and had planned to make them his "vessels"—heirs not only to his worldly goods but to his very being. After that failed, she had secreted away everything of value from Fiend's Fell.

Everything that rightfully belonged to Cormac, no matter Idris's intentions.

Cormac had helped acquire that collection. His blood sacrifice had kept Idris alive long past when other means had lost efficacy. What had Cassandra done compared to that? What were her thirty-some years compared to Cormac's centuries? Some two hundred and seventy five years of servitude to a man with a knack for cruelty.

He stopped after crossing the threshold. Waited. The steel door thunked shut, a scant inch from his back. Several bolts shot home.

Cassandra did not move, but her posture held new tension. She sensed an arrival—but did she specifically sense *him?*

Quentin, as had been agreed, leaned back against the wall. "Pretend I'm not here."

Not bloody likely, but at least he wasn't close.

Cormac, with his face neutral and his posture deliberately easy, rounded the table to sit opposite the woman made to be his rival.

Tonight, despite the sickly green jumpsuit, no makeup, and with her treacle-colored hair pulled back into a simple tail, she looked only a little worse for wear.

She had not gotten her glamour-magazine features from her father, that was for certain. There was nothing of him in her but the eyes. The same uncommon shade of amber. The same predatory gleam.

They narrowed, now, in the same way Idris's had—when he would study Cormac for vulnerabilities. For any weakness, no matter how slight, to use to advantage.

"Isn't this is a treat." Her lips curved, but not in what could be considered a smile. More in the fashion of a wolf baring its fangs. Idris had taught her well. "My only living relative come to call."

Leaning back, Cormac assumed a lounging pose. Idris had taught him too, and for far longer. He let his gaze flick over her manacled wrists.

Her hands fisted. "This should be you. You're the one who committed patricide, *brother dear.* A far worse crime than any of my peccadillos."

Even by his questionable standards, that term fell well short of the mark. But of course, if something negatively impacted her plans, if it hurt *her,* that was what mattered, not how her actions might have harmed others. Idris had been the same.

Below the table, Cormac removed his yew-handled folding knife from his jacket pocket. "I came across a compendium of sorts." He opened the blade, recently purified in a salt water bath. "You'd find it of interest, I think."

"I very much doubt—"

He lunged across the table, reached around to the back of her head to grab hold of her ponytail and yank her forward. Her face slammed down as, with a quick slash of the blade, he came away with a hank of hair.

He released her and was already back in his seat when she lurched up as far as the restraints allowed. She pulled against them, kicked a table leg, swore. Kicked again. The bolts held firm.

Cormac returned the knife to his pocket, then pulled out a square of white cotton. He unfurled that and carefully laid it on the table. Mindful not to touch the hair more than necessary, he coiled it upon the cloth.

"You're letting him assault me?" Cassandra shouted, looking to Quentin. When he merely shrugged, she let out an enraged shriek and gave the restraints one more go before dropping back onto her chair to sulk.

Cormac methodically folded each side of the cloth. He then folded that smaller square twice more before securing it with a length of silken cord.

"What will you do with it?" She had good reason to sound apprehensive. Innumerable awful things could be done to a person via their hair.

He shaped a precise smile, designed to infuriate and terrify, and stood, still holding the packet.

Quentin used his cane to rap twice on the door.

It opened while Cormac walked past the table, past Idris's daughter, without so much as a glance.

Her furious but empty threats followed him out.

● ○ ●

The Rowan Space, Eclectica
Granite Springs

"Since Imbolc is in two days, I thought we'd try divination," Abby announced as Thia settled onto a meditation cushion. It was covered in magenta silk, and a cheerful gold tassel had been stitched to each corner. Abby was already seated, facing her across a small arrangement of objects. Her cushion was done in purple, with silver tassels.

She and Abby were in Eclectica's upstairs activity space, the usual location for these guided sessions, and positioned in the center of the room's namesake: a circular inlay of rowan wood added to the historic building's original oak flooring.

Wary, she eyed the objects she would be asked to use. They looked innocuous enough, and unlike the past few sessions, there were not many: A box of small candles, familiar from Eclectica's shelves; a small bowl of water; and a stack of paper napkins. This might not be so bad.

She'd had a fairly smooth run of late—thanks in part maybe (she couldn't be sure) to a focusing wand from Quentin. He had given it after her inadvertently epic contribution to the parade events. She had intended to summon a single one of the explosive devices that had been placed along Main Street. Instead, she had brought them all.

If Cormac hadn't been there with her, she could have blown up an entire city block. And, of course, everyone in it.

Since she had taken to carrying the crystal-tipped palladium wand, there had been no unintentional levitations of objects, no accidental fires. No major losses of control whatsoever.

Still, she hadn't yet reached a point where she could enter into these practice sessions without anxiety (if not outright dread). She couldn't forget how things had gone before, when it seemed like the Cailleach's powers had intentions of their own—when they'd come up far too intense during a spell and refuse to settle. Or when they'd awaken without being called and then buzz along her nerves like an electrical current in search of an outlet.

That kind of power could be weaponized. She had seen it done. Had seen spheres of glowing, crackling energy form at peoples' hands. Had seen them launched at others, and the consequences.

To be struck by the energy's white form—*wanfȳr*—resulted in incapacitating pain followed by unconsciousness. The blue form—*wælfȳr*—was lethal.

These thoughts were not helpful.

Today's lesson was divination. She wouldn't be trying to use magic to move or transform things, or working to call power into tangible form at her fingertips.

Abby finished arranging the objects to her satisfaction. The bowl of water was central. To its left was the box of candles. Napkins to the right. There was no matchbook or lighter to be seen.

Of course not. To light a wick with focused intention was a basic skill Thia was supposed to be practicing because practice made perfect. Theoretically.

"Is Kendra not coming?" She glanced at her watch, a sturdy chronograph she had found in her great-aunt's dresser. Five minutes past six. Eclectica had been closed for half an hour.

Abby went to a supply cabinet. "She must be stuck at work. Or with the city manager." Her expression was mischievous.

"Are they officially dating yet?" Thia asked. "Or is she still claiming its just reconstruction business?"

"With her I'm not sure there's a difference," Abby said with a chuckle. From a drawer she took out four fat pillar candles, each of a different color. "But I think she's getting there. I'll set the circle."

"Do you want some help?" Thia moved to rise.

"Work on centering yourself. Clear your mind. The more clear you are, the clearer the message will be." Abby started placing the pillars at stations on the inlaid floor, one for each cardinal direction. Green, representing earth, at the north. Red for fire at the south. Air's yellow, east. Water's blue, west. From her pocket she took out a lighter and then, walking the perimeter, lit the wicks.

Envy became one more intrusion to be cleared away. Abby didn't carry power, or at least not in the way Thia did. That meant Abby got to use tools such as matches and lighters.

Oh, how Thia would have loved to never use magic. Not for lighting candles, not for opening a garage door. Not for anything.

She had not meant to claim the powers bound to the Stone of Shadows.

Yet she had, and ignoring them was not an option. Not only would the power not allow it, there were threats which went along with possession. People that would want to take them from her, or want something from her because of them—and would not hesitate to use her friends as leverage. She would be a fool not to learn how to protect herself and her friends from threats like that. And from the more present danger of her lack of control.

Thia could not rely on the focusing wand—on any item or person—to be ever-present or capable of preventing disaster. What if the wand broke? What if trouble came when she was alone? She needed to be able to control her power unaided. Until then, she remained a potential danger not just to herself but to everyone around. One day, the training wheels would have to come off.

This was not that day, though.

She removed the small wand from her cargo pocket, held it in front of her chest. At each tip was a clear crystal. The shaft was wrapped with gold-toned wire. She didn't know if it was actual gold. It quickly warmed in her nervous grip. The circle was almost set.

She engaged her Sight—so far the only new talent she could tap without concern. This use of it, anyway. There might be more, but so far she had only employed it as an overlay, to reveal magic and other elements not normally visible. That wasn't so much a matter of *doing* as it was of *allowing*. There was no engagement of power, no wielding, and therefore— she figured—no risk of backfire or loss of control.

As she attuned to it, the circle's energetic perimeter began to appear to her as a faint haze, similar to the soap-bubble-like surface of a protection ward, but less transparent.

Abby stepped inside, then took what she called a cleansing breath. Eyes closed, she extended her arms. "Bless this circle, cast today to keep all trouble far away while, safe within its unseen light, we do our work for good and right. As above, so below." She brought her hands in, palm to palm, as she bowed her head. "Lady of Silence, please hear these words and make it so."

Thia bowed her head in return, more out of respect for her friend than from any deeply held belief of her own. It wasn't that she did *not* believe, or that she felt conflicted about the loose "Christmas and Easter" Presbyterianism she had picked up from her parents. It was that all of this was too new.

And there were so many different ways and belief systems. Abby was a practicing Wiccan, with all the complexities that entailed. Members of The Retreat, a large spiritual complex outside of town (don't call it a compound, she'd been told) had their own thing. The Society of Brigantium followed an idiosyncratic mix of magic systems and folklore native to western Europe—or, more particularly, around the United Kingdom. Cormac was a figure out of those same myths. And Thia was walking around with power that had belonged to an ancient Celtic goddess.

"Right," Abby said, settling on her cushion. "What you're going to do here is some carromancy."

"Fortune telling from wax." Thia had read that on the box of candles. *For purposes of divination* was printed in Gothic font below a cartoonish rendition of a green-skinned witch and glowing crystal ball.

Abby removed three candles. Short and white and about a quarter inch in diameter, they resembled what Eclectica sold for use in German folk decorations around Christmastime at a third of the cost. Presumably these must have some special kind of wax.

"The process couldn't be simpler," Abby said, tying a black ribbon (included in the box) around the candle trio. "The key is in your connection to the energy—your own and that of the world around you—so that a communication channel is opened. The stronger the connection and your belief in it, the stronger the results will be."

There probably wouldn't be much result, in that case.

Oh, well. As long as she didn't lose control and damage the room or Abby or herself, she'd consider the exercise a success. Whether she got a clear result didn't matter to her so much as safety. She laid the wand beside her right hip, within quick reach should she feel anything beginning to go awry.

"I filled the scrying dish with Tara Water," Abby said, referring to another of Eclectica's popular items. "Otherwise we'd need to bless it first."

"Okay." Thia checked but, unsurprisingly, the water looked like water.

Yet it cost fifteen dollars an ounce.

"What you'll do," Abby instructed, "is pick up the bundle of candles, light them, let some wax melt, and then drip it into the water." She pulled a folded piece of notebook paper from beneath her cushion. "I wrote out what you're to say, but I'll cue you for each bit."

Thia took the paper, opened it to skim. There weren't many phrases, thankfully, and because Abby was meticulous, they were numbered. They were also in rhyme. That suggested the origin. "This is Wiccan?"

"It is. The coven does this one every Imbolc after the feast."

Thia balanced the paper on her knee. "Do I say the first one before lighting or . . . ?"

"Before." Abby sat straight. Intent. She might only be an observer in these training sessions, but she invested herself fully.

Thia rolled her neck and shoulders a couple of times, blew out a breath. So far her tension wasn't too bad, maybe a five on a ten-scale. Heck, she might enjoy this one. With her left hand, she picked up the bundled candles. From a lesson on color symbolism, she knew that the black of the ribbon meant protection and wisdom and worked to banish negativity.

She could use all that.

Reaching deep within herself, she called on the Cailleach's power. She would probably never find words to describe the process. Cobbled together from anecdotal advice, intuition, and total guesswork, it felt, in a way, like rousing something that slumbered in the marrow of her bones.

As the internal buzz began, she closed her eyes, the better to concentrate. Too much power and she would have no hope of maintaining control. Not enough, and she'd learn nothing of herself and her capabilities—or, rather, her limitations.

She had come across an internet video once of an artist who applied electricity to wood. The current traveled the grain, crackling and burning along paths of least resistance, similar to how the Cailleach's power acted within her, traveling the lines of her nerves, seeking the quickest, most efficient way out. Seeking a freedom she could not afford to allow.

The hairs along her arms prickled. She worked to reduce the flow—as if closing a faucet to a trickle. The power responded, thankfully not fighting the restriction. When it reached her hands and held steady, she opened her eyes. So far so good, but her discomfort over speaking the first phrase must have shown.

"Problem?" Abby asked.

"No, no. It's fine. I'm fine." But, really, why couldn't these things be done in plain language? Focus, she ordered herself. *Focus.* "Candles three the future see and share today to guide my way."

With her right hand above the candles, she snapped three times. In succession, the wicks caught fire. And, even better, nothing else had.

The finger snaps had been Kendra's suggestion. Before that, when Thia had tried using concentration and intention alone, she had lit all sorts of things—none what she had wanted.

"Let them burn a minute or so," Abby said, "until there's a good amount of melted wax pooled at the tops. When it feels right—intuitively—tip them over the water so the wax drops in."

"Okay." Thia glanced at the paper, prepared the next phrase in her mind while the flames ate noisily into the wicks.

The minute passed. "Air and earth to feed the fire. Water to shape and, through that, transpire." She turned the candles over the bowl. Three molten threads entered the water and, twisting around one another, solidified.

She quickly righted the candles. More wax slid down the sides, threatening her fingers.

"You can extinguish them," Abby said. "Then say the last bit."

Thia concentrated, holding the power-supported intention in her mind, and snapped. All three flames went out. So far so *great.* Relief felt almost like happiness.

She spoke the final phrase: "Imbolc is nigh, and the coming spring. Help me see what that may bring." She set the candles aside and looked into the water.

So much for her sense of triumph. Shouldn't the wax look more like *something?* In the amorphous blob that rested on the bottom of the dish, all she could see was failure. "That's it?"

"It needs to cool." Abby bent down, looking into the bowl. "But, yeah. That's it." She seemed excited.

Thia couldn't understand why. She tipped her head this way, that way. Squinted. Maybe the blob looked less blobby from Abby's side?

"That should do it," Abby said. "Take it out."

Gently, Thia fished the wax out of the water. It was about the size of a quarter and roughly the same shape. She set it on the napkin.

Abby leaned in again. "What do you think? Don't work at it. Just say the first thing that comes to mind."

"I think it looks like a blob of wax." With her fingertip, Thia turned the thing over. No help. She tried another squint. Her mind remained stubbornly blank. "Lumpish. Squiggly. Maybe I did it wrong?"

Par for the course—to borrow a favorite phrase from her golf-obsessed family.

"There is no wrong," Abby said. "Not in this, anyway. The connection might drop out or fail to form, so nothing would come through. But I could feel the energy here. Couldn't you? I'm sure there's something. We haven't seen it yet, is all. Try picking it up."

Taking careful hold with thumb and forefinger, Thia raised the blob first to eye level and then higher, peering up at it with the dark blue ceiling to serve as a backdrop.

"Oh," she said, pleasantly surprised. At one end was a hole crossed with spoke-like lines. "There's a wheel." She turned her hand to show Abby and her eye caught another distinct shape. Formed from ridges and shadow, it curved along the underside. So she pointed to that too. "Scissors."

"That's weird." Abby held out a hand. "May I?"

"You have to get the light just right." Thia set the wax on her friend's palm. "I know it's a goofy thing to see, but—"

"No, I'm sure you saw scissors." Abby lifted it to look at it the way Thia had. "Yeah, there they are. What I meant is that it's weird to have both of those signs together. The wheel is usually interpreted to mean the return of one who has been away. Scissors mean separation."

"Separation could refer to the present and a return is what's to come." Thia couldn't help but think of Cormac. Wanted it to be about Cormac.

Abby continued to frown at the wax. "Maybe."

"You don't think so?"

"It seems like unnecessary effort to form two signs for one event." Abby set the wax back on the napkin. "For someone to return after being away, obviously there was a separation. It's redundant."

"Right."

Granted, Thia's experience was limited, but fortune telling did tend to involve a lack of information, not a surplus. So it was more likely that a specific and unique piece of information was intended. In other words:

"There will be a return," she offered, "*and* a separation."

And possibly neither one had to do with Cormac.

"We can meditate on it." Abby smoothly arranged herself into lotus position. "See if more comes through."

With reluctance born of joints and muscles that had little patience for sitting on floors—special cushion or no—Thia straightened her spine and rested her hands on her knees.

She ought to feel good about what she'd done. The results might be unhelpfully vague, but hadn't her real goal simply been to do no harm? She, Abby, and the room were no worse for wear. No bruises. No scorch marks. No blood or broken glass. She would endure more meditation time and be grateful for it.

● ○ ●

Brigantium Annex
Whitehall, London

The door shut at Cormac's back as the two guards plus his security escort stepped close, hedging him in. Beatrice tore out of the observation room. "You said you would not touch her."

Who was she to tell him what spells he could or could not perform and what he could or could not take? She and her Society would benefit from what he was doing. Only incidentally, and not nearly as much as he would, but still. He needed no one's approval. Not anymore.

"So I did not," he countered, and let a glimmer of power

show in his eyes. A warning flare, there and gone. "I touched her hair." Using sleight of hand rather than actual magic, he made the silk-wrapped hank in question vanish.

"A breach of the spirit if not the letter."

"Surely in our line of work you understand the importance of specificity."

Beatrice glared but no power answered in her eyes.

He waited.

Not long. "The hair is not to leave our custody. Whatever you do, you will do under observation and only with approval. *My* approval." She turned and began walking, leaving him no choice but to follow like a damn servant. The other agents remained behind.

"You ought to be thanking me." He came up alongside her.

"Really." Said with infuriating condescension.

With some difficulty, he let that go. He required additional supplies. If the Brigantium would provide them, it would save him the time and effort of a trip home.

"No blindfold?" he teased. "And a direct route this time. I should think." When Beatrice didn't respond, he clicked his tongue. "No additional escorts, either."

"There are monitors should you try anything." A closed steel door lay ahead. She pulled out a ring of keys. "But why would you while I continue to be of use?" she asked shrewdly, then commenced work on the first of a tedious series of locks.

Each required its own key, kept in non-sequential order on the ring. This led to a lot of mucking about.

His patience at an end, he wove a spell in his mind and, with a swoosh of his finger and a flick of his hand, caused the door to open.

"A little antiquated, isn't it?" He preceded her into the next section of corridor. "All those locks?"

She closed the door—and commenced the infuriating lock and key process in reverse.

He should not have given in to impatience. The magic he had used on the lock was simple, but even simple could be revealing. He would not do it again.

That the Brigantium had not upgraded to biometric scanners seemed a curious oversight. He almost asked about it, but if they wanted to stay behind the times, that was fine with him. He had yet to meet a physical lock he couldn't pick.

Retinal and fingerprint scanners, however, were a different matter, and why he needed Cassandra's hair.

CHAPTER 7

Landmark Hotel
Granite Springs, Oregon
30 January

The sun having set, the Landmark's rooftop restaurant offered an expansive view of dramatic contrasts: bright and colorful Granite Springs set against the largely unlit backdrop of the Takelma Valley and its surrounding mountains. Inside, candle and firelight reflected off contemporary, upscale decor and tableware. Jewelry worn by many of the guests sparkled and flashed. Thia could not help feeling out of place while she and Abby waited by the hostess station. Her wool cargo pants and moss green cashmere sweater were nice and should have fit her in with the typical mix of locals and tourists. Tonight, however, the ambiance was "big city nice," reminiscent of fine dining in Los Angeles or San Francisco.

Granite Springs was changing in ways that went far beyond damage repair—and doing so quickly, if a relative newcomer like herself had noticed. What was the driving factor, money? Housing prices were skyrocketing due to high demand with severely limited availability. A number of long-time residents had already taken advantage, selling for three times what they had originally paid and leaving the area for one with a lower cost of living.

"The table is ready," said an unfamiliar voice, pulling Thia back from her mental drift.

Usually the hostess was an elegant young blonde, Samantha. This woman was also young and elegant but had sleek black hair, twisted into a glamorous updo.

"If you'll please follow me," she said, collecting several menu folios from the podium. Unlike Samantha, she did not engage in friendly banter on the way into the dining room.

Their destination was on the left, a four seat table adjacent to a bank of floor-to-ceiling windows. In the patio beyond, more diners sat in groupings of cushioned chairs and sofas. Outdoor heaters provided comfort while overhead strands of glowing crystals added sophisticated whimsy.

A uniformed server poured wine into glasses while another traded empty plates for filled.

"Tapas." Thia said, remembering Kendra had talked about it some weeks ago. "I hadn't realized you'd started that already."

"Not officially," the hostess said, waiting for Thia and Abby to settle in. "A number of hotel guests were amenable to a soft opening." She handed out menus, then laid the remainder at the unoccupied place. "I do apologize for your wait. This is Mr. Murphy's preferred table. Unfortunately, it is also favored by many of our returning guests. I misjudged the time the previous party would require."

"No worries," Thia assured her. They had arrived fewer than five minutes ago.

"It's not like *he's* here," Abby said with a tightness that boded ill. "Which means, table or not, we're still waiting—on him." She opened her menu and began to read.

With no change of expression, the hostess held up a slim black folder. "May I get you a beverage, or would you prefer to look over the list first? We're offering two special drinks this week—a blood-orange punch made with rum and bitters, and a sparkler made with pear cider and whiskey garnished with a stick of cinnamon."

"I'll have that one," Abby said, surprisingly.

"And for you?" the hostess asked Thia.

"Oh, I didn't think I'd—"

"Of course you will." Abby closed the dinner menu, set it aside. "He's paying, isn't he?"

"It's been a long day. And tomorrow will be another—okay, okay." She waved off her friend's insistent stare. "The punch, please."

"Very good," the hostess said. "I'll have those brought out along with a basket of our house-made rosemary bread."

Light and fluffy with a crisp crust and served hot from the oven. Already well acquainted, Thia's mouth watered. "I hope Murphy isn't much later," she said after the hostess's departure. "I won't have room left for the meal."

"He invites us and can't be bothered to be on time."

According to a clock above the bar, he was late by less than ten minutes, but Thia wasn't about to quibble. She pointed discretely to one of the larger parties seated across the room. "Isn't that Neil Amundsen?" So much for the idea that he and Kendra were on a date this evening.

Abby twisted to check. "Yep. City manager, mayor, and four council members. Parks and Rec head, too." She turned back, her expression wry. "Let's hope our tax dollars aren't picking up the tab."

Thia made a low sound of solidarity. She counted three wine bottles and several appetizer plates on their table. An extravagant night—unless they, too, were participating in the tapas event.

"I'm not sure what Kendra sees in him," Thia admitted. It had been bothering her. "But I've never met him, so I probably shouldn't judge. Have you?"

"No. So I shouldn't judge either—although I agree. She told me he has a great sense of humor, though, so who knows. Hey, Danny," she said as their server arrived with the cocktails and a cloth-covered basket of bread.

"*Thank* you." Thia immediately pulled out a piece, singeing her fingers. She let it drop to her plate and made an excited grab for a butter knife.

"Shall I tell you the specials?" Danny inquired. Unfailingly genial with a bean-pole build and seemingly endless energy, he was one of many aspiring actors on staff, drawn to the area by the Shakespeare Festival.

"Not yet, thanks," Thia said as she speared a round of soon-to-be-melted butter. "We're waiting for Murphy."

"I'll come back, then, in a—"

"No need." Abby paused her own bread-buttering to point with her knife. "Speak of the devil."

Rotating in her seat, Thia had the second Murphy-arrival experience of her day. The after-hours business casual of his shirt's open collar and absence of a tie ought to have looked shabby in comparison to the other diners. It didn't.

Confidence was a potent force. If only he could lend her some. She was tired of feeling decidedly *un*confident.

With his long strides, he was soon at the table. And because Thia had been watching for it, she'd noted how his gaze had been on Abby the entire way. Or on the knife she continued to hold.

"My apologies," he said, claiming the place in front of the window. "Bit of hassle with bonfire permits. Danny, I believe you were about to present the specials."

The young man proceeded to describe several complex and tempting entrées. Abby ultimately chose the most expensive, a wild-caught halibut, and then seemed vexed when Murphy chose the same. Thia ordered the fried chicken.

"Seriously?" Abby said as Danny left. "Don't you ever want to try something different?"

"I love it," Thia said, defensive. So what if she ordered the same thing every time? Every time was amazing. She picked up her drink, took her first sip. Rum, stronger than expected, burned a merry trail down her throat. "Oh." She stifled an amused cough. "Hello."

Abby grinned and took up her champagne flute. The cocktail lived up to its sparkler name, its copious bubbles catching the light as they streamed upward, fizzing off the surface like micro-scale fireworks. "Cheers," she said, then took a drink.

"*Sláinte,*" Murphy said. A glass of amber liquid appeared in his raised hand.

Thia tried not to react. She wasn't supposed to find this sort of thing—objects materializing out of nowhere—surprising.

"Show off." Abby set her glass down.

Thia did some peacekeeping by way of distraction. "What was that about a bonfire?"

"Ah." Murphy eased back in his chair. "I was forgetting that you weren't with us last year. We host one out on the patio there each Imbolc." His Irish accent gave the name a softer pronunciation than she had heard before.

Before she started working for Lettie, she had never heard the name at all. But many of Eclectica's customers had, and expected to purchase specific products ahead of it, in order to keep with their traditions. Objects for divination such as the candles used earlier; themed table decorations—runners, centerpieces, and recyclables—for those who wanted to hold a celebratory feast; supplies for crafting figures and crosses to honor the goddess Brigid.

"After the Yuletide trouble, the authorities aren't keen on any kind of rooftop gathering," Murphy complained.

"Understandable."

"It is, except I'm not a homicidal lunatic like that English *claimsech.* And many guests booked in expectation of it." He tossed back the rest of his liquor, put the glass down with a tablecloth-muted thump.

"You could take it up with the mayor," Abby said, directing

attention to the man himself. He appeared to be doing the lion's share of the talking, to good result. There were smiles all around. "He looked to be in a receptive mood. Maybe a bit too receptive," she amended as the group toasted with a clumsy enthusiasm that only made them laugh harder.

"I don't know." Thia reached for her bread only to discover she had eaten it. "He doesn't seem as far along as the others." She took another piece from the basket.

"Nevertheless, I'd prefer his undivided attention." Murphy's eyes narrowed as he continued to observe.

Whether he or Abby were aware, they were leaning toward one another, and their adjacent arms were resting between their place settings so that their hands nearly touched. "I'll get to him tomorrow. If we can't use the roof, there will be hell to—"

Kendra hurried in. She seemed distracted until she caught sight of them. Her hair stuck out haphazardly from the clips she often implemented in complicated—but always orderly— arrangements. Her face was flushed.

"You're together." She sounded both astonished and winded as she came to a stop behind the available chair.

"Together?" Abby quickly straightened away from Murphy. "No, not at all." Her hands made frantic sweeps of denial. "It's dinner. Business. With Thia, too. The three of us."

"Fiona is to showcase her baking," Murphy said, as if they all hadn't watched Abby mistake the question and overreact. He gestured to the chair. "Join us. Or were you on your way somewhere?" Asked with a nod toward the mayor's table.

"Oh." Kendra's focus drifted there and she frowned. "No, I don't—" She made a small shake of her head, then turned back to Murphy. "He's busy."

True enough, so involved in conversation, Amundsen didn't appear to have noticed her.

"Join us, then," Thia pressed. "It's perfect timing. We only just ordered."

"I shouldn't. At least . . . I think I shouldn't."

"Sit with us until you figure it out," Abby suggested.

"Look." Thia flipped up the bread cloth. "We've managed not to eat it all yet."

"No, I think I might—I'm supposed to meet someone. Not here, though."

"Working late?" Murphy helped himself to a large piece.

"I must be."

"You aren't sure?" Thia asked. Kendra was usually so on top of things.

"It's been a strange day, with the cancellation and—" She glared in the mayor's direction. "I'm surprised he dared show his face here."

"Kend, are you all right?" Abby asked at the same time as Murphy's, "Cancellation?"

"Didn't I tell you?" Kendra asked, facing him. "I should have. Pallister canceled the contract. He's using another caterer."

Murphy set down his bread. "Which one?"

Amazing how much threat a simple question could hold.

"I don't know." She began to rub her left hand, a massage of fingers which, Thia noticed now, were stained blue. As if they had been dipped up to the first knuckles in ink. "I was told but I can't remember."

"What's that on your hand?" Thia asked.

Kendra stopped rubbing to study the marks. "A pen must've leaked or something. I'll go wash. Although I think I already tried. Anyway," she said, backing away, "I need to go."

"Ross," Murphy called. "Have Jenkins see to those marks before you leave for the night."

"Sure. I have time." Past the hostess's station, Kendra gave them a wave of her blue-tipped hand and rounded the corner. Gone.

"Was that odd?" Thia asked. "That felt odd."

"It did." Abby continued to look in the direction Kendra had gone. "But I've been wrong with her before. If I push and she doesn't want to be pushed . . . ." She sighed, picked up her drink. "I don't want to overreact."

"She did say she'd had a strange day. Maybe she'd just tired," Thia said. "All that hassle with the mayor's party."

Abby nodded, but then, "Those marks, though. Ink might not wash off entirely but it doesn't stay so dark."

Murphy made pen and paper appear. "I'll have Jenkins see to her." When he finished writing a short note, he folded the paper in half and signaled the hostess.

● ○ ●

The closer they got to dinner's end, the more trouble Abby had making conversation. Thia and Murphy chatted amiably about business plans (his), and ideas on website design (hers), and surprisingly similar concerns over what was being done to the Plaza. By the time Fiona's baking had been sampled, the two were clearly enjoying themselves.

Abby was not. It was ridiculous. She was confident, intelligent, and perfectly sociable. She was also pretty and dressed to compliment what she and current fashion considered to be assets: a pair of long legs; an hourglass-shaped body that now went to Pilates twice a week along with the daily exercise of caring for her extensive garden even in winter. She had a head of glossy, jet-black hair. Her eyes, with their violet-hued irises, were an Elizabeth Taylor-esque rarity.

In short, thanks to a combination of fortunate genetics and practiced art, she did not lack for confidence when it came to her looks. She knew she was attractive. And she knew very well that Declan Murphy found her so. They had both been clear about where things stood on that front.

So why was she tongue-tied with him tonight?

Other than physically, she could barely stand the man. His

past was too mysterious; his nature too closed. Usually, she worried about picking up on too many emotions from other people. With Murphy, she rarely sensed anything at all. Either his feelings were locked down so tight that nothing escaped or he didn't have any. Repressed or psychopathic—not what she wanted in a partner.

But by Hecate, he was easy on the eyes.

Magnetism was the real trouble here, she concluded as the elevator doors opened to the lobby. No matter what her mind had already determined about him, her body held a different opinion. She exited first, leaving Thia and Murphy to follow her toward the side door. It would let her out across from Bloom's Alley, where she and Thia parked their cars behind Eclectica.

She wasn't nervous. That would suggest emotional investment, which simply was not the case. Nor was she avoiding him. She happened to be unsettled tonight, that's all. And she was concerned about Kendra. But if something were seriously wrong, Jenkins would find out, and tell Murphy, and Murphy would tell Abby. Probably Kendra was working too hard.

Murphy's fault, no doubt.

Since Thia was getting along so well with him, Abby left the social niceties of thanks and goodnight to her.

Outside, she checked for traffic, then began walking across the street's frost-slicked asphalt.

Instead of the single set of footsteps she expected to hear behind her, she heard double.

It became more difficult to convince herself that what she felt was not nerves.

"I'll walk you to your cars," Murphy said, coming up alongside. His nearness became a warm, magnetic hum along her left side.

"That's not necessary," she said, and checked to see where the hell Thia was. Staying a few steps behind, somehow. Not purposely, she hoped. *Please* not to give them space because of . . . vibes. She disliked that term, but she didn't want to put other words to it. Words like interest. Desire.

"Is it not?" Murphy asked. "Necessary?"

Damn his voice. The musicality of the Irish language with an intriguing roughness in its timbre. The kind of flaw that might result from hard use and only made her more curious about his past when she would prefer to not think about him at all.

"It isn't." She was proud of her tone. She dug her keys out of her coat pocket. "You can see the cars right there. No one at all around."

"This time."

Had she mistaken his intent? Was this truly about safety?

His smirk suggested her initial instinct had been correct.

Annoyed with him, with herself, she looked away. And sped up.

"What is it they say?" He kept pace easily. "'Better safe than sorry?'"

"More like, 'fortune favors the bold.'"

That surprised a laugh out of him. "To be sure," he said and snatched her keys. He began tossing them from hand to hand. "Am I to be favored, then?"

They arrived at her car, a second generation Mini Cooper that she had winterized with studded tires and several charms. Murphy leaned a hip on the fender and crossed his arms. The sleeves of his coat pulled, giving a glimpse of one of the two leather cuffs she had never seen his wrists without. Her keys remained in his possession, tight in his left hand.

She held out her right, palm up.

At night, Blooms Alley had several light sources—all high, attached to buildings. The contrast between light and shadow was sharp. Murphy's eyes might well have been black instead of the complex shadings of brown she knew them to be.

"I didn't say I agreed with it," she told him in a low voice. "'The cautious seldom err' is more my thing." Goddess only knew what Thia, unlocking her own car, thought of this. Abby kept her hand out for her keys.

"Virgil?" Murphy uncrossed his arms, held his closed hand above hers.

"Confucius."

"Right. Well." He uncurled his fingers. The keys dropped onto her palm. "'Never was anything great achieved without danger.'"

"Voltaire?"

"Machiavelli." He straightened away from the Mini. It put his face inches from hers and Abby was immobilized by want. "You know where to find me. On this night and most others."

Brushing past her, he began to walk back down the alley. "Goodnight, Thia," he said in a carrying voice. "I'll let Fiona know she can start next week."

"Fantastic," Thia called from the front seat of her vintage Datsun hatchback. She'd sold her car when she moved in with Lettie, and now Lettie's car, along with everything else, was hers. The driver's door was half open. "Thanks again. We— that is, I owe you," she amended with an uncertain glance at Abby.

"Nothing to it," Murphy called back, already halfway to the street. The lighting was less thorough on that end, making for lengthy stretches of pitch black. The sound of his unhurried steps was the only proof that he had not vanished altogether. He would reappear, moving through a patch of light only to merge back into the dark.

The universe was trying to send her a message, there.

A warning, undoubtedly. A reminder that Declan Murphy was a man with a dark past—and a dark present, much as he could make her forget. A man of shadows, rarely in the light.

"That was interesting," Thia said through the Datsun's open

window. Abby had been so entranced that she hadn't heard the door close.

Despite the frosty air, her cheeks warmed. She pretended to misunderstand. "The evening? Yes. Fiona is brilliant. The espresso mousse was phenomenal."

Laughing, Thia started the car. "Right, okay, I'll let you off the hook tonight. Tomorrow, though—" She grinned, rolled up the window. The headlights came on and, a moment later, the Datsun pulled away. Abby watched its slow drive down the alley. The Landmark's well-lit side door was in view. Murphy was probably back inside by now.

● ○ ●

Landmark Hotel
Main Floor

After an unknown time, Kendra returned to herself. She stood at the counter in the lobby's single-stall restroom. Water was running in the sink. Her hands were under the stream and she could not remember putting them there.

Hadn't she just been working in her office? She closed the tap, reached for a paper towel. Why were her fingers blue?

She brought them in for closer inspection and had a vague memory of . . . something. Of already doing this. A different restroom.

All her memories were vague.

That realization should've terrified but she couldn't manage more than distant concern. She felt outside herself, unable to reach much of anything within. Her memories, her emotions, her thoughts. Was she dreaming?

She stared at her reflection in the oval-framed mirror. That she made one meant that she existed, but she felt no more real than the image that faced her.

Pale, drawn skin. Shadowed, dull eyes. She didn't look right. Didn't feel right. Her reflection frowned and lifted her hand to study the blue marks.

It was extremely warm, wasn't it? She might feel better in fresh air.

«Outside.»

That was a good idea. Where to go became a picture in her mind.

"Yes," she said, and she was only slightly startled when her reflection shifted, turning into a different yet familiar form. "What are you doing in there?" she asked him. Her lover.

He smiled. So charming.

She couldn't help but smile in return.

«Hurry. You're running out of time.»

She felt herself nod.

● ○ ●

Blooms Alley

Abby unlocked the Mini, then took her time getting inside. The Datsun's brake lights flared briefly as it took a slow turn onto First. Thia would be home in a matter of minutes, the house she had inherited being only a few blocks away. Abby had a twenty mile drive ahead. Thirty minutes in good conditions; considerably more on a winter night. Her miles-long driveway was unpaved. She put the key in the ignition.

Unlit, icy roads, all to arrive at an empty house set deep in the woods.

She stared at her hands on the steering wheel. It would be a simple matter of turning the key, releasing the parking brake, and putting the Mini in gear.

She and Murphy had started down this same course when he had first arrived in Granite Springs. Afterward, they had been unable to be in the same room without doing damage. The Landmark's treasured crystal chandelier had been only one casualty of many.

Sure, he'd been considerate after her recent injury, and they had been getting along rather well, actually. Not so much as

one fight. She should leave it at that. Why mess up a good—
or at least tolerable—situation? Once burned, twice shy and
all that.

She turned off the Mini, removed the key as she opened the
door and swung her legs out. She'd go back to the hotel and
if he wasn't right there, easy to find, she'd take it as a sign and
go home. No harm, no foul.

She was full of clichés tonight, wasn't she?

Feet firmly on the ground, intentions clear, she stood—and
had to slam both hands on the Mini's hardtop when her vision
swirled. Her meal and all those sampled treats threatened to
come up.

She pressed her mouth tight—her eyes, too, as the vertigo
persisted—and tried to anchor herself to the feel of her hands
on the car's cold roof, of her feet squashed into less-than-sen-
sible shoes. The asphalt beneath. The winter air on the skin
of her face, dotted now with sweat.

Something terrible . . . Had happened? Was happening?

The feeling was overwhelming yet impossible to interpret.
It was all dizziness and nausea and frigid, awful dread.

She put a hand to her mouth. Tried to breathe slowly, calmly
through her nose. Just as she began to worry the sensations
were endless, they ended.

Eyesight stabilized, balance restored, head cleared—for the
moment. If things stayed true to form, she could expect one
hell of an ache soon.

The sick dread, however, lingered.

She turned, searching her surroundings but saw nothing out
of place, nothing to account for—

Sirens. Faint but growing louder.

As if drawn by an invisible string, she began moving, placing
one unsteady foot in front of the other until she was jogging
toward the Landmark.

She was not alone in that. When she reached First Street,

other people were converging from all around. Public parking garage, Pike Street, Main. They rushed in, their expressions ranging from curiosity to unease.

Like her, they aimed for the alley that ran perpendicular on the hotel's far side. A crowd was forming. Abby broke into a run, dodging obstacles stationary and mobile.

When she arrived at the crowd's edge, she pushed her way in. No one objected. That in itself was alarming.

"Sir," someone ahead was saying. "Sir, please. I don't think you should touch her."

Abby stepped free, the view clear. She staggered to a stop. The dread that had struck so terribly bloomed into panicked disbelief.

"No." She was unaware that she had spoken.

Several Landmark employees—kitchen staff, by their white uniforms—gathered near an access door. Murphy was on his knees, a woman laid out on the ground before him. He bent over her. His back blocked Abby's view of anything but the woman's lower half. Gray slacks. Sensible boots.

"No."

More became visible as she got closer. The woman's cashmere sweater had sopped up red liquid like a sponge. Kendra had one like it from a Portland boutique. Insanely expensive but too perfect to leave for someone else. Abby remembered telling her that in the dressing room. "It's perfect for you."

Hand knit, one of a kind.

She had been wearing it earlier.

As if in slow motion, Abby came around on Murphy's right. He lifted his bloodied hands from the woman's head and its tangle of blood-matted hair.

Abby's world stopped, even as she kept moving.

The sweater *was* Kendra's, of course. Also the hair and the bloodied face. The blanked, unseeing eyes.

"What did you do?" Abby's voice was raw. Agonized.

Murphy's head came up and turned so he could find her. She might have seen grief in his ink-dark eyes, but right now she didn't care to look. His mouth opened. She didn't care to hear what he might say.

Her world restarted with a vengeance.

She angled her shoulders for better torque and drew back her arm. Kendra had been particular about how the fingers should be curled, so Abby was mindful of that when she made her fist. There was no time to remove her rings, and maybe a part of her welcomed the idea of that pain.

"What did you do?" she repeated as her fist connected with Murphy's left temple.

CHAPTER 8

As the garage door rattled downward, Thia felt a twinge of guilt. She had stared at it, decided that she was tired, and used the remote control clipped to the visor. Tomorrow, she would try using magic. Tomorrow, for sure, both before and after work. She would leave extra-extra early in case she got the mechanism jammed again.

Her hand was on the side door's cold interior knob, but she needed to check first. She peered out the inset window.

Less than twenty feet of fenced garden lay between her and the house. As a matter of both welcome and safety, all exterior and some interior lights had come on hours ago, timed for dusk. She called up her Sight and, with an upward gaze, checked for gaps and other flaws in the wards surrounding the property. Against the clear night sky, they shimmered like a vibrant, rainbow-hued aurora.

From what she could tell, they were intact, with no signs of tampering.

She twisted the knob, pushed open the door, and stepped out onto the narrow brick stoop. She could not resist taking a moment of awed admiration: to stand in the crisp air with magic overhead in the wards and unfathomably distant stars beyond.

Supernatural shields were well and good but so was a sturdy deadbolt. She closed the door, picked out the right key from the others on the ring.

It was halfway in the lock when her front pocket vibrated. She startled wildly. The entire set of keys dropped, crashing onto the bricks.

Her phone, that's what it was, vibrated again.

She fumbled with her coat and then had to argue with the touchscreen. The cold of her finger made it slow to register.

"Yeah, Abby," she said, going by the ID when she eventually connected. "What's up?"

The voice that came through was Abby's, but not like she had ever heard her. And what was said didn't make sense.

Kendra. Alley. Dead.

"What?" Thia had no reason for saying that. No reason but denial. "What are you—" Abby had not paused and was not pausing, even for breath.

Thia struggled to concentrate, to make sense of the increasingly anguished torrent of words—

Police on scene.

Murphy with blood on his hands.

Threats to kill him—Abby's threats.

His fault. All his fault.

—while Thia's mind was stuck on three words already said: *Kendra. Alley. Dead.*

She began to shake. Dead? She needed her keys. They were somewhere at her feet. She bent down to search in the black of her own shadow. She was blocking the light above the door.

Kendra had helped install that light and set up the security timers.

Beneath Thia's scrabbling fingers, the bricks were rough and painfully cold. She hadn't worn gloves to drive. Her fingertips touched metal. Keys. She scooped them into a clumsy, painfully tight fist. The call had gone silent.

"Abby?" she fumbled with the doorknob. Fine motor skills were beyond her.

Inside the garage, the opener's automated light had yet to cycle off. She had only come home a minute or two ago, after all. How quickly everything could change.

With a pop, the bulb blew out, leaving her in the dark.

Her fault. Intense emotion was gasoline to the smoldering fire that was the Cailleach's power—exactly why she had been working to moderate her emotions and reduce stress. Once the power flared, it could be a huge challenge to tamp it back down. Much better to not give it fuel in the first place.

How the hell could she moderate *this,* she wondered, feeling her way around the car. The wand was in her pocket. Did she need to be holding it for it to help? Or was it enough to have it close?

"Abby," she repeated into the silence. "I'm on my way. Are you at home or—" Of course Abby wasn't at home; she lived miles away. They'd been together behind Eclectica not fifteen minutes before.

"H-hotel." Abby sounded as if she were choking. "They—they won't let me stay with her."

There was a sound like a sob and the call cut off.

● ○ ●

A police car blocked Main Street at Brick Lane, one street to the west of the Landmark. It was Thia's usual morning route to Eclectica. So, instead, she sped across the intersection and headed up the hill past the Shakespeare Festival only to find the turn onto Pike blocked too. An officer, strobed in red and blue by the lights of his nearby cruiser, was stringing a line of yellow tape from one lamppost to the next.

Crime scene tape.

With jerky motions, Thia shifted into reverse. She had the wand in her left hand. She made an awkward U-turn, then shifted back into first. The car's aging gears clunked roughly into place. The chassis shuddered, the engine on the brink of a stall. She popped the clutch.

The car leapt forward, the front wheel bumping a curb. She shouldn't have driven. She used to walk to work, before, and the hotel was closer to the house than Eclectica.

Backtracking her route, she weighed her chances.

Inside the car meant safety. On foot left her exposed. But street closures could include Eclectica's block, which would mean parking further away than that. If she was going to end up walking so much anyway, she was wasting time with all this driving. Four houses past her own, she whipped the car into an available space.

She wouldn't remember later if she locked it or turned off its lights. She would, vaguely, remember running. The jarring strikes of her heeled boots on the uneven, icy sidewalk. The harsh air sucked into her lungs through her dry mouth. The terrified pounding of her heart.

The rattle of gates and pop of streetlight outages as she ran by served as warnings: The Cailleach's power was waking. Her grip on the wand tightened, not that she could feel it for the painful burn of the cold.

Two blocks. Hardly any distance.

She dreaded her arrival. What if she lost control completely? If not for Abby, she would have turned back.

More police cars. More lines of police tape fluttered in the usual nightly wind from the forested hills beyond.

There was not a lot of civilization that side of Main Street. A few blocks up the hillside, housing density thinned as the terrain grew more rugged. The Victorians and Mid-Centuries of the older town stayed within a certain range. Only newer, larger, and more ostentatious homes dared to challenge the foothills.

Ultimately, there came a point where no amount of wealth was enough to conquer the rocky slopes and steep drops.

Thia's gaze was drawn to the contrast of night-black hills above bright, flashing pandemonium. *That way be monsters,* she thought unexpectedly, and turned away.

At the corner, a local TV reporter with a video camera on a tripod had waylaid the police officer stationed there to keep people out.

Thia put the wand in her coat pocket and then, reluctantly, withdrew her hand. She didn't want to look suspicious. *More* suspicious, she amended, as she ducked under the tape.

As she hurried across Main, she was so intent on what lay ahead that she didn't hear the reporter's shout of dismay or see his smoking camera topple to the ground.

A man from hotel security was struggling to placate a crowd under the marquee. "Thank you for your patience," he said over several protestations. "You'll be allowed to leave after we have your contact information."

Thia began weaving her way through.

"We were in the restaurant," a man complained. "We don't know anything about anything."

A woman yelled, "What about my car? I can't leave without it, now can I?"

At the lobby door, Thia grasped the ornate brass handle and pulled. The blast of heated air was the first shock. After she stepped inside, noise was the second—so many voices. People filled the grand room. Seated, standing, walking. Their faces showed bewilderment, fear, sorrow. Emotions were all around and they were raw. She reached into her pocket, clutching the wand as she zigzagged past several well-dressed groups.

Rounding the central table, she nearly bumped into a white-haired woman dressed in the familiar steel-blue suit of the concierge staff. It took some seconds for Thia to recognize her specifically. Natalie. Her face was distorted by grief, and tears were streaming.

Thia fought back her own. "Have you seen Abby?"

The table held a towering display—a bare, twisting branch decorated for the season with Brigid's crosses, green ribbon, and silver bells.

It began to tremble in its holder, jingling the bells.

"Have you seen Abby?" she repeated. "She called and I—"

When Natalie shook her head, Thia moved on, threading her way deeper into the congestion of patrons and employees and police.

Hotel security, she noted, stood along the lobby's edges as well as the railing of the first floor overlook. She knew a few by name; the others she could pick out by their uniform suits and forbidding postures.

Not far from the elevator, Neil Amundsen and the rest of the mayor's dinner party were talking to the police chief. Thia turned, desperate for Abby.

She found Murphy instead.

He stood at the fireplace, his back to the room. At a time when space was at a premium, he had more than his share.

The nearer she got, the more she understood why. Despite the fire, the area was freezing.

The cold seemed to emanate from him, but since that was impossible, Thia figured her dread had become so immense it was chilling her from the inside. Shivering, she stopped a short distance away. "Murphy?"

A slow inhalation, a subtle drop of his shoulders, were all the acknowledgment she got. And she had been mistaken— he hadn't been watching the fire. He was staring at his hands. At the blood dried on his skin.

Her head swam. And yet she could not look anywhere else. "Abby called me," she said, concentrating on breathing. Slow. Steady. Her voice sounded oddly distant to her own ears. She clutched the wand in her pocket so tightly she had the vague concern she might bend it. "Abby said that Kendra—"

Murphy's bloodstained hands clenched into fists.

She instinctively took a step back.

But he couldn't have harmed Kendra. He couldn't have. And he wouldn't have been left alone like this if he had. The only cuffs around his wrists were his own: sable leather with silver buckles, not police issue steel or plastic zip tie.

"Yes," he said, as if Thia had completed her sentence. His head turned toward her. His dark brown eyes appeared black. Impenetrable.

There was blood on his face. Not dried, as on his hands, but fresh. A thin line oozed from a cut near his left eye. The flesh around it looked angry.

"What happened?" In the silence that followed, she found herself half-hoping that he'd mistake the question and tell her only about his face.

By the dullness of his gaze, she knew he wouldn't.

"She's gone." He turned away, toward the fire.

Cold seeped into the marrow of Thia's bones.

● ○ ●

Brigantium Headquarters
Pall Mall, London

"What is this?" Cormac's tone made that less a question and more a statement. Dismay, disgust, disapproval. A trifecta of negativity that added up to an unwillingness to proceed.

His feet had, in fact, halted their forward progress and were set firm on the worn but nevertheless polished wood of the corridor.

His negotiations with Beatrice and Quentin had concluded a few minutes prior. Those had taken place over a four course meal in an otherwise deserted dining room. In keeping with a true society club, the Brigantium had a full-time gourmet kitchen on site.

Since then, they had been leading him along. *Stringing* him along, it felt like. Twenty steps ahead was a closed door. The room behind it was their obvious destination—and the origin of the sounds that had steadily increased in volume the closer he had come. The wall might be warded against the probing intrusion of his Sight, but it had not been sound-proofed. On the other side of the oak panels, a sizable crowd awaited.

While Quentin proceeded, the click of his cane as steady as a metronome, Beatrice paused to give Cormac a scowl that set his teeth on edge.

"It is *this*," she said with a sweep of her bony hand, "or it is nothing. Entirely up to you, of course."

He was loathe to have wasted all this time. She had him and they both knew it.

"*Under observation,*" he said bitterly. Words she had used and he had agreed to in their bargain.

"Exactly so." Her pale eyes narrowed as she mocked, "Surely you understand the importance of specificity in our line of work." *His* words from before.

"Ah, yes. Very good." Much as he would like to strangle her for this, she would not have bested him had he not handed her the opportunity.

When he had been most in conflict with the Brigantium, only one member had presented any challenge: Thia's great-aunt Leticia. She had proven to be knowledgeable, skilled— devious, on occasion—while her compatriots had hardly been able to ken magic from parlor tricks. Like children, they had been, not yet aware of the difference between make-believe and reality.

In the decades since then and now, their Society had grown up. This was not the first time Cormac had underestimated this current version. It *would* be the last.

Precisely what "this" entailed became clear when Quentin

opened the door, revealing the lecture hall beyond.

In theatre parlance, the house was full.

Eight rows of auditorium-style seating, tall enough so that there was a door behind the final row—leading to a second floor. Fifteen seats comprised each row, and despite the short notice and late hour, every one of them was occupied. When Cormac entered, voices quieted and he became the focus of one hundred and twenty pairs of eyes.

One hundred and twenty witnesses.

One hundred and twenty-*two*, with Quentin and Beatrice. He spun on his heel and blocked the latter from entering.

"I ought to tell you to go fuck yourself," he told her in an undertone, intentionally crude. Behind him, Quentin stifled what might have been a laugh. Beatrice simply stared.

Already, he could perform a glamour and get himself close to resembling Cassandra. With this ritual, though, he could be identical. Fingerprints, freckle patterns—even irises, when usually a fluke of his lineage meant his eye color could only be altered with contact lenses. Tonight's result would enable him to pass any scan that might stand between him and everything she had secreted away.

"No recordings." He had been adamant about this in their dinner discussion but he wanted it reconfirmed. "I *will* find another way."

"None."

A long moment passed while he decided whether to believe her.

He didn't, but the only other way he could think of involved returning home. To do this here and now was so much more expedient. Turning his back on her, he strode to the altar that sat in place of a traditional lectern or desk.

If he could not recover the Achill Bell before the deadline, his concerns about witnesses and recordings would be moot.

The requested supplies awaited, arranged on undyed linen

that draped halfway to the worn oak floor. Behind him, on a blackboard that stretched to the high ceiling, the list he had given had been copied in precise block letters. They would learn soon enough that it was not a complete accounting of what would be involved tonight.

"What is this ritual's origin?" Beatrice, having come to stand opposite him at the altar, tapped a manicured nail on the rim of a bowl of sliced lotus root.

He had asked for powder, but never let it be said that he couldn't adapt. "Had some trouble there, did you?"

It would seem that the Brigantium still dealt primarily with European folklore and occultism. He had wondered.

This ritual was his own, an amalgam of two spells bartered from a Manx buggane and then improved after the lotus plant had been introduced from southern Asia. He had never put the spell to this specific use, however—hence tonight's additional, unlisted ingredient. It ought to serve, but magic didn't conform to oughts and shoulds.

"In London," Beatrice said, "nothing is too difficult to come by."

He had been correct, then: The root hadn't come from their supplies. They had purchased it, most likely in Chinatown.

Beatrice pivoted, pitched her voice to fill the chamber. "We are now ready to begin"—she ignored Cormac's quiet expletive—"if you would be so good as to tell us what we are about to observe?"

He hadn't survived by being *good*. And he sure as *ifrinn* was not about to start now. He gestured to the chalked list. "Surely that makes it self-evident."

He lifted the amphora, held it over the onyx bowl.

"Lavender oil," Beatrice announced while he poured. "One half inch, approximately, into a black onyx bowl." By claiming the role of narrator, she presented him as a sort of performer, there at her behest and under her control.

He disliked it immensely.

She prosed on. "Once commonly used as a base liquid for its qualities of purification, healing, and clairvoyance, its use in that form all but ended after the discovery of the *Melaleuca alternifolia.* Why did you opt for it here?"

"You'd have to ask Idris." He said it strictly for effect; not even with his life at stake would he perform one of his father's spells for this lot. Yet it clearly thrilled them to believe so. Beatrice came around to his same side of the altar. Quentin, off to the side on a battered wooden chair, sat forward, newly alert.

Cormac uncorked a jar of dried edelweiss. Then, with silver tweezers, he picked out twelve blossoms and dropped them onto the oil, one by one. They floated lazily, looking like fuzzy, misshapen stars.

"Edelweiss." She held out her hand for the jar. After only a moment's hesitation, he gave it. If she was to stand so near, she might as well assist.

Capping the jar, she set it aside. "For invisibility?"

From the supply of lotus root, Cormac chose the smallest piece. Sliced, it resembled a telephone dial. He submerged it in the oil. Odd to think that these days he was more liable to come across lotus root than a rotary phone.

Belatedly, he answered about the edelweiss. "No. To create a blank canvas."

"And lotus for . . . ." Beatrice prompted the room.

"Protection?" someone responded.

Cormac tracked the voice to the first row, four seats right of center. A man with a substantial white beard. His robe was an absurd cliché: deep blue patterned with gold stars and crescent moons. He was recognizable from Brodgar. Along with Beatrice and Quentin, he had played a role in what Cormac had been made to do. The influx of power that had resulted in patricide.

"Indeed," Cormac answered, looking away. He pushed the root deep into the bowl. "And lock opening."

Idris Cathmor had been an abomination. Volatile, sadistic, and driven by a need to gain and assert power over all things. The ritual he'd planned for Brodgar would have granted him a veritable nuclear arsenal of power along with an existence akin to immortality.

Cormac picked up the jar of dried mugwort, tapped roughly two drams of the crushed mix of stalks and flowers in with the lotus and chamomile.

"Mugwort." Beatrice took the jar when he'd finished. "For a specific quality, or . . . ?"

A multipurpose herb, it could aid in everything from healing to astral projection.

"General use." Surreptitiously, he checked the room. If this *was* intended as a trap, its jaws would spring in the coming moment, when he would be completely focused on the ritual.

Speaking of that, "The altar area is protected?" If not, he would need to cast a circle.

"Of course."

He smirked. "Learned your lesson, did you?"

It was a gibe in reference to the Society's notorious initial disasters, but by the way Beatrice's face blanched there must have been a more recent one. More personal. She hadn't been alive during those early years.

Shifting his concentration, he called up his power.

Never far, it answered immediately, flowing as directed to his hands. With a snap of his fingers, the oil caught fire. Low, indigo flames danced across its surface as the burning herbs released a sharp, peppery scent.

Pleasant, but not for long.

From his jacket's inner pocket he retrieved several strands of Cassandra's hair, then put them into the flames. They writhed briefly, coiling in on themselves before turning to ash. Not so pleasant a scent, that.

"*Exs koutino*," he said, "*kele kom welo.*" Out of hair, conceal with deceit. The flames changed from indigo to amethyst.

Next came the tricky part.

He got his folding knife, held the blade over the flames to burn off impurities, and then set the tip to the middle line of his left palm. He heard Beatrice's quiet catch of breath as well as several murmurs from the crowd. This was what he'd left off the list.

Because of its *Sidhe* component, his blood made a frequent addition to his spellcraft. Here, however, he was banking on its human component—on a shared inheritance—to bind the spell. Success or failure, it would all come down to familial connection.

He extended his hands with the knife over the oil, into the rising heat. This could be a grave mistake. Should so little as a single drop go astray, he could be left open to any number of threats. Beguilement, hexes, genetic analysis. Idris had been able to call Cormac to him, physically, no matter Cormac's willingness or location. Ditto for psychic communication.

With one drop of blood, the Brigantium could make his life a misery.

Yet, what was life if not risk?

What was *his* life without Idris's collection? And, presently, the Achill Bell?

He made a quick slice in his palm. Deep enough to hurt but not so deep that he would bleed more than he could track. "*Tre moi waito.*"

Through my blood.

He made a fist, squeezed five drops into the flames as the wound closed—quick healing being another gift of the *Sidhe*. In a few moments, there wouldn't be so much as a mark.

If anyone expected a dramatic finish, they were to be disappointed. The flames flickered, died. The oil's surface stilled.

Cormac frowned at it. Nothing remained of the herbs, but the lotus root sat on the bowl's bottom, visibly unchanged. Had enough of its essence gone into the oil?

Beatrice bent close to see, then voiced a damnable echo of his concerns. "Should you have powderized it first?"

Possibly. Probably. Too late now.

From the altar, he took up eight wooden discs, each the size of a pound coin, and submerged them in the oil.

"Made of hazel," Beatrice announced needlessly. The discs were described on the blackboard. "Chosen for its quality of protection?"

Cormac allowed himself a short laugh. "Luck."

One by one, he removed the discs from the oil, dried them on his palm with a basic spell, and then deposited them in a drawstring pouch made of black velvet and silk.

"This has been a fascinating night," Beatrice said after the last disc went in. "Let's express our gratitude, shall we?"

The audience clapped.

Cormac made a perfunctory bow. No need to pretend that he hadn't been forced into this by circumstance and his own carelessness.

He secured the pouch in an inner jacket pocket and made a careful check of the altar cloth for any stray blood.

"Good night, everyone," Beatrice said as the applause died down. "See you tomorrow."

While the room emptied through two sets of doors behind the uppermost seats, Cormac prepared to burn off what was left in the onyx bowl. He held the purification spell's phrase in his mind, gathered the energy at his hand. The sooner he left here, the sooner he could—

"When was this?" Quentin's shocked question gave Cormac pause. Phone in hand, the agent limped toward Beatrice. His cane lay abandoned by his vacated chair. His face was grim. Beatrice walked toward him.

Cormac didn't have time for their problems. With power crackling at his fingertips, he refocused on what he needed to do: clear the altar of remnants, physical or magical. Anything that could be analyzed and used against him.

"Cormac."

Ifrinn. He banked the energy.

"Kendra Ross has been killed," Quentin said. "Outside the Landmark."

There was an odd lightness in Cormac's head. "Thia?"

"She's fine. They're all fine, except Kendra."

"Ah." His relief was dizzying.

But of course Thia could not be *fine.* Safe, perhaps, but fine? Not with her friend dead. Thia McDaniel was deeply kind. She cared for her friends. She loved, as much as such a thing was possible. She would not be *fine.*

The lecture hall was as good as empty, but a cluster of people remained near the upper doors; a similar number at the lower. Security agents, as proclaimed by the uniformity of their dark suits. The Brigantium had gone on alert.

"What happened?" Keeping his voice low, Cormac joined Beatrice and Quentin. "Is this the start of something more?"

"We don't know yet." Beatrice had a phone in hand and was tapping the screen. Texting. She darted Quentin a look. "Fill him in. I need to confirm that security has been raised at all locations." She walked a distance, held the phone to her ear.

"Our posted agent arrived at the scene shortly after police and emergency services," Quentin told Cormac, "but hasn't been able to speak yet with officials. She says the entire hotel is cordoned off, but it happened in the alley. Kendra, beaten to death."

"Evidence of magic?"

"Our agent couldn't get close enough to take readings."

"How certain are you that Thia is safe?" Cormac took out his smartphone and turned off airplane mode. "Where is she?

Who's with her?"

"She's inside the hotel. The agent has eyes on her—or *had* as of our call. The place is crawling with Murphy's people and police. Thia won't come to harm." Quentin was being uncharacteristically solicitous.

Which meant Cormac needed to get himself under better control. Emotions were weakness enough without his putting them on display.

"Emergency protocols are in place," Beatrice said, rejoining them. Her phone remained at the ready.

Three people, three phones—and while they remained half a world away from the trouble—useless, all.

Or were they?

"Cassandra." The others had to be thinking the same. She had sworn revenge. Many of Idris's followers remained largely unidentified or in hiding (or both). They would do whatever she asked—if she was able to contact them. In addition, she could have any number of other allies. She could've set something up before being locked away. A contingency plan. Hired assassins. Timed devices. Possibility after possibility.

Only one person could narrow them down.

Cormac put his phone back in his jacket. "Tell me there's a faster way than the tunnels."

Beatrice opened her mouth (to tell him off, if her face was any indication) but Quentin spoke first: "We can take a car directly to the holding facility."

"How long?" Cormac asked, but a third option had already come to mind.

"Ten, fifteen minutes."

"I'm not in favor of this." Beatrice tried to draw Quentin away. For a private chat, undoubtedly. Wasting more time.

Too long, any of it. Cormac returned to the altar and, with a wave of his hand, set the onyx bowl ablaze with *wanfýr*. A second gesture doused it.

Not a speck of ash remained at the bottom. He took up the amphora, poured a good centimeter's worth of fresh oil.

"What are you doing?" Beatrice stormed over.

"An experiment," he replied and, to Quentin, "You might want to ready the car regardless. In case this fails."

"Right." He flagged the attention of the trio by the lower exit, then limped out with them, talking quietly.

"Members of your security team are posted at all the doors, yes?" Cormac asked Beatrice and got a curt nod. "Good. Even though her powers are bound, she might see this as too good an opportunity." He had the pleasure of seeing Beatrice's eyes go wide.

With his energy concentrated on the room, he shorted out the lights and slammed shut the doors. Complete darkness.

"Just *what* do—" Beatrice's furious question stopped short. "No. You can't summon her. Can you?"

If he wasn't so apprehensive about what might amount to a disastrous stunt, he would have enjoyed her dismay. But the truth was, he didn't know.

What had worked for Idris might not work for him. Idris had held inherent superiority: father to son; more powerful; more experienced. Cormac and Cassandra were half-siblings. That might not be a strong enough link.

On the other hand, her powers were bound, which meant he was unquestionably superior. And he had centuries more experience.

On the *other* other hand, none of that experience included anything close to this.

Cormac pushed all that from his mind and floated a ball of *wanfýr* above the altar. It bathed the area in flickering light. He took Cassandra's hair from his pocket and separated out six strands.

When he moved to put the hank back, Beatrice held out her hand. "I'll keep that."

"Of course." With a show of reluctance, he put it on her palm. Let her assume that was all.

From her expression, she didn't. But she didn't press.

He held the six strands taut over the bowl and gazed at the oil. His faint reflection gazed back.

"*Akor kei waito lergo.*" He tied a knot in the middle of the strands, then raised them as if in offering. "*Nadske kwe fyera.*"

Open this blood path, said in ancient words. Bind and bring forward.

The oil rippled, the reflections on its surface fragmenting, then reassembling to show Cassandra in a rather bleak room. Cot, table, chair. No window. She was seated on the mattress edge.

Her head came up sharply. "Get out," she said, then began looking around wildly. Searching. "What *is* this?"

Cormac glanced at Beatrice. Like his, her attention was on the bowl but she showed no reaction. Did she not see what he did? Had she not heard Cassandra's voice?

Maybe this wouldn't be a complete disaster.

He coiled the hairs around his left index finger—twisting their owner to his will—and cast out a mind-to-mind line of communication.

«*Cassandra Swinton, daughter of Idris Cathmor.*»

Formality was key when establishing a new path.

After a tense moment, he felt a click, like the turning of a lock. The mental conduit opened. He watched as Cassandra shot to her feet.

"Guard!" She shot over to the door and put her face up to the narrow glass inset. "Alert the assistant director immediately. There's a violation of my right of—"

«*Tell her yourself.*»

With the looped hair tight around his finger, he curled his hand into a fist, surrounded it with red *fyr* as he focused on their blood connection. This needed to work. Had to work. He would talk with her, here and now.

"*Turete*," he said aloud. Come.

As shown on the oil, his half-sister stumbled backward, her eyes wild. "No!" She spun, her arms outstretched, as if she could physically fend off the spell.

Cormac knew all too well that once it got its hooks in, there was nothing to be done.

«*Turete.*»

Her image vanished from the oil and he turned, lunged to pin her solid and enraged form against the blackboard. She had materialized facing it, away from the room and from him.

Surprise was on his side. So was speed. He used one leg to pin both of hers while he grabbed her wrists, held one at the middle of her back while he raised the other, pressed it high up against the board. Her head was turned to the left, her cheek smudging the first letters of "edelweiss."

She struggled, but he had her. He set his mouth by her ear and spoke low and fierce. "Did you have anything to do with this?"

Her curses exhibited surprising variety. She might look like a supermodel but she had the vocabulary of a docker.

"I'm not here," Beatrice said. From the sound of it, she was near the exit. "I can have no part in this." The door opened and just as quickly closed.

"Alone at last." Cormac eased back only to push Cassandra more firmly against the blackboard. "It will go easier if you simply answer what you're asked."

"Oh, I doubt that." She had the gall to sound amused. "I doubt that very much."

"Here," Quentin said, his presence unexpected. With a tap, tap, tap he walked to them, then leaned his cane against the wall.

Positioning himself so Cassandra could see, he removed his

right glove, tucked it into his suit jacket. "Allow me."

"No." Her voice had gone small. Beneath Cormac's hands, she trembled.

CHAPTER 9

"Mint tea? Chamomile?" Thia shot the locks home on the back door. She felt so very helpless. Abby kept moving, passing through the kitchen and into rest of the house. Thia had driven Abby's car and, with her own parked up the street, put it in the garage despite the mess. She removed her coat, hung it on the rack. No answer about tea. She dimmed the kitchen lights and went after her friend.

The house was historic, built shortly before the twentieth century—and decades before "open concept" became a thing. The compact kitchen led to an open-ended room intended for formal dining, but in Thia's brief experience with it, was used more as an office. Beyond was the living room, spanning the front to include the main door as well as the staircase to the second floor.

Because this had been Lettie's main home for many years, the whole of it was crammed full of a hodgepodge of antique and modern. Crowded bookcases and glass-fronted cabinets lined the walls. Rare books, souvenirs from her travels (which, thanks to her Brigantium work, meant anything from coins unearthed at a Roman site to a Sèvres bowl purchased from one of her antique dealer contacts). It was a warm home, a welcoming home.

Thia still had a hard time thinking of it as hers.

She expected that to change after her own things were transported from storage in Los Angeles but she couldn't yet face doing that. The extensive curating and rearranging required would be a literal bringing home of the sad truth that Lettie was forever gone.

And now Kendra.

Thia found Abby standing at the central grouping of sofas and chairs, her vacant gaze on the front door as if someone were expected.

"Take your coat?" Thia asked gently.

"Oh." Abby shrugged out of the heavy wool. She handed it over along with her knitted scarf. "Thank you."

Thia draped them on a ladder-back rocker and then, since Abby hadn't moved, took the initiative to sit. She chose the red-upholstered sofa placed parallel to and several feet from the stairs.

Abby went to its twin along the front wall. The thick drapes behind it had already been pulled.

Keeping windows covered was another habit she had developed. After tonight, she might never open them again. She might never leave the house—No, of course she would. She had obligations to others, not to mention herself.

"I don't understand," she said, then felt terrible when fresh tears filled Abby's eyes. Her own were dry. She felt numb. The shock, and bound to wear off soon enough. In the meantime, she welcomed it. "Can you tell me what happened?"

She hated to push, but she still only knew that Kendra had been killed in the alley on the Landmark's western side.

Why had she even been there? It was a much-used shortcut between Main Street and the public parking garage. She had a designated space in the hotel's underground garage. And if she had wanted to go out onto Main Street, the lobby door would've done that more directly.

"Murphy found her," Abby said in a dull voice. With rough motions, she used what looked to be a restroom-dispensed paper towel to blot her eyes. "She—she was covered in blood. Her head . . . ." Abby shook hers. "I punched him. Murphy."

"Is he why she's—" Thia couldn't bring herself to finish the sentence. Dead. Gone.

"He has to be."

Thia pictured him, standing alone by the fireplace. "You're sure?"

"As sure as I need to be. He's dangerous. The life he leads—whatever it is—is dangerous. He pulled her into that. And it got her killed."

"The same could be said about me." There it was, out loud, what had been cycling around her mind. "*I'm* dangerous. *My* life is dangerous. What if this is more revenge against me? There are plenty of Idris's people left. And Cassie's. And the Rekkrs."

"Thia." Abby gaped. "You can't think this is your fault."

"Can't I? People have sworn revenge on all of us because of me. How can I not think this might be my fault?" She made a plaintive shrug. "I don't know what this is except that Kendra is dead."

"No one does. The police asked more than they answered."

When Thia had found Abby, she had been coming out of a meeting room off the Landmark's mezzanine, and had just given a statement to the police. She had seemed so wrecked, Thia hadn't pushed her to talk. She had simply suggested that Abby come home with her. "What did they ask?"

"Stupid things. What was I doing at the alley, how well did I know the . . . victim." Abby cleared her throat. "Routine stuff, it felt like. Because there are security cameras."

Thia felt foolish. Of *course* there would be cameras outside the hotel. And on the public parking garage too. Other nearby buildings. Whoever had done this would soon be known.

"Who will tell her other friends?" she asked, struck anew by the enormity of this loss. "And her family. There's a brother, right? And a sister?" Kendra hadn't been one to share many personal things. At least, not with Thia. Yet. Theirs was a new friendship.

Time had run out, unexpectedly and incomprehensibly.

"The police told me they'll handle the family," Abby said, sinking deeper into the sofa. "I suppose the rest fall to me. She and I have been friends here the longest."

"I can help. If you want." Such a difficult task shouldn't be on one person, solely. "Tonight? This will be all over the news by morning." The hour was late, but did that matter? There was never a good time for tragedy.

"I don't know if—" Abby closed her eyes as her tears overflowed, spilling down her cheeks. "I don't know if I can. Not yet." She turned into the couch's arm and covered her face. Her shoulders shook but she made no sound.

Thia went to sit beside her and laid a comforting hand on her back. "Of course not. I shouldn't have suggested it."

A news program or passing remark were awful ways to learn of a friend's death, but in Granite Springs, word of shocking events spread like wind driven fire. It might already be too late.

"Give me one person to call," Thia suggested. "I'll ask them to call another." And so on it would go.

Abby sat up to wipe her face with the wadded paper towel.

"I'll get tissues." Thia went to the half-bath tucked beneath the stairs. While there, she brought up Cormac's number on her phone. If this was part of a larger plot, he could be in as much danger as any of them. If not more.

She hesitated. To say that things were complicated where he was concerned would be to put it mildly. And, like Abby, Thia didn't think she could deal with anything more tonight.

She met her own gaze in the sink's gilt-framed mirror.

She looked an absolute mess. Auburn hair gone every which way. Pasty complexion. Sunken and shadowed eyes, the hazel's green more pronounced due to surrounding redness.

Given how uncommunicative Cormac had been, she knew he would not welcome the interruption of a call, no matter the importance. Would he even consider this important? She opened the messaging app to type the words instead.

How stark they looked. Her finger hovered over the screen. With the sending, she would be acknowledging that a friend was gone, taken by a shocking, violent act.

Once more, the world had changed. Irreparably.

● ○ ●

Landmark Hotel

The footage was full color and not at all grainy, being of the highest resolution available via digital technology and magic. The man now known as Declan Murphy expected the best in all things—security most particularly.

Because of that, he and the top tier of the local police force were able to watch in perfect detail as Kendra Ross went out through the Landmark's alley-side door to meet her fate.

Had anyone asked him beforehand, Declan would have said that scenes of violence were of no matter. He had witnessed too many, and experienced more besides. His physical form carried the proof, should his memories do the unlikely thing and fade. But, as it turned out, he was mistaken.

While events played out on-screen, he struggled.

And when they had finished, he swallowed against the lump in his throat and said, "Again."

The two officers looked to their chief, who then nodded, granting Declan permission as if they were not in *his* hotel, *his* security office. As if that was not *his* security tech at the controls.

His recently promoted director dead on the asphalt.

As if he didn't have more experience with murder than the whole of the city's force.

Chief Roland Nash was a bear of a man, about as broad as he was tall, and for what the job typically entailed, more than competent. (A touch too competent when it came to some of the activities in which Declan would have otherwise participated.) But murder was rare in Granite Springs. Hell, murder was rare throughout the whole, relatively rural county.

The footage replayed. Kendra Ross's killer hadn't bothered to conceal his face or keep out of camera range. For thirty-six minutes, the young man stood in full view of the Landmark's camera as well as anyone who might have passed by on Main or up at the parking garage.

Waiting, so it appeared, and not caring to be covert—which went some way as to why security hadn't rated him as a potential problem.

"Is he known?" asked Declan.

The overstuffed rucksack by a nearby tree proclaimed the youth to be a traveler or a local who was sleeping rough. Or someone who wanted to be seen that way.

"We'll check with patrol," Chief Nash said when neither of the officers responded. "Nice of him to give us such a good view."

"Mm," Declan agreed. "Too nice."

The killer didn't move like an operative. If he was one, if his behavior was intentionally misleading, then he was a skilled actor who had chosen to take seemingly unnecessary risks. His clumsy approach when Kendra emerged from the hotel had given her plenty of time to react.

That was another puzzle: Kendra Ross herself. The woman's hand-to-hand skills rivaled Declan's own. On top of that, she had been only steps from the side door. When the youth had moved on her, had she not wanted to engage, she could have been inside the Landmark in seconds.

On-screen, she turned toward the youth. The move put her back to the camera, so Declan couldn't see her expression, but the tilt of her head suggested curiosity more than concern. Even as the youth pulled the metal bar from under his puffy jacket, even as he raised it and lunged, swinging hard, Kendra never so much as flinched.

Full contact with the side of her head.

"Enough." Declan would not be able to withstand a second viewing of what followed. Nor did he wish to watch himself again, arriving too late, the youth gone and Kendra Ross gone as well. Forever. In token deference to the chief's authority, he asked, "We done?"

"For now, yes." The customarily stoic man sounded shaken. Looked it, too, when he turned from the monitor. "We'll be restricting access to the victim's office. Procedure," he added over Declan's objection. "From what this shows, it's fairly cut and dried."

"Seems so." For all except for motive and Kendra's behavior. Why the hell had she reacted that way? *Hadn't* reacted, more like. She had behaved as if in a trance, and Declan could only believe it had to do with the blue on her hands. She had been unlike herself earlier, too.

The room felt stifling. With a word of thanks to Lynnea at the computer and a nod to the three police, he left.

One of the Landmark's flaws—few though they were—was its lone elevator. Unless he wanted to climb the eight flights to his suite, he had to go through the lobby. Last he'd seen, it had been packed with police and reporters and guests and employees. Too many eyes. Too many demands.

He walked down the corridor, past supply rooms, laundry, employee break room and lockers. His office. Kendra's had a glaring-yellow "X" of crime tape across its door. Nearing the lobby, he worked a summoning spell, calling the elevator in advance.

He should insist that the yellow tape come down. Kendra Ross had been loved by all at the hotel. They didn't need the inside reminder of what had happened outside.

Declan could get that sorted within minutes, yet he couldn't bring himself to turn back.

Some of the lobby crowd had dispersed, he was relieved to find. Nevertheless, too many people remained. Those on his payroll turned grief-stricken faces his way. Two of his lieutenants—one who also worked security; the other a UPS driver and still in that uniform—joined him on his beeline for the waiting elevator's open door.

"What happened out there, *toísech?*" Huntly asked. "What are our orders?"

"Same as an hour ago." *Give me a fucking minute,* he wanted to tell his men, but they were his men and they were shocked and hurting too. He raised his hand. The bloodstains on his formerly white shirtsleeves were impossible to miss. "I'm after getting myself a change of clothes." His accent was slipping. Some time ago, he had determined that the less "foreign" he sounded in the States, the better. Second nature by now, it was, so that he rarely had to work at it.

Tonight he had to work at it.

Feet from the elevator, he used a power-infused gesture to trigger the doors so they were already closing as he got in, cutting his men off. The elevator began its ascent.

His hands tightened into fists. He squeezed his eyes shut— causing the cut from one of Abigail's rings to reopen.

A little while more, he told himself, counting the seconds.

A little while more.

● ○ ●

Brigantium Headquarters
Pall Mall, London

After the armed agents escorted Cassandra from the lecture

hall to return her to her cell the non-magical way, Cormac sprang to his feet, too frustrated to remain seated.

"That was a waste," he said—to himself, as it happened.

Beatrice and Quentin had turned their chairs toward one another and were leaning close, speaking quickly and quietly. Include Cormac when he was useful; leave him out when he wasn't. They and their whole Society could go to *ifrinn*. He didn't need them.

Besides, his hearing was excellent. They were arguing about interrogation methods. He didn't give a shit. Cassandra had known nothing.

He left the auditorium through the upper door. It opened onto a landing—the juncture of two corridors at the top of a grand staircase. The entrance hall stretched out below. By the banisters, a pair of security agents eyed him with suspicion but did nothing when he walked by.

Halfway down the staircase, he took out his mobile. The motion-activated screen lit, still showing the notification for Thia's text, received while he was busy with Cassandra.

KENDRA WAS KILLED TONIGHT, read the preview. He could put it off no longer. Facial recognition opened the digital lock while a hand gesture worked on the added hex. He pulled up the full message while he descended the rest of the stairs.

KENDRA WAS KILLED TONIGHT. I DON'T KNOW WHAT TO DO.

Did she think he would? It wasn't a plea, exactly. Thia wasn't seeking anything from him. Not outright. But that wasn't the problem; it was his *wanting* to do something. It was how he had reacted when he'd thought she had been hurt, or worse.

He should keep his distance. If she needed immediate guidance, the Brigantium's local agent was there.

But with the information in the O'Shannon's red book . . . Possibilities began to light in his mind. Flashes and glints of possibility. Advantage.

At the base of the stairs, he closed the message. Then he

placed a call.

On the fifth ring, Murphy picked up. "What."

"I need to renegotiate the terms of the bargain."

Tension crackled. "More time?"

"Under the circumstances."

"*Circumstances.* That's a word for it."

"One of them," Cormac agreed, then kept quiet. His position in this negotiation was to Murphy's benefit as well. It was only a matter of giving the man a chance to reach the same conclusion.

"Right." Murphy had not gotten to where he was in life by being slow. He continued in formal language and tone, "The bargain between Cormac son of Idris and myself as made on the eighth and twenty of October last shall be held in suspension until the coming full moon or justice has been served in the murder of one Kendra May Ross, whichever first comes to pass. Are we so agreed?"

There were twenty-five days till a full moon. Cormac would have preferred a longer extension, but this would serve. "We are so agreed."

"When should we expect you?"

"I'll ride the lines." As an answer, it was both specific and vague.

The call ended.

● ○ ●

Landmark Hotel, Granite Springs

Declan lowered his arm. The urge to hurl his phone against the wall was powerful. Acid born of rage pulsed through his veins, eating away at the usual ice.

His hand clenched. He allowed his control to slip, let a bit of wild magic run. The phone's metal case cracked. Glass and circuitry shattered. Adding intention to the magic, he opened his fingers. The phone's wreckage vanished in a burst of blue flame.

It was not enough. Power crackled at his hands. He surveyed his suite for objects available to throw. Furniture to overturn.

However good the destruction of his property might feel in the short term, it would not serve in the long.

Destroying Kendra's killer would.

But he had best not go about it while his temper ran hot. He knew well what could happen when he sought vengeance while emotion ruled.

He crossed the glazed concrete floor. An illusion of moonlight cast the open-plan space in cold blues and grays. There were no true windows. A combination of crystalline paint and complex spellwork gave a perfect view of the outer world as if the bricks and beams were floor-to-ceiling glass. The exterior gave a different illusion: a line of narrow, mullioned windows.

Inside, furnishing and fixtures determined the layout. Since he never had guests, he had no need to subdivide the whole to provide privacy. The term spartan might apply to the style—simple, modern lines and stark absence of clutter in favor of basic functionality—but couldn't be more wrong in terms of quality.

He entered what the designer had intended for the kitchen until reminded that room service ran twenty-four hours. With a few alterations (chiefly the removal of appliances other than a hot plate) it had become his workspace. He cued the overhead lights as he bypassed the oak cabinets that held supplies and grimoires. Until he could think clearly, coldly, he would not risk working with anything there. An easel stood near the end of the slate-topped counter. He stopped at it, stared at the canvas it held.

The landscape was only roughly blocked in. Swaths of tranquil greens and blues indicating the lay of grassy hills under a cloudless sky. Declan had planned for a stream to wend its way across the bottom third and had been looking forward to trying a technique seen on an old instructional program a local station broadcast for insomniacs.

There would be no stream. No hills. No sky.

No greens, no blues. Declan yanked open a drawer, tossed tubes of paint onto the worktop. Scarlet. Crimson. Venetian red to match the dried stains on his shirt-cuffs.

Fuck the fiddly little twist cap. He materialized a knife and slashed the tube. Red paint oozed, thick and sluggish. Not like blood. Blood spurted. Blood ran.

He threw the knife at the nearest wall. It hit where he had aimed, the blade embedded halfway to the hilt, but his attention had never left the paint tube. In his mind's eye, he saw only red.

Squeezing, he widened the split, then dragged the tube—no brush—across the canvas again and again. When that wasn't enough, he slashed open another. And another. And another.

Red. Only red until the tubes were empty.

Breathing hard, he took a step back. His throat was tight. Raw. He opened another drawer. This one held smaller tubes and yet more variety. Ultramarine. Viridian. Burnt sienna to match her hair.

"What did you do?" Abigail had asked him. Had *accused* him.

He didn't know.

What had he done? What *hadn't* he done? He didn't fucking know.

His hands were red to the wrists. Red paint on his leather cuffs and on his shirt cuffs to mix with her blood. Lovely, spirited Kendra Ross.

His vision blurred wetly. He blinked several times to clear it and pulled over a jar of brushes. He fingered through them, selected a blunt-tipped sable.

Now he would paint.

CHAPTER 10

Railroad District
Granite Springs, Oregon
31 January

Morning came much too soon. The sun had yet to rise when the clock rang beside Thia's bed. She grabbed it, slid the toggle, and then lay there with it clutched to her chest. Unusually, she was on her back. Interrupted, probably, in her typical cycle of side to side tossing. Her eyes were scratchy. Unwilling.

The window sheers let in the street lighting, so she left the bedside lamp off. Harsh shadows and muted color suited the day more than would the fully lit room: butter-yellow walls adorned with cheerful watercolors; a vibrant Turkish rug; a color block quilt. Lettie had been slightly more restrained in her own bedroom, which left this one to serve as an exuberant catch-all for whatever else had tickled her fancy.

The aging central heater cycled on, sending a faint hiss of air through two floor vents. Not a sound came from outside. But, then, it was a Sunday in winter.

Eclectica was due to open at eleven.

Thia didn't see how she could do that. Maybe she wouldn't. But her employees would arrive in a few hours and expect to work. She should call, tell them not to come for today at least, and that they would be paid regardless.

Their contact numbers were at the store. Unless Abby had the database linked in her phone—no, Thia wasn't about to wake her. Besides, a notice should get posted on the door to explain the closure to customers, which meant going there.

Imbolc was tomorrow. Hopefully everyone had what they needed. And if not, would be understanding. Eclectica could function without Thia, but not without Abby too. And Abby certainly would not be in any shape to work. Thia had heard her crying off and on through the night. Muffled sounds, as if she hadn't wanted to be heard—which was why, as difficult as it had been, Thia had left her to them.

And spent much of the time muffling her own.

She kicked off the covers and flung her legs over the side to sit up. The sun was rising rapidly, chasing away the room's deepest shadows. She returned the clock to the nightstand. Her phone's lock screen was blank. No alert to a missed call. No waiting text. On the other side of the world, the day was already half over.

She lurched to her feet and to the closet. A curtain served in place of a door. A string with a bead knotted onto its end hung just inside. One pull and the bulb would click on. She wrapped her fingers around the thin cord.

One pull and the day would truly start. The bead dug into her palm.

What did one wear the day after a friend's murder?

She yanked the string and then had to squint against the sudden stab of light and color.

● ○ ●

Eclectica

An hour later, Thia's eyes were the only part of her that had adjusted to the day. Everything was familiar—familiar objects, familiar settings—yet different. Edges were sharper, distances more pronounced, as if despite the vast, shocking changes of the past months, she had continued to view her life through a soft, comfortable filter. Kendra's murder had shattered that.

She felt exposed. What was it that stood between a person and absence? *Was* there anything? "Gone in an instant" could be said of anyone. Alive one minute; dead the next.

Life's precarious nature was not meant to be dwelled on, she told herself as she taped the closure notice to the inside glass of Eclectica's main door. To spend every moment of every day with this raw awareness—that the familiar, the loved could be gone in a blink—would be to go mad.

Yet she couldn't shake it.

She smoothed the final strip of tape and then turned around to consider the walking sticks that lay scattered on the floor. Every morning. Every morning, the sticks.

"Dammit, Thing," she called out, although she didn't credit the automated vacuum with sentience. What came across as personality was the result of glitches.

Although, might the same be said of people?

She righted the brass umbrella stand and then, one by one, returned the sticks to it. No matter where they were set up, Thing managed to topple them. She should probably locate him before she left. If he didn't begin each evening's routine from his charging base, he'd get up to even worse mischief in the night.

What was humanity's default setting, anyway, so many iterations down the line?

A hard tapping on the door startled her and she whirled. The stick in her hand swept a table clear of its *brídeóg*-making supplies. Baskets went flying, spewing their delicate, by-the-piece seashells far and wide while bundles of rushes bounced and rolled.

On the other side of the door stood Edith Wilkinson, the Brigantium agent stationed locally since November. She was trim in an athletic way, a few inches shorter than Thia, and seemed to possess both a youthful energy and a sharp if sometimes distracted intelligence. She had so far gotten along well in Thia's odd mix of newfound friends and acquaintances.

Despite the day being unseasonably mild, she wore matched ski jacket and pants along with scarf, hat, fur-topped boots, and gloves. She gestured for Thia to come.

"Just a second." Thia laid the walking stick aside before stepping carefully through the new mess she had made. Two deadbolts and a latch later and she pulled open the door. "We're staying closed today, but if you need to get something—"

"Oh, no, no, no," Edith said in a rush. "I saw you through the window as I was driving by."

A sleek Mercedes SUV idled at the curb not far from Thia's parked Datsun.

"Please accept my deepest condolences. Kendra was such a—such a force." Tears glistened in Edith's brown eyes. She grimaced, shook her head. "That isn't helpful, I'm sure. And isn't what I meant to say. Assistant Director Meriwether has sent Quentin with a team. They should be arriving soon—I'm on my way to collect them. But when I saw you, I wondered if you might like to come. I'm told Cormac is with them."

At the mention, Thia felt a jolt of conflict. To have had no response to last night's text had been disappointing but also worrisome. *He didn't care to reply,* had been one theory. He did not care about Thia or Kendra or any of them. *He was unable to reply,* had been another. He was hurt, seriously hurt, maybe dead. Those two theories had been cycling around for hours.

He could have told her he was coming. One damn text.

"I shouldn't," Thia said, in the way of someone who didn't have time. It was more that she didn't feel up to it. She had been *afraid* for him. "Thanks, though. Abby is at my house. I should get back."

"Of course. Please extend my—*our* condolences." Her brow

furrowed as her mouth thinned. "We haven't been able to get much information beyond what was publicly released, which of course sheds almost no light. Probable mugging. Here? In the off-season?"

That was the story running on the local news sites. Thia had checked, hoping for more. "It's hard to understand."

But did that mean she *shouldn't* believe it? Was there such a thing as an understandable tragedy? There would always be disbelief that such a terrible loss had occurred.

Edith began to walk backwards toward the SUV. "We'll get to the bottom of this, I promise. I'll let you know when we're back, and we can all meet straight away."

"Right," Thia said, and tried not to feel overwhelmed. How many different emotions could she process at the same time without short-circuiting? She wasn't a computer—or a robot vacuum—but she felt dangerously overloaded.

"Oh, and Thia?"

With the door halfway closed, she paused. "Yeah?"

Edith dodged street slush as she rounded the SUV for the driver's side. "Keep to well-protected areas as best you can."

Watching her, Thia wasn't exactly having second thoughts about going along—more like half of one second thought—but she'd already missed her chance. Edith was barely settled behind the wheel when she pulled the door shut and sent the SUV speeding away from the curb and across two lanes to narrowly beat a red light.

● ○ ●

Abby stormed up First Street toward Main. She had Thia's spare house key clutched in her gloved fist from when she'd locked the door. It felt good to crush something. That Thia had single-handedly decided to keep the store closed—and told her in a note—was more upsetting than it ought to be. Eclectica was, after all, hers, not Abby's. Her hand squeezed tighter. She couldn't stop getting angry.

Anger had gotten her out of bed. Anger had made it possible to strip off the borrowed pajamas and, with a few more items borrowed from Lettie's dresser, to put on yesterday's clothes. Anger let her eschew the coffee left too long on the machine's burner and decide to make her own latte at Eclectica, closed or not. She was headed there now. It felt right to be outside and moving.

Despite having spent more hours crying than sleeping, her mind was clear. Sharp. She expected to find Thia at Eclectica where, together, they could then make a plan. What was being done? Were there any suspects? Had he, she, or they already been caught? Abby hated not knowing. Kendra was her friend. Her best friend, if she were made to rank such things. She needed to—

Her steps slowed. Kendra *had been* her best friend. Never again present.

Sorrow brought her to a standstill just past the ice cream shop.

The *former* ice cream shop.

Abby would not cry. Anyone driving by would see. Anyone looking out a front-facing window would see. It was early for stores to open, so the street was essentially deserted, but still. Tears were a private matter. Her own.

She focused on the Landmark, ahead, so much taller than anything for miles around.

Anger got her moving with a change of plan. She crossed Main and soon her hands shoved open the lobby door and she was storming in, her boots unusually loud on the polished stone floor. Never had she seen the place so vacant.

Only one guest was taking advantage of the morning coffee service. An older man and not familiar as a customer at Eclectica, he sat by the fireplace. An unopened newspaper lay next to him on the sofa seat. Wisps of steam drifted from a cup on the table before him. He stared vaguely in its direction, his expression sad.

That's what sorrow did to a person: Inaction. Anger kept Abby moving across the lobby.

Behind the reception desk, a clerk noticed her approach. "M-Miss Collins. Please, may I say how sorry I am. Kendra— that is, Miss Ross, was such a—"

"Is he in?" she asked, not slowing as she turned left to walk past.

"I-I don't—that is, I'm not sure if Mr. Murphy—"

She was already into the hallway that led to the administrative offices. Kendra's door was the first of several. Bright yellow police tape had been strung across it. Murphy's office was farther down. Its door was also closed. No tape there, she noted when she stood at it, and dove deeper into her anger.

Curling her fingers around the brass knob, she noticed her other hand still gripped Thia's key. She released it into her coat pocket as she flung open the door and entered.

Murphy sat behind his desk. She had expected as much, but the bruising around his eye was a surprise.

Oh, she remembered hitting him. She remembered it well. The surprise was that he had done nothing about the bruise. If he lacked the particular magic himself, he had a healer on staff. At the least he could have concealed it with a glamour. She knew he could craft those. Yet he had kept it, a purpling crescent that went from the outer corner of his left brow to the top-center of his cheekbone.

As she got closer, she noticed the scabbed line of a cut.

He made a slow circle in the air with his pen before he set it down. "Collins."

The way he spoke her name, the bored expression on his face . . . Abby's anger surged, hot and bright.

Behind her, the door closed with a muted, controlled click. Cued, she realized, by his move with the pen. Wand work? Or was the tool irrelevant to the gesture? Part of her itched to ask, although he never discussed magic. He never discussed much of anything.

She could hate him.

The year before last, the two of them had all but destroyed the ballroom—the result of a discussion that had escalated. One of many, but by far the worst.

And she hadn't felt nearly as upset then as she did now. She shouldn't have come. Not today. Not like this. But it was too late. She was too furious to leave.

"There's crime scene tape across Kendra's door," she said in accusation. "Is that because whatever she was doing—for you—got her killed?"

His expression didn't alter.

How dare he remain so cool. She closed the distance to the desk. "My best friend is dead. Murdered not a hundred feet from here, and if you are in any way the cause, so help me, I'll—"

"I can't do this now," he said, blandly cutting her off.

Abby's teeth clunked together on a wave of pure, white-hot rage. The desk dug into the tops of her thighs as she leaned in, planted her hands on the papers strewn across the blotter. "*You* can't. *You* can't." Her throat burned. "How do you think *I* feel? How did *Kendra* feel? I'm sure she would have loved to say, 'Sorry, I can't do this now, maybe you could murder me another time?'"

Never let it be said that anger was rational.

"She worked for *you*. Why is she dead? Does it have anything to do with—with whatever it is that you really do?" She noted a subtle change in the impenetrable dark of his gaze. Finally a reaction. Faint lines of tension formed at his mouth.

Encouraged, she leaned closer. "Tell me why she's *dead*. Is it because of you?"

"You'd prefer that, I see," he said coldly. "When the truth is it could just as well be because of you."

She jerked back, her mouth opening—only to feel the argument die in her throat.

"You and Thia and the bloody Society of Brigantium." He broke eye contact to retrieve his pen and pull over a sheet of paper. "But you don't see me going around accusing. I've got her wake to prepare and her family to host and the murdering bastard to find. I don't have time—*jaysus,* Collins." He sprang up, came around the desk to wrap his arms around her as she began to shake, her anger swept away in a flood of grief.

Abby couldn't see through the tears. Then she couldn't see because her face was pressed to the plush wool of Murphy's suit coat.

"*Tá brón orm,*" he murmured while his hand came to rest on the back of her head. She wasn't familiar with the words, with whether they were comfort or curse, no matter how kind his voice sounded. She didn't care. Kendra was going to have a wake. After a wake would come a funeral.

A *funeral.*

If Murphy had not been holding her so securely, she might have collapsed. She wanted to. His hand continued to stroke the back of her head while she sobbed. She had left her hair loose. His fingers worked their way through the curls.

"Don't," she managed to say with her face mashed against him. "Don't be nice. I need to stay angry." She felt his chest expand on a slow breath and then deflate on a sigh.

"I'll not argue that." He sounded resigned. "But you might consider a different target."

She did, for a time. Twelve comforting strokes of his hand. Then, "Show me one."

His hand stilled.

"Security cameras," she said, and pulled back to study his face. Whatever expression she expected, she found only coldness. Yet his touch had been so warm. "You must have some out there. Show me the footage. I need to know."

"There's a phrase people use in jest, about not being able to un-see a thing. I'll use it with you now, Abigail, and not in jest. This is a thing you can never un-see."

She laid a light hand on his cheek, let her thumb skim the red line one of her rings must have cut into his skin. Then, lowering her hand, she stepped out of the strange comfort of his arms.

"Show me," she said.

● ○ ●

The Vale
Near Granite Springs

In Cormac's estimation, the only mode of travel worse than hurtling through the sky inside a winged metal cylinder was hurtling through time and space inside a leyline. As miserable as airplanes could be, they didn't transform matter into amorphous energy.

He dropped out of the line, instantly reacquiring physical form if not his usual finesse. He landed awkwardly, could not correct in time, and toppled face first into snow. Nearby, he heard an impact similar to his own accompanied by a shocked grunt. There was no graceful way to exit a line.

"All here?" Quentin's voice came from a distance. From even further than that, the two accompanying agents answered in the affirmative.

A limited contingent, which suited Cormac. If more were needed, they could be sent through.

He raised his head. His vision refused to settle yet, but he could determine his surroundings well enough. Snow covered meadow. Mountains to the left. Pine trees. Road to the right. He was becoming all too familiar with this particular portal.

Never again, he promised himself (as he suspected he had done before, as well).

"There's no toll?" One of the agents' voices carried as, under Quentin's supervision, luggage and gear was collected from where it had dropped around the field.

"No keeper," Quentin replied, and the other agents reacted with amusing yet forgivable astonishment.

This portal was at a juncture of several major leylines—lines which had been controlled by some organization or another for centuries, or even millennia. So, yes, the absence of a toll keeper was unusual indeed.

The cold was seeping through Cormac's outerwear despite the warming spell in its weave. He pushed to his feet, brushed himself off as he looked for his canvas holdall, retrieved from a rented locker in London. Prior to this he had never gone through a line with more than what he had on his person, but the Brigantium had loaned him a charmed tag.

And it worked. His well-worn bag was amongst what the agents had gathered. He made his way over.

"Unbelievable." Quentin was slowly circling the collection, poking at nearly identical black cases. "Not bloody again."

Remembering what had happened to the agent's luggage in December, Cormac grinned. "Lose something?"

He said nothing, just continued to glare at the field where his agents continued to search.

"I'll go on ahead, shall I?" Cormac shouldered his bag and began the snowy trudge to where a black SUV idled on the roadside. The woman who stood beside the open driver's-side door was familiar . . . but was not Thia.

He should not feel disappointed. He hadn't told her he was coming.

He hadn't told her anything.

Fat snowflakes began to fall as the wind picked up. He heard Quentin direct the others. "Load what we've got. Let's go."

When Cormac reached the road, the woman—Edith Something-or-Other—reached inside the SUV and caused the rear hatch to open. He placed his bag within.

"What's the issue?" Through a pair of horn-rimmed glasses,

her wary gaze met his only briefly before it returned to the field.

"Missing suitcase," he said, and secured the ends of his scarf against the wind.

"Quentin's?"

"Seems so."

"That happened last time. He'll be in a mood." She watched a moment longer, then opened the rear passenger door for Cormac.

He remained where he was. The others could go first. He wasn't about to trap himself in a middle seat.

He could fly into town. His raven form was well-insulated from the cold, and there were spells that would do even more.

But that would be an energy expenditure at a time when he should conserve. Also, he would be unable to carry his holdall. The Otherworldly process would not consider it as being "on his person" and therefore would exclude it—which meant he would have to entrust it to the Brigantium.

Arms folded across his chest, he leaned against the SUV. Quentin was having difficulty with the slope up to the road. No one had dressed for snow, and his shoes in particular were proving to offer inadequate traction.

Edith met him halfway down the berm. "Here, let me take that." She reached for the wooden case he carried.

"It's fine." He hastily moved it out of range and almost over-balanced himself.

She didn't argue, but she stayed close until he stepped onto the road.

"We need to fix the transport tags so they stay the fuck on," he said tautly, and shoved his case in with Cormac's bag.

"Was your personal luggage the only loss?" Edith inquired.

"Only?"

"You know what I meant."

"Yes." Quentin blew out a cold-clouded breath. "And yes, only mine." He got into the front passenger seat but left the door open. "I suppose the Landmark has records of what they supplied before."

"I should think so." Edith passed by Cormac on her return to the rear of the SUV. "I rather liked the hoodie."

"Indeed," Cormac said, wry. "After all, who doesn't 'heart' Granite Springs?"

Quentin's door slammed.

CHAPTER II

"Hours before her death, the victim phoned you"—Quentin's voice rose steadily despite the close proximity of his target—"and you didn't think to share this before *now?*"

Cormac regretted his choice back at the portal. Crammed into an overheated vehicle with four Brigantium agents, two of whom were more intent on argument than the road and its potential hazards—he should have flown himself into town.

Edith jerked the steering wheel into a sharp turn and the combined weight of the men seated to Cormac's left pressed into his shoulder. Not getting inside sooner, before the rear bench seat had been filled with overflow luggage and supply cases, was another regret.

"I hadn't the chance." Edith wrenched the wheel the other way. Cormac braced himself so as to remain upright.

"Nonsense," Quentin countered. "That took you, what, all of five seconds to convey? Surely you've had five seconds to spare prior to this. Text or email would have done the trick as well. Unless you're an abominable typist. *Are* you an abominable typist?"

After a charged pause, she said, "I apologize." But it had been tightly done, and Cormac had a view of her hands. The wheel might well have served as a stand-in for Quentin. "I was given to understand that my priority was threat assessment, in addition to making arrangements for the team's arrival. I assessed that my having received a message concerning land records was less critical than everyone's safety. I had honestly forgotten about it until I was on my way to meet you. *Sir.*"

The road straightened. She stomped on the gas.

"*Brid* help us," the agent to Cormac's immediate left whispered in prayer.

"You *forgot?*" Quentin's disinterest in self-preservation was unfortunate for them all. "That you qualified to be the solo field agent here defies comprehension. You *forgot.* A message from a murdered woman and you f—"

"What was said, exactly?" Cormac asked. Loudly.

Edith met his gaze briefly in the rear mirror. "She wanted to know if we'd learned more about the trust that owns the land beneath the Valhalla."

Not a reference to the Norse realm of the dead but rather the trash heap of a tavern that he, Murphy, and Kendra had broken into while investigating the Rekkrs motorcycle gang in December. He clutched the armrest as the SUV sped into another turn. "Did she mention why?"

"No. She asked if our research had turned up anything, told me to call back, then hung up. That's it."

"Presumably you called back?"

"No answer." She slowed to a stop at an intersection. They had reached the outskirts of town. Well below the snow level and with posted speed limits, the drive ought to be a hell of a lot safer.

Cormac leaned forward. "What were the times? When she left the message and when you returned the call."

"Hers came in at ten forty-six." Edith took the left tine of the road's fork. "I wasn't able to call back until the afternoon. Two o'clock, maybe three."

"She was killed when—about half past nine? Plenty of time for her to respond if she'd considered it vital."

"By accounts, she was in her office all afternoon and evening until she went to the restaurant. During that time she took no meetings or calls, at least on her office line. No outgoing calls on that either."

The transformation really was remarkable. The Brigantium had gone from a purely academic, social club to something akin to an intelligence service.

"What of her mobile? Other than your missed calls?"

"I haven't been able to get those records yet."

"No?" Quentin interjected.

These people. As the squabbling recommenced, Cormac sat back, observed the scenery out the side window.

At the drive's start, Edith had recounted eyewitness statements. Each presented Kendra Ross as acting strangely prior to her death. Distracted, unfocused, vague. There had been marks on her fingers. Blue, like ink, according to description.

The closer the SUV got to downtown Granite Springs, the more Cormac's own focus drifted. He had left on good terms with Thia—whatever that meant. But he had not stayed in contact.

How annoyed might she be by that? And, worse, how upset that he hadn't so much as acknowledged the text she sent last night?

At least he didn't have "read receipts" turned on. He could claim that his phone's battery had run down.

It didn't matter to him personally if he had upset her, but for what he needed to do it would be better if she did not hate him.

The red notebook was a strangely heavy weight in his inner breast pocket. The doppelgänger discs, too.

● ○ ●

Main Street, Granite Springs

Outside Eclectica, Thia reconsidered the temporary closure announcement's placement on the door. Taped to the inside of the glass at average head height, it might be better closer to the handle. People would be bound to see it whether before or after they tried the locked door.

They would see it where it currently was, too, either before but definitely after the door didn't budge.

She knew she was overthinking. She tended to do that when stressed. The feeling that something she had done (or hadn't done) might have contributed to a terrible wrong made her hesitant to decide anything at all. Fear that she had made a mistake, small or gargantuan, made her afraid that she might make another. All morning, she had been second, third, and fourth-guessing herself through the most basic, inconsequential decisions.

Enough. The sign placement was *good enough.* If it wasn't, too bad. She locked the door.

She was nearing her car when her attention was caught by bright, erratically moving color.

Madame Demetka, adorned in her usual yards and yards of fabric, had entered the block at the lower end. She saw Thia and waved both arms wildly. "Miri mora!"

The voluminous skirt made it difficult to tell, but from the bounce of the older woman's shoulders, she might have been jogging. "Such happenings," she cried, her cloak flaring out behind her. "Terrible happenings!"

Clearly, she knew about Kendra. The Sunday paper, word of mouth, local websites—Thia needn't assume this to be due to clairvoyance, although that was how Madame Demetka made her living.

Until recently Thia had believed that to be more show than substance. Skillful guesswork done with a good deal of flair. After the past few months, she wasn't so sure—but, for good reason, not ready to fully believe.

"I have not the right words," Madame Demetka announced, spreading her arms wide as she neared.

Thia braced for the impact that came a moment later, cushioned by the other woman's ample bosom. Strong arms and patchouli-scented fabric enveloped her, a hug and a swaddling all at once. Fine hairs prickled the skin of her face.

Cat hairs, she realized when she was abruptly released and able to swipe a hand across her lips. She could see many more where those had come from on the cloak's burgundy velvet.

Thia could also see moisture beaded in Madame Demetka's mascara-augmented eyelashes, and damp tracks marring her face powder.

"You heard?" Thia asked her gently.

"No! I had to read of it. I am much put out."

"I'm so sorry—I should have called you when—"

"*Pshaw!*" Madame Demetka briefly looked to the sky. "My Guides, they are useless today. They leave it for the morning news. No warning. Nothing. Is complete shock."

"A shock, yes."

"Is tragic."

"Yes."

They shared a moment. Two women, not well acquainted, standing in the windless cold of morning. One confused as to much of what the other said, whereas the other might simply be confused.

Madame Demetka eyed Thia up and down. "There is difference, yes? Energy." She waggled her fingers. "Shut up."

"Excuse me?"

"Ah! No, no. Sorry. Your energy is shut up. Closed. But you know this, yes? You do this on purpose."

Thia hoped whatever that referred to wasn't important. "I need to be getting back to the house. Abby's there, and I don't want her to be—" Her phone rang and vibrated in her pocket.

"That is her now," Madame Demetka said, and sure enough, Abby's name was on the screen.

"Did you—"

"Easy enough guess, sugar." Said with shrug and a half smile. Gone was the outrageous Madame Demetka persona with its Eastern European-esque accent; Sally Wilson and her deeply southern drawl had taken its place. Alter ego, maybe, or the real person beneath the role.

This was why Thia wasn't ready to fully believe in Madame Demetka's messages and visions.

She picked up the call. "Abby, did you get my note? I'm on my way back."

"I'm not there." She sounded awful. "I'm at the Landmark. You need to come."

"The Landmark? What are you—never mind. I'll be right there."

Abby clicked off.

Lowering the phone, Thia started to say that she needed to go, but Demetka-Sally was already halfway up the block.

"I heard," she said as Thia caught up. "I've got good ears."

Apparently. And, because Thia couldn't come up with a way to dissuade her, they walked together.

"You're not opening the store today."

"Oh, hell." Thia felt like an idiot. "I'm sorry—I should have called you. Your appointments. I didn't think." Didn't think of any of the bookings, let alone Madame Demetka's. Weekends were the busiest. "You don't happen to know who else is using the Rowan Space today, do you?"

"Sorry, sugar. Only that I'm scheduled from midmorning to three." Sally stopped as Thia did. "I've already canceled with my clients, so don't you worry about that."

"I'll go get the schedule." Thia turned around.

Sally halted her with a hand on her arm. "You go on to Abby. I can make whatever calls need to be made. And I'll be sure to lock up after."

Thia held out her collection of keys. "Thank you, that'd be so—" The protection wards. *Good grief.* She hadn't reset the wards when she left.

Just as well, since Sally would have been unable to get past them; but it was a disturbing thing to have forgotten. Resetting them had become routine. A vital one.

"Sorry," she said with a shake of her head. "Lost in thought." She finished handing over the keys. She would go by later and do the wards. "I appreciate this."

"No trouble at all." Sally jingled the keys. "I'll return these to you at the Landmark."

"Okay, thanks." Thia set off. She was not particularly tall— five foot eight—but much of that was leg. She could cover ground quickly when needed.

What was Abby doing at the hotel? She hadn't sounded in any shape to be out, let alone *there.*

The police tape had been adjusted since the night before. Instead of the entire street, it blocked off only the alley.

Thia stepped into the lobby. The building's heat came as a shock after so much time spent outside. Her face and hands tingled, acclimating. She could not say the same for herself. Here, Kendra's absence was profound. Thia felt as if she were drowning in it, although she realized the inherent contradiction—how could one drown in a void?

Never again would she meet her friend for drinks through that doorway, there, to the Alchemy Taproom. No afternoon breaks by the fireplace. No dinner conversation that extended well past the meal and covered everything from folklore to politics to movies. And what of the conversations that would have—*should* have—been to come? All that, as of last night, they would never get the chance to say. The truly personal talks of established friendship. Childhood. Family. Romantic love and all its chaos and angst. Dreams and aspirations.

Thia walked past the central table. Abby had not told her where in the hotel to meet her, only to come. She went to reception.

"Hi," she said to get the attention of the young clerk, head down as he tapped on a mounted tablet.

"Yes?" He looked up, blinking reddened eyes. Recognition slowly dawned. "Miss McDaniel, sorry. It's been a horrible—" He composed himself. "If you're looking for Ms. Collins, I'm pretty sure she went to Mr. Murphy's office."

"Thanks." Thia took a step but then paused. She might not know the clerk's name (because she was terrible with names, and from now on, she promised, she would make more of an effort) but she knew him both from being a daytime fixture here and a regular customer at Eclectica. "How are you?"

"Oh." Fresh tears filled his eyes. "I don't know. It's—I don't understand how this could happen. It's so awful."

"It is."

They shared a look of commiseration and then Thia walked on, taking the turn into the narrow hallway that led to the offices. Kendra's was first, on the left. Its door was closed and had been crisscrossed with yellow tape. There was a notice posted—multiple typed paragraphs on official police department letterhead. Thia didn't stop to read.

The door to Murphy's office was also closed. She didn't hear raised voices inside, which was good. He and Abby were not fighting. Probably. She raised her hand to knock only to have the door swing open.

Abby stood on the other side, and looked as wrecked as she had sounded over the phone. Her hair had been pulled into a messy pony tail; curls stuck out like a freeze frame of a violent explosion. Her eyes were deeply shadowed.

Thia was ushered in with obvious impatience. Not even ten

minutes had elapsed since the call, she thought, and waited for some cue as to what was expected of her.

Seated behind the imposing desk at the back of the room, Murphy was fully absorbed in whatever was on the screen of his open computer.

The space was curious for such a successful businessman: Tight, windowless, and devoid of the objects people of high status tended to display. No awards, degrees, press clippings, or photos of him alongside other successful and/or celebrated persons. No photos whatsoever, she realized.

A taupe area rug; a couch against the left wall with a coffee table before it which displayed brochures of the Landmark's sister hotels and resorts; two round-backed chairs before the desk and a third by the right-hand wall; on the back wall, a wooden cabinet which held labeled binders and narrow file boxes. No curios, no books aside from travel guides.

Abby closed the door but made no move to sit. Thia took her cue from that and remained standing.

The room's austerity made the painting that hung directly behind the desk all the more stunning. Verdant, rolling hills and a glimpse of what could be a lake or cove. Someplace in Ireland, she would bet.

She would also bet it had been done by the same artist as several other paintings placed throughout the hotel. A rain-slicked city scene hung in a hallway off the mezzanine; a field of poppies, in the nook between the elevator and the lobby restroom. She'd identified at least seven more by style—and by the mix of admiration and envy that each viewing inspired. Much as she had tried, she couldn't paint worth a damn.

She realized the silence was going to stretch until she broke it. "Abby," she said gently. "What am I doing here?"

Abby ducked her head, avoiding eye contact, and rubbed a hand across her mouth before replying. "I saw the footage."

"Footage? What foot—" Security footage. *Good lord.* "You

watched Kendra?"

Abby said nothing. She might not have been capable, with all the tension in her jaw and her lips pressed so firmly, like she was trying to hold herself in, or together, or—

Something clicked behind Thia. She turned.

Murphy had closed the computer. Had *that* been what he'd been looking at? The hotel security footage?

Oh, no. *No.* Was she supposed to watch? Her mouth opened, a protest on the tip of her tongue. But what if she could help catch Kendra's killer? With her mouth shut as tight as Abby's, she sat in one of the desk-front chairs.

Murphy looked up, and she shivered from a sudden chill. He showed no emotion. The cut below his left eye had scabbed over. The skin around it and most of the socket had purpled.

"Okay." Thia gestured to the computer. "I'm ready."

"No!" Abby lunged, putting herself between Thia and the desk as if the computer posed a physical threat. "Absolutely not. I wanted you here because nothing makes sense. And I panicked, thinking of you out there unprotected." She sank onto the adjacent chair.

"Are we in danger? This wasn't"—what was the term—"an isolated incident? A mugging gone wrong?"

"It wasn't a mugging," Abby said darkly, matching Edith's earlier skepticism.

"Cassie, then?"

"We don't know."

"But you don't not know? So it could be?"

"We don't know bloody anything," Murphy said, breaking his silence. "But Collins here has the right of it. Better safe than sorry."

"Kendra let the guy walk right up," Abby said in bewilderment. "She went into the alley and let some maniac come at her with a pipe and she didn't even try. She stood there. As if . . . as if she were waiting for it. Looking for it." Her voice broke.

Thia ached for her. "Oh, Abby."

"It doesn't make any sense." Tears slid down her cheeks. She began swiping at them with her knuckles. "Shit."

Murphy pushed a box of tissues across his desk.

Grudgingly, Abby took it.

"Kendra acted oddly in the restaurant," Thia said to Murphy. "You told her to see someone about the blue marks. Someone that would make sure she was okay. Do you know if she did?"

"Jenkins, that was," he replied. "She did not. Nor was he able to locate her himself. In time."

"We should have made her," Abby said, tossing a wadded tissue into a nearby wastebasket. "We shouldn't have let her leave."

"That's on me," Murphy said tightly. "She was one of mine. She should have been safe within the hotel."

"But she left," Thia said, and Abby pulled a fresh tissue out of the box.

"Aye," Murphy said. "She left."

Regret. Guilt. Self-recriminations. Those things could kill if left to flourish. And none of them could bring Kendra back.

"She seemed—" Thia struggled. "I don't know how to put it. Not herself. Less focused, less . . . present. As if she had been drugged." She couldn't imagine Kendra willingly taking anything. Thia had known her to turn down aspirin. "Could the marks on her fingers have carried a toxin? No," she nixed her own idea. Far too coincidental. "She then just happened to wander out to be attacked. Never mind."

"Wait, though," Abby said. "If we can assume this was not a random attack—and I believe we can—then we have to figure she was the target. Last night, at least. Whether this is only the beginning, we—"

"The beginning?"

"The beginning," Murphy answered before Abby could, "of any number of larger possible schemes against any number of targets. Myself included."

"Cassie."

"Or," he said, "someone after those new powers of yours. But, as killing your friend is an odd first step to take for that sort of thing, I should think we can rule it out."

"Consider me reassured," she said dryly, feeling nothing of the sort.

"In any case," Abby said with force, "Kendra was targeted last night. Something caused her to go into the alley where her killer waited, and something made her not defend herself when she could have."

"*Easily* could have," Murphy emphasized. "She was one of the best fighters I've seen in—Well. In a long time."

"It has to have been the marks," Abby said. "A toxin, like you said, Thia. Something that made her open to suggestion, maybe? Which got her to step beyond the Landmark's wards. That would explain why she didn't react. Suggestion. Outside influence."

"Sure, it's possible," Murphy said, "but why make it obvious with the blue? It's counterproductive if the aim is to render a person helpless. Anyone might notice the marks—as we did. Not that we did a fucking thing about it."

"We tried, though," Thia said, despite knowing it was weak. They should have tried harder. She would carry that burden the rest of her life.

"We need to find out how she got them," Abby said. "The marks. If we know the how, we might come to know the what and the who. And the why."

"We?" That came out sounding frantic, Thia knew. But she was starting to feel frantic, actually. "What about the police?"

"I've got a contact," Murphy said, although that wasn't at all what she had meant. "He'll keep me apprised of any progress.

Such as it might be." The implication being that not much was expected.

It was true that when Zoe went missing, the police hadn't been much help. The Brigantium and Cormac, on the other hand, had been invaluable.

"If Kendra was made susceptible to suggestion," Thia said, using Abby's phrase, "how did those suggestions get to her? She was inside the hotel. Inside its wards."

"Inside." Abby straightened. "Whoever sent them could've also been inside. You have cameras all over the public areas, I assume," she said to Murphy. "We can check that footage."

"I do and will," he said, "but if the marks were *cumachtae*—infused, that is, with magic—they could have been part of a connection spell. A link. Kendra had top security clearance. Anything she brought with her would pass through the wards without registering as a threat. Any bespelled link would have been maintained."

Would there ever come a time when Thia didn't feel lost? She had been studying all things magic for three months yet had only scratched the surface. "Someone can make another person do things they don't want to do through a spell that gets on their skin?"

"With enough power and skill," Murphy said. "At its base level that would be a tracking spell. I've seen a variation used in fox hunting—not approved, mind. It tracks the fox, and if the hounds lose the scent, the hunt master can coax the fox back in." His expression abstracted, his fingers drummed on the desk. "Not visible to the eye, though, that one. The Sight, sure, but not the eye."

"Blue like a bank robbery," Thia thought aloud.

"Ah." Murphy's fingers stilled. "Blue ink as from a dye pack. Sure. Sure, it is."

Abby was frowning. "If Kendra was looking into something, somewhere—somewhere that she shouldn't have been—and got stained with a spell which allowed someone to influence her, why have her killed in the alley? Why not keep her in place and deal with her immediately?"

"Right." On a heavy sigh, Murphy tipped back in his padded chair. "*Fuichecht.* We're back to where we—"

"The spell wasn't enough." Abby stood and began to pace. "Not at first. It might've started as a tracker, with just enough of a connection to maintain it, and the deeper influence came later. But how?"

"He got to her."

"Right. Somehow he made contact outside the spell and was able to weave another layer. The one that gave him control."

"Risky."

"Desperate," Abby corrected him. "It must not have taken hold immediately. We wouldn't have seen Kendra at all if it had." Her voice faltered. "She would have already been dead."

"She fought." Bitterness laced Murphy's tone.

In the ensuing quiet, Thia's mind went back to a pronoun used. "He?" she asked. "You both said 'he.'"

"Force of habit," Murphy shrugged.

Abby considered that a moment and then shook her head. "I probably picked it up from Murphy. Generic use. I'm not getting any specific feeling—" She resumed pacing. "Got to Kendra *how,* though. In person? He could have done more in person than cast a spell."

"He could *try,*" Murphy said. "He might have been afraid to attempt more and risk drawing notice."

"By phone, then."

"Do the police have it?" Thia asked. "Kendra's cellphone."

"Sadly not," Murphy said. "He took anything of value."

"The killer did? The one in the alley, I mean."

"As opposed to whoever—man, woman, or group—did the spellwork, yes."

"Is it possible the guy in the alley did that, too?"

"Crafted the spells?" Murphy frowned. "Not unless what we saw was a disguise. Young man, early to mid twenties, looked to be a vagrant. Not the sort who would have something to go to such lengths to protect, even if he had the ability."

"We're back to nowhere." Abby sat heavily on the sofa.

"Call records." Murphy made a quick twisting gesture, and a smartphone appeared in his hand. Thia startled. *Dammit.*

"Again with the showing off," Abby said with a roll of her eyes.

Ignoring that, Murphy used both thumbs to type rapidly on the screen. When finished, he pushed back from the desk. "I set people on it. In the meantime, let's see if we can narrow down where those blue marks originated."

● ○ ●

Outside Kendra's office, Abby hugged her arms around her middle and tried to anchor herself while Murphy made short work of the police tape. A wave of his hand caused it to fall away, drifting to the floor to lie like molted snake skin. The lock seemingly clicked of its own volition and the door swung open. To a man such as him, such feats must be child's play. He entered, no hesitation. No remorse?

Thia followed, while Abby could only continue to stand at the threshold. She looked to her feet, encased in the same heeled boots she'd worn last night, and willed them to move.

"*A dhiabhail.*" Murphy's voice. She raised her head, saw him standing behind Kendra's desk; Thia, in front. The habitually cluttered surface was bare.

"The police took everything?" Abby asked, incredulous. It felt like a violation.

Kendra had kept personal items there, objects which had no possible bearing on what had happened to her. A desk set inherited from a grandmother. Family photos. A small clock Abby had given to celebrate Kendra's promotion.

The office's other furniture was equally bare.

"Is that normal?" Thia asked. "To clear out everything?"

Because Murphy was bent over while he opened and closed desk drawers, his reply was muffled and punctuated by slams. "It might be when your employer has, shall we say, a complex relationship with the law."

"Oh, right," Abby said, furious again. Furious about so many things. She focused on one: Him. "Will they get anything on you this time?"

"From confiscated documents and files?" He had the gall to act astonished. "My businesses are entirely legitimate. It's not on me if some people are determined to doubt."

"Haters gonna hate."

Thia turned to mouth a silent plea at her: "Don't."

But how could Abby not? Her fury needed an outlet, and here was the perfect target.

"It would seem so," that target said agreeably, failing to take the bait. He kicked shut what must have been the last drawer.

If the police had bothered to take every object from the room, Thia supposed it followed that they would have taken all the papers too. She returned the empty wastebasket to its spot beside the desk. "What now?" she asked. "How can we retrace her steps?"

"More security footage," Murphy said. "First here, interior and exterior, then expand the radius. Traffic cameras, banks, shops. I'll get people on it."

Persuading retailers to hand over their security recordings to the man whose hotel was largely responsible for drawing so much business to this section of Main Street would be easy enough, Abby supposed, but a bank?

Murphy checked his watch, a chronograph with even more subdials and pushers than Thia's. Its wide leather band was a match for the unadorned one on his right. She had never seen him without either.

"Your police contact," she began, skeptical, as he typed on his phone. Instructing his minions, no doubt. "They will tell you what they find on any of her 'to do' lists, schedules, and whatever?"

He grunted an affirmative.

She wasn't convinced he'd actually heard her.

"Did Kendra sync with the cloud?" Thia asked. "Calendar, text messages, email."

Abby should have thought of that. "With her account name and password, we could access from any computer."

"Do you know them?"

"No." Abby glanced at Murphy, still texting. It was safe to assume, though, that if Kendra hadn't given the information to her closest friend, she hadn't given it to her boss.

Not that the two hadn't been friendly, but she found it hard to believe he could be friends with anyone. Friendship took trust.

"We might not need to," she said. "I have her key." Sorrow surged back to the surface—and brought with it more than a little anxiety. If she couldn't bring herself to go into Kendra's office, how could she go into her home?

She would have to, that's all.

What would have been here was Kendra's work laptop. At her apartment was a trove of personal, interconnected tech, from the latest iPad to a giant-screened iMac Pro.

"The police won't remove things from her home, will they?" Thia asked.

If the office had been cleared out because of its proximity to the crime scene, then, "Probably not," Abby said. But if Murphy was correct and it had been cleared out because of its connection to him, then, "They might."

Kendra's apartment was miles distant, but Murphy was still Murphy.

"Only one way to find out, right?" Thia suggested, despite

looking as if she regretted the whole idea.

"Right." Abby's voice came out a bit rough. They were really going to do this. Go to where Kendra had lived for the past three years. Where Kendra would never be again.

"I parked in front of Eclectica," Thia said. "Should I drive, or . . . ?" She looked back at Murphy, who hadn't so much as glanced their way until then.

Abby hadn't thought to include him—and was annoyed that Thia had. His resources and experience made him invaluable; what did she and Thia know of crime, of evidence-gathering, and so on? He was steeped in all of that . . . which was also why he should not be involved. Because he likely *was* involved, as the catalyst for Kendra's murder.

He was putting away his phone. "Thanks just the same, but I'll sit this one out. I've got—" Mouth closed, a muscle worked in his jaw. He appeared, rather shockingly, to be fighting raw emotion.

Abby promptly squelched a pang of sympathy.

His fight was quickly won, in any case. When he met Abby's gaze, his held nothing but ice. "Along with everything else, I've got the Ross family due to arrive."

"Today?" She shouldn't be surprised. They would have begun making arrangements the moment they had heard.

Kendra had loved her family so deeply. That had been her way: to love deeply, fight fiercely, live fully. And someone had taken that from her. Someone had taken that from all who knew her.

Turning away, Abby began walking down the hall. She called back to Thia, "You don't mind if I drive, do you?"

Her Mini Cooper was in Thia's garage, which meant a little more of a walk than to the Datsun, but she needed to feel in control of *something* even if it was only her car.

CHAPTER 12

No sooner had Abby taken the turn onto Kendra's street than she swore under her breath and slowed considerably.

Thia didn't need to ask why.

Halfway down the block and directly in front of their destination sat a squad car with an open trunk. One uniformed officer lowered a file box into it while a second stood on the strip of winter-frosted grass that accounted for the entirety of the landscaping. No amount of plants could increase curb appeal, so management hadn't bothered.

The two-story, rectangular building looked like it had been carved off a late seventies budget hotel and plunked down in the middle of an otherwise quaint neighborhood. Its beige stucco badly needed a power-wash; the curlicued metal railing along its balcony, a new coat of paint. Rust showed through the white.

"The police are being incredibly thorough," Thia remarked. Rather than feeling encouraged, she felt shaken. Granted, her experience with such things was limited to what she had seen on TV—but there had been a *lot* of TV. Her father's love of serial mysteries bordered on obsessive. Thanks to that, Thia had been raised on them from the cradle.

Not once in the hundreds of episodes of *Verdict: Guilty* had Detective Sloan cleared out a victim's office as thoroughly as Kendra's had been. It seemed that the same was being done to her home. Was that a difference between fiction and reality, or was this unusual? And if so, why?

Abby pulled the car over to the curb, put it in park.

"We're getting out?" Thia asked, surprised when Abby began to do just that. "They won't let us in. They certainly won't let us use"—from outside, Abby shut the door—"her computer."

Reluctantly, Thia got out to follow.

"They'd seen us," Abby said when Thia caught up. "It would be more suspicious if we didn't stop and get out."

She probably had a point. The officer at the car had shut the trunk and was observing their approach while his partner moved to head them off. "I'm sorry ladies, but this—"

"That's all right, Officer Simons."

Everyone turned toward the voice.

Neil Amundsen stood on the balcony. Behind him, the chief of police himself walked out of Kendra's apartment.

"Ladies," Amundsen greeted. "I'll be right down." He spoke to the chief, who then returned inside, closing the door.

Thia and Abby waited, silent, as the man Kendra had been spending time with descended the stairs. He looked weary, as if he hadn't slept any better than they. She hadn't considered how he might be taking the loss.

She hadn't considered him much at all, and obviously she should have.

"You came hoping for an update?" he asked, closing in with his arms extended in a way that made Thia think he meant to embrace them both. Her surprise must have shown—or perhaps it was due to Abby's swift step back—but in any case, his arms lowered to his sides. "That's why I came as well," he continued, doleful. "I was hoping for progress. And I needed to . . . well. This is all such a shock. More so for you both,

I'm sure, being such longstanding friends." He paused, giving them a chance to respond.

Thia, unsettled and conflicted, made a noncommittal noise. They weren't here to talk to anyone—they were doing their own investigation. Which was probably wrong in the eyes of the law. By comparison, Abby's solemn, "Thank you," came off as masterful.

"Things were only in the early stages, of course," Amundsen continued smoothly, "but I had hoped to get to know Kendra and her friends better. She was a special woman. So bright and full of promise."

He said the right things, and in the right way. His pale eyes conveyed the right emotions. Why, then, did Thia feel something was off? She looked to Abby, whose barometer for other peoples' moods was superlative.

Nothing showed beyond a neutral attentiveness.

"I called the chief to make sure the investigation had been given top priority," Amundsen was saying. "When he told me he was here, I wanted to see that her property was treated with the utmost care. Mugging." He made a slow shake of his head.

"Is that what they're still saying?" Abby asked.

"Yes, but—" In the manner of someone with an awkward secret, he leaned in, lowered his voice. "My understanding is that Kendra's employer—how can I put this? That not all of Mr. Murphy's dealings are on the up and up. It makes one wonder."

"It certainly does," Abby agreed. "I've lived here for years and never heard of anyone being mugged. Before."

"None reported," he confirmed.

Thia's odd feeling persisted to the point of nagging. What could it hurt, she decided, and tapped into her Sight.

Flickering colors of the protection wards in operation over Kendra's apartment despite the comings and goings caught her eye first. Did they remain intact because a key had been used in the locks? The landlord would have one for emergency access, which was probably within the wards' parameters. She would ask Abby later.

Amundsen's voice—"I'll do all I can to see justice done"—recaptured her attention and she looked over.

And she *saw*.

She felt her eyes widen and then it was like one of those glaucoma tests that jets a puff of air onto a person's eyes. She recoiled, blinking wildly, and stumbled off the curb.

Against the skin of her upper chest, her Brigantium pendant was hot. An unmistakable warning. She and Abby needed to go—now—before whatever she had seen superimposed over Amundsen realized that she knew. That she had *seen*.

"Thia?" Abby reached out. Thia took a small step back.

"I'm okay," she lied. She felt dangerously close to panic. "I got dizzy or something. Must not have eaten enough today." She tried to smile—at Amundsen in particular so he wouldn't suspect.

Both he and Abby regarded her strangely.

It was becoming impossible to behave as if her heart wasn't pounding, as if terror wasn't racing through her nerves like a colony of ants out of a collapsing hill.

"We should get going—right, Abby?" Widening her attempt at a smile, she began easing toward the car. Internally, she was shaking. She had seen that *creature,* felt that pressure-punch to her eyes, and then her Sight had shut off.

On its own, she wondered, or had the creature done that? Creature—what a horrible thing to say, but what else to call it? Neil Amundsen and something, *someone* bigger. Startling and hideous with sallow skin and bulbous features and a wild tangle of hair sprouting from an outsized head. Did it know she had seen it? Oh, God. *Oh, God.* She had lost her mind.

"Right," Abby said slowly. Unsure, but playing along. Thia

could have hugged her in gratitude. And she would. Later.

"Don't hesitate to contact me," Amundsen said, walking the short distance with them. "I'll be keeping a close eye on the investigation. That's a promise."

Thia didn't listen to any more. She was too intent on getting into the car, and all but threw herself onto the seat. What a relief that she didn't have to drive; she wasn't sure she could. She got the door shut and then, as surreptitiously as possible, mashed the lock down with her arm as if resting it alongside the closed window.

After a brief, muted exchange with Amundsen, Abby got in, turned the ignition key.

They didn't speak until they were in the next block.

"Before you tell me what the hell just happened," Abby said, sparing her a look of concern, "where do I drive us now? Back to your house or—"

"My keys." The seatbelt dug in when Thia sat up. "I'm such an idiot. Madame Demetka or maybe it was Sally—whoever, she has my keys. She was going to give them back to me at the Landmark."

"Okay." At the Boulevard, Abby turned the steering wheel to the right, toward the hotel. "Now, what happened? Are you all right?" She accelerated through a yellow signal. "Why does Sally have your keys?"

● ○ ●

Landmark Hotel

The drive wasn't long enough to cover all three questions, as it turned out. Riding the elevator up from the Landmark's underground parking, they were still covering the first two.

"Can you access it now?" Abby asked. The Sight.

"No."

The elevator opened to the lobby. A quick survey failed to yield any sign of Madame Demetka (or Sally), so Thia headed for reception.

She had tried to use her Sight in the car. Instead of seeing the Landmark's many wards, she had seen the building as she always had, before. She had been holding onto the focusing wand as if it could protect her, fix whatever had gone wrong, calm her down. At least her pendant wasn't hot and warning of danger anymore.

"Nothing at all?" Abby asked.

"That's kind of how it is. All or nothing."

Abby didn't have the Sight—at least not in the same way Thia did.

At the front desk, they waited for the clerk to finish with a telephone reservation. It was the same young man from the morning. A uniform tag that she hadn't been able to read then gave his name as Chuck.

"Could it be because of—of what happened with Kendra?" Abby asked quietly, her back to the desk. "Trauma can make even the most dependable magics act weird, and yours aren't anywhere near that. Yet," she added, too late for comfort. "It could've made you hallucinate or whatever. An overload—not real—before it short-circuited and went out."

"My Sight *is* dependable, though," Thia argued. "Up until this. I don't know." Dammit, she had thought she could count on that one thing. Just *one* thing. "If it was a malfunction, and that's why I can't get it to work now, what was that vision right before? If it wasn't real, why did my pendant react as if it was? Or maybe that was a malfunction too. It's not like I got the new and improved version."

"Could your pendant have been reacting off of you? To your reaction?" Abby asked, but Thia would have to consider that later. Chuck had hung up the phone.

"Ms. McDaniel," he said. "Ms. Collins. If you're looking for Mr. Murphy, he isn't—"

"No." Abby cut him off so sharply that he flinched.

The elevator chimed, announcing its arrival. Quentin exited first, taking large strides despite—or due to—the cane held in his left hand. Edith hurried alongside, talking rapidly as they took a direct line to the fireplace. Abby moved to join them.

"I'll catch up," Thia told her, and then asked Chuck, "Did someone leave a set of keys for me?"

Cormac stepped out of the elevator. The shock of it was like accidentally touching an electrified fence. It held Thia in place, incapable of speech. Incapable of anything. He caught sight of her.

His stunning, blue-gray eyes widened and he halted as if he had struck a wall—or touched that same electrified fence.

That was the sum total of his visible reaction: stillness. He was a master at giving nothing away. Cool, calm, collected.

His short, mahogany-brown hair was stylishly disarranged. His layered clothes were a study in muted tones and varied textures. He was recognizable as himself, at least. When he had arrived in Granite Springs in December, he hadn't been. He had been in disguise, pretending even with her.

She had not seen him since before Christmas. Hadn't heard from him. She had worried, whether consciously or subconsciously, for much of that time. And now here he was, fifteen feet away, clearly no worse for wear, and leaving it for her to make the first move.

Typical.

"Hello," she said, and was proud of her control.

"Thia." His hands were in his pockets. Quietly, he cleared his throat. "We came as soon as we could."

He spoke in a mellow baritone, and with an accent that her limited American ear could identify only as "British"—similar to what she had heard in the Miss Marple mysteries of her childhood or on BBC News. Smooth yet distinct consonants. Round vowels.

"Yes," she said belatedly. "Thank you."

She was upset, she realized. Last night, he could have damn well acknowledged her text—or texted anytime since then to let her know he was all right.

She was also flooded with relief to see him, as if they were the best of friends or more, reunited after a long separation.

Illusion was a powerful thing.

And Cormac was a master of it.

December's subterfuge had not been the first. The first had been in October, when he had threatened her outside Lettie's house. He had appeared to be an innocuous, older man. The next time, when they "met" on the plane to London, he had looked like himself and been delightfully charming in another attempt to take the Stone of Shadows. At Lettie's townhouse, another disguise—followed by a frightening reveal. She could go on, listing all the disguises, the ulterior motives, the lies.

● ○ ●

She had caught him off guard. He hadn't expected to encounter her so soon and his wits had scattered. It was one thing, Cormac learned in that moment, to have been told that she was unharmed. It was quite another to share space with her, to see her, feel her standing there before him. The relief had crashed like a wave, and while he had withstood the impact, he had yet to regain his balance. The sand kept being pulled away beneath his feet.

He found her attractive. Beauty, wit, charm—how could he not? But this was more than simple want. He had missed her. Much as he had tried not to, he had *missed* her.

The pain of loss was writ plain in the shadows beneath her hazel eyes and the tightness of her bow-shaped mouth. Her hair had been put up in some disordered way at the back of her head. The tips of multiple tendrils stuck out like hedgehog spines.

Another had avoided restraint altogether and hung temptingly alongside her neck.

He knew how silken that hair was. And the equally enticing feel of the skin it touched. His hands tensed. Hell, his whole *being* tensed as the silence stretched. His fault. If she were his target in a con, he would have no trouble coming up with what to say. Instead, he was at a loss.

She was going to think he was here for her.

It was, after all, what everyone thought. He was here with the Brigantium; the Brigantium was here for Thia—ergo, so was he. It was an ideal cover except for this one unforeseen complication: He hadn't expected it to bother him.

He could at least mention that he had additional business. Keep it general. He needn't tell her of the red notebook and the pages concerning Founders Hall. But he could say *something.* Condolences first, though.

"Thia," he began, "I'm so— "

"Hail, hail, the gang's all here," quipped her *not*-dead friend and business associate, rushing over from where she and the Brigantium agents had been conversing. She linked her arm possessively with Thia's. The glare she fixed on Cormac held a warning. Or perhaps it was a threat.

"Abby," said Thia, seeming surprised.

"We're going out to examine the alley," Abby said, and with arms still linked, prepared to set off.

Thia balked. "Isn't it cordoned off? By the police? We can't be out there. Can we?"

"I never pay that sort of thing much mind," Cormac said. In his experience, legalities mattered only in terms of potential consequences attached to disregarding them.

Abby tugged Thia's arm. "The police got everything they're able to. The Brigantium has different equipment. Different skills. Please," she added as Thia continued to look uncomfortable. "They'll do it with or without us."

"It's a crime scene."

How different Thia was to Cormac--and how ill-suited to

the world in which she now found herself. It was no place for rule-followers. "The sooner we move on this," he said, "the better."

Abby's look was arch. "Oh, it's 'we,' now is it? After weeks of silence, you come back as if—"

"Okay, okay." Thia drew her friend away. "If we're going to do this, let's get to it."

● ○ ●

Trailing the Brigantium agents past the reception desk, Abby kept her arm linked with Thia's. Normally, physical contact was not Abby's thing; it risked triggering her so-called "gift" with flashes of the other person's emotions, thoughts, memories—it was random, what came. And rare, thankfully. But it could be so disturbing when it *did* happen, she preferred not to take chances. This, though, was for Thia's sake. Cormac, behind them, was trouble, and Thia was drawn to him like iron filings to a magnet—no, a different cliché was more apt, since there was no risk to the filings. Thia was like a moth to a flame.

With Cormac, hurt was inevitable. And, knowing Thia, so was her forgiveness. She had a generous heart, and more problematically, she was attracted. Abby knew the symptoms well; she suffered them too, didn't she, over a different enigmatic, devious, no-good man? She was also worried about whatever had happened outside Kendra's apartment. Whether real or not, it had frightened Thia, and so did the current loss of her new powers of Sight. Fear caused all sorts of vulnerabilities— which someone could exploit.

How easily Cormac could ingratiate himself with offers to help, to comfort.

Ahead, Quentin was leading them past the offices and into the employee-only part of the hallway. Lighting was harsher, more industrial. Behind one of several closed doors, laundry machines hummed and bumped.

Contrary to romantic fantasy, enigmatic men did not make good partners. Thia deserved someone who appreciated her. Who did not confuse her, make her worry, and leave her to wonder where she stood in his life.

Until Thia realized that, it would be up to Abby to protect her. She would make sure that Cormac didn't break her heart.

Or get her killed. Like Murphy, he led a dangerous life. Abby had lost one friend; she would not lose another.

"He's got a lot of nerve," she said to Thia in an undertone.

"Cormac? How do you mean?"

With the man in question walking only a few feet behind, Abby didn't answer. She'd wait till later, in private.

Not far from the hallway's end, Edith stopped, held up a hand. "Wait there, please," she said when the others would have kept on. "I'd like to scan. If that's all right." That was directed at Quentin, and rather snide. He lifted his hands—cane included—in a mockery of surrender and stepped back.

"Thank you," Edith said to everyone else. From her satchel she took something that resembled an old graphing calculator with a clear quartz point mounted on its top edge. Gripping the whole unit in one hand, she began moving it to and fro, as with a metal detector—or, Abby supposed, a Geiger counter. Scanning, obviously, but for what?

"Interesting," Cormac said from close behind her and Thia.

"Clear quartz." She could direct Thia's attention away from Cormac, and her own away from the hallway's end where the door to the alley waited, criss-crossed with police tape. "Do you remember its qualities?"

"You're turning this into a teaching moment?"

"Humor me. Please." Across Kendra's door, the yellow tape had seemed a mild request to keep out. The tape ahead was a bellowed demand, and despite how she'd presented the idea, she was having serious misgivings.

"Clear quartz," Thia said, watching Edith, "amplifies energy, draws away negativity, balances emotions . . . enhances psychic abilities. There's more, but that's all I've got right now."

"Very good," Cormac told her. "Only that isn't quartz, it's apophyllite."

Smug son of a—Abby took a deep breath.

"An easy mistake," he added, not doing himself any favors with her temper. Then he leaned closer to Thia. "The lighter varieties offer many of the same qualities as quartz but work at a higher frequency. They have a higher water content as well, which makes them an excellent conductor." He raised his voice. "Getting anything?"

Edith's reply was immediate. "There have been too many people through here to pick up on Kendra, specifically." She ran the scanner across a door labeled as linen storage. "But the bleed from the wards around this is fascinating. Layers upon layers—It's incredible. If I had an hour, I'd scarcely get past the surface."

Abby doubted Murphy would allow so much as a minute.

"I'm getting *something,* though." Bending at the waist, Edith held the scanner over one spot near the handle only to flick it away, then return. "Definitely. I'll know more after I analyze all the readings and compare them with my database."

"You *have* been busy," Quentin said, not at all nicely. "I do wonder, though, that you haven't been down here before."

She did not acknowledge this—if she had even heard it. Her entire focus was centered on a closed, unmarked door to the left of the linen storage. She scanned along the frame. Unlike the other doors, this one had been painted to match the wall. "This is extraordinary."

"Oh, here we go," Cormac said with a chuckle.

"What?" Thia asked, turning. "What do you see? My Sight isn't working."

"She's triggered an intrusion alert. What do you mean your Sight isn't working?" With a hand on Thia's shoulder, he spun her around to face him, breaking Abby's hold.

"Let her go." Abby pressed in. "Now."

"Abby," Thia said, "he isn't—"

There were footsteps beyond them, then Murphy's cold, carrying voice: "And just what do you think you're doing?"

He stood at the start of the hallway. Two security guards flanked him. They all held guns as if to shoot.

While Abby was too shocked to speak, Thia said, "Nothing. We aren't doing anything," and Cormac released his hold to put his hands up. Unlike Quentin, earlier, he meant it.

But Murphy wasn't talking to them. He was glaring past, at Edith.

His expression shifted from hostile to disgusted. He tucked his gun into what must have been a shoulder holster beneath his suit jacket and, at his nod, the other men put theirs away too.

It didn't make Abby feel any better. *Guns.* All this time, had hotel security been armed? Had he?

"We're tracing Ms. Ross's route," Quentin told him. "Care to join?"

"You should have bloody well asked first." Murphy stalked toward them. "You set off an alarm." He brushed past Abby as if she wasn't there and, with a glance at the knob of the unmarked door, positioned himself between it and Edith. He held out his hand for her scanner. "If you don't mind."

"I do, as it happens." She hugged it to her chest. "It's calibrated to me. If anyone else touches it, I'll have to do a full reset before it'll be of use again. That would take at least an hour."

"No." Abby stepped forward, forcing him to notice her. She was almost unbearably upset.

"No?"

"No." She made herself hold his gaze. "We need it. We're going outside." Her misgivings were all but forgotten in the face of Murphy's cold rage. He wanted the scanner, therefore she opposed it. He and his men had come with guns drawn. Someone could have gotten shot. "We're going to search for clues," she said, and hated how amateurish she sounded.

But that's exactly what she was. An amateur. For goddess's sake, Murphy carried a gun.

"Do you not think my people and I have gone over everything?" he asked, likely reading horror on her face. Yesterday when in Eclectica, last night when they had dined, when they had walked along Blooms Alley—had there been a gun?

What about before? All those times before.

He had been in her *home.*

"You haven't been over the alley with *this,*" Edith said. "It registers and analyzes energy. Active spells, remnants—"

"We have something like."

"Made by Brunhoff?"

Murphy's scowl could be taken as an affirmative.

"Right. Mine's more sensitive by a factor of ten. And more accurate."

Abby's patience was gone. "Declan, you're wasting time and being ridiculous. What can it hurt?"

He fixed her with a stare so hard that she recoiled, feeling the force of it like a physical shove. "You have no idea what you're—" He broke off as something started beeping.

The scanner. Edith moved it in a slow arc, extending her arm outward. "It seems to be coming from"—she looked up at Murphy—"you."

His backward step was fascinating for its haste. He pointed to the alley door. "Go on, then."

The machine continued to beep. "These readings are—"

"Go." He took another step back. For Murphy that counted as a full retreat. Shocking. His back was against the unmarked door. A hint of power shone in his eyes, turning them from brown to bronze. "Outside. Before you set off anything else."

Edith's face blanched. "Of course. Sorry," she said, lowering the scanner and turning away, to the exit door. With her other hand she gestured at the tape strips. "If someone could help me with this."

"Fuckssake." Murphy reached over and ripped them down.

At Kendra's office door that morning, he had used magic. Why had he not done so here? It had to be the scanner.

Edith gestured. "And the lock?"

Muttering under his breath, Murphy reached into his pants pocket and pulled out a set of keys. As he unlocked the door as most people would—key to deadbolt, hand on bar, push— it occurred to Abby that she had never seen him do that. A wave of his hand, a flick of his wrist, that was how Murphy opened doors.

Edith went out, followed by Murphy, then Quentin. Abby's feet felt as if they had been cemented.

"You don't have to go," Thia said.

Cormac walked past, leaving them behind.

The door drifted closed on Abby's view of Murphy pointing to the left and then at the ground. Recounting the events.

"No," she managed. "I need to do this."

"Okay."

The walk felt endless and too brief. She pushed the exit bar, shouldered the door open. Her body felt heavy. Robotic. She stepped outside.

Edith was crouched in the middle of the alley. She held the scanner only a few inches above the asphalt. The three men stood around her, intent.

A gust of wind rattled the lids of the hotel's dumpsters and bins as Thia stepped out. She went no further than Abby. The door closed with thump and a loud click of its latch.

Abby could only nod. She didn't trust her voice.

● ○ ●

Thia suppressed a shiver. The outside air seemed much colder than before. In the alley's center, Cormac and Murphy stood by Edith while she knelt at one of a multitude of splotches on the aged, battered asphalt. Holding the strange scanner over it, she frowned and then adjusted settings.

Quentin left them to walk further up the slope.

"My men took samples last night," Murphy said of whatever was on the ground.

"I would appreciate having access to those," Edith told him. "But there is a usable amount, still. It froze overnight. That helped with preservation."

Blood, Thia realized. They were looking at Kendra's blood. Abby must have realized that too; she made a low sound. She shouldn't be putting herself through this.

Edith, apparently, had experience with forensics. The others likely had applicable skills as well. But Abby and Thia? They didn't need to be here. They could wait inside. She suggested as much in a whisper.

"No," Abby said. "But you go if you need to. I'll be okay. I shouldn't have asked you to do this."

"Nonsense. Of course you should." That was what friends did, right? Supported one another despite misgivings? If Abby truly needed to be here, Thia would be here too.

"Inconclusive," Edith announced. Shifting her weight, she adjusted the lay of the satchel slung across her chest so she could reach into the main compartment. She took out a slim white cord.

A set of earbuds, Thia assumed—wrongly. Instead of splitting into two near the end, the single cord became at least six. At the tips, small crystals of various shapes and colors had been attached with silver wire.

Edith plugged the main line into the scanner and then, with

the excess cord held in her right hand, dangled the crystals a few inches from the asphalt.

Tentatively, Thia reached for her Sight—and found it. A bit weak, but present. "Oh, thank God."

Heads turned her way, including Quentin's. He stood a good twenty feet away, leaning against the trunk of a tree by a short row of empty parking spaces.

"Sorry," she said, flustered. "I just—No, it can wait. I didn't mean to interrupt." She let the Sight go. Knowing that she could access it again was enough for now, and she remained concerned that the episode with Amundsen was what Abby had suggested: A glitch brought on by trauma and stress. If so, she would only risk experiencing another episode here—and to what purpose? The real experts had no need of her inept and likely malfunctioning efforts.

Attention had returned to Edith's crystals. Everyone's, that was, but Cormac's—he was walking in Thia's direction, his hands behind his back, unhurried and deceptively casual.

Beside her, Abby leaned close. "You got your Sight back?"

Cormac's brow quirked. He had heard.

"Yes," she said, and Cormac's mouth tightened.

"What did it show you?" Abby asked.

"The hotel wards," Thia said. "I didn't look further. Before I really try to use it, I want to talk to everyone. Tell them what I saw, what happened. If that was real, what does that mean for Amundsen? What *was* that? Could it mean that he's involved?"

"If what you experienced was real. He's lived here for years and what you described is—"

"Freaky? Terrifying? Insane?"

"—bizarre. Someone else would have noticed."

Granite Springs had no shortage of residents with extraordinary abilities, that was true. Why would Thia be special? She wouldn't.

"Still," she said, "I need to talk about it. Even if it's just so everyone knows my Sight went crazy."

"I'm sorry to say it," Abby said grimly, "but I'm hoping that's what happened."

"If Amundsen *is* whatever that thing was, what would that mean? Not only for Kendra but the city in general? He's the city manager. How many decisions has he been involved in and—" She broke off as Cormac closed the final few feet of distance.

Aligning himself beside her, he turned to observe the others as she was. Ostensibly.

"So," he said. "What's this about your Sight and who—or what—is 'Amundsen'?"

"Maybe you could tell me," she said to Abby's undisguised dismay. "We went to Kendra's apartment. We wanted to get into her computer to check her messages, email, that sort of thing. But the police were there and so was the city manager. Neil Amundsen. He and Kendra were seeing—or they wanted to start seeing—one another." She knew she was rambling.

It had been weeks since she had seen Cormac, and here he was, standing so close, and he smelled so good. Like quality, woodsy soap or fine cologne.

"It doesn't matter. He was there and while we were talking I got a weird feeling. So I used my Sight and have no idea what went wrong. I saw a—I don't know what I saw. It didn't make sense, and then it was like something pushed my eyes. Like those tests at the eye doctor's—oh, you might not know. You probably have no need for an eye doctor."

"No."

Being able to heal all sorts of grievous wounds in a matter of minutes, he would have perfect vision and no need for a glaucoma check.

"Right." She felt a bit of envy. "So, some have a machine that puffs air at your eyes. That's what I felt right after I saw that—that *thing*."

"What thing was that? Specifically."

"A nightmare." She worked to separate the visual memory from the visceral. "It was two simultaneous images, one on top of the other. Neil Amundsen and an overlay. It was so fast I might've imagined it. Although why I'd make up something so awful, I have no idea. And the pendant got super hot. I didn't imagine that."

"Describe it."

"A monster. It looked like a *monster.*" She struggled for calm. "But I only saw it for a second—less than—and the image in my mind isn't clear anymore. I thought it would be seared in there forever, but I can barely—"

"Humanoid or beastly?"

"Humanoid."

"Smaller or larger than the man, or the same size?"

"Larger." She closed her eyes. Covered them with her hands as she strained to recall. It really was odd how vague it had become. But she remembered what she had said immediately after to Abby. That helped to bring it back, and a few more details besides. "Huge head. Horrible eyes—they bulged. The pupils were red. Or glowed red, maybe. Sickly looking skin. Yellow-brown with a greenish tinge. Crazy hair."

"Crazy how?" That was from Abby. "Like Leo from the job interview?"

"No." Thia opened her eyes. "Like Ronald McDonald on an extremely bad day."

"That's a fast food mascot," Abby explained for Cormac's benefit. "A clown."

"I know who Ronald McDonald is," he said.

Edith sprang excitedly to her feet. "Definite indications of a spell," she announced. "Most likely a type of influence hex but not one that I'm familiar with. I could do a lot more with those samples your men took," she told Murphy.

He was stone-faced for a strained moment. When he spoke, the words were slow. Reluctant. "And if you had the delivery agent? The transmission material. Could you work on that?"

"You know what it was?"

"We suspect. She had marks on her fingers. Like blue ink."

"You have a sample?" Edith began putting away her equipment. "We could rush it to our lab."

"I do not. But I can get you access."

"No," Quentin objected from his position against the tree. "You refer to the morgue, presumably. To Ms. Ross's body."

Beside Thia, Abby sucked in an audible breath.

Murphy glanced over, then back to answer Quentin. "I am. But not at the morgue. She'll be released to me as soon as can be arranged. For the wake."

"There's no need to wait for the release," Edith said, her smartphone in hand. "Assistant Director Meriwether can set things up with the coroner. You might have mentioned this sooner—but since elements remain detectable in the blood here, we can expect the source hasn't degraded much." She began poking the phone's screen.

"No," Quentin insisted. "Stop. I won't permit it."

She was clearly stunned. "You're pulling rank? That's not—I can go over your head. The assistant director *will* allow it."

"Such a thing is not for you."

"My specialty is the analysis and detection of magics. I am more than qualified."

"Qualified." His laugh was harsh. "How many corpses have you dealt with—outside the classroom? How many of those were people you knew?" He came slowly forward, the metal tip of his cane making a deliberate click . . . click . . . click. "How many died a violent, malevolent death? No, my dear. You may have the qualifications, but that does not make you ready. It makes you dangerously naïve."

Edith closed the distance with several quick steps. "How

dare you—"

"Okay, okay, hold it." Thia said, hurrying toward them. Yes, Quentin was being an ass and Edith deserved to stand up for herself, but the two of them could battle it out on their own time. And hopefully not in front of Abby, who looked ready to break down. "You don't need us here for this. So, what can we be doing? What's the plan?"

And wouldn't it be better left up to the police, she could have added. But she knew what the overwhelming response would be. She hadn't jumped in to stop one argument only to start another.

"We didn't get into Kendra's apartment," Abby said roughly. "The police were there. Which means we still have no idea who she might have met with, or what she might have gone to do, or where."

Murphy sighed. "How she picked up the marks."

"She called me." Edith sounded defensive. "I missed it, but she left a message. She wanted to know if the Brigantium had learned more about the trust that owns the Valhalla property."

"The biker bar?" Thia asked. It wasn't just any biker bar, of course.

"As part of our investigation into Cassandra's revenge plot, we've been trying to learn how the Rekkrs became involved."

"Why would Kendra ask about that now?" Thia turned to Murphy. "Was she also looking into it?"

"I did task her with looking up a fair number of land records. This has been an opportune time to expand my holdings."

"You want to buy a biker bar?" Abby asked, incredulous.

"Why not? It's in an excellent location on a lovely piece of land."

"So," Thia said, "she was asking about the ownership as part of researching a potential deal?"

"Sure, but it isn't high priority. I have others in mind that—"

"She found the same name on an additional record," Edith

broke in. "The Carl Verner Trust. That's why she'd wanted to know if we had got anywhere on it. Because she had come across the name again."

"Where?" Abby asked.

"No idea."

Abby focused on Murphy. "What other properties are you considering?"

"Numerous." He had taken out his phone. He put it to his ear. "Smitty, have you anything to report on the neighboring cameras?" Then, clearly displeased, "No, no, stay at it. What about our own? From earlier in the—oh, have you now? Keep it cued up. We'll be right in." Ending the call, he headed for the hotel door.

"What?" Abby glared at his back.

"The front cameras show Ross diving into some shrubbery yesterday afternoon." He pulled open the door. "Shrubbery near a property that *is* high priority. Founders Hall."

CHAPTER 13

Quentin could not wait to sit down; so naturally Edith made herself an obstacle on his way to the hotel door. At the moment, he was incapable of dodging her. Besides, he suspected she would only move to block him. Hence the rest of their odd coterie went inside, too intent on the intended destination to notice two members remained behind. Possibly they didn't care.

Brigid, his hip was screaming—as he himself would be, and fairly soon, if he didn't get some relief.

He couldn't do that with Agent Edith Wilkinson around.

On the best of days, he couldn't trust her not to report his every action. Considering her current mood, she would likely relish it.

He had been trying to protect her. To work with the dead carried immense risk. She might have an intellectual understanding of that, but she didn't *know.*

"Mightn't we take this inside?" he asked, risking a shift of weight so he could lift his cane. He pointed it past Edith, the shaft a few inches from her waist, as if he might brush her aside. Not precisely a threat.

She widened her stance and put her hands on her hips. Her eyes were two narrowed, angry slits. "How dare you," she said, picking up where she'd left off.

On a sigh, he lowered his cane, set it to take weight. "Surely this can—"

"No." She took a step forward, coming so close he could smell the floral scent of her . . . perfume? Shampoo? She thrust a finger at his chest, all but making contact. "You might be my superior—in rank—but you were completely out of line. Not to mention wrong." She did make contact then, a sharp jab to his sternum, but he'd be damned if he would step back.

He would likely fall down if he tried. Beneath his clothes, he had broken out in a sweat.

"I respect your training, your skills, your knowledge," Edith went furiously on. "It shouldn't be too much to ask that you do the same for mine. Especially in front of others."

"Is that what this is about?" His own temper ignited. "Your feelings were hurt?"

Behind the lenses of her horn-rimmed glasses, her brown eyes flashed amber.

"Careful." Quentin allowed a bit of his own power to show. He believed hers had been unintentional. She wouldn't be so foolish as to challenge him. In that way, at any rate. She knew he had far more power than she, so that flash of amber was more liable to have been a loss of control—emotion rather than outright threat.

Her eyes remained brown. Brown topaz ringed by a darker smoky quartz, to be exact.

Lustrous, intelligent and rather lovely, actually. He tended to overlook that, what with the lenses of her glasses and the fact that he didn't have time for such things.

He banked his power. He had not called much, so his eyes would have only glowed a faint blue. Edith would be seeing the usual gray of his irises now. "If you're quite finished," he said, and shifted his weight in preparation to pass.

She mirrored the move, still not breaking eye contact. "How bad is it? The pain, I mean."

Shock rooted him to the spot. "Nothing I can't handle." He willed her to believe him as cold dread ran down his spine.

Had it been so obvious? He was already on thin ice with Beatrice for suspected overuse of pain dampening spells. She likely also suspected that he had been finding it necessary of late to augment those with pharmaceuticals. Confirmation as provided by Edith with her sharp eyes and present antagonism would put paid to his time as a field agent, either by demotion or dismissal, and then what would he have?

"All right," she said, apparently believing him.

She turned the wrong direction—walking up the alley, away from the hotel. The sunlight played on her short, light blonde hair. "I want to scan by the tree. Where the attacker stood." She glanced over her shoulder. "Where you stood, earlier. But I don't want to be out here alone."

His grip tightened on the cane's chased silver knob. If he didn't move, he could manage a few minutes more. "I already went over that area."

"Yes, I didn't think you were lounging." She held her little device at the ready but appeared to be waiting for him to join her.

It didn't take her long to understand that he would not. She dropped to a crouch and began moving her device over the tree's exposed roots. "What did you find here? I understand that as my superior"—sarcasm did not suit her—"you aren't required to share, but that seems an ineffectual way to run an investigation."

"Won't that risk skewing your results?"

She made a noncommittal sound. Her attention was almost fully on her invention. Its crystals dangled, swaying on their cords while the unit itself emitted a series of soft tones. After a moment, she straightened. Quentin envied the quick, lithe movement.

"He waited a long time," she said, returning. Her expression reminded him of a cat who'd got the cream. "Half an hour."

Not bad. He briefly inclined his head. "And a bit."

Her lips curved in a smile. Lovely lips. Had he noticed that before? She came to a stop before him.

"His strength was augmented," she said, pleased with her toy. "By what reads to be a charm based in *seidr* traditions."

Good lord. *Not* a toy. Not hardly. She had every right to be pleased.

Yet her smile quickly faded, and something harsh took its place. "I got that information without risk to myself. Can you say the same?" She pointed to his right hand. The hand he had placed, ungloved, on the tree trunk and by which he had made himself vulnerable.

He'd thought no one had noticed.

"I'm good at what I do," she said, and walked away.

● ○ ●

Landmark Hotel (Inside)

Leading a veritable parade into the security hub was a bad idea, Declan knew, but the sooner they watched the video, the sooner action could be taken. At the unmarked door between the linen and janitorial closets, he pressed the button on the frame's side. Cream on cream, it was virtually impossible to see unless one knew to look.

Inside the room, a bell would sound but the guards would already be aware of his presence. When accompanied, that he rang only once signaled he was not under duress. The pose of his left hand gave a second assurance. In this case, since he wore a suit jacket beneath an open winter coat, he held his hand so his thumb touched the jacket's topmost button.

The door opened, sliding leftward into the wall. The knob

was an illusion.

"Which screen?" Declan, entering, asked the three guards. The room was tight, designed with technology in mind, not people. Twelve monitors stacked three rows high took up the length of the facing wall. The work surface below the screens and its accompanying three chairs accounted for practically the whole of the room's depth.

"Six," answered Smitty, the older man seated on the far left. He moved to rise.

"You're fine." Declan kept his position near the doorway.

Smitty's eyes bugged as the rest of the group—minus the two Brigantium agents—fit themselves into what little space remained.

Because Declan's day had apparently not yet been wretched enough, Abigail pushed in next to him. He felt her like the warmth of a fire after a hard slog through winter mud. It had been that way from the first, with her. For someone who did not feel much anymore—the past twenty-four hours aside—it was intriguing and infuriating and entirely inconvenient.

Currently, antipathy came off her in waves. She blamed him for Kendra's death.

Since Declan also blamed himself, he didn't take it well. He lifted his hand—because it forced her to move, slight though it was. She bumped up against the wall. With the snap of his fingers, he triggered the doors to close.

When they had, he gave Smitty a nod. "Play it."

Monitor Six's screen came to life, showing a bird's eye view across Main and down several blocks of First. Detail was lost at that distance, but where it mattered, where Kendra Ross came into view, the picture was crisp.

She darted out of Founders Way, crossed the car park, then dove into a cluster of overgrown shrubs. She remained there, hidden from camera view.

Declan studied the entire frame for cause. An infrequent

vehicle drove by, none near enough to be of interest (although he'd have people track those down anyway). On the recording, Kendra remained in the shrubbery. "This was at what time?" he asked. His estimate, by the sunlight's angle, put it around one in the afternoon.

Smitty confirmed that with the exact time stamp. "We have her entering the Way roughly ten minutes prior," he added, "but there's nothing notable. We figured you would want this part first."

Declan grunted, the whole of his attention again fixed on the screen as Kendra extricated herself from the shrubs and began to walk in the Landmark's direction. She was agitated but doing a passable job of pretending. Anyone who didn't know her well would see nothing amiss.

Aside from the curious blue on her fingers.

Abigail pressed against his arm to get a closer look at the monitor. "Did she have those when she ran out? Before she went into the bushes?"

"She did." He had no room to move away. Warmth flashed across his skin, danced along his ribs.

On-screen, Kendra prepared to cross Main. Although traffic was one-way, she checked both directions before she walked out. Halfway, she answered her phone. Stopped.

"What is she doing?" Abigail asked. "Why doesn't she keep going?"

To be sure, there were no cars anywhere near, but as Kendra had been fearful of her safety only moments before, it seemed highly suspect that she would then leave herself exposed in the street. Safety was less than ten meters ahead.

"How close are we to having her records?" he asked Smitty as they all watched Kendra put away her phone and continue toward the Landmark.

Kendra went under the portico, again out of camera range. The recording continued to play, showing sparse street traffic and a handful of pedestrians. Nothing at all suspicious.

"The cops are giving us the cold shoulder," Smitty replied. He indicated the younger man seated on his right. "But Cleve here has a call scheduled with someone at the cell provider."

"In an hour," said Cleve.

"Unlimited funds," Declan told him in case that hadn't been made clear. "Should it come to that."

"Bribery?" Abigail pulled her attention from the screen to fix him with a stunner of a glare.

"Whatever it takes." He shifted his stance, forcing her to acknowledge their proximity. "Or are your ethical standards more important than your friend?"

He regretted the taunt instantly. Hurt filled her violet eyes and her lips parted to suck in a short, pained breath. He had wanted to wound, as she had wounded him, but as usual he had gone too far. Struck too deep.

It was not in his nature, however, to apologize.

Nearby—everyone was nearby in the tiny, damned room— Cormac cleared his throat. "I should think the Brigantium could assist with call logs. Government contacts and all that."

Correct. Prior to its recent internal troubles, the Society of Brigantium had been assisting a number of British agencies, one or two of which could be of use. Declan made a mental note to push Quentin in that direction.

"What about Ross's activities after she returned?" he asked his men. "Anything to see there?"

The third guard, Grafton, swiveled his chair so he could say over his shoulder, "Nothing unusual. She goes straight to her office, stays there until she goes up to the restaurant."

Declan had already watched all that. "What of—"

"The others are done outside," Smitty interrupted, directing attention to Monitor Four. Quentin and Edith were entering the corridor from the alley.

"There's no room," Cormac objected when Declan reached

to press a button on the wall. The door slid open.

Cleve stood. "We'll wait outside." He rolled his chair with him as he went. Grafton followed.

That left Smitty. Declan asked him, "What's the status on footage from the other businesses?"

"We sent people out to check with anyone who might have an angle on the parking lot and alley. It's a shame Founders Hall doesn't have any cameras up. They'd have the best view. As for additional footage of our block, the cops beat us to it. Took storage cards from everyone there except the movie theater and the Festival. Those use cloud-based services." He paused to allow for the Brigantium agents' arrival.

When they were in, Declan shut the door.

Smitty resumed. "We backtracked the killer, picked him up by the Festival. Came in from the Plaza's south end. Looked to have had the Landmark in mind. Didn't linger elsewhere, moved at speed. We're working on locating him before that."

"Where did he go after?" Thia asked.

"Ran down Main Street," Declan said, "took a right on Mill. Went out of view from there." He'd been over, and over, and over every frame of that, looking for anything and anyone. A dropped scrap of paper. A face in a car window.

"How much of downtown do your cameras cover?" Abigail asked. "This seems more like spying than security."

One and the same, in his experience. "It's proving its use, though, isn't it?"

As expected, his patronizing tone made her livid, which was a sight better than the hurt he'd done her minutes before.

● ○ ●

Oh, Abby could kill him—with her bare hands, she was that angry. Except that Murphy had power, skill, and as she knew now, a gun. She'd have a better chance with a spell. Poison. Black magic. But of course she would never do anything like that, not really. Not even to Declan goddess-damned Murphy, no matter how furious he made her.

Tempting, though.

That he was right made it worse. The Landmark's cameras recorded the activities of everything downtown, intruding on people's privacy—yet instead of proving him to be paranoid or devious or any number of the negative qualities she would bet had motivated the installation, it had proven to be vital. She refused to credit him for it. His "business interests," his mysterious, dangerous life were why they were all here, in this room, and Kendra was not.

Kendra never would've gotten involved in anything illegal—not knowingly. Some element in Murphy's life had spread like powdery mildew in a summer garden. The physical act had been carried out by the young man in the alley, but Murphy's life must have drawn him there.

While Abby fumed, Quentin and Edith were brought up to speed; when they asked to view the recording of Kendra in the parking lot, everyone was made to rewatch.

The pain of viewing did not lessen with repetition. To see her friend reacting as if she were in danger; to know that only a few hours later there would be no escape; to be in this close room that wasn't meant to have so many people at once, using up the air—

"All right?" Declan asked quietly as the recording continued to play. His hand made for a light, steadying pressure on her back.

"Fine." She didn't want his concern. His care. "It's stuffy in here, is all."

His hand left her back—and the air changed, a fan coming on. Coolness rushed in.

He had done that.

She mumbled her thanks, but his interest remained on the screen. Kendra had come out of the bushes and was walking along First.

"What building is that?" Quentin asked.

"Founders Hall," said Murphy.

"That's one of the properties you intend to acquire?"

"It is. Highest priority."

Abby frowned. "Owned by the same trust that owns The Valhalla? That's what we think she found out, right?"

Instead of answering, Murphy turned to the nearest of his security guards. "Smitty, access the record, would you?"

The man was already typing. On a screen directly before him, he pulled up the website for county records, entered the address. The result popped up.

"Carl Verner Family Trust," Abby read aloud. "That's it, isn't it? That's the one."

Beside her, Murphy had tensed. "It is."

On Abby's other side, Quentin shifted, rebalancing himself, to tell Murphy, "I'll get London to prioritize their work on that. If your people need assistance here, the other agents are at your disposal." He turned to Edith. "Fancy a stroll about town? With your equipment." She looked surprised but game, and they moved to leave.

When Murphy reached to push the button on the wall, his arm brushed Abby's upper back. The door opened. "Try not to trigger any wards while you're at it," he told them as they walked out.

Edith held up her smartphone. "I have an app for that."

A different phone buzzed—Murphy's, in his coat, and Abby tried to give him room to access it. Other than a one-word greeting, he didn't speak.

She couldn't glean anything from his face while the caller—whom she could not hear, despite being so close—did all the talking. Then, with Murphy's curt, "Right," the call ended.

"Get the Brigantium back," he ordered the security guard

waiting outside.

"What?" Abby asked. "What's happened?"

"The police located the traveler in Elkhorn Park," he told her. Told them all. "Dead."

CHAPTER 14

Try as she might, Thia could not get comfortable with what they were on their way to do. Poking around the alley after the police had already examined it had felt risky enough, but to go to an active scene? Where someone had been found dead? But she didn't want to abandon Abby, so here she was, accompanying her, Murphy, and Cormac to Elkhorn Park in order to . . . Well, as usual, she wasn't entirely sure. To ask questions, presumably. And to study the scene—if they were allowed near it. Things they had already been doing because, as uncomfortable as that made her, to do nothing felt worse.

She did another compulsive check for her most important items: protective pendant, secure on its chain; crystal-tipped wand, in a coat pocket. Wallet, phone, house—*keys!* Madame Demetka still had Thia's keys. And Eclectica's wards still had not been reset.

Not only was Thia in danger of losing control of the Cailleach's power, she was losing control of her life.

At least the pendant hadn't reacted since that scare outside Kendra's apartment. It might not alert to all threats, but since it had alerted to that one, it would do so next time, wouldn't it? If there was a next time for that particular threat.

She still didn't know what that might have been. Since the alley, there hadn't been a moment that wasn't taken up with some revelation or discussion that felt equally important if not more. And she wasn't about to sidetrack the group with something that could have been a stress-induced glitch.

The pendant did seem to indicate that there was more to it than that, but last October the Brigantium had come to learn of a major flaw. They didn't alert to threats when the person doing the threatening also wore one. She could have experienced another flaw. Members and novices had received new versions. Since she was neither of those things, she continued to wear the old.

It had been a gift from Lettie years ago—with no mention of magical powers or secret societies. Thia had thought it an amusing curiosity, nothing more, and had taken to wearing it as a whimsical reminder of a favorite relative. Lettie had been larger than life to Thia as a child. Someone who lived in far off places like London and Oregon and sent her amazing and amazingly odd gifts. A true eccentric, doing as she pleased. It had been completely foreign to Thia's experiences at that point, and inspiring.

The pendant had been given to Lettie during her training. Done in silver, it had been replaced by the gold version when she attained full membership.

Her death in October was what had revealed the flaw.

Thia had been invited to join. To follow in her great-aunt's footsteps, she supposed. In a way. It would mean two years of full-time training—which she saw as a very good thing, given her difficulties—followed by sworn allegiance and permanent membership. That's where she got less sure. And there would be mandatory employment, either as an agent sent out into the field as Lettie had been, or as what? A researcher? Neither suited her inclinations.

What would happen to Eclectica? Lettie had managed to be both shop owner and agent—but in her later years, after she had semi-retired from field duty.

Adding more weight against joining were concerns that the Brigantium's interest was not in Thia but in the power she held. She couldn't help fearing she would be less a member and more a guinea pig.

"A penny for your thoughts," Abby said, giving her a nudge as they walked side by side up the park trail. Their group of four had been silent until then. Busy in their own minds, or taking a needed mental break.

Thia had always found the park to be soothing, but today the rush of water through the central creek was terribly loud. Winter scenery that only yesterday she would have described as starkly beautiful struck her now as bleak.

"I forgot to reset Eclectica's wards." She didn't want to get into what she'd seen with Amundsen again, not while she was already keyed up, with nothing new to add. "Please help me remember when we get back. And my keys are at the Land-mark, if Madame Demetka left them like she'd said."

"Hm." Abby loaded a lot of skepticism into that one little sound. But she didn't pry, and they relapsed into silence.

Elkhorn Park was often spoken of as Granite Springs's true heart—and what a beautiful heart it was. The lower half was a blend of cultivated landscapes, ponds, and recreational areas placed amid a mix of native and specimen trees and connected by meandering walkways and trails. Elkhorn Creek ran the whole length, its deep, rocky bed crossed by numerous arched bridges. The land sloped the entire way, gradually—and then not so gradually—heading into the granite foothills for which the town had been named. The slope meant the water moved quickly, especially when high.

Beyond the rustic structure of the park's office and mainte-nance sheds, what was considered the upper half began and things were much more akin to a woodland hike. Aside from a trail with a couple of bridges, some benches, and a couple of drinking fountains (out-of-order, in Thia's experience), the landscape was mostly left to itself. Coniferous trees towered while deciduous ones arched over the trail, with grasses and low-profile shrubs filling the land to either side.

Given the season, the trail itself was frosted-over dirt and patches of ice. If Thia had known she'd be doing this today, she would have worn boots with better treads.

When her foot skidded yet again, Cormac took hold of her upper arm, stabilizing her.

She hadn't realized he had been so close, or that Abby had gone ahead—closer now to Murphy. Better footwear allowed them both to walk faster. "Thanks."

He made a brusque sound of acknowledgment, as if most of his attention was elsewhere. Gradually, his hand shifted, threading the bend of her arm, drawing her in.

"Your friend is none too pleased with me," he said after a moment. "Is that a sentiment you share?"

Her initial reaction was that she was far too tired for this, and her emotions, too battered. Yet this promised to be their first conversation in weeks. She wasn't going to waste it with grievances.

"It is good you're here," she said. "I hadn't expected it."

Their pace had slowed. Murphy and Abby were twice as far ahead.

"I didn't even know you'd gotten my text." She wasn't sure why she was bringing that up. "Had you? Gotten my text?"

"I had." He spoke carefully. "I was in London. At the Brigantium. I saw it after the news had already reached them." He glanced at her, out the side of his eyes only. Checking. "We interrogated Cassandra."

"About this? What did she say? Was it believable?"

"Yes, taking the third question first. And no, this wasn't her doing."

"You're sure?" Thia pulled him to a stop, forced him to look her in the eyes. He was so often impossible to read, but she would always try. And, evidently, would always feel a connection when their gazes met. She might never understand it or him, but it was there. Something in her clicked with something in him, and so she could not help feeling glad—despite everything—that he was here. "This wasn't another revenge attempt?"

"I'm certain." His pupils were black and fathomless within the North Sea colors of his irises. "Whatever this is, it is not because of her. Or you."

Thia felt her shoulders sag, released of a burden she hadn't needed to carry. "Kendra wasn't killed because of me?"

"Nothing indicates that. Nothing at all."

At some point she had taken hold of Cormac's lapels, which made it easy to step forward, against his chest, when a rush of relief and sorrow threatened to undo her.

"In fact, that vision before your Sight went out—"

Tears spilled out of control, running down her cheeks. She dropped her forehead to Cormac's collarbone, let her head rest as she fought internally to hold herself together. She felt a sob build—but she couldn't give it release. There was work to do. She had to stay focused, had to—

Slowly, his arms lifted to enfold her. Stiffly. One hand went to the back of her head and held firm when she might have considered pulling away. She was making a mess of his jacket, and they needed to get on. But it was nice to be held—only for a while, she promised herself—even as awkward as that hold seemed to be.

He was not a comfort hugger. The tension in his body, the hesitant way he had come to it, his immediate and ongoing silence confirmed her prior suspicion. He had no issues with physical contact, she knew. That he used it to advantage was another of her suspicions.

This was not one of those times, and in a self-serving way she was grateful for his being so patently ill at ease. She also appreciated his effort. It was no small thing, that he would try to give her this without benefit to himself.

Unless he thought to benefit by getting her to believe that he had no other motives, which was a kind of double-motive, wasn't it, or at least a—She was ruining this for herself, whatever it was. What did his intention matter, really, if she got something out of it?

It mattered because it would not be genuine.

The sorrow of that rose up, joined with what was already at the surface, and she cried all the more. Which was a shame, because it caused her nose to clog up, and Cormac smelled so good. She let go of her hold on him and then, sniffling, reached into her jacket pocket.

He did the same with his. "Here," he said, "I have a—"

"Handkerchief." In her hand was the one he had given her weeks ago, when he'd arranged to sit next to her on her flight to London—before she knew who he truly was, and that he was trying to take the Stone of Shadows from her.

He returned an identical cloth to his pocket. They resumed walking. Abby and Murphy were nowhere in sight.

"You kept it."

"It's a quality piece," Thia said lightly, then used it to blow her nose. "You don't want it back, do you?"

He made the short, almost soundless huff she had come to know was as good as a laugh.

He often made a show of amusement but it was just that: a show. The real thing was rare—and, no matter how annoyed she might be with him, she treasured it. Plus it usually meant she had surprised him, and there was kind of triumph in that.

Ahead and across the creek, patches of yellow could be seen through the trees and bushes. Police tape.

"We should cross." She indicated the bridge that became visible as they rounded a curve. Multiple footprints marked the frost on its wooden planks. The sound of voices became audible—only just—over the water and rocks.

She gratefully accepted Cormac's renewed offer of support. Her boots were not the only things that threatened to skate out from under her. Her nerve was, too. She wanted to turn around. Go home and hide under the covers and pretend that nothing terrible had happened or could ever happen.

But she was not here for herself; she was here for Kendra and for Abby, who believed this was necessary. Thia would be here for her in case she needed a steadying arm—actual or metaphorical.

That was what friends did.

As she and Cormac stepped off the bridge onto the trail's continuation, she asked, "What was were you saying before my meltdown? About my Sight and what I thought I saw."

"It'll keep." His attention was fixed ahead, where the trail turned and disappeared behind towering rhododendrons. He pulled away. "I have an aversion to law enforcement," he said wryly. "And you need to get on."

"Okay, sure. But why did you come if not to—"

His index finger went up, pointing skyward. "I won't be far," he said mischievously.

It took Thia a moment. "Oh. Oh, right."

He could transform into a raven.

It was entirely possible that she would never adapt to her life. Magic and spells and fairytales-as-reality. It would be year after year of shocks and feeling overwhelmed.

Well, year after year if she survived.

"Murphy and Abby are around that turn," Cormac said, and, tracking his gesture, Thia turned her head to the right.

A rushing blur of motion to her left had her whipping back and she gasped as winter cold air displaced by black-feathered wings blew across her face and ruffled her hair.

Cormac was gone but for the sound of flight, and soon that was gone as well. A black bird within a dense tree canopy. He could be anywhere in there, and she had missed the moment, misdirected with a magician's skill.

A feather drifted down.

She caught it on her upturned palm. It was only about two inches in length and rounded at the top. There was silky fluff before the shaft. A contour feather, she believed it was called.

Black was a misnomer. Depending on how she held it, there was blue and purple and green. Subtle, beguiling colors.

Fortunately, she hadn't really blown her nose into the handkerchief. The linen, other than a damp spot or two, was clean. She set the feather on it, folded the cloth with care, and then slipped it into her pocket. Another memento.

Magic, spells, and folktales-as-reality. No, she would never get used to this.

She rounded the trail's curve and it was like walking into *Verdict: Guilty,* absent the familiar cast. The ubiquitous yellow tape marked off a large area, starting at a mossy grouping of boulders on one side to stretch across two sections of trail and down a steep, overgrown bank to the creek. Within, police and park patrol along with several people in white coveralls went about their work. Beyond it on the other side, past the boulders and on an uphill slope, a fair number of onlookers had gathered.

There was no visible body. No tarp-covered one, either. She hoped it had already been removed.

At the nearest line of tape, Murphy spoke with an officer. From the amount of gestures both were making, their conversation was not going a way either liked. Abby stood at a short distance, her attention on the fern-bracketed entrance of a trail down the bank. From where Thia had stopped, it was impossible to see down to the creek.

"He was in the water," Abby said dismally when Thia joined her. "The body is still down there."

"Oh." Thankfully, the view from here was not much better.

The angle was wrong; the undergrowth, too dense.

"So far Murphy hasn't been able to convince the police to let us—" She broke off when she turned and caught sight of Thia's face. "You've been crying." Her frown went from one of concern to one of anger. "What did Cormac do?"

"What?"

"Where is he? If he said anything to—"

"No. No, I just—All this. It got to me, that's all. Do you have any Kleenex?" she asked to change the subject. She waggled her hand at her nose. "I'm a mess here."

Abby's eyes narrowed, a clear signal that this would be revisited later. She reached into her duffel coat's side pocket, got a travel pack of earth-friendly bamboo tissues.

"Thanks." Thia pulled out three, stocking up.

"I took them from your place this morning."

"Huh." She blew her nose—for real this time. "They must've been Lettie's." Like almost everything there. "I need to figure out what to do with my stuff."

"Aren't you having it all shipped?" They had talked about it a few weeks ago.

"I am—I will." But after it arrived, she would have to sort through everything. Lettie's things, her things. They wouldn't all fit in the house. She wiped at her nose. "I'm not ready."

"You can't put it off forever. You won't be going back to Los Angeles, right? That's your house now. And you're Eclectica's owner. You're in charge."

They both knew that was more of a technicality.

"No, I'm staying," Thia said. "I'm definitely staying."

"You could at least transfer your things to a storage place here. Prices are bound to be better."

"Yeah, that's true—Ah, geez."

There was a frenzy of movement involving the onlookers uphill. Madame Demetka was pushing her way through.

"Oh!" Catching sight of Thia and Abby, she waved. Something jingled in her hand. "Is good I find you!" She skirted the police tape on her way down the brushy slope. The fabric of her garments caught on numerous twigs, breaking them off and dragging them along.

"Madame Demetka." Thia noted the attention given by the nearest police officer. "What are you doing here?"

She again waved a jingling hand. "Keys!"

"Of course." Feeling her brain break a bit, Thia stepped past Abby to reach for them. "And you came here to give them to me. Now. Not at the Landmark."

"I was meditating in the Rowan Space." She placed the keys in Thia's hand, then paused for breath. "I ask for help with catching the killer, and my Guides tell me, 'Go. Go to Park.' And next thing I know, I find body."

"What?" Thia missed her pocket and the keys dropped to the ground. She scooped them up. "You found the body?"

"Yes! Was most incredible." With a sweep of her arm, she pointed past the onlookers to the road. "I have been sitting in warm patrol car. My clothes, they get wet." She shivered, or maybe shuddered, given her next words. "The young man was at water's edge. Not easy to see. I slipped." She cast a furtive glance toward where Murphy stood at the police tape. In place of the officer who had been talking—arguing—with him was the chief.

"Closer." Taking hold of Thia's arm, she pulled her in for what might almost pass for a whisper. Her breath smelled of fennel. "We will do a reading when coast is clear. My Guides, they say there is restless spirit . . . or something." She frowned skyward. "Is not clear."

Abby joined the huddle. "We can't stay here the whole time, waiting for the scene to clear. It'll look suspicious."

"Yes. Already they are upset that I leave car." She aimed her frown at a different target: Chief Nash.

"Miss Wilson," he called over. "We have not finished taking your statement."

"Of course, sugar," the former Madame Demetka said with a broad smile and broader southern drawl. "Be right there."

To Abby and Thia she said, "Here, at midnight. Be sure to bring your friend with the limp."

Giving no chance to argue, she set off in a flurry of twig-bearing fabric to join the chief on the other side of the tape. A moment later, the two walked away, leaving Murphy on his own—and clearly furious. He strode toward Abby and Thia.

"The *cáeptha* seems to believe this wraps things up," he said as he neared. "Kendra Ross's death is the result of a mugging, he says, and this a fatal mishap. Drug overdose, likely heroin. The investigation is done but for the technicality of a toxicology screen. Done up all neat and tidy like a present, this is. Might as well put a damned bow on it."

● ○ ●

Founders Way

When Edith had begun her studies with the Society of Brigantium, Quentin had been a hale and ascendant star among his fellow novitiates, a literal golden boy with hair the color of a newly minted sovereign. He aced every exam, surpassed every expectation, mastered every challenge as if it were no challenge at all.

Every novitiate had wanted to be him.

Every novitiate had resented him immensely.

He had been popular in the way people became when others viewed them as a means for raising their own stature, which meant that he had needed to put no effort toward making or maintaining friends. He had never spared Edith a glance or, she was sure, so much as a passing thought.

All things being equal, they should have attended at least a few classes and seminars together. They were not far off in age and she had entered the novitiate program only a term or two after he had—nearly six years ago, directly following her doctorate from Cambridge. But all things were *not* equal where Quentin Sigmund Aloysius Reynolds was concerned. He had breezed through the lower levels, tested out of every first-level requirement and most of the second, and had done it all with easy charm, good looks, and none of the nepotism that had been so readily available to him. Edith had found it infuriating. She still did.

He became a member a full two years early and continued his meteoric rise. Bets had been made as to how many—or rather, how few—years it would take before he ran the whole Society. Everyone knew he was being groomed for it. How could he not be, with talent and skills such as that?

Then came The Accident, as it was now called, and every-thing changed. An unauthorized ritual gone horribly wrong, it was said, although no one knew for certain. Or, if they did, they weren't talking.

Nine dead, that night; all but the Brigantium's golden boy.

There were rumors, of course, as to the cause. Catastrophic error, some said. Icarus flying too close to the sun, attempting a feat beyond his scope. Unsanctioned use of black magic.

In the aftermath, Quentin all but vanished. Other than as a whispered cautionary tale to new recruits, it was as if he had never been.

Fast forward to five months ago, when he returned.

No fanfare. No announcement. No clear explanation of his role, either in The Accident or within the Society's current hierarchy. He had simply entered through the main doors and begun issuing orders as if he had every right, and everyone behaved as if he had. It was as if his absence had never been.

But his golden hair had turned gray, and he no longer both-ered with charm.

He often didn't bother with conversation.

This was one of those times. He and Edith had walked up

Main Street, passing in front of Founders Hall to enter the Way at the opposite end from the shrubbery where Kendra had taken refuge. They were halfway down that, all without having exchanged a word.

No one would take them for friends on a leisurely outing. In addition to the pronounced absence of conversation, no one could see Quentin, his limp growing more pronounced by the yard, and believe he was doing this for leisure.

"We won't fool anyone," Edith said, her patience at an end. How could his silence be anything but antagonistic? Clearly, he resented her. At best he saw her as a mere subordinate; at worst he believed she didn't belong in the field. He made light of her inventions and apps, and thought little of her contributions. She was no more to him today than she had ever been: incidental.

"Pardon?" He sounded as if he'd forgotten she was there. He didn't look over. Couldn't be bothered to make eye contact, no matter how fleeting.

"If this is supposed to pass for a casual stroll," she said, her jaw tight as she maintained her pleasant expression—playing *her* part—"we're not doing a good job of it."

He grunted.

In agreement? Dismissal? How the hell was she supposed to tell. "It's like working with a blooming sphinx."

He side-eyed her.

"Well, it's true." She hadn't meant to say it aloud, though. But what was said, was said. She wouldn't back down.

After a few steps, he asked, "I present you with a riddle, is that it?" Instead of the anticipated anger, she sensed a ghost of his former charm. It lifted the corner of his mouth and put a teasing gleam in his grey eyes where condescension usually resided—although that might have been a result of the afternoon sun, reflecting off the buildings to highlight him just so.

"You *are* the riddle," she said, annoyed.

Another grunt, timed with the strike of his cane. They were passing a tiled entry marked by a flickering neon arrow. There was no door in evidence, presumably having been plastered over. The tiles and the stucco were stained and cracked, their better days obviously having been several decades prior. "Was this once a club?" Not that she expected him to know.

"Good location for it." He slowed, dropping the pace from leisurely to glacial. To justify it to any observers, he made a show of studying the arrow. "Are you getting anything?"

"No." She held the scanner close to her thigh, the crystals hanging inconspicuously alongside her knee-length coat. The fringed ends of her scarf served as further camouflage. "A few things along the way, but nothing now. The closer we are to the building, the less environmental noise there is."

"A dead zone."

His tone made her glance over, and she noted how much more he leaned on his cane when he believed her attention was elsewhere.

She had suspected he was in pain back at the alley. That was before walking more than a half mile. Dammit, this had been *his* idea. What he did to himself was not her problem.

"You're not picking up anything either?" She wouldn't admit to it, but she had been worrying that there was a glitch in her equipment or, worse, a flaw in her design.

"Nothing outside. It—" His voice caught and he came to an abrupt stop.

"Quentin?"

His eyes were closed. Sweat beaded on skin gone pasty.

Tangling the crystals' lines, she stuffed the scanner into her coat pocket and then took hold of Quentin's right arm. His left had gone rigid on his cane as if that and only that could keep him upright.

"I'm fine," he said, the roughness of his voice proclaiming the lie. "It's nothing."

"Come on, then." She lifted the arm she held, ducked under it, and then, setting it across her shoulders, tucked herself up against his side. Keeping a tight grip on his wrist, she put her free arm across his back. His entire body was rigid. He had yet to open his eyes. "Is it your leg or your hip?"

"Don't."

She tugged, arguing with his refusal to shift his weight. "I've got you. Lean on me."

"No."

"It's this or you pass out and I leave you here. *Language,*" she scolded when he swore.

A word even saltier followed, but some of his weight eased her way. Not enough.

"I might be petite," she snapped, "but I'm not fragile. Give over." She pulled.

His breath hitched. "Wait. It's—it's a spasm. It'll pass."

"In how long?"

There was time to watch a car pull out of the distant post office lot and drive away before he answered.

"A while."

"Oh, that's fine," she mocked. "Just brilliant. What about a pain spell?"

"My method of choice, certainly, but not here." A tremor ran through his lean frame. "It'll attract attention."

As if this wouldn't? Edith nearly rolled her eyes, but he was right. Some kind of craft was at work to create this dead zone. Use of magic within it would undoubtedly draw notice.

"What about—" She paused. That issue was tricky. But they couldn't stand here much longer. If he did collapse, no way could she take his full weight. "What about something else? For pain."

Use of pharmaceutical painkillers was forbidden to all active members. As a field agent, Quentin was denied those and also most herbal concoctions. Such things dulled responses and, almost without exception, suppressed magical talent.

Assistant Director Meriwether had suggested that he might be using and had asked Edith to report any signs. This would be more than a sign. It would be an out and out admission.

He let out a quiet sigh. "If I tell you it's in my shirt pocket?"

For a moment, they simply stood together in what was not an embrace but was intimate nevertheless. She could feel him breathe. He likely could say the same of her.

Edith's career-journey to this point could be summed up in one word: challenging. The Society was patriarchal. Most of its leadership also held prejudices against her area of expertise. And then there was her lack of social station and family connections. After years of determined, strategic effort, her ideas were at last being heard. In the fall, her side projects (derisively termed "gadgetry" by many) had been given a bit of funding, and then she had been posted to Granite Springs—a promotion-track assignment.

Her loyalty was to the Society, in general, and specifically to Arthur Barnstable and Beatrice Meriwether.

"I'll have to report it." Each word pained her. "I—I'm sorry."

How paltry that sounded.

Quentin's chest expanded, then contracted as he blew out a resigned breath—her only warning before his weight came heavily against her and he took a lurching step forward.

"You aren't going to . . . ?" She let the question trail off while together they took another awkward step. At this rate, they would reach the hotel—right over there—in an hour.

"No."

She felt him gather himself, preparing, and she braced for the move that would follow. It got them another foot or so. "We could call for a ride," she said, thinking of the two other agents. "They're not far. They could get here in—"

"They look like what they are," he said through clenched

teeth. "Brigantium."

"And we don't?"

"You, certainly not."

She bristled. "I'll have you know that I—"

"It's a good thing, Edith." Another lurch forward.

"Not thus far." She hadn't meant to sound so bitter.

"Because most of your peers got assignments before you?" He made a dismissive sound. "Arthur has antiquated notions. You're a favorite with Bea. She'll sort him out soon enough." He used his cane to point across the parking lot to the hotel. "Shorter this way."

"But the shrubbery where Kendra hid is over there." The other direction. If they continued to follow Founders Way, they would go right by it. Yes, he was suffering, but they had a job to do. "It could hold vital information."

"I can read it from here."

"It's at least fifty yards," she argued, helping him negotiate the angled change in direction, to cut across the lot to the street corner.

"Fifty five." So smug, he sounded. If he were steadier, she would have been tempted to shove him.

Well, all right, she was still tempted.

Especially after he asked, in that same smug tone, "Does your device not work at that range?"

"I'll do it," she grumbled. "I swear I will."

"Pardon?"

"You're intentionally antagonizing me."

"Am I?"

She might have growled.

He chuckled.

They reached the sidewalk, and she had been pushed past caring that, while he lacked the authority to end her career, he could make things extremely difficult. "You're infuriating."

"I thought I was a sphinx." He was grinning.

Grinning.

She looked away. There had been a time when she'd found him almost insufferably attractive. She might, still.

CHAPTER 15

Shakespeare Festival
Granite Springs, Oregon
31 January

"Why was he there?" Thia asked, interrupting the low-level squabble Abby and Murphy had begun as soon as they'd left the taped-off clearing. Since they were now passing the Shakespeare Festival, that meant they'd spent almost none of the return walk to the Landmark in productive discussion. Thia had questions and she was fed up with their bickering. "What was he doing? Was he part of a transient group?"

Granite Springs, being a popular tourist town with a central retail and entertainment district, attracted a lot of buskers and panhandlers. Most had moved on, what with the drop in business, but they'd return in the spring, when reconstruction had finished and the Festival plays were running.

"Security footage can give a rough idea." Murphy dropped back to talk alongside her. Abby stayed ahead. "He hadn't any run-ins with local police, so he wasn't known to them."

"Do they now know him now? From his wallet or . . . ?"

"No. They'll run his prints."

Thia frowned. "He didn't have any kind of ID?"

"Apparently not."

"And they don't find that suspicious?" She certainly did. He might have been someone who had not wanted to be identified. Someone with outstanding warrants. Someone who had killed before.

"It is and it isn't," Murphy said. "He was living rough. He could've been an earlier victim of theft. Or he was on the run. Or he wasn't a suicide or an accidental overdose, and whoever killed him saw to it that we wouldn't have an easy time."

Some distance away at the Plaza, an industrial tree chipper roared to life, shrieking and grinding its way through what must have been a huge branch. Thia grimaced. Murphy said something in a language she didn't recognize. By his tone, it was profane.

"You really do hate the redesign," Abby said as she slowed to join them.

He strode ahead. "The loss of those trees will be a long time felt."

"Too bad you didn't try to convince city government," Abby spoke to his back.

"Who's to say I did not? This time, their minds were made up."

Abby sighed. "Yeah, that's the impression Loretta got too. A woman in my coven. She wrote letters, spoke at city meetings, threatened to chain herself to the mountain ash—the one presumed to have been planted by one of the founders. She had a protest scheduled. A lot of the coven signed up."

"Nothing came of it?" Thia hadn't heard about a protest— and the tree was gone.

"The removal crew arrived a week early. It was down before anyone else could get there. Like the library tree, but worse."

The sounds of another large branch's destruction reverberated off the alley's buildings. The parking garage's open floors acted as amplifiers.

Cormac strolled out from the ground level and smoothly fell into step beside Thia.

"Are we buying what the police are selling with their over-dose theory?" he inquired after the noise died down.

"We are not," she said, and then realized they had not yet discussed that as a group. "Are we?"

"Too tidy," Murphy agreed from several feet ahead.

Abby made it unanimous. "Too convenient."

At the intersection of the two alleys—the one they had just used and the one that ran beside the Landmark—they ducked under the police tape and re-entered the scene of Kendra's death. If Thia never walked through this alley again it would be too soon.

She moved closer to Cormac to ask quietly, "What did you see while you were . . . overhead?" She didn't know how public he wanted his transformation to be.

Unfortunately, she hadn't accounted for Abby's interest and acute hearing.

"How's that?" the latter asked, moving to stand in front of Cormac. "Overhead where?"

Forced to either sidestep or stop, he stopped. So did Thia. His mouth quirked. "I had a bird's eye view. And a bird's ear as well." His amusement faded. "I'm not ware of heroin use in this age, but that seems an odd setting for it."

"It's isolated," Murphy offered, walking back toward them. "Secluded. Little chance of being caught."

"Plenty of closer locations fit that criteria," Cormac countered. "The whole scenario feels off. We're to believe that the morning after he kills a woman, he goes deep into the park to take what amounts to a fatal dose so close to the creek that he tumbles into it, striking his head multiple times, and landing in a way that would drown him if he wasn't dead already? It's a bit much."

"This morning?" Abby asked. "How do you know he hadn't been there all night? He could have gone there to hide after he—After." She pressed her lips together.

"He could have, but he did not. I asked around."

"You found witnesses?"

"Ravens." One shoulder lifted in an uneasy shrug. "There was a mated pair at the scene. I consulted them, as it were."

"You can talk to them?" Thia supposed it should not have come as a surprise, considering how he could *become* one.

"In a fashion. They didn't see the deed itself, but they could give a rough time frame of when it must have happened. Body not there, body there." He held up his hand when Murphy looked set to interrupt. "I asked if there might've been other witnesses. Nothing came through. I'll go out later, ask around. It's approaching tea time." He checked his watch. "If I'm not mistaken, we all missed lunch."

Thia hadn't wanted to say anything—it felt selfish to make an issue of it when there was so much going on. But despite grief dulling her appetite, her stomach had been gnawing on itself for the past half hour.

"I'll sort it," Murphy said and began texting.

Thia returned to something Cormac had said. "He hit his head multiple times?"

"Rather curious, given the path his supposed fall took. Not much between the top of the bank and the water that could do that kind of damage."

Abby eyed him with suspicion. "The body was submerged, you said. Yet you could get all that detail from wherever you were?"

"When he was laid out," Cormac replied easily. "Yes."

Murphy used a key to unlock the Landmark's side door. He held it open.

Abby spun on her heel, went inside. Thia followed, stepping over the yellow tape left on the floor from earlier.

"Staff at the Taproom are expecting you," Murphy said after he had locked the door. He led the way down the hall. "I'll see you settled, then I have business to attend to the rest of the day."

"Thank you," Thia said, the only one to do so. She was so tired of navigating the interpersonal dynamics. "What should we do about Madame Demetka's thing tonight?" she asked, letting her frustration show. "Should we meet up beforehand? Go together?"

"What thing?" asked Cormac.

"She wants to hold a reading. At midnight. In the park."

"Ah, shit." Abby came to an abrupt stop. "My coven. We're finalizing our Imbolc preparations tonight. I've got boxes of supplies at my place. Even if I don't attend, I need to bring all that in."

"Couldn't someone else do it?" Thia suggested. The night ahead would be challenging enough without that round trip drive.

"I hate to ask them," Abby said. "They've been calling all day and I've been sending them straight to voicemail—which I haven't checked. I just—" She made a small, defeated gesture. "I can't handle all their sympathy right now."

Thia understood that. It was hard to hold yourself together when the people around you expected and at times encouraged you to fall apart.

Stopped a distance ahead, Murphy offered, "Make a list of what you need and where to find it—the supplies, a change of clothes and such. I'll send concierge staff out."

"I don't know," Abby said. "I'm sure they have better things to do than to—"

"Kendra was a favorite here, as if you didn't already know. They would consider it an honor to be of service to her closest friend."

"Oh." Abby ducked her head and resumed walking, but not before Thia had seen fresh tears.

Murphy stepped aside, giving room as she hurried past.

Thia followed, but slowly. At the end of the hallway, Abby

turned toward the lobby and soon went out of sight.

"See that she makes that list, would you?" Murphy said to Thia as Cormac trailed further and further behind.

"I will." They rounded the corner, the lobby's open expanse coming into view. "She should stay with me tonight, too, as late as it might run. Why don't we all meet there before—"

Near the central table, Abby was involved in a group hug with an older, gray-haired couple and man and woman closer to Thia's age. Each face was lined with grief.

There was a notable break in Murphy's stride. He recovered quickly and went to greet the strangers.

Except they weren't strangers to Abby. Nor to him.

There *was* something familiar, Thia noted as the hug split up, although she didn't know them. It was in the red of the younger man's shoulder-length hair, and in the young woman's height and slim, athletic build. And in the fury that came over the older man's face when he caught sight of Murphy.

Thia had seen that same expression on Kendra's face a time or two. The same red hair. The same slim, athletic build.

"Mr. Ross," Murphy said and extended his hand. The older man—Kendra's father, no doubt—rejected the gesture. After a beat, Murphy let it drop, then acknowledged each family member in turn. "Mrs. Ross. Fiona. Jack."

The Ross family said nothing. The younger woman, Fiona, slid her arm under Abby's, holding her in place within their group. A silent, formidable wall.

"I-I sent a jet," Murphy said with an uncharacteristic verbal stumble. He cleared his throat. "And there was a car for you at the airport."

"We made our own arrangements," said Kendra's father. His deep voice matched his large frame. He was of a height with Murphy, and broader across the shoulders. If he had been a sculpture, Thia might have said he had been carved in haste. His face was rough. Craggy. Kendra might have inherited her expressions from him, but she had gotten her features—her beauty—from her mother.

Not her height, though. Kendra's mother was only a hand's breadth past five feet.

"We want nothing to do with you or your riches," she told Murphy. Her eyes were a vibrant, identical green to Kendra's. "Not your jet nor your car nor your hotel, even if our girl did choose to work in it. She's gone and we don't need to pretend we approved. We did not." Thia couldn't tell if the flash of the woman's eyes was a trick of the light or the force of emotion.

Or was it power? Did Kendra's family work with magic?

"We did *not* approve." Mrs. Ross jabbed her index finger at Murphy, who stood as if frozen. "We told her to have nothing to do with you—and more fool us, we believed her when she said she would be fine. We believed *you* when you swore you wouldn't involve her in any of your dark business. That you would not let it touch her." Her volume had risen, attracting the attention of staff and several guests.

"Henrietta," Mr. Ross tried, but she wouldn't be warned off.

"You got her killed," she accused Murphy, whose face might have paled. The bruise and scabbed cut near his eye stood out in starker contrast. "We'll allow her wake to be held here, in a place where she spent so much time and energy, but you're not to have a thing to do with it. It's for us to arrange, from the candles to the flowers to the—" Her voice cracked and she covered her face with her hands.

"Henrietta." Her husband gently drew her into an embrace. Her shoulders shook.

"I'll have someone take you up," Murphy said, then went to reception. After a quick word with a clerk—Chuck, Thia reminded herself—he walked out, going back the way they'd come. To his office, presumably.

Only then did Thia realize that Cormac was absent. Not in the lobby, and not in what she could see of the overlook.

Where the hell had he—

"Thia." Abby, no longer arm-in-arm, waved her over. "Thia, these are Kendra's parents, brother, and sister." All but Mrs. Ross, who was blotting her eyes with tissue, turned to meet her.

"Hello." She felt incredibly awkward. What could she say? What could anyone say to people who had lost so much?

"Thia?" Kendra's sister quickly enveloped her in a firm hug, then stepped back. "I'm Fiona. Kendy spoke of you often." Her eyes were the same green as her mother's. As Kendra's.

"She did?" Thia recovered her balance, physically at least. She didn't know what Kendra might have told them. Did they know about the Cailleach's powers? About magic at all? Did they know about the parade attack, and how that connected to Thia? Oh, how she hated secrets. "Kendra was a wonderful friend," she said lamely. "She helped me so much."

"How's that?" Kendra's brother asked. The first thing she had heard him say, and it sounded accusatory. He was staring at her in a way that felt accusatory, too. His eyes were a pale, intense hazel.

"Thia only moved here recently," Abby explained. "Kendra and I were sort of her welcoming committee."

Mrs. Ross gave Thia a watery smile. "It's very nice to meet you. I'm terribly sorry you saw me lose my temper."

"Hardly." Abby briefly touched the woman's arm. "Besides, you didn't say anything that didn't deserve to be said."

"No, but my timing could have been better."

"Seemed more than fine to me, Ma," Kendra's brother said, and then turned to Chuck who had come from reception to stand nervously by. "What?"

Chuck flinched. "I'm to escort you to where we have been setting up. When you're ready. Please allow me to say how sorry I am for your loss."

"We're ready now," the brother said, ignoring the sympathy.

"Of course." Chuck gestured toward the elevator. "This way, please."

"There is so much to do," Mrs. Ross said to Thia. "I hope we get a chance to talk more. After." She reached out, gave Abby's wrist a squeeze. "Be strong. Kendra would want us all to be strong."

"Yes," Abby said.

The Ross family followed Chuck into the elevator. When the doors closed, Thia felt some of the tension ease.

"You've met them before?" she asked Abby.

"A few times. When I'd go with her to the Bay Area. Never here. They never came here."

Thia hadn't known where Kendra's family lived. She hadn't known their names before now, either. How could she know so little? She was a horrible friend. Horrible.

The lobby's air changed with the opening of the main door, and Edith and Quentin struggled inside. He leaned heavily on her, his face drawn and ashen.

"What happened?" Thia, along with Abby, hurried to them.

With the door's closing came an electrical surge. The lobby lights brightened, flickering, as the telephones rang at reception—and almost immediately returned to normal.

So did Quentin. He straightened, lifted his arm from where it had been across Edith's shoulders. The look she gave him was odd. "Did you just—"

"Pain dampening spell." He blotted perspiration from his face with a handkerchief pulled from an inside coat pocket. "Completely above board."

"Do *they* know that?" Edith asked as security guards rushed in from several directions.

With a low oath, Quentin tucked his cane high under his arm and walked to meet them. He held his hands out, fingers splayed. Empty. "Sorry to alarm," he said. Whatever followed was too quiet for Thia to hear.

"What happened out there?" she asked Edith.

And, to herself, where the hell was Cormac?

● ○ ●

Edith admired Thia McDaniel. For a number of reasons, but especially for how she was facing the challenge of unexpected magical power. At the Ring of Brodgar, she had experienced a fundamental change, yet instead of allowing it to overwhelm her, she was attempting adapt and work with it.

To possess magic was no trivial thing, regardless of quantity. Not only had Thia received a substantial amount, but it was of an ancient strain not well understood. A goddess strain—with the particular goddess being the Cailleach, of all things, credited with shaping mountains and valleys.

Edith also *liked* her. She was smart, funny, kind—someone who would make an excellent friend.

So, when Thia asked, "What happened out there?" Edith's instinct was to answer fully and honestly.

Unfortunately, she was constrained by duty, and the rule on information sharing with non-personnel was simple: Do not.

"Quentin's old injury was bothering him," she said, picking out what she *could* say. "Other than that, it was fairly straight-forward. I'll analyze the scan data, confer with headquarters, and then hopefully have some useful results to share." That bit skirted the edge of falsehood. She already knew she had useful results. "How did it go at the park?"

"I don't know." Thia seemed subdued. So did Abby. The day had been long, and it was only the afternoon. "The area was cordoned off, so we didn't see anything. Murphy spoke with a policeman who said it looked like—"

"Accidental death." Scorn laced Abby's words. "Heroin over-dose coupled with a fall into the creek."

Edith asked, "You have reason to doubt?"

"Yes." Abby didn't elaborate.

Thia did. "Cormac saw the body. He thinks the injuries are wrong for that. Plus it *feels* wrong, doesn't it?"

"It does." Edith had a specialty in forensic analysis—but of magic, not murder. Yet there *was* something off. It felt hasty and convenient. "What does this mean for Kendra's case? If the local police believe her killer's death is a simple matter, will they stop looking into hers? Motives, connections—" She shook her head, perplexed.

"They don't want to investigate," Abby said. "That's what I think. They're afraid they'll connect it back to Murphy."

Thia frowned. "You can't really believe that."

"Can't I?" Abby glanced around, stepped close to say in a low rush, "He's responsible, directly or indirectly—and he's got the police afraid of him and his organization. I can and do believe both those things."

Edith was well aware of Declan Murphy's reputation. Before she had left London, she had been shown the thick file kept on him and his businesses. Nothing had indicated outright criminality, but there was a workable gray area between legal and illegal, and while Declan Murphy might not overtly break laws, he had long associated with those who did.

"Murphy is as bothered by the police's conclusions as we are," Thia argued. "Or do you think he's pretending?"

"I didn't say he *told* them to stop investigating," Abby said (grudgingly, to Edith's mind). "I think they're afraid of what they might uncover. Things that don't necessarily tie in with Kendra's death but that they'd have to act on."

"What is it that he does?" Thia asked with obvious frustration. "No one has ever told me outright. Drug dealing? Smuggling? Murder for hire? Good god, Abby. If you know, what *is* it?"

"I don't know *anything*," she exclaimed. "That's the problem! But he has enough security here to qualify as a military unit. You saw some at Brodgar, and saw what they're capable of at the parade. Imagine what he might have at his international properties. And he's carrying a gun, for goddess sake. A *gun*."

"And he wields magic," Edith added, although they were all aware. As to what more she knew about him, she would need to check with the assistant director about sharing that, too.

"*Wields*. Exactly," Abby said, newly energized. "Not just uses magic but wields it. Like a weapon."

"So do a number of people," Thia said, and turned to Edith almost pleadingly. "Wielding power isn't bad, right? It's a skill. A thing some people can do. Right and wrong depends on what is done with it. Right?"

"Right." Edith needed to tread carefully. She knew the assistant director wanted to recruit Thia. It wouldn't do to scare her off. "Sometimes—for defense—force becomes necessary. So, for example, at the Society, those who have the talent for it learn how to do it well. It's a matter of safety. Protection."

"It's one thing for the Brigantium to defend itself," Abby countered, "but Murphy is not a member. Neither is Cormac."

Thia frowned. "What has Cormac got to do with—*Abby*." She gaped at her friend. "He wasn't even here until today. He had nothing to do with what happened."

"I don't trust him. Him or Murphy."

Knowing what she did, Edith thought that wise.

"But—"

"I'm sorry, Thia." Abby, closing her eyes, rubbed her forehead. "But you know they can't be trusted. Neither one."

"Overall, of course. I know that. But in this? Surely we can trust them in *this*."

Using two fingers, Abby continued to massage the area of the third-eye chakra—and Edith truly must be tired for that particular tidbit to spring to mind. Her sister was the New Ager, the one making their parents proud. Edith had left all that behind.

She shifted her attention. "You said Cormac saw the body

in the park. Do you know where I might find him? I'd like to ask him about that."

"No idea. No idea at all." With sudden exasperation, Thia flung up her hands. "He was with us when we got back here, and then he wasn't. No word. Nothing. As usual."

"Seems like he made himself scarce," Abby said, "when we met up with Kendra's family."

"They're here?" Edith hadn't had time to read the digital file she had received on them. "Quentin will want to take the lead on our interviews there, presumably. I should tell him they've arrived. Do you know their room number?"

Abby grimaced. "Ohhh, yeah, no. They're not staying here."

"I think they'd rather burn the place down," Thia said.

"With Murphy in it."

"Goodness." Edith should have made time for that file. "Do you know where they *are* staying?"

"No," Abby said. "But they're upstairs now. Second floor, in one of the event spaces."

Thia explained, "They've taken over the setup for the wake."

"Ah. Of course." Edith hated the timing, but it wasn't her place to decide. She prepared to go. "I need to tell Quentin that they're—"

"Wait," Thia said. "Madame Demetka is doing a reading in the park tonight. She was emphatic that Quentin be there. Of course, she's always emphatic."

"I'm not sure that—"

"I thought we could all meet up before we go. Things feel so scattered," she said. "Different people taking on different parts and finding out different things. Seeing different things. There hasn't been time for it all."

"Has something happened?"

She exchanged a look with Abby, then, "I had a—a vision, I guess? While talking to Neil Amundsen and using my Sight.

And then my Sight went out."

"Out? Is it working now? What sort of vision? Did it relate to—"

"If it's okay, I'd rather wait until tonight to go over it all."

"Of course." Edith considered apologizing for the barrage of questions, but it felt easier to simply move on. "What time?"

"Ten?" Thia checked with Abby, who nodded. "Okay. Ten."

"Ten it is." Edith back-stepped to the elevator. She had even less time to do what was already too much work. "If you hear from Cormac, please tell him I need to talk about what he saw." She pressed the call button. "I'd like to include that in my update to the assistant director this evening."

"Oh sure," Thia said, with a cynical laugh. "If I hear from him."

"Thanks." Edith entered the elevator, gave a small wave as the doors closed her in. She would be surprised if Thia didn't hear from Cormac. He certainly hadn't come all this way to assist the Society. Nor was he here in the pure-hearted pursuit of justice. Why else would he have come but for Thia? Something nefarious, Edith supposed, answering her own question as the elevator slowed to a stop.

"You're too soft." Said under her breath as she walked left down the corridor. "And hungry." She hadn't eaten since early morning.

Quentin must be starving too, unless he had since ordered a meal to his room. He had been going nonstop since his leyline journey. It was said that the transatlantic lines were grueling. Edith had never ridden a line bigger than a regional—the one into greater London from the Wiltshire training center.

At his door, she lifted her hand. Hesitated. She should have texted to make sure he wasn't resting—but, no, there was too much to do. She knocked.

Waited.

She knocked louder. And waited some more.

Quentin had seemed fine after he had used the pain dampening spell, but all spellwork was an energy drain and if he was already exhausted, it might not have worked for long.

"Hello?" She knocked again. "Quentin?"

What if he'd used what he had alluded to carrying in his pocket? Some medications warned against taking them on an empty stomach because of side effects. Some could be quite dangerous. What if he'd taken too many than was safe in any condition?

She got her mobile, quickly placed the call. As ring followed ring, she pressed her other ear to the door. She couldn't hear any sounds from within. Not footsteps. Not moans for help, either, or the ringing of his mobile. He could have set it to silent but maybe he was—

A simple explanation came to mind.

—not in the room at all.

"Right." Edith canceled the call. "Of course he's gone off on his own. Because why not? Why should the golden boy follow protocol."

She composed and sent a brief text before she could reconsider its tone.

BLOODY WELL CALL ME.

CHAPTER 16

Skati's plan for the mayor's party was flawless, with each carefully selected component placed in perfect alignment. As with an elaborate domino effect, when the first piece tipped into motion the rest would play out in a glorious chain reaction. His painstaking preparation was set to pay off with nigh automatic implementation.

Or it *would,* once rid of the intrusive flaw which was threatening a cascading failure.

Difficult to say when that flaw had been introduced. If Kjeld had not left the door open; if Kendra Ross had not entered through it; if she had been corruptible; or if there had been more time—then Skati would not have been forced to devise such a rushed, drastic means of ensuring her silence.

On the plus side, the police would not present a problem. He had been working them since he had first arrived. And even if he could not count on their susceptibility (he could), he had provided them with a clear case: A troubled youth with no community ties, living on the edge and addicted to illicit substances, had committed a heinous, opportunistic act and, not long after, caused himself a fatal mishap. It was a tragic tale—wrong place, wrong time for the lovely and well-loved victim—and Skati had supplied all the right ingredients for a quickly closed investigation. If only she did not have such troublesome connections.

Annoyingly, those troublesome connections were what had drawn him to Kendra Ross in the first place. It was a shame there hadn't been more time. Her trust had been slow to win, and only recently had she begun to speak more freely about her work and her friends.

He glared at the scene playing out on the scrying mirror. Althia McDaniel, getting out of a Mini Cooper—driven by Abigail Collins—and into her vintage Datsun. Soon both cars continued down Main, then turned left at the intersection.

If he had not been away, coordinating with the family for most of November and December, he could have started on her sooner. More, Idris Cathmor's daughter would not have been able to abuse their business connection, embroiling his *rekkrs* in her short-sighted scheme and drawing all manner of unwanted interest.

For five execrable years Skati had been dutifully attending to the family's interests here. Having created a persona that would hold up under the most intensive scrutiny, he had not only been accepted into the highest strata of the citizenry, he had attained a position within Granite Springs' government that could fast-track the family's goals.

It all hung on the Welcome Center proposed for the first interstate exit to the south. As it was to be under city control, Skati would ultimately be in charge, whether through official position or unofficial influence. A high-traffic amalgamation of rest area, information kiosk, and souvenir shop, the Center was to become the family's North American hub. Their black market goods would arrive via the unattended leyline portal to then be taken to the Center in the guise of supplies. From there the distribution possibilities were limitless.

Thanks to him, he and his family would dominate the entire Pacific Coast.

With that, the family would be forced to stop holding his youngest brother's death over his head. And, they would have to acknowledge that Skati had done far more than his older brothers ever had—and done it with less.

Three strong-minded council members were all that stood in his way. With Alma's assistance, the mayor's party was to be the solution to that. It had only taken a false promise to protect the Warden Trees.

He felt himself smile. Despite what he had told Alma, the *vordtré* would be down within the year. All of them. He had already filed the paperwork.

At the party, while members from her Retreat entertained with an Imbolc ceremony, she would help Skati weaken the guests' minds so that he could exert his full influence. Not only would the hold-out councilors be his, so would everyone else in attendance. He would have the whole of city leadership: mayor, council, public works, parks and recreation, fire, police—with many of the most powerful citizens as a bonus.

Then Alma and her associates would replace the memory of that part of the evening with an illusion. Partygoers would remember only what Skati wanted their memories to be.

It was a brilliant plan. A glorious plan. And it was why he had needed to take such a drastic step when it had been threatened. In only one day more, Granite Springs would be his.

In the mirror, he watched the two cars turn onto the street where the McDaniel woman lived. He could safely presume its destination. He prepared to close the session. He had left Kjeld's punishment unfinished.

The raven caught his notice.

It could be nothing, but he knew what was said about the *lethsíd* son of Idris Cathmor. He pulled for a closer view.

Ah. Yes. Cormac did a good job of concealing the power he carried, but the aberrant eye coloring gave him away.

● ○ ●

Above Granite Springs

After seeing Thia and Abby safely enter the house, Cormac angled his wings and banked out of the circle he had been making over the block. He slipped into a strong current, let it take him west toward Mill Street.

Kendra Ross's killer had run that way for a reason.

No one had been in pursuit at the time, so it had nothing to do with evasion. Furthermore, if that had been the young man's aim, he would have more logically gone in the opposite direction. Interestingly, that was the forested park where his body had been found. If he had deemed that area safe enough for drug use, why had he not sought refuge there after the killing?

If he had been high at the time, if he had panicked—all of that could explain his erratic, illogical behavior. Yet Cormac could not shake the feeling that there was more to this. The killing itself made no sense.

If Kendra Ross had been targeted specifically, if the young man had been paid or coerced to kill, then it might figure that the route he took afterward was deliberate. He could have gone to meet with whoever had given the orders.

That could be why he was dead now too. A tying up of loose ends.

What was Founders Hall in all of this? And for how much longer could Cormac conceal his own interest in it?

Keeping secrets was how he survived. And these secrets in particular? He would be a fool to volunteer them if there was no connection to Kendra Ross's death.

He also hadn't told Thia what her Sight had revealed, but that wasn't intentional withholding. That was timing.

Although, granted, he could have made more of an effort. "Your dead friend was involved with a *huldrekall*," he could have said. A matter of seconds.

He was unfamiliar with the ways American cities organized

themselves, but "city manager" sounded like a high position of influence—exactly the sort of thing *huldrefolk* were drawn to, but not necessarily with nefarious intent.

As with the *sidhe,* a few bad apples, so to speak, had put the whole tree under suspicion.

That Neil Amundsen was a *huldrekall* could be important or it could be a meaningless distraction. He hadn't been in a hurry to get into that with Thia.

What if it connected with his interests? *Huldrefolk* outside of northern Europe were not unheard of but they were rare. How did one come to be in Granite Springs? The nearest city to an unattended leyline portal?

He did not know who ran the facility where Cassandra had placed part of Idris's collection, but there was one particularly nefarious family that had been heavily involved in the shipping trade (among other activities) for centuries. A possible connection could not be ruled out—yet. That he would tell Thia what she had seen was inevitable, but his instincts were screaming at him to take care.

A late afternoon smog had settled over the whole valley, the product of woodsmoke and heavy interstate traffic. Cormac flew higher, into colder but cleaner air.

The sun was low, ready to sink behind the mountain range to his left. It cast a gentle, rose-gold light and turned the thin smog into a visually pleasant, pinkish haze that softened the crisp lines of buildings and other man-made objects.

Discomfort, as if someone poked the back of his mind with a stick, caused him to call on his Sight.

He could identify no immediate threat. Nothing directed at him specifically. He narrowed his focus to that single feeling of quiet, persistent unease.

There. He would have noted it earlier if he hadn't been so muddled by other things. Other people.

Cormac altered course, headed toward a magnificent black

cottonwood. Its winter-bare branches provided a visual feast of twists and angles, an elaborate dance of nature, performed at a tempo slower than an eye could measure. She stood alone in a grassy lot within a chain-link fence, protected from the neighborhood that had sprung up around her.

No, not protection. As Cormac drew closer, the better he understood.

There had been a fuss, the tree told him in the montage of memory and sensation that the oldest, strongest specimens were able to convey. A man had come and told the children not to play on the branches and the adults not to rest against the trunk. The tree was dangerous and its time had passed, the man had declared. She was to be cut down so houses could be built. The city needed more homes for its people.

The tree's friends had resisted. The fence had been put up instead, to protect the people from the dangerous tree.

But the tree felt as vital as ever, she told him. Her branches were strong; her trunk, sturdy. She did not *feel* dangerous, and could not comprehend why the man had called her so.

She disliked being separated from the neighborhood, but that was better than being removed altogether. Other trees had not been so fortunate. In a matter of months, some of the oldest guardians had been felled.

That's what Cormac had detected—the faint unease which ran beneath the surface. The trees were afraid.

● ○ ●

Landmark Hotel

Quentin had not gone off on his own. At least, not in the way Edith meant. He was, in point of fact, corporally inside his hotel room. Consciously, not so much.

From where his physical form lay in the gap between bed and wall, he had heard Edith outside the door, but in a vague way, irrelevant to his present, trance-like state. He might have heard his mobile and judged that slightly more relevant had he not neglected to retrieve it from the bathroom sink after his attempt to shower the agony out of his hip. The resulting humidity had been soupy despite the automatic fan, which was why he had been in a hurry to shut the door on it, and why neither he nor Edith had heard the ringing.

In the place where his consciousness had gone, a fetid mist rolled in, swiftly obscuring the graveyard landscape. Noxious droplets clung to his skin and soaked into his hair and clothes. Back in the hotel room, his pulse picked up.

Hoofbeats and the distinctive, squeaking rattle of a specific horse-drawn coach grew louder. Closer. He turned toward the sounds. Braced himself, little good that it did.

The coach-and-four emerged from the mist. Not a single lantern or bit of gilding relieved the varnished black.

When the Coachman drew his team to a halt, the lead horse was near enough for Quentin to feel the breath from its flared nostrils. No average carriage horses, these four, but colossal, intimidating beasts whose eyes could flash red to match their master's mood.

"You disturb my work."

At the voice, Quentin suppressed a shudder. He would not cower, not this time. Nor would he look at the coach windows. It would not do to see what—who—might be inside.

"You are always working," he said.

"True." The cloak's deep cowl hid the Coachman's features. His skeletal hand, starkly white amidst so much black, made an impatient gesture. "On with it, then. Ask what you will."

"Two deaths. Murders. Both in the heart of Granite Springs. Both within a day. *This* day."

"I do not collect all the world. As you well know."

A chill ran down Quentin's spine. Illusion, or his consciousness affecting his physical form. Either way, he would want a second shower after this was done. "Did you collect these two?"

With a snort, the lead horse bobbed its massive head. The feathered plume it wore grazed Quentin's cheek.

He flinched.

The coachman laughed, and then, "Names."

Quentin's breath had frozen in his chest. He forced a cough. Inhaled. "Kendra May Ross. I do not know the other—that of her killer."

Time passed with nothing but the breathing of the horses, the stomp of an impatient hoof, the jingle of a harness, the flick of a tail. Not a sound came from inside the coach itself. It might be empty, its registered passengers not yet collected. He hoped that was the case.

Memories of his own ride were too fresh. Always too fresh. The velvet of the bench seat. The stifling, musty air. Brocade curtains had been drawn across the windows. He had grabbed hold of the nearest one, flung it aside so he would know where he was, what was happening.

He had been at the annex near Covent Garden. He had just recited the trigger words, and then . . . there he was, inside. The door's brass handle had been cold. Cold and immovable. No matter how he had tried, he could not—could not—

"Not mine," the Coachman told him now. He had said something similar that night as well, later. Much later, presented as an error when the reality had been an arrangement.

"Do you know *of* them?" Quentin pressed.

"I will inquire." The Coachman clucked his tongue, a signal to the horses. Quentin stepped aside as they began to move.

"My thanks," he said, and manifested a drawstring purse of gold coins. He had to hurry. The horses were almost past him; the coach itself—its windows—neared. He tossed the purse toward the Coachman. An easy catch, quickly tucked inside the cloak.

"Until next time," the Coachman said, and cackled.

Quentin jerked awake.

The spectral laughter lingered in the disorienting seconds before sensation returned. His body was shaking, chilled to its bones. Most of its bones, rather. The ones that bore the damage of his Great Mistake burned like fire.

For all that, this could have gone much worse, he judged before giving some consideration as to whether he would be able to stand or if it would be better to pull the duvet down from the bed and remain on the floor for a while.

He had learned nothing. Yet, payment had been taken. If there was information to be had, the Coachman would get it.

Which meant Quentin could anticipate another encounter. Another chance for things to go worse.

On a groan, he rolled over, began the awkward process of rising. His watch gave a time hours later than expected. By rights he should be ravenously hungry. Terror was a fine appetite suppressant.

He staggered to the bathroom, the first shower's steam long cleared. He was preparing to strip when he caught sight of his mobile. A series of notifications lit the screen. "Damn."

Propped against the sink, he scrolled through the missed texts. Several from Edith, perturbed to start and culminating with a threat to contact Beatrice. She had followed through on it, as each missed call proved: Beatrice's office, mobile, and home phones.

Thrice damned.

He picked the most recent number on the call log. On the second ring, Beatrice picked up, her voice so shrill that he struggled to make out the words.

Immeasurably tired, he interrupted his mother's tirade with a low, resigned, "I'm here."

● ○ ●

Yet again, Edith was having to knock on Quentin's door. Ten minutes prior, she had received a texted order from Assistant Director Meriwether: GET THE HELL UP THERE AND STOP HIM.

Stop him from what, Edith could only guess. Pills? Illicit magic?

The assistant director hadn't responded to questions sent, which had only added to Edith's bewilderment—and alarm.

There were no sounds from inside the room. How could the assistant director be sure Quentin was in there?

Edith gave up on the knocking and instead used her fist like a hammer. Too bad she hadn't the talent for pain dampening spells.

Had he been inside when she was here before? She hoped not. That was two hours ago. She hoped he hadn't been inside this entire time, possibly in distress. He hadn't responded to her texts. Two hours.

"Quentin!" She kicked the door. "Open the bloody—" Her next kick sent her stumbling past the abruptly yanked-open door and into the room.

"Do come in," he said from behind as she quickly recovered her balance. No one in the midst of a crisis could sound so bored.

Therefore, there was no crisis.

She turned around, glaring.

Quentin was smiling, damn him. He released the door. The hinge mechanism drew it closed. The deadbolt automatically engaged with a loud snick.

Curtains were drawn across the windows and there were no lights on, but Edith could see him well enough in the glow cast by the mobile phone he held to his ear.

"Yes, she's here," he told the caller. "Do you wish to speak with her?" His gray eyes were so intent on her that she felt pinned. "No? No helpful advice to impart on how to *handle* me?" He spoke the word as if it tasted foul, and she flinched. His smile returned.

"I believe you alarmed poor Agent Wilkinson," he said. "She reads like an open book—really, you ought not to send her out until she can better school herself, Bea. It's dangerous." Some emotion glinted in his eyes, there and gone yet so startling that Edith stepped back, bumping against the closed door of the closet behind her.

Something was off with him but she couldn't discern what. His pupils seemed normal given the low light. If he had medicated his pain, wouldn't they be constricted?

Really, it was unfair of the assistant director to have put this on her. She was an agent, not an adult minder.

"I will hold you responsible, of course." Said with such calm menace while his gaze remained fixed on her that Edith felt a spike of alarm. She was alone with him. Isolated.

He disconnected the call, slipped the phone into his jacket's inside pocket. Breaking eye contact at last, he walked past her into the room. It was only then that she noticed the cane in his left hand.

His limp was neither the best she had seen it nor the worst. What level of suppression might that indicate, she wondered, unconsciously flexing her knock-bruised hand.

She was trained in self-defense and, given his compromised hip or leg—whatever the injury was, she didn't know but it didn't matter. In a purely physical fight, she knew she could debilitate him enough to escape.

But with Quentin, no fight would be purely physical. And while Edith had some skill with magic, it was nothing to his.

"I need to sit," he announced, and promptly did so in the nearer of the two armchairs by the curtained windows. "Stay there if you prefer, although it's rather far for conversation." He set his cane aside, propping it against the small table to his right. "But perhaps you're here to lecture. That *is* why she sent you, I suppose."

His tone set her teeth on edge. She suspected he knew that and was doing it on purpose. He reclined in the armchair and, with fingers interlaced, settled his hands on his lean middle.

The picture of nonchalance if not for the fine tremor before he stilled. That decided it.

"I came by earlier," she said, and slowly entered the room. "You didn't answer, either the door or your mobile. I thought you had gone out." She felt his attention on her as, passing the foot of the bed, she deposited her phone into the side pocket of her satchel for easy access. She set that on the floor within reach and sank into the other armchair. "What were you doing?"

"No lecture?"

"Assistant Director Meriwether only said to stop you. She didn't say from what."

"Ah. Well. Too late there, but we can assume she had already gathered that."

A darkness had settled around him—one that had nothing to do with light or shadow—and Edith felt a sharp foreboding. The brittle tension, the mercurial moods. She wanted to take back her question.

She and Quentin might be sitting like two people having a casual chat after a tiring day, but her fear remained relevant. If he were to lash out, she had nothing to match his power. Her pendant might protect her to some extent, but *he* had been the one to craft the improvements. What if he had put in a failsafe for himself? A way to get past what he'd done? What did she really know about him?

Cassandra Swinton and her brother had been taken to be entirely trustworthy, and look how that had turned out. The Society of Brigantium continued to reel from internal corruption. The process of removing traitors was ongoing. Unknown numbers remained.

"Why did you come back?" she asked, and the color drained from his face.

"Come back from . . . ?" His voice actually shook.

"You were gone almost six years from the Society. Why did

you come back?"

"Oh, *that*. Of course." He laughed bleakly. "There isn't much else I'm suited for, is there? I am as yet her golden boy, after all. Despite having lost my luster." With a wave of his hand, he indicated his silver-gray hair. An attempt at a joke?

"I'm sorry," she said, wary. She couldn't gauge his true mood. "I shouldn't have asked. It's none of my—"

"It's a living," he said as if she hadn't spoken. Another laugh. "A life."

She knew her discomfort was plain on her face, and that he'd think less of her for it. More training, he had complained to the assistant director. Would that be enough? Could she change her nature?

"Why would you want to?"

She startled. She hadn't meant to say any of that aloud. It was an unfortunate tendency when under stress and lacking sleep. And when she was nervous. But it had never been this bad. "I want to be good at this," she found herself admitting. "I've wanted it as long as I've known such a thing was there to be done. And I . . . I don't know if I'm—" She gritted her teeth. Of all people to reveal her insecurities to. For Brigid's sake. Had she not just been chastising herself for being too open? Could she not manage to keep—She closed her mouth. The mouth that had only then stopped talking.

He was watching her closely. Too closely.

She noted the slight, malicious curve of his elegant mouth. The faint glow that changed his irises from gray to a light, luminous blue. It was not only that she was stressed and tired.

"You're *bespelling* me," she accused. Her hand went to her pendant. It hadn't warned her.

"No harm intended," he said by way of explanation for the failure. "And it's only fair. Tit for tat."

She fought to hold her temper. For practical purposes if not official assignment, this man was her supervisor. It would not do to get into an argument—even when one was merited.

Her mind locked on a word he had used: fair. She had asked questions; he had used spellwork to manipulate. There was nothing fair about that. "It was an intrusion," she told him, incensed.

When had it started? She recalled his awkward joke, when he'd gestured—at his hair, but potentially doing double duty as the cue to a spell. She had misinterpreted that moment as one of openness. She had offered him her sympathy! She had felt *sorrow* on his behalf. And he had been working her with a spell.

"The next time you wish to learn about me," she said tightly, "just ask."

His slight nod did not reassure. Nor did the flattery which followed: "Not every agent would have noticed it. Good for you." He retrieved his cane, positioned it as if to rise. "You can assist me in the alley."

She remained seated. She wanted to leave, yes, but not with him. And the assistant director had sent her rushing to *stop him*. Did that instruction include this?

"We've been over the alley," she said. "But we haven't shared our analyses from this afternoon. And I have updates—do you know about the meeting later, at Thia's? And the reading?" Without waiting for a response, she launched into a lengthy retelling of her lobby conversation with Thia and Abby.

After she had mined that for details, she moved on to one of food. "Have you eaten at all since London? You should." She had. "Room service is excellent. There's a halibut fish and chips with an amazing jalapeño batter." At last, she risked a glance.

His hands remained atop his cane, but he had reclined in the armchair. His eyes were closed. Beneath them, the shadows had deepened, emphasizing the contours of bone.

"Quentin?"

He twitched, as if rousing from sleep. His eyes remained closed as he languidly set his cane to the side. "Perhaps the alley isn't . . . necessary. Just yet." His head dropped back as he slid lower in the chair.

"Quentin," Edith asked, "did you hear anything I said?"

"I wasn't sure . . . " He was dozing off again. " . . . if it was wise." His breathing deepened, his head lolling as he relaxed.

She went to fetch a chenille throw from its decorative place on the bed.

"You'll want to eat before the meeting," she said, unfolding the blanket. She draped it over him, taking care to tuck the top edge behind his shoulders. The depth of her concern was as surprising as it was ridiculous.

He made a noise, sinking deeper into sleep, and she paused.

They were not friends. They were not even friendly. How could they be? Him, with his three first names that screamed (in as genteel a fashion as possible) old money and nobility; her, with her third generation Clapham roots and family-run yoga studio above, currently, a Thai restaurant. (Last year it had been a pizzeria, and the year before that a curry house.) He could destroy her career—her future—and hardly realize he'd done it, she ranked so low in his world.

His hair looked soft. Edith suspected that, if left to grow longer, the waves would curl. What had happened for it to go from golden to silvered gray? The Accident, of course, but what specifically? Nine dead. How had he survived?

She itched to ask. Everyone did, who had been around at the time. Yet no one dared. Afraid of his reaction? Or was it his answer they feared? First-hand knowledge of how dangerous the matters they worked with could be.

Belatedly—far too belatedly—she lifted her hands from his shoulders and stepped back.

No harm intended, he had told her earlier, about his intrusive spell.

In retrospect, it felt like a test. He hadn't remarked on *what* she had revealed, only that she had detected the spell. He had commended her on having done so and then told her to assist him in the alley.

What the hell had he intended to do there?

Unwise. As he drifted off, he'd said he wasn't sure if it was wise. Despite that, he would have gone there and performed spellcraft. What risks would that have involved—to himself but also to her?

She checked the time, made some calculations. Then she leaned in to keep her voice low. "I'll wake you in three hours." The air around him was warm. She touched the back of her hand to his forehead.

"Hm," he mumbled, stirring only slightly. "I'm all right."

She doubted that. But he didn't feel feverish. She lifted her hand—and instead of backing away, did what she had sworn she would not: She touched his hair. With light fingers she brushed errant strands from his brow, returning them to their proper place. Tidying, she told herself it was. She knew his appearance mattered to him a great deal, which was why the loss of his clothes and toiletries struck such a blow.

His breathing had slowed. She watched as his chest gently rose, then fell beneath the blanket. Her fingers rested near his left temple. Spellwork wasn't her talent, she reminded herself. Analyzing it, yes. Performing it, not so much. But the energy gathered, almost of its own doing, so she might as well put it to use. She spread her fingers, spearing them through his hair so that her hand cupped the side of his head.

"*Vitae et requies.*"

A basic healing spell. She sent the intention along with the power. Glowing white tendrils, startlingly bright. The room had darkened considerably since he had let her in. Little light crept past the curtain edges. The sun had nearly set.

Quentin shifted, his brow creasing as the energy began to

move along his scalp, following the contours of his skull. That was not what was meant to happen, but Edith should have expected it. Rejection. She withdrew her hand and the energy dissipated. She didn't have skill enough to reclaim it.

She turned away, went to where her satchel awaited with her equipment. The bed would make a comfortable place to work. Her room had an exact match, but it was less effort to stay.

While Quentin slept, at times fitfully, she reviewed the day's findings. She was afraid of overlooking something, anything, so she triple-checked all the data. If she were to misinterpret a reading or miscalculate an equation . . . .

Two lives had been lost. A mistake could cost another.

● ○ ●

Founders Way

Below where Cormac perched atop the electric pole, a vision crystal had been embedded in the wood. It had been cannily done, placed within the visual distraction of a cluster of transformer bushings. If he had not flown in the way he had, and landed how he had, he might not have located it so easily. If he had not expected to find something, he might not have noticed it at all. The pale crystal's surface was unpolished, not liable to catch the light.

Presumably it belonged to the O'Shannon.

How long it had been in place? Shortly after Founders Hall had been identified as being in operation, no question—but when had that been? It didn't matter to Cormac's purpose; he was merely curious. Granite Springs was proving to be a surprising nexus of international and Otherworldly intrigue.

That the vision crystal had undoubtedly been active during the past few days meant that Cormac might soon owe the leprechaun a second good turn. A weighty one, depending on how much had been shown of events related to Kendra Ross's death.

He almost regretted having located it.

How could he explain having come into whatever information the O'Shannon might provide? He would have to give that very careful consideration.

He had wanted to be done with his part in this tonight. He was prepared to attempt the doppelgänger charm and enter the building here and now. It would only require returning to human form, holding one of the discs, and triggering the spell. Once inside the building, once he located Cassandra's storage unit, he would either remove the goods immediately or set them up for later transport.

Then he could search—there must be at least one office for the running of the storage business—for evidence, details on the owners, and anything else of use.

It had seemed almost too easy, so of course it was.

Instead of a closed, darkened building and a deserted back alley, for the past half hour there had been a near-constant parade of people through a guarded doorway. Back and forth they went, carrying boxes from a white, unmarked van.

Cormac wasn't sure he should trust what had been printed, variously, on the boxes: Books, mugs, t-shirts. But those were things one might expect in a gift shop, and Granite Springs was a tourist town. To work this late on a Sunday was odd, certainly, but who was he to say when some retailer needed to load goods into storage? So far there was nothing to connect this to any other events of interest. And there was no way for him to get inside while it was going on. The slightest chance that Cassandra was known to anyone present was a chance too great.

The genuine Cassandra could go about her business, freely walking about the building. Cormac as Cassandra could not risk even a minor social encounter. Depending on the wards, mere suspicion could trigger alarms, lockdowns, or worse. He would have to wait.

CHAPTER 17

"I should offer coffee *and* tea, both," Thia said as she opened the wrong cupboard. This one held jars of spices and, randomly, a set of vintage ice cream dishes. Closing it, she moved on to the next—and found the familiar multitude of boxes and tins of tea, precisely where she usually knew them to be. She was nervous. She hadn't hosted a gathering since she had come up from Los Angeles. It felt significant. Proof that this house was to be her home.

To christen it with this group, for this reason? No wonder she was a mess.

Cormac took his tea with honey.

Thia left the tea cupboard ajar, crossed to the tall built-in Lettie had referred to as the pantry. Tucked amidst bottles of extracts and baking chocolate was a glass, bear-shaped jar. The substance within was pale; vaguely yellow and cloudy. "Is this still good?" She tilted the jar side to side. The stuff didn't budge.

"Honey lasts forever," Abby decreed from across the room. She sat at the bistro table in the nook beside the back door. The takeaway boxes of leftovers from the Taproom waited to get put in the refrigerator.

Ruffled curtains had been drawn across the many windows. The cheerfully pink-striped fabric was a stark contrast to the picture of exhaustion and grief Abby presented. She looked as if she hadn't benefited from her nap any more than Thia had from hers.

"It's really okay to serve it like this?" Thia held the jar upside down.

Cormac struck her as having refined tastes. Murphy was in the business of luxury hotels and fine dining establishments. When she met Quentin, he had been in formal evening wear, and for all she knew, Edith wrote British etiquette books in her spare time.

"This looks fossilized." She twisted off the lid, poked the purported honey with the tip of a spoon. "It *is* fossilized. I can't serve this. It's embarrassing."

The organic grocery was less than a block away via a public cut-through between two houses—but, no, it had closed at eight. Why hadn't she started getting ready sooner?

"Is there a way to re-liquefy it? Hot water?" She got a sauce pan, filled it from the tap.

"Why are you in such a state about this?"

"I'm not." Thia put the jar in the pan. "Am I?"

"You are."

"I am." Sighing, she set the pan on the stove. "I really am. I can't seem to help it." She turned on the gas flame, stared at the flickering orange and blue. "Cormac puts honey in his tea."

Abby's silence held palpable displeasure.

"It isn't just him." Thia turned to face her. "It's everyone, and what we're doing after. Someone died there, and Madame Demetka plans to *communicate*"—she used air quotes—"about it. You know how weird things get with her in *normal*"—more quotes—"situations. Of course I'm in a"—she stopped herself from a third use—"state. I'm scared."

"So am I," Abby said. "About tonight in the park, and what happened to Kendra, and what kind of danger we might be in. And what makes it worse is that it's brought *him* back into your life. It would've been better if he had stayed gone—hear me out," she said when Thia would have jumped in. "Cormac is *Otherwordly*. How many centuries has he been alive—and doing what? What sorts of things for his mad-sorcerer father and no doubt for himself too? Stealing? That would be the least of it. I'm not saying he's a bad *sidhe*-person or whatever, but he has done bad things."

"Right. You're right." It wasn't anything Thia hadn't already told herself. She should give more consideration to Cormac's past, about which she knew next to nothing.

"The more time he spends in your life, the more his life will end up in yours," Abby said. "How many Cassie-types do you think there might be for him, waiting to take revenge? How many people—and Others—do you think he's pissed off over the centuries? And, unlike with Cassie's thing against you, he probably actually wronged them. He's an invitation to danger, and you have enough of that already. More than enough. Look at what's happened."

Thia nodded. What could she argue? Everything Abby had said was right—yet it wasn't *everything*.

She had presented negatives. There were positives, too. Not as many, maybe—but they weren't talking about columns to be tallied on a balance sheet.

And people were more than their past deeds. What about the grays of extenuating circumstances? What about who the person had become? Thia wouldn't judge someone on their past alone.

Maybe she had no business judging someone at all.

She had been over and over and over these same arguments with herself already and gotten nowhere. She would not pick them up again, tonight, with Abby. They were both too tired and too stressed.

She checked the stove. The honey's color had changed. Its clarity, too. She poked the spoon through the open top. Much more pliant. "Good enough," she declared and turned off the flame. Using a hot pad, she took the jar from the pan, set it beside the sugar bowl.

"He's not worth the effort."

Thia stiffened. It seemed Abby was determined to walk into a conversational minefield. "Please let it go, Ab. For tonight? I just—I can't help what I feel." She went to the refrigerator. "I'm attracted to him. Drawn to him. I miss him when he's not around." She poured milk into the pitcher from Lettie's tea set, returned the carton to the fridge, and then jammed the pizza box in after. "He matters to me, and this is the first time he'll be here, inside what I'm trying to make my home."

"He *matters* to you," Abby parroted. Her disapproval hurt more than Thia would have expected. Probably because Thia shared some of it herself.

She hadn't told Abby everything—all that Cormac had done in his attempt to get the Stone of Shadows, how he actually had been to the house before, but outside because he hadn't been able to cross the wards. He had worn a glamour, and she hadn't known who he was, and—if she was to be exact—he had attacked her. She and Cormac had never spoken of that either, although sometimes she wondered if he still had her old phone, dropped during the scuffle.

She hadn't told Abby the magnitude of her feelings, either. How she had told Cormac that she loved him when she had believed he was dying, and another time after inadvertently summoning the explosives. Also the next day, when she had invited him to spend Christmas with her and believed that— Well. She had assumed that he had been trying to say he felt the same. But he had left, and . . . flash forward to tonight.

She placed the already-filled teakettle on the stove. After a moment of consideration, she lit the burner. It was early, but water that was already warm would be easier to bring to a boil when it was time to serve.

"He saved my life," she said, adjusting the flame's height. "A number of times. I know he's done bad things, Abby. I do know that. Even if I don't know what they are."

What if they were truly awful? She knew he had killed— she had seen it, when he'd defended her against attackers and fought at the Ring of Brodgar. But had he ever *murdered?* She couldn't imagine it, but what if that was a failure on her part? What if her instincts were wrong? He had been in service to Idris Cathmor, after all. Or as Abby had put it, his mad-sorcerer father. Had he inherited that same madness—that same need for power?

Yet if he had been acting in service out of self-preservation, could she blame him? If his choice had amounted to "do this terrible thing or be tortured or die," should she judge him as irredeemable?

It was too many hypotheticals with too many unknowns. What she *did* know was that, "He's risked a lot for me. For all of us."

"Gained a lot too." Abby was not wrong there, either.

Cormac had absorbed some of the power, too, when he had helped Thia with the Stone. Idris's death had meant Cormac's freedom. His half-brother's death—and his half-sister's later imprisonment—meant there were no challengers to his being Idris's heir. Yes, Cormac had gained a great deal from helping.

Preparing to brew a fresh pot, Thia emptied dregs from the coffeemaker. "I am aware that he could be using me."

That was the history of the whole of his life, wasn't it? Using people? Close to three hundred years spent in manipulation and deception and, when he could, self interest. She'd learned that much from the Brigantium, if not the specifics. Of course he could be using Thia. He could be using everyone.

"I can't help what I feel."

For a time, the kitchen was silent but for the hiss of the

stove's burner, the growing rumble of water in the kettle, the rattle of coffee beans as Thia poured them into the grinder. The click of the lid. The scrape of Abby's chair when she got up.

"We can't help what we feel," she said, joining Thia at the counter. "But we can guard against it. Here." She nudged Thia away from the grinder. "Let me."

"Is my coffee really that bad?" Thia asked, dismayed but not surprised.

"No," her friend said, and then smiled. "It's worse."

● ○ ●

Cormac knew countless ways to kill. Poison, slow or quick or something in between. Weapons. Bare hands. At a distance. Up close. He had faced more lethal threats than there were days in a year. He could summon ancient power to his fingertips. He could call down a storm to ravage the whole of this valley. With a single thought-driven spell he could set fire to the tree upon whose limbs he perched as a raven. And, not twenty-four hours ago, he had walked into Brigantium headquarters at risk of capture, torture, and death—and done it with barely a fraction of his current reticence.

Should he come down from the cedar branch, there was but a short walk through Thia's front garden to her door. He was expected, so the wards surrounding the property should be a nonissue. Yet here he remained.

Much as he would prefer to ignore the root of this astonishing cowardice, he could not. Survival often depended on eradicating weakness—whether real or perceived.

He was nervous.

Early in his acquaintance with Thia, he attempted a *leanan sidhe* enthrallment. Instead of binding her to him, for a time he feared he had done the reverse and bound himself to her. How else to explain what he had then done for her, against his own interests? The decisions he had made, the way he had endangered himself and his plans. Never before had physical attraction so clouded his judgment.

Never before had he lost sight of who and what he was and what he wanted.

He had since determined that a botched enthrallment was not to blame. Or, he had *mostly* determined. He did revisit the possibility from time to time.

But he could not deny that there had been something from the start. Before they had met, even. Her bright, smiling face in a photo. Her voice speaking through Leticia's phone. *I love you,* she had said then. Words intended for another, yet, inexplicably and irrevocably, they had sunk into him like hooks.

More had since joined them; the same words, repeated to him directly—perhaps to bind him to her as thoroughly as any *leanan sidhe* spell.

Cormac caught sight of Murphy entering the block from the southwest. The Irishman's manner was deceptively lazy; his power uncloaked to serve as a warning and a taunt, both, for anyone attuned to such things. *Stay away* or *go ahead, come at me.* He stopped at the base of the cedar and looked up.

"I hadn't taken you for a coward," he drawled, and Cormac launched himself off the high limb.

Tempting though it was to put talons to Murphy's power-illuminated eyes, Cormac aimed for the ground and reverted to his native form. His boots hit the pavement with a force that jarred from toes to teeth.

"I was early," he said as he straightened. "I've been meaning to say, that's quite a shiner you've got. Anything we should know?"

"Fuck off." Murphy reached over the short picket gate to lift the latch.

Laughing, Cormac followed him up the path to the covered porch. His amusement was short-lived, subsumed by a resurgence of anxiety and his internal debate over the O'Shannon's red book. Time, there, was ticking.

It was his private business. Emphasis on private. Yet if it should be revealed in the course of events, better it should be done by him, and sooner. Later would mean more . . . mess.

As to the O'Shannon's vision crystal, Cormac's phone call had gone unanswered and as yet there had been no response to the message he'd left. Since he had no way of contacting the leprechaun directly, all of that would have to be conveyed via whatever notification system was in place. Time, in other words. It could take some time.

At the sound of an approaching vehicle, he looked back.

The Brigantium's SUV pulled up to the curb. If someone had told him a few months ago that he would be working with agents from the Society of Brigantium, *Deglán Murchada,* and two amateurs to solve the murder of a woman to whom he had no connection, he would have recommended that same someone for Bedlam. Yet here he was. Here they all were. He joined Murphy at the door.

Edith bounded up the steps while, back at the street, the motor shut off. She came to a stop on Cormac's left. "Were we meant to bring anything?"

"This isn't a dinner party," Murphy groused, then twisted the mechanism on an old fashioned bell. A cheery peal sounded inside the house. Behind them, Quentin's cane thumped on the wooden porch boards.

"It is not," Edith agreed, undaunted. "But we're guests. It would've been polite."

This was not a dinner party, no, but it *was* an occasion of sorts. And novel, considering how Cormac usually visited a home: breaking and entering; slipping uninvited into a party for reconnaissance or theft; to take part in acts of a purely physical nature.

Wine? That was a typical gift on a social call. On the flight to London, Thia drank a Merlot, but as the choice had been between "red or white," that wasn't precisely informative.

As shown through the door's leaded glass inserts, a figure approached, easily identifiable by how she moved. A seductive combination of efficiency and grace.

Spells learned in youth were second nature, a simple matter of power and decision. The bottle materialized in Cormac's left hand. Beside him, Edith's startle drew attention.

That was the problem with those early spells: They were so quick to perform there wasn't time to reconsider the impulse.

"For fuckssake," Murphy said.

"Mead." Quentin's brow arched. "Really."

"I think it's nice," Edith said, and Cormac's humiliation was complete.

At the snick of a deadbolt being undone, his pulse trebled. The door swung open and there was Thia, bathed in gentle, welcoming light, and even as Quentin jostled him on his way by, Cormac found himself unable to move.

As the others filed past with easy greetings, Thia directed them in the taking off of coats and scarves. Her hair had been pulled back more neatly than earlier and gave emphasis to the simple beauty of her face. "Abby is in the kitchen—please go on through, you can't miss it," she said with a gesture to the left.

Turning back to Cormac, she cocked her head. They were alone for the first time in weeks. A smile played about her lips. Her eyes sparkled. "Do you need special permission? For the wards?"

"No." Weakness, not spellcraft, kept him outside. He held out the bottle he'd summoned.

Her smile widened, discomfiting for its honesty. Whatever she presumed about the gift, he should tell her she was wrong. She was wrong about him.

But he didn't, and a blush rose on her cheeks. "Thank you," she said as she reached out, covered his hand on the bottle's neck with her own.

The contact sparked, or perhaps that was simply Cormac's surprise when she leaned in and touched her lips to his cheek in a brief kiss. A customary greeting, so often perfunctory, but it rattled him.

In the second it took him to recover, she slipped the bottle from his grasp and slid her arm beneath his. Thus linked, she brought him across the threshold.

Inside was warm, bright, and unnervingly familiar because he had known the house's prior inhabitant, Thia's great-aunt. Not well—they had been face to face less than a handful of times—but there had been a string of years when their paths frequently crossed as a result of competing interests. Despite the stakes, he had enjoyed matching wits with her.

"There's coffee and tea," Thia said, leading him past a staircase and into a sitting room reminiscent of Leticia's London townhouse. There was no design to the choices, but there was undeniable style: furnishings from the early-to-mid twentieth century, of good quality and numerous. A pair of sofas and several chairs, end tables, side tables, a coffee table, and—of most interest—a multitude of glass-fronted cabinets, filled to bursting in a kind of visual anarchy of curios and books. Dark-stained woods and richly autumnal colors.

The wall art was whatever had captured the buyer's fancy: a watercolor of the Thames here, a pencil sketch of a terrier there. It was all very much Leticia, and in some ways, Thia too. Bright, complex, vastly interesting.

"Abby made the coffee," she said, as if he should find that reassuring. She must have noticed his confusion because she smiled. "Mine is horrible, apparently." She laughed.

He suddenly felt too warm. With his free hand, he unzipped his jacket. He had been distracted, to say the least, when he'd entered and hadn't thought to remove it.

Thia was taking him toward an open turn. The front room

flowed into a dining area—more crowded cabinets lined the walls. Adjacent to that was the kitchen, from which voices and sounds of activity emanated. Through the doorway, he saw Abby attend to a kettle on a gas range.

Cormac stopped. And because they were arm-in-arm, Thia stopped with him.

"Would you rather I opened the"—she checked the bottle's label—"mead? Oh, that's brilliant, thank you. I've only had it one time before, and that isn't a good memory." Her pleasure dimmed. "Not that tonight will be good, either. Maybe we could wait? I'd like to remember it well. Do you mind?"

She had mistaken his reason for stopping. Coffee, tea, mead, he had no preference at the moment.

"Here." He slid his arm from her grasp and took the bottle. "For another time." He went to place it on a sideboard. The move took him out of view from the doorway and next to a corner cabinet. Its open shelves were filled with anything and everything. Art deco sculpture, Roman glass, a set of salt and pepper shakers proudly hailing from someplace called Gold Beach, and—

"Bloody hell." Grouped with a clockwork mouse and a rusty coin bank was a chunk of sandstone no bigger than the palm of his hand. Its top jagged for having been broken almost a thousand years ago, the front and sides were covered in runic script. So was the back, as he had cause to know.

In 1953, he had been sent to collect it from an archaeology club in Trotternish.

"See something important?" Thia joined him. "Lettie has— *had*—so many things. I'm clueless about almost all of them. I should have asked her when she was here, but there was so much to talk about the store and the website and family, and future plans, and almost anything else. Then she went away on her trip, and . . . ." Was killed. She didn't need to say it.

He picked up the stone. It was cool, the surface rough. The

carvings were worn; some, nearly worn away. The weight, or the association with his past grounded him. He took his first easy breath since he'd stepped inside.

"Leticia got there first," he said, idly running a finger over the symbols. "A crofter happened upon it while repairing a drystane wall. He took it to a group of amateur archaeologists and made the local paper. This was well before the internet, so Idris didn't learn of it until a full week after the printing. He sent me. I missed Leticia by two days. Too late to catch up with her."

"What would you have done if you had?"

Perilous ground. "Taken it from her."

"Yeah, I figured. I meant how."

"Any way I could," he said, irritated. This was what he did. This was who he was. "Leticia knew the risks. Unlike those archaeologists on Skye, she wasn't an amateur. She knew what she was getting herself into when she went after artifacts."

"I'm sure she did." Thia's hazel eyes sparked—not in a show of power but with temper. "I guess what I want to know is if you would have hurt her over a chunk of carved rock. Maybe I need to know how far you'll go to get what you want."

"*I* didn't want it." Unaccountably bothered by the implied accusation, he thrust the stone toward her so she was forced to take it. "What was it to *me?* It's a list of names, probably a practice carving—which Idris could damn well see from the newspaper photos. But he wanted it. *Idris Cathmor* wanted it, and what Idris Cathmor wanted, Idris Cathmor got."

For a time she said nothing and Cormac had the fascinating experience of watching Thia's mind at work. Thoughts played across her face as easy to read as a children's primer. He had a sinking feeling that she had experienced something similar with him.

His outburst, he feared, had been revealing.

Thia was fiendishly perceptive. Her inexperience made that

easy to overlook. Lack of knowledge, however, did not equate to lack of intelligence.

"Idris didn't get what he wanted *that* time," she said, all trace of temper gone. "He would have been very angry, I imagine."

"Idris was always angry."

"I did get that impression, yes." Unexpectedly wry, she startled a laugh from him.

"Well." He smiled. "It was rather hard to miss."

She smiled back, and then stepped close in order to put the stone back on the shelf. "Did you and Lettie do that a lot? Go after the same things?"

Again she surprised him. She had seen what Idris could do when in a rage. She must wonder what had occurred when Cormac had returned empty-handed to Fiend's Fell.

But instead of prying, she asked about her great-aunt.

"I'd love to hear what she was like," she said, as Cormac had more and more difficulty concentrating. They stood almost exactly eye to eye, thanks to her heeled boots. Her face was mere inches from his. "As a kid, I only knew Lettie through quick visits and phone calls and presents wrapped in extreme amounts of tape. It feels as if I was only here with her a little while before she was gone—and now all her things are mine. This house, the one in London, and everything in them." She gestured widely to the room, to the house and its shelves and cabinets. Its walls covered in framed paintings and sketches and photographs. "I know there isn't time tonight, but maybe you could tell me about her?"

He should have anticipated this. Leticia made for a natural topic of conversation. What would be in it for him, though, other than the risk of exposing parts of his own past?

Goodwill and access.

"Of course," he said. "And if you need help with her various collections, we could go through them." He paused. "If you'd like."

"Funny you should offer that. Beatrice did, too."

"How kind of her."

"Isn't it?" Thia seemed perfectly naïve—until she rolled her eyes. "But, really, thank you. I *will* consider it."

"If you can trust me."

Sounds from the kitchen intruded. A kettle nearing boil.

"I have missed you," she said, as if burdened. "It would be so much better if I hadn't."

"It would."

The tea kettle whistled; the stove was shut off.

"If you don't mind," she said, stepping up to him, "I've been wanting to do this." She slid her arms under the open sides of his jacket to wrap around his waist.

It was a simple matter of closing his arms to bring her snug against his chest. Her head settled on his shoulder, her face turned toward him. Her exhale feathered over his neck.

Ifrinn. Ah, bloody *ifrinn.* His head tilted, the angle somewhat awkward, so he could breathe in the scent of her. She felt so right, pressed against him. A perfect fit. "Thia."

Sounds of kitchen activity increased and she moved to pull away.

"Wait," he said, even as he let her go.

She stood beside him, braced for the audience to come. "I hoped my feelings would change," she said in a rapid near-whisper that cut like a knife. "I wanted to feel differently the next time I saw you. If there was a next time. But I don't. It's the same. My feelings haven't changed at all."

From the kitchen, Abby brought out a tray of fruit, crackers, and cheese. "All set," she said cheerfully while glaring murderously. At Cormac, of course, not her friend.

He would think it amusing if he *could* think. Thia had no need of assistance from anyone on that front. Consider how, with only words as her weapon, she had gutted him.

She was smiling at the others as they exited the kitchen. "I'm sorry." She gestured to the steaming mugs they held and to Abby's tray. "I meant to do all that. Cormac was telling me about a piece in Lettie's collection."

Not a lie, but not easily sold as truth, either. Not to this group. There wasn't a one who struck him as being particularly unobservant.

● ○ ●

Obviously, Thia had said too much. Cormac was looking as if he'd been stabbed. She could almost find humor in it, since the first time she had told him, he *had* been stabbed. Bleeding out, or so she had believed.

Why had she said all that now? It was like her brain had shut off and she'd gone on autopilot. A malfunctioning autopilot.

"I'll just grab my drink," she called to the others, already in the front room, and went into the kitchen.

Cormac followed.

Of course he did. This was where the drinks were.

"Coffee or tea?" she asked, choosing one of two remaining mugs for herself. Emblazoned with the image of a sea lion, it was a souvenir from a city on the northern California coast.

She had done it again. She had told Cormac that she loved him and his response, as before, had been . . . less than ideal. What was the saying, the one about the definition of insanity? Doing the same thing over and over and expecting a different result? She pushed the carafe back into position with more force than necessary.

There was a minor difference this time; she hadn't said the words outright. As if allusion would protect, what, her pride? It hadn't protected her heart, that was for sure. That felt as bruised as it ever did coming out of these exchanges.

Someday she'd learn.

But, really, would she? Moreover, did she want to? Love was

love. Whether or not it was reciprocated had nothing to do with what she felt.

She could change what she *did* with it, though. She could put an end to moments like these, when she took her deepest emotions out of their protective packaging and offered them up for display. She could stop inviting rejection.

Cormac had yet to answer about his drink preference, and Thia was done. Done fixing her mug of coffee, done being alone with him this way, done with his non-responses.

"You should be able to find everything you need." She waved vaguely at the things on the counter. "The honey is probably okay." With that, she turned to leave.

"Wait."

Shock—and hope—rooted her to the spot. But what he said next was such a non sequitur she couldn't make sense of it. Literally. The words made no sense. "Hold or call."

"I'm sorry?" She turned back around to frown at him.

He stood as he had been, but seemed even more uncomfortable. "What you saw earlier,. The city manager. It's a kind of shapeshifter." He spelled the strange word, then repeated it. "A *huldrekall.*"

"Seriously?" Her mind was short-circuiting, thoughts versus emotions. "I've never heard of—You couldn't have mentioned this earlier?" She managed not to shout. Barely.

"There wasn't time."

"Only because you haven't tried. What the absolute f—You could've just—You know what? Never mind." He was staring, his eyes wide. Too bad she was too furious to enjoy having so obviously unnerved him. "It's fine. This is fine. I'd wanted to talk to everyone about what I'd seen, and you can tell us all about . . . ." She couldn't recall the word.

"*Huldrekall.* That's the male. *Huldra,* female. *Huldrefolk* for the plural."

"Great, thank you. That's great." She left to join the others.

<h1 style="text-align:center">CHAPTER 18</h1>

"All is in readiness for the morning?"

On the other side of the desk, Eindride stood at attention. "*Já*, Skati. We are coordinating the transport of supplies to the mayor's home with the scheduled arrival of your brother's *fjolmenni*. We should have everything and everyone in place by ten."

"Fine. I want anyone who is not directly involved with the party deployed on site, armed and ready. But for the love of *Vánagandr*, be covert about it."

"You expect trouble, Skati?"

"Always expect trouble. Then you'll never be disappointed." Skati flicked his hand in dismissal and his adjutant backed out of the office. After the door closed, he locked it with another flick of his hand, then checked the room's wards. He pulled over the scrying mirror, removed its leather cover.

He did not have to wait long. His eldest brother was invariably punctual.

"It's all set," he said after Agnar's face was displayed. There was no need for greetings. They no longer had that sort of relationship.

"*Så langt, så godt.* My people will complete the transit by nine fifteen local time."

"Our people, brother." Always, they would try to cut him out. "*Our* people."

Agnar's ice-blue eyes narrowed. "You may make that claim should you prove to be successful, Stig. Not before."

"And so it shall be."

"Time and experience have not yet taught you the dangers of overconfidence."

"The plan is brilliant," Skati said. "You know it is—you and father had enough of a hand in it. With flawless execution, it cannot fail."

His brother's laugh was not born of amusement. "It is to be *flawless,* then? You give us no margin for complications? For unforeseen obstacles? Already there have been two events of significance which have brought unwanted scrutiny. Ah, Stig," he said when Skati failed to hide his surprise. "Did you not think we would receive reports on your handling of the task we set before you? Come, come. For your many faults, you have never been a fool."

"No," Skati said through clenched teeth, "I have never been a fool. I am aware of the threat from Declan Murphy and his allies—and I assure you it is *in*significant." He watched his brother's face closely to see if he bought the lie. "My *rekkrs* outnumber them. Even if they work out what is planned, they will be unable to stop it. And afterward, they will present no danger."

"You understand why we continue to have concerns."

He did, but it grated. "I am handling this, *bródir.* For years, I have been handling this. If father had not summoned me to Nidaros for so long, the yuletide stupidity with Idris Cathmor's daughter would not have occurred. That posed more of a threat to our plan than this." So he hoped.

Agnar studied him for a troubling stretch of time. Yet at the end of it he said only, "I will relay your confidence to father. Do not fuck this up, little brother." The connection ended.

With a roar, Skati sprang from the chair. The scrying mirror was in his hand. He came to his senses halfway through the throw and instead returned the relic to his desk.

● ○ ●

Elkhorn Park

"Remind me why this approach is necessary," Thia grumbled as she and Abby descended the trail from the reservoir at the park's elevated southern end. After the Brigantium's vehicle had deposited everyone there, Cormac went to act as "eyes in the sky" while the rest split up to arrive at the scene from different trails. Thia's booted toe hit something on the trail and she stumbled.

The moon was out, which gave enough light to see by, but not as much as a flashlight would. "When I fall and break my leg and an ambulance has to come get me, it'll attract all sorts of attention."

"Just because I didn't argue against it," Abby said, sounding just as annoyed, "that does not mean I'm in favor. Not that I mind getting away from *him* for a while. Even if it's only for a few minutes."

"Cormac?"

"Him too."

Ah. Since there had been no clashes at the meeting and relative quiet in the SUV on the ride over, Thia had presumed that Abby no longer held Murphy in active contempt. Wrong again.

Abby remained upset with Murphy, Thia was newly upset with Cormac, and Edith and Quentin—she didn't even know what the mood was between them. Never a smooth sail, from what she'd seen, tonight had been all swirling undercurrents and treacherous swells. It was a wonder the meeting had gone as well as it had. ("Well" being a relative term, she supposed.)

Much information had been exchanged—about Amundsen being a shapeshifter, Edith and Quentin's analysis of the area around Founders Hall, and Cormac's discovery that Granite Springs' oldest trees were afraid.

Yet what did they really know? They had a puzzle and they had pieces, but did those pieces go to that puzzle?

A raised wooden walkway along an eroded bank was coated with ice, forcing them to walk single-file in order to use both handrails simultaneously.

"We picked the wrong trail," Abby complained, performing a skating-like glide instead of lifting her feet.

Behind her, Thia opted for short, precise steps. What they lacked in length she made up for with speed. "No. The upper trail is crazy narrow." She had tried it in summer daylight. The views were amazing, but with so much time spent watching her feet and worrying, she barely noticed. "Narrow and steep, too. The paved road"—tonight's third option—"is better for Quentin." Although parts of that could be iced over, too.

"He was walking fine at your house."

"True." Thia caught herself as her foot slid. "But I think it costs him."

Abby grunted, either in agreement or to mark the end of the walkway. She stepped onto the dirt path, waited for Thia to catch up.

"We should have left sooner, though," Thia said moments later as they hurried down open trail. The absence of cover aided visibility—which wasn't necessarily a good thing. Easier to see meant easier to be seen. "I didn't realize how long this would take."

"Madame Demetka won't start without us."

But Thia could tell Abby was uneasy. "Won't that depend on her Guides? Has she ever said who or what they are? Do they even exist?"

"You're just asking that now?" Abby laughed, then, "But, the answer to all that is, 'who knows.' I'm not even sure she could tell you."

Entering wooded cover, they slowed to a walk, their breaths pluming—Abby's less so.

"How can you not be winded?" Thia's lungs were burning.

"I've been working out. Since I was—since what happened up at the lodge." She didn't like to talk about when she had been hurt. It had been serious enough that she'd taken a week off work.

"You joined a gym?"

"Oh, goddess, no! I mean, not really. The owner of Circle Fitness is in my coven, so I get a discount."

A portion of washed-out trail had completely frozen over. Using low branches for balance, they crept around the edges.

"It's mostly Pilates and yoga, but there are a couple of weight sets and a few cardio machines," Abby continued. "The tread-mill has been great for taking out frustration."

"I should try that," Thia said. "Clearly I need more cardio."

"I can probably get you a guest pass."

Thinking she would rather be outside—parks, hiking trails, neighborhoods—she was about to turn down the offer, but then remembered she had switched her work commute from walks to drives for good reason. Of course she couldn't start walking more around town.

"Security is good?" she asked.

Past the ice, they picked up the pace.

"It's not great," Abby said, "but I could get it increased."

Thia figured that was a good idea regardless of her joining. While suspicion in Kendra's death may have fallen away from Cassie and Idris Cathmor's followers, that didn't mean they wouldn't be trouble in the future. They or anyone else might target Abby as a way to get to Thia.

There was a short bridge ahead. "We cross here, right?" she

asked.

"Yep. Almost there."

"And nobody fell down." Taking firm hold of the rail, Thia stepped onto yet another icy plank.

"Don't jinx it," Abby joked, again implementing her skate-like glide.

"What would Kendra feel about this?" It had been nagging at her. "What we're doing, I mean. Not just tonight, but all of it."

Halfway across, Abby stopped and leaned her arms on the rail. Thia joined her. It was true, Madame Demetka wouldn't start without them. Moonlight sparkled on the fast moving water below. Brilliant flashes of silvery white on liquid black.

"She'd be afraid for us. She'd want to rush in and defend us from whatever threatened. She'd be furious that she wasn't here to keep us safe." Abby took an audible breath, blew it out to mist over the creek. "She'd feel guilty if we put ourselves in danger on her account."

"How can we not?" Thia wiped at the tears about to spill down her cheeks. "Especially if we're already in danger."

"Yeah."

"This is bigger than her, bigger than any one of us, isn't it." Not a question, to Thia's mind, but rather a reluctant under-standing. "It's bigger than any business of Murphy's, legal or otherwise." She spoke over Abby's quick objection. "There's something in the way things are changing. Things such as the mess of the Plaza's redesign process. The new welcome signs. All of the public art installations that have most of the public upset. Tree cutting, when there are still more benefits from those trees than drawbacks—and despite protest. As if citizen input doesn't matter. There's something off. Fundamentally."

"I feel it too. And he's not responsible for those things. He's pissed about the Plaza." Abby's sigh was nearly lost amid the creek sounds. After a moment, she turned, set her lower back against the rail. "Have I been too rough on him? No, don't answer that. But I won't apologize. I'm still not sure."

● ○ ●

Amazingly, they were not the last to arrive. That honor fell—literally, by the looks of him—to Murphy. Dirt-streaked and dotted with bits of leaf and other debris, his clothing told the tale of at least one significant tumble.

"What?" he snapped in response to several bemused looks. Cormac chuckled, and Murphy's eyes flashed bronze.

Moonlight could have done that, coming through the trees at a particular angle, but Thia still braced herself when Abby walked toward him.

"Have you seen the state of that upper trail?" Head down, he was shaking leaves and twigs from his wool coat. "A right fucking hazard it is." He straightened at Abby's approach. His eyes were definitely glowing. "What now?"

"Just this."

He flinched when she reached up, took a leaf from his hair. She handed it to him and then spun on her heel to return to Thia's side near the same stretch of tape they had stood by earlier. Beyond it, Madame Demetka used a lengthy stick to mark a circle into the frosted ground.

Murphy had not moved. But his eyes had lost their angry light. He looked, Thia thought, rather lost himself.

"Is good we are all in attendance now," Madame Demetka boomed, straightening. Her volume made a mockery of their attempts at stealth. This part of Elkhorn Park was secluded, but there were homes within that kind of sound range. Fancy homes whose occupants might not appreciate after-midnight disturbances and wouldn't hesitate to phone in complaints.

"Please to enter now." Tossing the stick aside, she stepped into the circle's center. "I will close this behind you and—"

"A moment," Cormac said mildly. "If you'll indulge me."

"The old magics!" She stretched out her arms and whirled to face him. Her cloak billowed. "Of course, of course. Please, be guest."

From all directions, fog began to roll in, thick and white.

"Oh, brilliant," Edith exclaimed.

Druid Fog. Thia was fairly sure, anyway. She had been in it twice before. Old magic indeed, and perfect for this. Unless a person had permission to be inside, the fog would confuse and disorient. It would also mute and conceal whatever took place within.

"Did you know he could do that?" Abby asked her.

"No."

Whatever was done within the circle—no matter how loud Madame Demetka became—the fog would contain it. Should police intend to patrol the area, they wouldn't be able to get near. And, most likely, they would never realize why; they'd simply believe they had misremembered the right way.

"*Misto!* A most excellent addition," Madame Demetka said. Extending her arms above her head, she looked to the night sky. Her wide sleeves dropped, exposing elbow-length, purple knit gloves.

Thia hoped they were lined. The night was bone-chillingly cold. She pulled her scarf up to cover her mouth and nose.

"My Guides are amused by this fog trick. Children they are at times." Madame Demetka lowered her arms only to then make a frantic sweeps. "*Av akai*—Come. Come, come, come. They are impatient."

In typically chaotic fashion, she arranged everyone—"boy, girl, boy, girl"—around the circle's inner perimeter and then returned to its center. "I will be focus. Like rod of divination. Excuse please, I now close circle." She shut her eyes, tipped her chin to her chest.

The Druid Fog was a white wall around them, with none of it above. Moonlight was absorbed and reflected, brightening everything within.

Thia tried to gauge reactions. Did the others think all this was legitimate, or were they simply humoring a charlatan on the off chance she might get lucky?

It was impossible to tell.

The arrangement had placed Cormac to her right but with roughly three feet between them, too far to talk. She would ask him later. Murphy was the same distance to her left. Abby stood to *his* left, and Quentin to hers—directly across from Thia. Edith completed the circle on Cormac's right.

"Is excellent time in year." Madame Demetka opened her eyes. "Imbolc is almost upon us. A time when omens abound and answers may be freely given. My thanks for joining here this night. Your talents and energies add to my call. I do so now." She picked out one necklace from the mass of crystal pendants, charms, and beads she wore. At the chain's end was a silver bell. She rang it, the sound no louder than what a cat might be made to wear.

She shut her eyes so tight that her brow furrowed. "We seek answers, if it pleases to give. Answers to sorrow and tragedy. First, the death of a friend, killed by the young man dead in this place." She gave the bell another shake, then released it.

Her body snapped to attention. "My Guides, they warn of *wafti* schemes. An egg rotten beneath a plain shell. Not to be trusted, but in a position of trust. *Pah!*" She shook a fist toward the sky. "You tell me all this before! Is nothing new. I ask about the young man, the one who—" On a gasp, she staggered back a step. Her hands clutched at her necklaces, held them out as if they might ward off whatever she saw, or believed she saw.

It hadn't occurred to Thia to use her Sight. Now that it did, she didn't want to. *Really* didn't want to.

"I-I bring message. From spirit realm." Madame Demetka's volume was as absent as her confidence. "Message from the

Coachman." She turned around, putting her back to Thia, to tell Quentin, "He has answer for what you asked of him."

Murphy swore—foreign words that conveyed shock, maybe even alarm, and Thia's fear spiked. Her view was the absolute worst. She couldn't see Madame Demetka's face, couldn't see past her to Quentin. She turned to Cormac; his view was better and maybe he knew—as Murphy seemed to—who or what this Coachman was.

Cormac's brow was furrowed, his mouth tight. Not abject fear, but revealing enough tension to kick Thia's anxiety up another notch. Noticing her attention, he looked over.

Silently, she mouthed, "What's happening?"

He made a slight shake of his head. Either he had no idea, either, or this wasn't the time to explain.

One thing, however, was clear: This was no longer Madame Demetka's reading. The Coachman—whomever or whatever that was—had come seeking Quentin.

"The b-boy," Madame Demetka said thinly, "was corrupted. Weak of mind, easy to use. He was not himself. He knows not what he has done . . . or what was . . . done to him." On a moan, she bent forward at the waist.

Instinctively, Thia stepped forward, prepared to put a stop to this. That's what she wanted, anyway. It wasn't easy to read faces at a distance by moonlight, but she could tell that no one else had moved. Maybe it wasn't her place to rush in.

"Last he knew, he was seated by Plaza." Madame Demetka remained folded over with her hands braced on her thighs. "Waiting outside pizza place. Sitting on sidewalk. He finds it funny, to sit near to the City Hall door. Fun to heckle people there. Good money will start when the tourists return and he'll be ready. Leonard Jackson DeWitt. Age—" She sucked in a loud breath and arched back, her arms flung wide as she did an extreme version of jazz hands. Her bracelets jingle-jangled wildly. "*Kite m 'pou kont li!* Away! You got something to tell this

Society man, you tell him yourself!"

"Son of a biscuit." Sally dropped to her knees and pressed her hands to her face. "Give me a minute, y'all."

● ○ ●

There would be no more from Madame Demetka—or Sally Wilson—that night. When she felt able to stand, she declared that her Guides had fled, and then she asked for a ride home. That threw a wrench into their exit plans, but Murphy volunteered to accompany her to the road above the park, to be met by a Landmark car.

Thia tried to keep her face from freezing while those who had things to do went about doing them. Edith was running her scanner over the circle's center; Cormac was down at the creek where the body had been found.

They had a name, if the hijacked reading could be believed. Leonard DeWitt, who had not been in control of his actions.

So, who had been? No progress had been made whatsoever on that front. They were all to go to Kendra's apartment next. That had been the plan, anyway, before this.

"You'll meet us there?" Abby asked Murphy.

"I will not, no. I've arrangements to make, whether the Ross family likes it or not." He offered Sally the support of his arm.

"Didn't they take over . . . everything?"

"It's my hotel." His jaw clenched. "The vigil will be in my conservatory. The wake will be in my ballroom. And besides that, she was one of mine. My responsibility."

She looked at him a long moment, as if she might speak, but then she walked away without a word. Nearing Thia, she held up her wrist, tapped her watch. "We should get going."

Checking her own, Thia groaned softly. Nearly one in the morning. As Murphy and Sally/Madame Demetka headed out into the Druid Fog, she gauged the others' readiness. Cormac was presumably still at the creek—or maybe he had left the country, who the hell knew. Edith, scanner no longer in hand, was approaching Quentin where he leaned against a boulder.

"I'll see if we can get a move on," Thia told Abby and began to walk to them.

In the windless cold, Edith's voice carried. "What *was* that?" So did her anger.

His response was a mild, "What was what?"

"You know what I mean."

"Not now." He looked pointedly at Thia, nearing.

She felt her own anger. They were supposed to be working together. All of them, equally. She was fed up with feeling left out of a loop she was meant to be in.

"When?" Edith pressed. "I won't be put off forever."

Quentin used his phone to place a call. "I am not walking all that way again," he told whoever picked up. "Meet me at the second car park from the top." Pocketing the phone, he projected his voice toward the creek with the skill and precise diction of an actor trained to the stage. "Cormac. The driver needs to get through the fog."

"I'll involve the assistant director if I must," Edith said. A clear threat. For her to do that, the situation with the reading must have been bad. Bad enough to have been dangerous?

Quentin set his cane to take weight, then pushed off the boulder. "I am well aware, Agent Wilkinson." He limped past Thia and onto the path between towering rhododendrons.

"What's going on?" she asked Edith.

"It's nothing," the agent said, only to then shake her head. "No, it's not nothing. I'm meant to keep an eye on him and he knows it. I feel like a failed spy and a disloyal friend—not that we're anything like friends. But he needs watching, doesn't he?" Pensive, she turned toward where he had gone, no longer visible through the fog. "And after this . . . I don't know what that was in the reading, but it came to speak to him. As if it was familiar."

"Familiar? As in 'a familiar'?"

"Oh, *Brigid,* I hope not. That would be—" She visibly shook off the unfinished thought. "I only meant that the entity was familiar with Quentin. And of course he won't talk about it."

"Of course." No one ever wanted to share.

● ○ ●

Dogwood Lane

The night was definitely going to count toward cardio, Thia thought as they walked toward Kendra's street. It could also count as another exercise in stealth. The SUV had deposited them several blocks distant where it and Paul, the Brigantium agent driving, would await their return.

"Can you cloak the neighborhood in Druid Fog?" she asked Cormac, at her side.

"I could," he answered, "but it might draw attention. By the creek in the woods on a night like this, fog could be expected. Not so much here."

In the lead, Quentin raised a closed hand. Everyone quickly moved off the sidewalk into deep shadow. There was plenty to be had thanks to Granite Springs' erratic relationship with public lighting. This was one of the many residential blocks without.

At the three-way intersection ahead, a police cruiser eased by, patrolling Kendra's street.

After the sound of the engine faded, walking resumed.

"Does this mean they aren't parked there," Thia asked, "like with a stakeout? They're doing patrols instead?"

"Could be both," he replied. "These things usually depend on priorities and resources."

"It's a small force."

From behind, Abby said, "To do both would pretty much put a lie to the mugging-gone-wrong-followed-by-accidental-death theory they're going for."

"Even so," countered Edith, glancing back from her position near Quentin, "we shouldn't chance it. The police might not be watching all the time, but someone else might be—from anywhere."

"Right." Remote means, either through cameras—drones—or magics. If Thia wasn't pretty much asleep on her feet she might've thought of that; but the caffeine from her pre-park coffee had long burned off. She was operating on willpower alone, and even that was flagging.

Several feet from the intersection, they took another pause. The lighting by Kendra's apartment, unfortunately for their task, was excellent.

"Allow me." Cormac studied the sky. "I should think I've got more experience in this sort of thing."

"Undoubtedly." That was from Quentin, and wry.

"Be careful," Thia said. She didn't waste the effort of asking him what he was about to do.

He might've smiled. "Naturally."

To her surprise, he hurried back the way they had come.

Abby glared after him. "Where does he think he's—"

He stepped into someone's yard, out of sight behind a tall wooden fence. A black shape took flight. A raven, briefly illuminated when it flew past a lighted window.

"Oh," Abby said.

"Amazing." Edith sounded awestruck, and Thia felt better about her own reaction. If a trained Brigantium agent could be awed, Thia might not be as hopelessly naïve as she feared.

A *pop!* drew her attention to Kendra's street. A second *pop!* and a streetlight at the intersection went out. Down the line, the next light caught the silhouette of a passing bird. Then it too went out. *Pop! Pop!* The length of the street.

Being as covert as their particular group of four could be, they made it to Kendra's building and up the stairs without apparent incident.

When they reached the balcony, Cormac spoke, startlingly, from somewhere ahead. "The wards are intact."

Thia began to make out his shape as she neared. Together, they moved to the other side of the door so Abby could use the key.

Her hands shook as she selected one, struggled to insert it in the deadbolt. "I'm hurrying," she said, then missed the first two tries with the knob. "I'm hurrying."

Her shaking had gotten worse.

"Let me." Gently, Thia took the key from her. She unlocked the deadbolt, then the knob. Twisting that, she pushed open the door. "Do you need to go through the wards first? Or can you stay outside?"

"I should go in. Otherwise they might trigger. I'll be okay. I can do this."

"Of course you can."

Abby took a moment, like a diver on a high platform, before she took the plunge. She didn't get far inside, remaining shy of the door. Everyone else followed, with Cormac and Edith going to different windows to draw the blinds. Abby shut the door, set the deadbolt and an extra security latch.

"Is it safe to use lights?" Thia asked. "I can barely—"

The room brightened.

"It won't be visible outside," Cormac said. A glowing white sphere hovered above his upturned palm. *Wanfýr.* It remained where it had been created, floating, when he turned to take in the layout: main living area on the left; open-plan kitchenette and dining on the right; bedroom and bath ahead.

He went over to Quentin and Edith. She was making broad gestures and saying something about needing scans.

Thia couldn't shake the feeling that they should have asked permission before intruding. Like Kendra might walk in and demand to know what the hell they were doing. At first, that was the only change Thia noticed—the pressure to hurry.

Kendra had only ever been welcoming.

As Thia looked, she saw only what she expected. Sectional sofa. Glass-topped coffee table. Shelf unit. Furniture that was on the spartan side of modern, with the overall impression softened by decorative touches like framed Monet prints and vases of silk flowers. There was a pom-pom fringed throw on the back of the sofa,

Upon closer inspection, the police's work became evident. A trio of framed family photos were absent from their place on the low television cabinet. Books were no longer in orderly lines on shelves but in haphazard stacks.

"Well, shit," Abby said, drawing attention to the worst of it: The computer was not on the dining table. A printer, plug strip, and cup with scissors and pens were the only evidence that Kendra had used that spot as her home office.

"This can't be normal procedure," Thia said, going there—as if standing at it would make a difference. Gone was gone.

Cormac joined her. "For a mugging, I imagine not."

"This was a waste of time." And emotion, she added silently, looking to where Abby leaned against the closed door.

Cormac's attention followed Edith as, scanner in hand, she went into Kendra's bedroom, but he asked Thia, "Have you tried your Sight?"

"I didn't think of it." And she didn't want to, not after what had happened earlier.

Which must have shown on her face. "Don't trouble yourself," he said. "Mine's not showing anything. Kendra wasn't a practitioner?"

"No. At least, not that I know of. Why?"

His gaze idly traveled the room. "No evidence of spellcraft aside from the external wards. So, either the space has been thoroughly cleansed or there was never anything."

"No readings," Edith announced, leaving the bedroom. "I'm sorry. I'd had higher hopes for this." She gave her scanner a disappointed shake before stowing it in her satchel.

"The point was her computer," Abby said. Her voice was unsteady. "But they've taken it too. I don't understand this."

Nor did Thia. "What will the police do with it all? They're ready to close the investigation, right?" That's what Murphy had said. "If they return her computer, we could access it. But will they?"

"And when would that be?" added Abby. "*Now* is when we need it. Tomorrow might be too late if she was killed as part of something bigger."

"Do you think Murphy could use his influence to get us into the station?" Thia checked the time. Good grief. "At half past one in the morning."

"Could you get us access?" Abby asked Edith. "Through the Brigantium? Pull some international, legal strings?"

"I'll call the—"

"There are two mugs here," Quentin said from the kitchen. Thia hadn't paid much attention when he had passed behind her. He stood by the drying rack. "She had company on her last morning."

That brought Abby in from the door. "I didn't know things had gotten that far."

"With Amundsen?" Edith asked.

"Yeah," Abby said. "I'd have thought she'd tell me."

"Does it matter if he was here with her?" Thia asked. "Or when? That wouldn't necessarily tie him to the—" She rubbed her forehead. A dull ache was making it impossible to think. "He's not . . . ."

"Thia?" Cormac's hand came down on her shoulder, gave a gentle squeeze. The headache cleared. She opened her eyes— and was surprised to find him so near, his face inches from hers. In the *wanfŷr*'s soft glow, his irises were a rich, twilight blue. "Better?"

She focused on the deep black of his pupils. That and his

touch helped anchor thoughts which wanted to scurry. "I was remembering this afternoon, when Abby and I were talking with him outside and—"

Behind her, a heavy object slammed onto the kitchen floor accompanied by breaking glass and a clatter she would later attribute to a dropped cane. She spun around.

The eat-in counter obstructed her view.

"Shit," said Cormac, who had gone around. He was bumped by Edith, rushing in past him. Thia followed as far as space would allow. More *wanfýr* appeared overhead, lighting what had been deep shadow. Quentin lay supine on the beige linoleum, his body shaking as in a seizure.

Edith dropped to her knees, reached out as if to grab his arms. She stopped before contact was made. "I don't know if it's safe. Is it?" she asked Cormac, standing behind her. "What am I able to do?"

Quentin's eyes were shut tight, his mouth a thin line as the muscles of his jaw and throat strained. His right hand gripped what was left of a ceramic mug, his spasms making the jagged edges a danger to himself and others. The way his hand kept striking and shifting along the floor, he'd be lucky if he didn't cut himself on the shards scattered there, too.

"Get that out of his hand." Cormac had also noticed the mug. "Try not to touch his skin. Here"—reaching, he tossed her a black leather glove from the counter.

Edith's hands were trembling, making for a clumsy attempt.

Thia's sense of helplessness intensified. "Should we call an ambulance? I could—"

"No," they said in unison. Abby had abstained.

Edith hadn't gotten the glove on all the way, so the fingers were flopping, half-empty; but she was proceeding. While her other hand pinned Quentin's lower arm—his clothing must act as enough of a barrier—her mostly-gloved one worked to pry the handle from his grip. "Let go. Let go, dammit."

"Allow me." Cormac set his booted foot above her hold on Quentin's arm. That solved the problem of erratic motions but not his grip.

"Really, I think we should call an ambulance," Thia said.

This time, she was ignored. She ventured a couple of steps into the kitchen. Maybe there was something she could use to help. A towel might not be enough protection, but what about an oven mitt?

She looked to the counter—where the dish rack held only one mug, not the two Quentin had mentioned. That had been *his* glove on the counter, she realized. He had removed it to take a reading, as he had done in December, when they had been trying to locate Zoe. It had rendered him unconscious then, too, but not for long, and not like this.

But no wonder no one wanted to involve paramedics.

"I can't," Edith said. "I can't get it. Not without—I'm sorry. I'm sorry." With her bare hand, she took hold of Quentin's wrist.

His eyes shot open as he gasped, his body gone rigid. Edith fell back, the broken mug in her hand.

"That got you back, did it?" Cormac asked with a smirk as, lifting his boot, he stepped away.

On a low groan, Quentin rolled over, planted his hands in preparation to rise.

"Careful," Thia warned. "The broken pieces."

"Stay down," Edith said with more force. "Give yourself a minute, at least, you bloody—"

Surging to his knees, Quentin lunged for the counter, pulled himself up to get his face over the sink. He retched.

"Can we call an ambulance now?" Thia got her phone. Now that they had moved past the magical-mystery element of the emergency, maybe they could get to the medical help part.

She was voted down again with the addition of Quentin's garbled, "Don't," as he spat and turned on the tap. He cupped his hand beneath the flow but enough of a tremor remained that not much water reached his mouth.

"Glasses are in the cupboard above," Abby told Edith, who had begun to search.

She found one, filled it. Because Quentin now used both hands to keep himself up, she held it so he could drink. He swished loudly, spat that out, and then let himself slide into a slouch against the under-sink cabinet.

"He needs an ambulance," Thia insisted to Abby, who had come to stand beside her.

"Or the Retreat."

"I'm fine," Quentin said, doing such a poor impression of it that Thia's concern only increased. His voice was faint, his skin a pasty white.

"He's not walking to the SUV, that's for sure," Abby said.

"No," Edith agreed. "But we can't just have it pull up outside and all of us get in. Not unless we want to give up on stealth."

He might have said, "I'll be fine." The words were so slurred it was difficult to say exactly. "Just need . . . minute. Or . . . two."

"Before you pass out"—Cormac used the toe of his boot to nudge Quentin's shin—"tell us what you saw."

"Bland looking fellow. Neil."

"Neil Amundsen," Abby said. "He *was* here with her."

"Spent the night. Made coffee. His mug." Quentin made a slight gesture with his right hand.

"You picked the mug he used."

"Random . . . luck." He seemed to rally. "I went—I looked deeper. What Thia saw. Two faces. One he wears. One he is."

His head tipped forward and his body went limp.

"Quentin?" Edith dropped to him and, heedless of her bare hands, touched his cheek as she leaned in, her ear near his mouth and nose. She took hold of his wrist, set fingers to a pulse point.

"He's all right." Cormac sounded bored.

CHAPTER 19

Headlamps off, the Brigantium SUV left Kendra's street. There had been no option but to call for a ride, with Quentin in and out of consciousness. Cormac kept close watch out the windows. He didn't pick up on anything of concern, but that didn't mean their actions had gone unnoticed; it only meant that no immediate action was being taken against them.

At the boulevard, the driver switched on the lights.

Cormac made a final check through the rear window, then settled tensely onto the bench seat. He and Thia were in the last row, the middle seat empty between them. Not much of a separation, but it might as well have been a chasm.

He wanted her.

It was as simple as that, physically, and more complicated in a way that was so unfamiliar to his experience that he could not put words to it. Or perhaps his incredulity prevented it. He had little experience with that category of emotion.

Thia noticed his attention. Her frown suggested that she was annoyed by it—or by him, full stop. She leaned forward to peer over the back of the middle bench. "How is he?"

Edith's head came into view. "I don't know. I wasn't trained for this."

"He's fine," Cormac said. He had been the one to carry the agent to the SUV. He had placed him inside, laid out on that seat with Edith. And all it had gotten him was a crick in his neck. He rubbed at it.

"So you keep saying." Edith turned her brown, worried eyes his way. "How do you know?"

Uncomfortable, he shrugged. "I checked."

"You had better be right," Abby said from beside the driver. She held her smartphone. "There's no answer at the Retreat, so that's out." They had intended to take Quentin there.

"To the hotel then, Agent Wilkinson?" asked the driver.

Edith was frowning fiercely at Cormac. Trying to gage his truthfulness, he assumed.

"He's fine," he repeated. "He needs rest, is all."

Her eyes narrowed. Such was Cormac's lot in life—tell the truth and still be doubted for a liar.

"Okay," she said, at last. To the driver, she said, "Yes, Paul, back to the hotel."

Before Cormac could think better of it, he moved forward, reached over the bench-top. "Lift his arm."

"What?"

He waggled his fingers. "Here."

"Why?" But Edith was already doing as told. Quentin's arm came up, his hand flopping limply as the SUV jounced its way through an obnoxious series of speed humps.

Cormac wrapped his fingers around the wrist. The skin was cool but not cold. The agent was not in great shape, but he wasn't too bad off, either.

"If you hurt him," Edith said fiercely, "his pendant will kill you."

Cormac almost smiled. "It can try."

He knew (was almost certain) that it would not. Whatever

danger he faced here was not from a bit of charmed jewelry but from suspicion—Edith's and that of the armed driver.

Normally, he would perform this spell silently in Cumbric. In the interest of not getting shot, he used the Latin common to Brigantium spellcraft. And did so aloud.

"Quiesce et accipe hoc donum. Dormi pacifice usque aurora."

Glowing white threads of energy snaked from his hand to Quentin's wrist where they flickered, crackling faintly as the correct neural pathways were sought.

Found. The energy sank into the skin, faintly illuminating its path up the arm before going out of view under the agent's sleeve. Muscles tensed, then relaxed. The gift, as it were, was accepted.

"Doing all right back there, Agent Wilkinson?" the driver asked. He was watching in the mirror when he should have been concentrating on the road. Edith bent down, dropping out of Cormac's sight below the seat-back.

"Yes," she answered after what he felt was an unnecessarily long moment.

Her head reappeared briefly. "His color is better," she told him before going back out of sight. Pulse was better, too, as Cormac could feel.

"Satis," he said. *Enough.* He cut the energy and let go.

"You spelled him to sleep." Edith, lowering Quentin's arm, again looked over the seat. "Until dawn, you said. Is there a failsafe?"

"If there's need, he'll wake. It's a true sleep, not a coma."

"Right. Good." She turned to face front. They had reached the town center.

Cormac slouched back and folded his arms across his chest. He had not given anything he could not afford—the energy could be replenished soon enough when he was away from prying eyes—but it *was* a loss. Not unlike the experience of a quick drop in blood volume, he was left feeling a bit woozy.

As he allowed his eyes to close, he wondered, vaguely, why he had made the effort.

"You all right?"

He opened his eyes. Thia leaned as close to him as her seat-belt allowed. Light and shadow played across her face as the SUV passed beneath and between streetlamps.

"Fine," he said, but he wasn't, really, and her being within reach didn't help. She was so beautiful, in a way that had as much to do with how she looked and how she moved as it did with who she was. He craved the gentleness, the generosity, the genuineness of her. Everything, really. At times, he feared she might be everything he could want.

This. This was why, at times, he suspected the enthrallment in London had been turned back on him.

She frowned, pulling away. Likely she had seen something in his expression and he didn't dare consider what. With the energy loss, his defenses were not at their best.

She turned to call up to the driver, "Can you drop us at my house first?" To Edith she said, "You don't need us to help get Quentin inside, right? The other agent is at the hotel?"

"Should be. If not, the staff can assist." Edith, too, called to the driver. "Paul? She's right, we should let them off first."

"Thia?" Abby asked. "What's going on?"

"I'm exhausted," she said with a glance at Cormac. "We all are. There isn't anything we can—or should—do tonight. And if we don't get some sleep, we won't be any use for anything tomorrow, either."

"True enough."

The SUV turned down First Street. They would be at Thia's house shortly. For a second time, Cormac let his eyes close. Whatever he felt about the prospect of parting for the night, of going to his impersonal, empty hotel room, Thia was right about the need for sleep.

A light touch on his sleeve startled him—he truly was tired

if he was allowing his awareness to drop off so entirely. Twice she had startled him in the past ten minutes.

"That was kind," she said in a low voice. "What you did for Quentin. Generous." She took her hand from his arm. Such a slight thing, but he felt its absence keenly.

"Doesn't sound like me."

"Doesn't it?" She studied him a moment, then her hands, clenched in her lap. "I was hoping to ask a favor."

He waited.

"Would you mind staying at the house? With *us*," she said with particular emphasis. "Abby and me. There isn't a guest room available, but the couches are comfortable. It's just that . . . . I don't know, probably we should all stay at the Landmark, but I'm sure"—her voice lowered further—"that Abby would rather not. I know the wards on the house are strong, but with you there, it would be even safer. Will you stay?" She was so earnest, so without guile.

The SUV slowed, turned into the gravel drive alongside her home.

She trusted him. Him. How ridiculous, given their history— which she knew as well as he.

And their present, which she did not.

● ○ ●

Railroad District

Exhaustion meant Thia couldn't think straight. Couldn't walk straight, either. She was a pinball, ricocheting off one stationary object to the next. From the SUV door to the hood; hood to gatepost; gatepost to porch railing; railing to door—where she had coordination issues with the key.

Hearing the SUV begin to back out of the drive, she paused to wave goodnight. Abby was coming up the steps. Cormac had latched the gate. Both moved slowly, as if they were as weighed down by the day as Thia. In Abby's case, it would be surprising if she weren't. But Cormac? He had extraordinary healing abilities. Thia had known him to recover from an otherwise fatal wound in minutes.

Her suspicions were likely correct: What he had done in the SUV had come at a cost.

"Why is he here?" Abby asked, not moderating her voice as she crossed the narrow porch.

"I invited him." Finished with the locks, Thia opened the door, gestured for her to go ahead. "I didn't think you wanted to stay at the Landmark, and we could use someone with his abilities. In case of trouble."

"Is that the only reason?"

Thia trailed her into the kitchen. "What?"

Abby grabbed the coffeemaker's carafe from the collection of clean dishes by the sink and began filling it from the tap. "You know what I mean. You said it yourself. Despite everything, you're attracted to him. Drawn, was your word." She poured the water into the coffeemaker's tank, set the carafe under the drip chamber. "You're using safety as an excuse."

Sounds behind her made Thia turn.

Cormac, having closed and locked the door, leaned against it. He had to have overheard, but all Thia could perceive was weariness—the same weariness that had prompted her invitation. Abby was partly right: Thia used the security offered by his presence as an excuse to get him here, but not out of desire. She was concerned.

"The wards are excellent," Cormac said blithely. "Some of Leticia's best work."

"With augmentation," Abby told him curtly, and proceeded to deal with the coffee filter and grounds in the noisiest way possible. Every action involved a bang, tap, or slam. "We're capable of protecting ourselves."

His only response to the antagonism was a slight tilt of his head. The control he had over what he did and did not reveal was masterful—and fascinating. Thia was a poor card player for the same reasons he would make a brilliant one.

He crossed one ankle over the other. "Have you linked them to your mobiles?"

"What?" Thia asked. "We can do that?"

"There's an app. The Brigantium could have put you on to it. Then again, I expect they dangle knowledge like a carrot. What better way to get you to join?"

"Thia will make up her own mind." Abby, jabbing at buttons on the coffeemaker, programmed it for the morning that was only a few hours away. "No one pressures her into anything."

Thia was far too tired for this. "I'll get sheets and things for the couch," she told Cormac on her way from the room.

"Do you, uh, need help with . . . ?"

She turned, and he made a vague gesture. "The sheets and things?" she repeated, and almost laughed. Centuries old, able to transform into a raven, and helping with such a mundane activity. "No, thank you. But they're upstairs. I'll just go—"

"*I'll* get them." Abby walked out past her. "Since I'm going up. I'll toss them down. Meanwhile, Cormac," she said from the dining room, "why don't you tell Thia more about *huldre-folk?* For instance, what they have in common with the *leanan sidhe.*" She stormed out of view.

The sound of her foot-stomps declared her path through the house. Living room, stairs, upper landing—

"I'd better be there to catch," Thia said, rushing. She arrived as a pillow landed on a heap of top sheets and a lilac fleece blanket at the base of the stairs.

Despite Abby's fury, on her way upstairs she had turned on two lamps. The living room looked cozy. Inviting.

"Goodnight, Ab," she called, although Abby was nowhere in sight.

After a pause, there was a faint, "Goodnight, Thia," and the bedroom door's surprisingly docile closing.

Thia bent and gathered up a sheet. When she straightened, Cormac stood near the end chair of the dining table, a few steps shy of the living room. She was alone with him—truly alone—for the first time in weeks. In her own home, in the very late hush of night. She used the material in her hand to gesture between the two couches, identical with red velvet upholstery. He could take his choice: the one along the front wall or the one set perpendicular to it and serving as a room divider, with the staircase and front door several feet behind. "Which would you prefer?"

"Either." He approached with his hand extended. "I can do this. You don't need to—"

"We'll both do it." She gave him the sheet. It was patterned with daisies and cornflowers. From the couch parallel to the stairs, she removed the back cushions, stacked them on the floor. While Cormac worked to lay that out, she went to get the other. It had red poppies.

"Here."

He took the two corners she offered; together they spread the poppies over the daisies and cornflowers to make a floral mismatch. Next went the blanket. "What did Abby mean," she asked, "about *huldrefolk* and *leanan sidhe?*"

"They're both shapeshifters." He tucked the bottom edge of the blanket between the couch arm and seat cushion with efficient, practiced motions.

"And that's all?"

His hands stilled and he tilted his head up to meet her gaze. His eyes caught the lamplight.

They were the sole feature he could not transform—their color, anyway. A mixture of grays and blues surrounded by a darker ring. Thia found them beautiful. Found *him* beautiful, really, in the fierce, thrilling way of storm clouds and roiling seas. Unpredictable. Dangerous.

Currently, as struck by the light from Lettie's Murano-glass lamps, they were a piercing blue.

"They both seduce," he said, and returned to his work with the blanket.

Thia went to collect the pillow from the floor by the stairs. Its case was from yet another floral set. Wisterias.

"But *huldrefolk* must shapeshift in order to do it," Cormac continued. "The *huldra* is said to be inherently alluring but she needs to hide a tail. The *huldrekall*—thank you," he said when Thia handed him the pillow. He took it to the other end of the couch, where the sheet and blanket were turned down. "He has to do much more than that. You saw why." Instead of placing the pillow, he held it against his chest almost distract- edly as he looked at the readied bed. He was frowning.

"I can get another pillow," she offered. "I use two myself, so—"

"No." His shoulders moved as he took a deep breath, sighed it out. "No, I'm just . . . tired, is all. Not thinking clearly."

"I know the feeling." When he looked over, she gave him a rueful smile. "I've been struggling since before we left the park."

His gaze returned to the makeshift bed. "What is this?"

She considered being snarky by mistaking his meaning, but because he sounded genuinely confused and "genuine" from him was such a rarity, she instead asked, "Between us?"

He nodded, still looking at the bed.

Earlier, a compact barrel chair had been set opposite the low table in the middle of the seating area. The joins creaked when Thia lowered herself into it. "Speaking for myself," she said, knowing she shouldn't but doing it anyway, "I'm caught in an intense attraction and not thinking clearly because of that coupled"—she had *not* meant to say that—"with extreme exhaustion. I won't dare speak for you, since you're cagey and an excellent liar. So if it's one-sided, that's—"

Fine, she would have said but for his muttered oath.

He dropped onto the couch, much in the way of a puppet after its strings were cut. His head tipped back and he lifted the pillow, pressed it down over his face.

"Of course this isn't one-sided," he said, extremely muffled. "I wouldn't be here if it were."

"Here, tonight? Or here, in Granite Springs?" She needed to know if this was about a short-term opportunity she had handed him on a metaphorical platter when she had asked him to stay the night, or something potentially more that he had initiated when he had chosen to accompany Brigantium agents through the portal. Had he, in fact, returned because of her?

The sound he made could have been a groan or growl. He flung the pillow aside but kept his head back and eyes closed. Hidden. The hollows beneath were pronounced. "I need to— there are things that need doing. Things I can't afford to put off."

It wasn't a direct answer—hindsight and rumination would later reveal that it wasn't any answer at all—but Thia was too caught up in her own emotions to notice now. And perhaps she wouldn't have cared if she had. What she heard, what she responded to, was that Cormac had admitted an attraction to her, and with his return, had again put aside his own interests in favor of her safety.

"I'm sorry," she said, although she hadn't been the one who started this whole chain of events. Idris Cathmor had, when he sought the Stone of Shadows. To a lesser degree (or was it the same degree, but Thia felt lesser resentment) Lettie had set portions of the chain in motion as well. It was Lettie who had sent Thia the Stone. Lettie had caused Thia to become a target, first of Cormac and his father, then of Cassie, and who knows who else at this point. If not for Lettie's choices, Thia would not have ended up with the Cailleach's powers.

Thia was her own person, yes, and made her own decisions, but the initial events, the larger scheme—it was as if she had been set in motion on someone else's chessboard. This was not the life she had arranged on her own. "Do you ever feel like a pawn in someone else's game?" She asked, and startled a laugh out of him.

It was not the good kind: the short, nearly soundless huff. This one lasted for some time and held such bitterness that she cringed.

"You saw how he was," he said eventually.

She had. A cursed charm had transported her to where Idris Cathmor was. She had witnessed him berate and then assault Cormac over perceived slights and failures.

No wonder Cormac had laughed. He had been a pawn until the night Idris died.

"I learned early," he said, "to deny anything that mattered. Otherwise, Idris would use them. What I liked, what was—" He swallowed visibly. "What was dear. He would make it into a weapon. To punish, to control. Always to control."

Such cruelty was so far outside Thia's experience, she could scarcely comprehend it. He had lived it for centuries. Words were woefully inadequate.

The rise and fall of his chest was the only indication that he was not as calm or as detached as his features presented. The rate seemed slightly fast; the motion a bit shallow.

Cormac had killed Idris on Orkney and he had been dealing with the repercussions ever since. He could have stayed away, doing what he said he needed to do, yet he was here, involving himself in whatever danger surrounded Thia and her friends. He had done the same back in December, but that had tied directly to the events on Orkney and to the Stone. As far as Thia knew, this did not.

Cautiously, she went and sat beside him. He tensed slightly as, matching his pose, she reclined. Their shoulders touched, warm and mildly electric even through layers of clothing. Her pulse picked up as attraction flared, but her intention was to soothe.

His hand rested between them on the blanketed couch seat. The palm was broad; the fingers lithe. A capable hand. She covered it lightly with her own. His fingers tensed. Gradually, his hand shifted, turning to put palm to palm. That same electric warmth built at this additional point of contact, and this one was skin to skin. There was nothing mild about it. Thia closed her eyes.

"I don't act on this," Cormac said as their fingers interlaced, "precisely because it does matter." She felt a fine tremor run through him.

"Idris is gone" she reminded him. "He can't use me against you." Again. For surely Idris had done so when he'd lived.

"Others can." Cormac's grip tightened. "They will."

Such was her life now, apparently. Not only was she endangered because of magical power she was stuck with as a result of someone else's maniacal plan but also because she could be used as a means of getting to the half-*Sidhe* son of a deranged wizard.

"How many others might there be?" she asked. "Cassie is in custody. And as for Idris's followers, they'd more likely target me for what I've done, myself. Not to get to you." She had contributed to Idris's downfall, and to Cassie's defeat—twice. She had caused Matthew's death. She was trouble in her own right.

"I'm three centuries old." Cormac's baritone held a note of resignation. "Minus a few decades. I didn't spend that time making friends."

"You have enemies outside what you did for Idris?"

"Certainly."

She gave him time but he didn't elaborate. "Well." Shifting to lean against him, she rested her head on his shoulder. "You made one friend."

"Thia, don't." But he didn't move, either to push her away

or to avoid.

"Don't what?" Drawing her legs up, she tucked herself more comfortably against his side.

Her hand remained clasped with his. If he didn't want this, he could let go.

She rested her other hand on his arm. It wasn't the physical that he objected to, it was the rest. "Don't be honest? Whatever else there might or might not be between us, Cormac, I *am* your friend."

An audible intake of breath was her only warning before he twisted toward her, dislodging her hand from his arm, as he cupped her cheek and pressed his lips to hers.

She was the one to break their handclasp—in order to use both of hers to grab his shoulders and draw him down with her onto the blanket. The pillow was in the other direction but she didn't care.

Cormac stretched alongside, their legs twining as she drew him closer, closer, closer, his chest a welcome weight upon her own. His tongue grazed the seam of her lips.

Five. Five times, they had kissed before. This made six. She opened her mouth. Two had been quick, giving no opportunity to explore, to revel. But when there had been the luxury, as now—

"The colors," she whispered when their mouths parted for a change of angle. The beautiful colors, as she had seen before, flashing and sparkling behind her closed eyes.

"Only with you," he breathed. "Only with—"

Thia's tongue and what she did with it prevented him from finishing that thought.

● ○ ●

Landmark Hotel

More disturbed than he let on, Declan tucked his hands in his pockets and leaned a hip against the chest of drawers that doubled as the room's television stand. He was staying well out of the way while Brigantium agents transferred Quentin from one of the Landmark's wheelchairs to the bed.

Yesterday, he had read the names of the two agents doing the transferring, but he couldn't be bothered to recall them. As for the fourth agent present, he was quite familiar with her name—and other details, all compiled in a dossier locked in his office cabinet. As she was living in his hotel, it was his business to know everything about her.

Not one mention of her infernal scanning device.

"Thanks for the use of the chair," she said. Edith Wilkinson. She stood at the foot of the bed. "I was afraid we would have to put him on a luggage trolley."

"I treat my guests a fair sight better than that. Even those from the Brigantium."

Her Society would jump at the chance to see him put away, he supposed, and his assets seized—as long as it was to do the seizing. Yet here he was, willingly in its agents' midst, having accompanied them up from the parking garage. He had met them there himself, when any of his security team would have served.

To not find Abigail among them—particularly after he saw the state of Quentin—had given him an awful, black-hole-to-swallow-him-up moment. But it was no matter: Abigail was uninjured and to stay at Thia's another night. She would have her friend for company and be under warded protections, and have Cormac there as well. (Not that the *lethsídhe* could be trusted to protect much more than himself.) That was better than were Abigail to be at her own home, isolated and alone in the mountains. Declan should feel satisfied.

He should. But Abigail would be safest at the Landmark, where he and his people could watch over her.

As strong as the wards were around Thia's home, the hotel's were better—as Abigail knew. She could also do basic maths:

Cormac made for one additional level of protection, whereas Declan and his people were multiple. Her choice stung like rejection.

Under agent Edith's supervision, Quentin's shoes had been removed and the blanket pulled to his chin. That done, the other two moved to leave. One pushed the empty wheelchair.

"Leave that in the hall," Declan said. "My people will see to it." Since Edith had obviously stepped into the role of agent-in-charge, he made the offer to her: "I can have Jenkins see to your man, there." He tipped his chin toward the bed.

"He isn't *my* anything," she objected with undue force, then tried to cover her slip. "Well, he is my boss, yes. Sort of. And no, thank you. I'll set up a video consult with our chief healer. They'll have access to his medical records, presumably. If they need them."

The room door closed with a discreet click, the other agents having managed to get the chair out to the corridor. This one looked none too pleased to be left on her own. Her fingers fidgeted with her sweater cuffs.

"If you change your mind," he told her, "dial the front desk. Bevins is on call."

"Right. Thanks." Said grudgingly. Clearly she did not trust him any more than he did her.

He knew damn well she had been tasked, at least partially, with keeping tabs on him. Yet he had allowed her to remain a presence in the Landmark. He could have fabricated any number of reasons to "justify" her expulsion. But he hadn't. Instead, he had made sure that she had been treated with the respect afforded to all his guests.

What had his generosity and personal risk gotten him? He had unknowingly given access to her damned machine. And if she and her entire, blasted Society had done better, Kendra might be alive tonight instead of lying dead a few floors down in the Ogham Room.

"A *huldrekall*," he said, going back to what she had relayed in the elevator. "You told me everything Quentin here said of his vision? You've left nothing out?"

"He didn't tell us much," she said, her gaze going to the man on the bed and staying there. "Maybe when he wakes he'll be able to tell us more."

Declan wouldn't count on it. "Have you any experience with *huldrefolk?*"

"No."

"Has the Brigantium?"

"I haven't had time to contact London since he—" Her voice thickened and she stopped. Ducking her head, she removed her glasses and began working on them with a tissue pulled from her pocket. "Have you encountered them before?"

"A time or two." That Declan knew of. He had not known with Amundsen. "Never outside *Lochlann*—Norway, that is. Until now."

"What does he want? He's the city manager. But what does he want?"

"What does anyone want?" His laugh tasted bitter. "Power. Money. Control. I'll leave you to your night." He headed out. "What's left of it." At the door, he couldn't resist a look back.

Edith had not moved, but she had finished with her glasses. They were back on, likely enabling her to better observe the man on the bed. *Not my anything,* she had insisted, yet everything about her suggested otherwise.

It was amazing what people could deny, even to themselves.

Had his own expression been similar, when he had kept vigil at Abigail's bedside at the Retreat?

Closing the door quietly, he thought to return to his office and pick up work where he'd left off. But when the elevator deposited him in the lobby, he walked straight through and out into the icy night.

A stroll to clear his head, he told himself, even as it became plain that he had a specific destination in mind. He would go past, that's all, to assure himself that the wards were fully operative and that no one—no *thing*—was skulking about.

Yet when Declan got to the house, he stopped. The downstairs lights were on. He could take a minute, see for himself that she was unharmed.

● ○ ●

It took Thia an unknown amount of time to realize someone was lightly rapping on the door. Her every molecule preferred to focus on more tactile input. Cormac's mouth, his hands, the soft rasp of his breath, the press of his body. His skin and hair beneath her hands. His lips on her lips, on her throat, or lightly between her teeth, depending.

But someone was at the door. She managed words to that effect but then Cormac did a thing that caused her to gasp and arc her neck.

Her grip tightened reflexively. His hair was warm silk. Her fingers curled through it, anchoring her. Anchoring him. His tongue located a surprisingly sensitive spot where her neck joined her shoulder.

"Door," she said. The kaleidoscopic show of color continued behind the closed lids of her eyes. "Someone. At."

His exhale on the skin he had just laved made her shiver. She tightened her legs around his hips. She had never wanted anyone more.

His hand glided down the side of her chest as he nipped at her earlobe.

Releasing his hair, she cupped the nape of his neck with her left hand while her right went to his upper back. Firm muscle shifted beneath his cotton shirt. She needed to know the feel of his skin. She moved her hand from his back to his collar, slid her fingers underneath.

Oh, yes. Yet not enough. "Off," she insisted, tugging on the fabric.

He stilled, his head dropping to rest on her collarbone. His chest expanded on a deep breath. The sigh which followed was full of disappointment.

She kept her left hand on the back of his neck. Her fingers stroked through his hair, the strands there delightfully short. "I meant your shirt," she said, sorry that she hadn't been clear. The dance of color was fading.

"I know," he said on another sigh. "I know, but Murphy isn't leaving."

How quickly she had forgotten about the door.

She opened her eyes and the dazzling colors vanished. There was the living room. There were her hands. The normality of them seemed strange after . . . all that.

This close, she could make out the different shades in the brown of Cormac's hair. Unlike her own, there wasn't a single gray. Would there ever be? He aged at an Otherworldly pace. If they were still acquainted when she was seventy, would he have visibly aged at all?

A silhouette showed through the door's glass insets.

"You're sure it's Murphy?" She answered her own question. "You used your Sight."

"As you could have done." Cormac lifted his head. Concern clouded his beautiful eyes. "Unless it continues to give you trouble."

"No. I didn't think of it, is all. I should have."

His expression was wry. "You were considerably distracted."

"Considerably." Her smile felt bittersweet.

How often would she get a chance such as this? Cormac's weight, his presence. The conversation they had before. The honesty. Words she had told him previously sprang to the tip of her tongue, but she would not say them. Not this time.

He shifted to one side. She reluctantly disentangled herself and went to answer.

"If it was urgent," she said, hastily putting her clothes and hair to rights (or near enough) on the way, "he would've called. Or rung the bell"—instead of the light taps and, following, this bizarre, silent presence?

She unlocked the door, pulled it open. "Murphy, hello, has something—"

He brushed past, striding into the living room. "Even if we assume Kendra knew, Amundsen wouldn't have had her killed simply because she could out him as a *huldrekall.*" If he was surprised that Cormac should be there, seated on a rumpled, bed-made sofa, it did not show.

Thia closed the door, redid the locks.

"His being Other wouldn't endanger him outright." Murphy took to pacing. "There has to be more to it, to be worth the risk of two deaths."

Thia avoided him on her way by. "Are we sure that he *did* kill? Just because he's—" A noise at the top of the stairs drew her attention.

Abby, in one of Lettie's nightgowns and mint green terry-cloth robe, descended. "Why was he interested in Kendra in the first place?" She stopped on the lower landing, her hand on the newel post. "She was gorgeous, inside and out, sure. But she was also the director of your hotel. Privy to all sorts of information, right?"

Murphy took a step toward her. "She would never—"

"But Amundsen wouldn't know that, or maybe he decided it was worth a try anyway." Her eyes narrowed. "How far would *you* go for what you wanted?"

"I wouldn't kill an innocent." His voice was glacial. His back was to the room in order to talk to Abby, so only she could see his face—and she looked stricken.

"I—shit—I didn't mean *that.* I meant seduction. But that's not any better, is it." She sighed, her shoulders drooping. "You have to admit, though, you do have a reputation."

Thia shivered. The room's temperature had plummeted. "Is

everyone else freezing?" she asked, alarmed. "Did the furnace break?" It had been running fine a few minutes before. And if it had just broken, the house wouldn't chill this fast.

"*Murchada.*" Cormac stood. His irises were a brilliant blue—aglow with undisguised, summoned power.

"Don't worry about it," Murphy said.

Abby clearly did not believe him. She rushed down from the landing and then, with a hand on his back, guided him toward the seating. Thia could see his face now. It was blank, like a mask. She shivered again.

The closer the two came, Thia realized, the colder the room felt.

"Nice trick," Cormac said. His breath was misting. Everyone's was. They might as well be outside.

"Beats the alternative," Murphy said in an undertone, and Thia began to comprehend. *He* was responsible for the cold.

Abby took hold of his arm and pulled, getting him to sit with her on the nearest sofa, which happened to be the one made up for Cormac, where only a few minutes ago he and Thia had been—She turned away before anyone noticed her blush. Going to the empty sofa, she sat on the end farthest from the lamplight.

"What is the alternative," Abby asked between chatters of her teeth, "that this b-beats?" She tucked her legs up beneath her and pulled what she could of the blanket over her lap.

"It's about control," Murphy said. Unlike Cormac's, his eyes were not glowing.

Thia recalled the cold she had felt around him right after Kendra's death. "My power stopped acting up since I talked to you last night. Was that your doing?"

"Not directly, no." His hands unclenched. Clenched. "But as you can feel, the effects extend a certain range. I've yet to find a solution for that."

"*Hléowe.*" Cormac made an odd circling gesture. The room

warmed. He went to the opposite end of the couch from Thia and sat. "It warms the area," he said when everyone continued to stare. "That's all."

Thia rubbed her temples, her brain awash with a stupefying cocktail of frustrated desire and lack of sleep. Cormac was too far and too close, simultaneously. "We don't know for sure that Amundsen is connected to Kendra's death, or the other one"—she fought off a yawn—"do we? Just because influence spells or whatever were involved, and he's got that talent."

Cormac had slid further down in his seat so he was near horizontal. "If he is connected, it wasn't related to his probable interest in her as a source of inside information. No one gets rid of such a high quality prospect—and certainly not in that messy, public way—unless she had become an immediate threat."

"It was done outside my hotel," Murphy said. "My home. And timed so I would be the one to find her. It was to show me how close he could get."

"Not necessarily. Your part in the discovery could have been incidental. A bonus, if he's got a grudge against you. But not his main intent. *If* it was his doing."

Thia grimaced. "We're back where we started. We have no idea if Amundsen is involved at all, only the assumption that Kendra knew something she shouldn't have."

"And we don't know what that might be," Abby said. "Or about who. Whom." She made a face. "Except that it probably involves Founders Hall."

Thia lost the fight against her yawn. "Sorry," she said when it finished. The room remained quiet, no one having anything more to say, evidently.

They made such an odd group—not odd for having fallen silent, not at this time of night after such a day. No, she meant they were odd for the combination, that they formed a group at all, even temporarily.

Every one of them had become important to her despite knowing almost nothing about two. Every one of them had helped her, at great risk and some cost.

The shadows under Abby's eyes were purple and she blinked with such frequency that she was probably more than halfway asleep. Murphy showed no emotion but did so with a brittle intensity that Thia had to suspect was ultimately unsustainable. Especially if this mysterious cold was all that kept him from—what? Losing control of his power?

How much did he hold? More than Cormac? Thia turned her head to her right. Cormac had spent centuries adding to whatever he'd already had at birth.

His eyes were closed.

They all needed sleep. "We're not going to figure this out by talking. There's a couch left, Murphy, if you want it. Cormac has that one." She pointed to the sheets and blanket beneath him and Abby. "I'm sure I can find more bedding."

For a moment it seemed like he would accept, but then his shoulders slumped. "My thanks, but I shouldn't." He rose. "I have business yet to do."

"I'll see you out." Abby scrambled to her feet. She preceded him to the door, held it open while he walked out. Neither one spoke. She said nothing to Thia, either, after closing the door and engaging the locks. She simply turned on her heel, then walked upstairs. The floor above creaked as she made her way to Lettie's old room.

She had left them alone again. Did she think they would pick back up where they had left off?

"It's late," Thia said lamely, embarrassed. She made herself stand. "There's another long day ahead, and we—*I* should go to bed. My bed." She made the mistake of meeting his gaze.

His eyes no longer glowed with magic, but they were no less magical.

Without at least a few hours of uninterrupted sleep, the day ahead would be even more of a misery than it already promised to be. Yet she had no desire to go take them.

When it came to making the wise choice, her impulse was to choose Cormac.

He was complication, aggravation, and deceit. Mystery and shadow. What sort of fool would choose that over her own best interest?

He was studying her. Had been, all the while.

"You should," he said, and she had to work to recall what she'd said only moments before. She was beyond exhausted. She absolutely had to go to bed.

Because she was choosing to be wise, it felt important to be honest. "I don't want to."

"Nor do I want you to."

It seemed he was also making the wise choice. She let that settle a moment, or tried to. It was like trying to coax butterflies to land. She wasn't alone in wanting. It was thrilling and terribly, terribly complicated.

"Okay, then." She turned away to walk to the stairs and up. From the landing, she looked down, saw him seated on the couch. Watching her. "Goodnight."

"Goodnight, *muileach.*"

CHAPTER 20

Here she was again, like yesterday, staring into the closet and contemplating what to wear. Her emotions were no less tumultuous this morning. In some ways they were worse, so she would make damn sure she kept the crystal-tipped wand close. Her powers seemed to have been tamed by coming into proximity with whatever Murphy used on himself, but how long might that last?

She felt a decade older but no wiser. What did one wear two days after a friend's murder, when going after who- or whatever was responsible? And when the man to whom she was wildly, insensibly attracted was just downstairs, having spent the night on the couch? The couch where she and he had . . . and then almost . . . .

She felt ridiculously awkward.

Physical attraction could make such a mess of things under normal circumstances. None of the circumstances since she had met Cormac could be considered normal.

She took a pair of casual slacks with ample pockets off their hanger.

Was it love that she felt? She had said so—both to herself and to him—but was that accurate? Or was it more a muddle of fascination, chemistry, and gratitude?

And was that gratitude misplaced, she wondered, choosing a black turtleneck along with a dove gray cashmere sweater.

She could counter the times that Cormac had come to her rescue with times that he had actively worked against her. If she went to the bedroom window, she would see the picket fence that he had tried to pull her over when had wanted the Stone. That could be considered assault. It had been. And she had been terrified.

The times that he had helped, in fact, had also been to his benefit, not hers alone. His motives were always murky. She should never forget. Cormac acted in his own best interests—whatever those happened to be.

She set her planned outfit on the bed, then eased the door open to quietly make her way to the bath. The door to Lettie's old room was closed. No light shone underneath. Since there had been no sounds yet from within, she presumed Abby was still asleep.

A shower would be noisy, so she did the basics at the sink. Then, staring into the mirror, she lowered her expectations. She tended not to wear much makeup, so her supplies were limited, and the challenges of stress with not enough sleep looked to be immense.

She began with the bruise-like crescents beneath her eyes.

So what if what she was feeling was love? What good was that for her? There was no present relationship, and likely no future. Not a healthy one, anyway.

She set the powder brush down, picked up a tube of mauve-tinted gloss for her lips. It was a moisturizer too, not just for looks.

Passion could easily be mistaken for romantic love, as her younger self could attest. She knew, despite not having much actual experience with either, that she could do that in her mind. In her heart. Physical desire, not emotional connection.

That made much more sense, she decided, pulling her hair back and up into a basic twist held by a butterfly clip. Nothing special, that style. Or the care she had taken with her face. Not really. She gave herself one final check in the mirror.

She was still in pajamas.

She returned to the bedroom. Good thing she hadn't spent too much time on her hair and makeup, because when she pulled on the turtleneck, she'd make a mess of both.

Her disappointment a few minutes later when, fully dressed and retouched, she crept downstairs to find the living room abandoned suggested that she had been fooling herself after all; she'd wanted to look good, not for herself but for Cormac. And he had gone. The sheets and blanket were neatly folded and stacked by the guest pillow on the coffee table.

Had he even spent the night? The deadbolt was engaged on the front door, but he probably had a magical way of manipulating that, or he could have left from the back door.

Almost to the dining room, she smelled coffee—and had to remind herself that Abby had prepared the machine and set the automatic timer when they'd arrived last night.

Foolish, foolish, foolish to have forgotten, and to have felt a jolt of anticipation.

The light was on, she noticed as she rounded the corner. Had they forgotten it last night? She heard the coffeemaker spurting out the last of its water. Through the doorway, she saw movement in the faint shadows on the kitchen floor.

Had he not gone?

Another jolt of anticipation, this one large enough to pass for anxiety. Foolish to be so nervous, she told herself. Foolish to be feeling these things, these selfish personal things, when the situation around them was so tragic and dangerous. This was a distraction, and probably and inappropriate and hopeless one, at that.

Yet, despite knowing this, her pulse continued to speed as

she entered the kitchen. Cormac stood at the sink, his back to her. The pendant light overhead picked out bronze glints in his short-cropped hair. How could the line of a neck be sexy?

Before she could fully ponder that, he moved, returning one of Lettie's glass unicorn figurines to its place in the garden window and turning to face her. The same light that was doing wonders to his hair turned his irises to an almost cobalt blue.

If only he wasn't so handsome, it would be easier to hold onto her resolve. But he was, and she couldn't help thinking how it might be to see him in this kitchen on more mornings, in better times.

Foolish, foolish, and more foolish.

"Morning," she said.

"Isn't it," he said and she couldn't tell if he was mocking her inanity or making a joking reference to the early hour.

The toaster popped. He went to it, pulled out two pieces of bread. "You don't have oats," he said, setting the toast on a plate. He knifed up a liberal amount of butter.

"No," she said, and her opinion of it must have been in her tone, because he gave her a frowning glance.

"You don't like porridge?"

"Oatmeal? Not really."

The twelve-cup coffee carafe was full; Abby had prepared enough and then some. Travel mugs, probably, for later. She had not set anything out, however. Cormac had. There was milk in a whimsical little creamer jug, small spoons, and an array of mugs.

She picked one. "Thanks for this."

They stood side by side while he finished buttering his toast and she stirred sugar and milk into her coffee.

She almost offered to pour him some, but remembered she intended to distance herself. They were not friends. She took her mug to the short counter beside the stove. Leaning back on the tiled edge, took a sip.

Literal distance.

She closed her eyes as the milky, sweetened deliciousness went down. Abby was right, and here she had proved it. Thia made terrible coffee. Was it the ratio? The grind? She'd have to ask. She couldn't go back, not after this.

Cormac went with his to lean on the sink counter. Facing off with her, the whole of the kitchen between them. He was smirking behind his mug—one with a photo of a moose—as he drank. Amused by her discomfort, no doubt.

It wasn't just their situation. Thia had never been a morning person. Even under ideal conditions, her sunup conversation ranged only from strained to nonexistent.

"Nothing happened last night," came out of her mouth, and she regretted it instantly when he cocked his head, laughter in his eyes.

"Nothing, was it? I'd have said it was at least—"

"With the wards, I meant. No sign of threats. Intrusion. I didn't mean about what we—"

Abby rushed in, making a wordless beeline for the coffee.

"Hey, Ab," Thia said, but didn't expect much response. Abby was not a morning person either.

She put enough milk into her mug to turn the French roast beige. One swallow quickly followed another.

"You're right about my coffee," Thia said. She was worried about Cormac and Abby being in the same room. "I guess I figured the taste was from the brand or the machine and I got used to it. But yours is so much—" Her cellphone rang. "It's Edith," she read aloud as she took the call, and then, into the phone, "Hey, how are—"

"London sent information." Edith was all business. "How soon can you and the others get to the Landmark?"

● ○ ●

Murphy's Office
Landmark Hotel

For the past several minutes, with a hip set against the corner of Murphy's desk, Edith had been sharing information sent by the Brigantium. Cormac was not so gullible as to believe she shared everything, but he did trust it to be accurate. In these circumstances, Beatrice would gain nothing from giving them doctored information.

"As we suspected," Edith said, "the Carl Verner Family Trust is a front—rather, part of a series of fronts. The name behind it leads to another name, which leads to another name, which leads to another—you get the idea." She consulted her tablet: "Amund Egillsen."

Well, now, *that* was a headache. Shifting his weight on the chair he had relocated closer to the door, Cormac pinched the bridge of his nose.

"He helms Knarr and Skeid," Edith read. "It's a Norwegian import—"

"—export firm," Murphy finished from his seat behind the desk.

Knarr and Skeid was also one of the O'Shannon's primary competitors. Cormac casually returned his hand to where the other rested on his midriff. *This* was why Founders Hall had been in the leprechaun's red book.

"Ostensibly an import/export firm," Edith said, getting back into it. "Interpol has had an eye on them since the mid-fifties. They were founded only a few years prior. By a man named"—she checked—"Egill Hemmingsen. Amund Egillsen's father."

Cormac felt like he was walking along a windy precipice. To tell them outright what he knew, or to try to lead them to the it? He said, "They use the old naming conventions."

"Right." Edith swiped. "Egill, son of Hemming. Amund, son of Egill."

He gave that a moment but no one made the connection. It

was damnably early and all were short on sleep, but come on. "Neil Amundsen," he said, gesturing in frustration. "Amund's son."

"What?" Thia, on the sofa, sat forward. "Amundsen?"

"Not possible," Murphy said. "I had that *mac conlón* vetted when he was up for city manager. Every aspect of his life was investigated. Thoroughly." His hand slammed down, sending a pen off the desk. "Background, associations. What he had in his refrigerator. His first car and how he paid for it, and all the vehicles after. There wasn't so much as a hint linking him to Knarr and Skeid."

"There wouldn't be, though, would there," Edith said with care. "It doesn't come up outside specific property records— and those wouldn't be part of research on Amundsen. It's only with the names and the old conventions that it clicks. Might click, that is. I'm not finding a Neil mentioned anywhere in here." She tapped and swiped on her tablet. "Sons are Agnar, Fritjof, Stigander, and Trym. There are photos of Agnar and Fritjof—no resemblance to the man we know. Trym died in a road accident. Nothing on Stigander other than the sugges- tion that he was banished or ran off around that same time. Almost a decade ago." She lowered her tablet. "That's it for sons."

"Could Stigander have changed his name?" Thia asked, only to then shake her head. "No, that doesn't work, does it. Why would he change his first name but not his last? That *is* the surname, right?" she looked to Edith. "The one the sons use?"

"It is."

"Might they have middle names that aren't in your files?"

Murphy was still not having any of it. "My people verified Amundsen's birth record—and that of his christening. Every school and all his grades from kindergarten through college. Where he lived, where he worked. There were no gaps. There was not a damn thing to suggest he could be anyone other than the son of Harold and Marlena Amundsen of Norfolk,

Nebraska. Nothing at all. My people were thorough."

"So were his," Cormac pointed out. "That family has done this far longer than any one of us. Knarr and Skeid might be their latest public face but they have operated in the North—in Scandinavia," he clarified for the modern age, "since the collapse of the Hanseatic League—1669. Given what they're said to be, that's likely off by centuries, but Idris hadn't much interest in trying to trace them back farther. His interest was in the Shetland portals, which they controlled at the time. Forging documents, faking records—I saw what they could do in 1807. Would you say they're more likely to have gotten worse at it or better?"

Murphy continued to glare.

"Import/export on the surface," Edith said, back to reading her tablet. "Varied forms of racketeering suspected beneath. Protection, extortion, smuggling. There's a lengthy bit copied from an Interpol report, about how going after Egillsen and his lot is like trying to grab smoke. Leads disintegrate. What little evidence they find vanishes soon after. People disappear or end up dead." She lifted her tablet as if entering it at a court of law. "They're capable of fabricating an entire life's history. One that could withstand the most rigorous scrutiny."

"What are we saying?" Abby asked, gesturing wildly. Beside her, Thia flinched. "Some mafia-like family in Norway owns properties here and somehow they were so threatened when Kendra started looking into that, they had Neil—maybe no relation—*kill* her? While the two of them just happened to be dating?"

"It took Interpol to get to the base layer of all the trusts and shell companies," Edith said. "No disparagement of Kendra's investigative skills, but the family would not have seen her as a threat in that way."

Abby made an exasperated noise. "So if she was not killed because of the research she was doing or because she might have learned that Neil Amundsen was a *huldrekall,* then why the hell *was* she killed? We've gotten nowhere."

"What if," offered Thia, "she learned he really is the third son what's-his-name—"

"Stigander," Edith supplied.

"Right, thanks. Stigander. Maybe he didn't want his family to find out where he was—No, sorry, that doesn't work, either, does it. Again, because he kept the last name. Like he wanted the connection." She sat back. "But it fits, because Stigander disappeared. It has to fit."

"Pride." Quentin spoke for the first time. Slouched at the sofa's far end, he had been giving whatever was in his thermal tumbler the whole of his attention since the meeting began. He appeared to be wearing yesterday's suit, with enough wrinkles to suggest he had slept in all but the jacket. "He wants the family name but doesn't want the trace to be so obvious, back to them. How long has he lived here?"

"Going on five years," Murphy answered before Edith could look it up. She nodded.

Quentin set his tumbler before him on the low table. His hands were gloved. "Did Knarr and Skeid buy the properties around that time, or before?"

"Before." Edith tapped. "Long before. Both are listed under the Carl Verner Family Trust since the early eighties. Why? What would racketeers operating in Scandinavia want with Granite Springs?"

Cormac could answer that—he *should* answer that—but he wasn't going to. Nor did he expect Murphy to answer, given his own interests. He had to be aware, generally, what about the region would attract such an operation. After all, his had a substantial presence here, and not just to take advantage of the tourism.

Quentin disregarded that question entirely. "How long have the Rekkrs operated out of that roadside bar?"

"Five years," Abby said slowly. "But they're only here in late autumn through winter."

Murphy reached into a desk drawer, pulled out a set of files. "They spend the rest of the year traveling around the Pacific Northwest. We've been keeping watch on them in case they tried anything locally. Up to this past December, they hadn't."

"They didn't want to draw attention," Thia tried. "I mean, other than by being jerks when they roared around. But that's not unusual, is it, that sort of stuff. What did they do outside this area?"

Murphy pushed the file forward. "Similar to what is alleged of Knarr and Skeid, as it happens. Protection rackets. Transport of illicit goods."

Edith picked it up, began flipping through the pages inside.

"Quite a coincidence," Thia said with heavy irony. Despite frequent naïveté, she had a knack for suspicion.

She was also terribly adept at making connections.

In this case, connections were all too easy to make. Knarr and Skeid owned the land beneath the Valhalla, the Rekkrs' bolthole. Both were known for or suspected of the same class of criminal enterprise. Knarr and Skeid was based in Norway. The Rekkrs emblazoned their motorbikes and jackets with *Mjölnir,* otherwise known as Thor's hammer. Their name was old Norse for "warrior."

Neil Amundsen and the Rekkrs had first come to Granite Springs at roughly the same time—although that in itself was hardly a link.

"Who runs them?" Cormac asked. "The Rekkrs."

Murphy leaned back and glowered. "All we have is the name you gave us. The one you overheard in December. Skati. Most likely it's a title or an honorific."

"We hit a wall there too," Edith said, and returned the file to the desk. "Cassandra was questioned about him. She claimed they had never met, and that he had not been involved with her deal with the bikers."

"Try her again," Cormac said. Knowing what he did, it was a certainty that if she had not lied outright, she had withheld. But he needed to tread carefully. "Offer to release some of her finances. She's at risk of losing Idris's collection if she misses the next payments to the groups hired to store it."

So was he.

"Know that's what she did with it, do you?" Murphy asked, too alert for comfort. "She hired minders?"

"So it seems. Generally."

Along with the troublesome reliance on Munster Irish, the O'Shannon's notebook was cryptically esoteric. That it was a compendium of comings and goings at various locations was clear. The problem was in the identification of the locations themselves—the where and what. Cormac recognized some, like Founders Hall, thanks to prior familiarity. He knew what they looked like and where they were, so the obscure descriptions served as prompts. The rest, however, needed further research to identify.

Yet more frustrating, the notebook did not detail what each location might hold. It listed dates and times of arrivals and departures, and described the people involved along with any receptacles—crates, boxes, bags. It did not inform as to what business took place within the locations, or what had been brought in or out.

Murphy's eyes narrowed. "You *will* locate it."

"Of course." Not for the first time, Cormac considered that Murphy himself might be familiar both with Munster Irish and the locations mentioned. And, as in the times before, he dismissed the idea. He was not yet that desperate. After the reprieve, however . . . .

Their exchange had been observed with various degrees of curiosity. Thia spoke first, asking, "What are Knarr and Skeid reputed to be?"

His mind was slow to shift off the Achill Bell.

She prompted, "You said the family probably has been in operation longer than 1669 because of 'what they are reputed to be.' What is that?"

Oh. Right. "It's there in the name Hemming, if one goes to the Norse root, *hamr.* I can't be the only one here to have heard the rumors."

Yet Edith had made no mention of it, and Murphy appeared annoyed—and defensive when he said, "I've never dealt with them directly. And as you may or may not be aware, I do my best to steer clear of that area of the world. I've no cause to go looking into what they do in actuality, let alone whatever tales might be going around."

Incredible. So, it would seem Cormac *was* the only one.

"*Hamr*—shape. Shapeshifting. Even as they forcefully deny the rumors, in every third generation the family names one son Hemming."

"Shapeshifting," Thia said, "as in they're *huldrefolk?*"

"Precisely."

"So, it *does* fit. Neil has to be Stigander." She abruptly sat straight. "Could he also be Skati?"

● ○ ●

Alchemy Taproom
One Hour Later

If Thia were to ponder what her life had become, it wouldn't get her any closer to understanding. She could only acknowledge that she had experienced such a series of drastic changes after leaving Los Angeles that there was little left to recognize of her past self. Contemplation would do nothing to return any of that familiarity. Her old self was gone; there was only this. She had to hope this new version might one day feel less new. She couldn't return to a few *minutes* previous, let alone a whole year. She could only ever go forward.

Please, though, could forward involve less trauma? Not only for herself but for everyone around her?

But that was life, wasn't it? Risk and potential disasters and unexpected tragedy? She was not blind to the news, to world events. She broke off another piece of cranberry orange scone with her fingers. Stared at it. The other pieces had not gone down well, delicious as they were.

"I can't stop worrying," she admitted to Abby, seated across from her. They were at a small table in the closed Alchemy Taproom, the bar and lighter-fare restaurant adjacent to the lobby. At Murphy's direction, they had been served individual pots of coffee and offerings from the Landmark's mezzanine breakfast buffet. So far she'd had more caffeine in the past few hours than she normally did in an entire day. "We're not the police. I know I keep saying it and it doesn't do any good, but we're not even investigators or agents or any sort of trained professional."

"No, we aren't." Abby was idly turning her cup on its saucer. "But Edith and Quentin are. Whatever the Brigantium does, exactly, this sort of thing seems to be part of it. And Murphy certainly seems to be in his element. It's you and I that don't fit. Literally." They were here instead of crowding in with the others in the security room to watch the monitors.

And Cormac was out risking his life, again.

He was going to break into Founders Hall. There was no other way to learn what made Kendra run out or how she had picked up the blue stains, he'd said. The building was at the heart of all of this. In the hope that evidence remained within it, he would try to retrace her steps.

He had fought the idea of anyone else going with him. He had the skills to get inside, plus the Sight and could hold his own against threats. Quentin would be hampered by physical limitations. Edith, by her own admission, would have been more hindrance than benefit. And, if Amundsen or his allies noticed Murphy near the building, suspicion would be raised.

Abby or Thia would be more of a hindrance than Edith, as unfortunately gendered as that appeared to be. Kendra would have been brilliant. If only she were here to avenge her own murder.

So, it would be Cormac and Cormac alone. Edith had given him her scanning equipment and shown him how to record.

"I'll analyze the data afterward," she had said.

He had not wanted to, Thia could tell; but he'd taken the device.

She checked her watch. Almost a half hour ago. He would disguise himself, he'd explained, and approach the Hall from the opposite direction of the Landmark. Give him at least an hour, he'd said.

"Be careful," she had told him. Foolishly, in retrospect. Of course he would be careful. It would have been more honest of her to have said, "Stay safe." *Please don't die.*

She had hoped that it would be less stressful for her to wait somewhere other than in the security room where she would be helpless to do anything about whatever she might see in the cameras' limited coverage. It was not. She worried just the same.

Abby speared a melon ball with her fork. "He knows how to take care of himself."

"I wish I could say the same for myself."

"Same." She stared at the melon. "I feel so useless."

For the first time that morning, Thia saw her friend clearly. The shadows under—and in—her eyes. The strain. "I'm sorry I haven't been more . . . *present* for you. I've been caught up in my own mess. I haven't even asked how you're doing."

"Oh." She made a soft laugh, then wiped away a sudden tear. "I'm not one for talking about my feelings. You know that." Her smile was muted but genuine. "Which is why you *are* a good friend. You've let me stay in your home. You keep me company but don't push. And even when you're in the midst of a crisis too, I know you'd be there if I asked. You're a great friend, Thia. Honestly."

"Oh." She had to blot sudden tears of her own. "Thank you, Abby. Ditto. What would I do without you?"

"You'd figure it out. You're good at that." She caught sight of something through the bank of windows. "That was fast."

Cormac was walking by, headed for the hotel entrance.

"Too fast." Thia stood.

She got to the lobby as he was halfway to reception. Edith, Quentin, and Murphy were coming in as well, from the left side hallway. They must have seen Cormac's approach on the monitors.

"What happened?" Thia called out, and he turned toward her, changing course. She couldn't see any signs of distress or damage.

"I'm fine," he said, doing a better job, obviously, of reading her than she ever did, him. "And *nothing* happened, is what." Some annoyance showed as the others arrived. "The place is a hive of activity. I couldn't get in." He looked to Murphy. "I didn't need to."

● ○ ●

Murphy's Office

Rounding Murphy's desk, Cormac set down the Brigantium's scanner. "I didn't get a chance to use this."

While active, the device would scan him as well as anything else. He had never intended to use the damn thing.

He *had* intended to use the doppelgänger charm, get into Founders Hall as Cassandra, locate her storage unit, and plant a summoning token so he could later retrieve whatever was inside. Just like he had intended last night. And just like last night, there hadn't been a damned chance.

He pulled out his smartphone, selected the photos he had snapped from inside a ramen shop with an unobstructed view of Founders Way and later from the roof of a building almost directly across from the Hall.

"Is your computer enabled for air drop?" he asked as Murphy met him behind the desk and took possession of the padded chair.

"It will be." Seated, Murphy opened the laptop and logged in with a fingerprint scanner. Too bad, that. Standing at his side, Cormac had a clear view of the keyboard. He could steal a sequence of letters, numbers, and symbols. He couldn't steal a fingerprint.

With the exception of what he had done to Cassandra.

"Go," Murphy said.

Cormac shared the photos. The images immediately began opening on-screen.

"I've enabled my tablet," Edith said from the other side of the desk. "If you would."

It appeared on his mobile's list of available devices. Thia's was there as well. He sent to both.

"You can see why I didn't go in," he said as they all focused on various screens. "And also why it wasn't necessary."

Necessary for *their* interests. In regard to his own, he was maddeningly frustrated. Alone and in the guise of helping the group, this had been his perfect chance. He would not have another.

"None of this was visible until I got close. We should assume they didn't want it to be." They hadn't been so concerned last night.

This had been a version of that same activity, but in reverse and much more covert. The same white van had been parked outside but with doors closed and, it seemed, no one around. It wasn't until Cormac had a view into the recessed doorway that he knew his plan was fucked.

People were bringing boxes from the building to stack them there in preparation for loading. Same people from last night. But not the same boxes.

"The fifth photo," he said. It was a close-up

"Blue splatters," Thia said. "Like on Kendra's hands?"

"Exactly."

"These are catering supplies," Murphy said, clicking rapidly through the entire array. "Tableware. Serviettes. Chafing dish fuel. Pallister's party is tonight. The one the Landmark had a contract for that he canceled last minute."

"Kendra didn't remember who got the job," Abby said, and glanced at him briefly before returning to her study of Thia's phone screen. "Did you learn who that was?"

"Ledberg Events, according to Pallister's assistant. There's no business with that name registered with the state."

"Well, we know where they operate from, anyway. If we can for sure connect it to the mayor's party." She looked over at Cormac. "Did you follow the van?"

"They were still preparing to load when I left. What's this about a party?" He would have felt excluded but for Edith and Quentin's equally befuddled expressions. Some particular bit of knowledge among Kendra's friends, then. Hotel business that seemed insignificant before. "I could go back to the Way if—"

"No need," Murphy said tiredly, and finished dragging both hands down his face. "Where the hell else would it be going but to Pallister's? If I hadn't been so distraug—*distracted,* I'd have pegged it straight off as a likely target."

"This is why Kendra was killed? Catering supplies?" Abby's voice trembled, and Cormac noted how Thia briefly touched her friend's arm. Kindness. "A party?"

"Pallister has been bragging to all and sundry that there's to be an Imbolc ceremony performed by the Retreat," Murphy answered. "He hosts a party every year, but that's a first." He slammed the laptop closed with enough force to fracture the screen.

Then he swept it off his desk altogether, sending it crashing against the wall.

The room's temperature held steady, so it would seem he was otherwise under control.

Quentin spoke into the uncomfortable silence. "None of us have been at our best on this one."

"I should have been."

Cormac was surprised to find himself forgetting that he was not here to help. Not truly. "Who is on the guest list?"

"I am, for one," said Murphy. "Every year. He invites the most influential citizens. Government, business, philanthropists. Money and power."

"Is he behind this?" Thia asked. "Kendra's death, getting rid of her killer . . . Is Mayor Pallister working with Amundsen?"

"It would explain why the official investigation is so strange, right?" Abby said. "Why they took all her papers and devices. Why her death was so quickly ruled a mugging."

"By order of the mayor?" Cormac couldn't see this as being so straightforward. "The chief of police and the investigating officers would have to be in on it. And then there's the forensics team, evidence storage—too many people."

"Corruption," offered Quentin.

"Bribes, blackmail, and other pressures are always possibilities," Cormac agreed, thinking aloud. "But this is large scale. I'd look to Amundsen for it, not your mayor. Corruption via influence. That fits with the talents of a *huldrekall*. Which he could augment with any number of spells, obviously."

"Oh, yes," Thia muttered. "Obviously."

He didn't take her remark—and the bitterness it carried—personally. For him, such things were as obvious and expected as gravity; whereas, until a few short months ago, Thia had believed magic and folklore to be pure fantasy.

It was to her credit that she was adapting as well as she was to what amounted to the entire shift of a worldview.

"No matter who is behind it," Quentin said, "something is planned for the tonight. We need to find out what that is."

"And stop it," said Abby.

Murphy turned to Edith. "If you're still wanting to examine the marks, she's in the Ogham Room."

"What?" Abby recoiled. "Kendra is here? How is that poss— For the wake. You should have said. Damn it, right when I got here, you should have said."

CHAPTER 21

"I really appreciate this, Loretta," Abby said into her phone. "I know how busy you all are." She had hoped there would be enough coven members willing to drop their Imbolc preparations at a moment's notice, but it was a huge ask.

While she listened to the surprisingly long list of who had agreed, she watched Thia's determined effort with Jack Ross outside the Ogham Room. She was doing her best to persuade him to let Edith and Quentin in to examine the blue marks.

She really was good, even if her retail sales experience was limited. Solicitous yet confident expression and mannerisms; excellent use of eye contact—steady but not so constant as to turn into a challenge for dominance. She was a natural, and Eclectica had benefited from the moment she had arrived to set up the website.

Yet, she was not making the sale. Jack Ross crossed his arms almost belligerently and shook his head.

Loretta finished with her list. "Will that be enough?"

"Better than I could have hoped," Abby assured her. "I need to go now and set things up here. Blessings."

"And to you," she replied as Abby ended the call.

Putting her phone into her tote, she hurried to Thia.

"Jack," she said, extending her hand. "Thank you so much for understanding." Sometimes the best way to persuade was to act as if you already had.

"Abby, hello." Confusion skittered across his youthful face. He clasped her offered hand. "I haven't agreed to anything."

She was relieved to find that he had shielded himself; she received no unwanted sensations or visions from the contact. He made to pull away, but she held firm, used the handclasp to step close.

"We wouldn't ask if this weren't so important." She lowered her voice, as if this was just between the two of them. "I'm not sure how much Thia was able to explain. We're concerned about what might be on Kendra's fingers. The blue."

"She did say. And we've been careful," Jack said. "Ma had a bad feeling straight off."

"I promise they won't disturb Kendra or your preparations. We want to be sure there isn't a lingering danger. If there is, the Brigantium can neutralize it." She hoped. It wasn't her intention to lie.

Jack gave her hand a light squeeze. "We hadn't thought that through. We should have. *Would* have, I'm sure, if we weren't so—" His mouth, its shape a masculine version of Kendra's, pressed into a tight line. "We don't want to have anything to do with *him*."

"Murphy? No, he doesn't—It would be the two agents, no one else."

"My parents . . . they don't want us to get involved. We know you're looking into what happened, that you don't believe it was a mugging." He spoke rapidly. Fervently. "And we know that *he* won't just let whoever is behind it get away. We want in on that. Fiona and me. We want in."

"Jack, I don't know if I can promise something like that."

"You can if you want the Brigantium in the room with her."

Emotion, hot and bitter, lanced into Abby.

She pulled her hand from his grip and, unbalanced, rocked back on her heels.

"I'll get the family to agree," he said as she plunged both of her hands into her pockets. "If you can."

His face held a kind of apology. For the ultimatum, or for the dropping of his shields? Had that been intentional?

She was safe, she told herself. Safe. The emotional intrusion was already dissipating. "Fine. That's . . . fine."

It would have to be.

"She was the best of us, you know," Jack said, turning toward the door. "We're feeling pretty lost right now."

She supposed that was also a kind of apology. And she could certainly understand that feeling, and acting out of grief and anger, and causing hurt as a result. And so she could forgive. Especially the much-loved brother of her friend.

"We all are," she said. "We'll find our way. In time."

"Oh, I don't know." He turned the knob, cracked open the door. "Some things, once lost, are gone forever." He began to slip inside.

"Jack."

He looked back.

"Members of my coven will hold a protective circle while the Brigantium agents do their work. I'll let you know when they arrive." So the family could then leave the room.

"We would like to join that. Too."

"Of course." After he was back inside the room, she turned, leaned against the closed door to steady herself.

"You okay?" Thia asked. "I'm sorry I didn't do a better job— When he came out instead of Kendra's parents, like we had expected, it threw me."

"You did fine," she said. "We should have known it would work better with both of us. Like when we finally got that pewter chess set sold."

"Yeah, well. I'm still sorry. I know how hard that was, even before he took advantage."

"You noticed that?"

"Hard not to, the way you reacted."

Abby had to laugh. "That big, huh?"

"Like you'd been burned."

Abby nodded. "Near enough. And my own fault for giving him the opportunity." She still couldn't believe Jack had done that on purpose. "I thought—Well, I thought it might work both ways. If I could receive, I might be able to send." But she hadn't tried to send *emotions*. "I thought if he could tell how important I felt this was, it would help convince him."

"Did it work?"

"I don't think so. He agreed because we made a deal."

● ○ ●

Was it ever possible to be comfortable in the face of death? Inside the room with its incense-laden air, Quentin couldn't help but wonder. He'd seen enough that he should at least be inured. Yet his heart beat uncomfortably fast and hard, as if he were running uphill instead of sedately, reluctantly limping toward the form laid out at the end of a perfectly level ballroom.

The body of Kendra Ross was on a cloth-draped platform centered between a pair of pine votive stands. Arrangements of winter greenery formed a backdrop, while the foreground was lined with vases of cedar boughs and dried white statice flowers. It was a lovely and loving display. Could the same be said of the memorials for Roddy and Anisa and Lyle and the rest, lost the night of his Great Mistake?

He hadn't attended any of those services. Even if he could have gone, he would not have. The shame of that cowardice burned almost as hot as the guilt of their violent, terror-filled deaths.

As his heart continued to pound and his chest grew ever tighter, he considered that this could be the least of what he deserved. This, the chronic pain of his hip, and all the other changes—what were those compared to what he had caused? The choice to participate had been theirs, of course. But they had been friends, all, and far too trusting.

They had encouraged him and been excited to take part. He should have known better, even if they hadn't.

Enough. With effort, he focused on the task at hand.

Kendra Ross had been beautiful in life. Quentin would not say she remained beautiful in death; the absence of spirit was too jarring.

Her family had prepared the body with meticulous care. An intricately patterned quilt, doubtless an heirloom, had been pulled up to just below the shoulders. The arms were outside it, hands together on the chest and posed to hold a bouquet of yew and rosemary sprigs, dried lavender, and roses of deep crimson. It put him uncomfortably in mind of a bride.

He startled as Edith came to stand on his left.

"It's almost as if she could be sleeping," she said.

Except where cosmetics failed to conceal the blue marks on the fingers, the body's flesh glowed with false vitality. The lips held the pink of health and the soft smile of a sleeper whose dreams were happy.

Quentin did not believe that Kendra Ross's final expression had been anything like this.

Edith studied the bouquet. "Remembrance, mourning, and love." Traditional European floriography.

"Did Beatrice's packet include information on her family?" he asked. The dead woman was not sleeping. It was almost cruel to have laid her out as if she might be.

"Basic things, yes. They have a successful investment firm and serve on several San Francisco boards. Music, charities, arts." She took out her scanner from her ever-present satchel and began untangling its crystal pendulums.

"Interesting that she didn't stay within the fold."

"It couldn't have been easy. For any of them." The depth of emotion in Edith's voice gave her away.

"Speak from experience, do you?"

Her shoulders rose and fell on a sigh. "Unfortunately."

Nothing more was forthcoming. They both knew he would have no trouble getting the details. Likely it was all in her application records. That she didn't want to tell him herself suggested discomfort or even pain.

"If only I'd done the same," he said, thinking to give some solace. He shifted weight onto his cane to make his point.

"Didn't turn out so well for Kendra, though."

"No."

"Do you—" She stopped only to start over. "Do you think she regrets it now?"

Was she asking his opinion, or something more direct?

"That's complicated, isn't it," he replied, wary. "First, does consciousness exist after death? Then there's the question of form—what sort of afterlife one might encounter and how it compares to life as the person knew it. If she's in a better place, would she experience regret?"

Behind her glasses' lenses, her eyes were too keen. "I think there *is* a kind of regret. But not for themselves. Regret for those they left behind."

Quickly, he turned away. What regrets might his lost friends hold for him? Easy enough to imagine. That he had not died along with them.

"Shall we?" Beside him, Edith lifted her device and began to move it toward the corpse.

He readied what protections he might offer should the scan trigger anything in the marks. "Proceed."

● ○ ●

Edith flicked the toggle to the active position. Almost immediately, she could tell this was not going to work. The readings were glitchy, alternately spiking and bottoming out. But she had pushed for this, even against her own reluctance. She was sensitive to disrespecting anyone's grief and the sanctity of this memorial and of what had once been Kendra. But this was for the greater good—for justice, and making sure no one else came to harm.

Vibrant, spirited Kendra, quick to laugh, and always with a ready ear to listen to Edith droning on and on about gadgets and apps.

She closed her eyes and promptly shut her sorrow and her second thoughts in a mental box. What she was doing here was not desecration, not disrespect. It was necessary—if only it would work. It had to work.

Eyes open, she adjusted the frequency of the second and seventh crystals, then swept the array over the blue marks in a slow tick-tock motion. The readings spiked. Bottomed out. Spiked.

"Nothing?" Quentin leaned close to get a look.

She willed herself not to react. She hated when teachers had stood over her to observe and potentially criticize. She was long past those days, and this man was not her teacher—but he *was* highly critical. And, annoyingly, his opinion mattered.

He also smelled intriguing, a darker musk to blend with the more dominant scents of the memorial greenery and herbs. Cologne, was that, or soap?

"Shower gel," he said, so close that she could feel his silent laughter. "Courtesy of the hotel. Doesn't your room have the same?"

Oh, no, not again. "The staff have been leaving rose-scented products."

"*Intriguing,*" he said pointedly, to Edith's mortification.

"How much did I say?"

"Of your thoughts? I have no means of comparison. And before you accuse me of making you talk, let me assure you that was all you. An interesting habit—but not ideal in a field agent. Not a criticism," he added quickly, chuckling.

Was there a stage beyond mortification? If so, Edith had reached it. She lowered the scanner. "It's no use. The readings are all over the place, which means none are reliable."

He turned back to the platform. "Explain."

"All I can say with certainty is that the resonance is similar to in the alley." Miserable, she walked to her satchel, left on a chair in the first of twelve rows. "I'm sorry. I truly thought this would work." She dropped the scanner into the satchel's main compartment. "I don't know why it didn't. Maybe if I added a rose quartz? It isn't as reactive. I might have made the set too sensitive." She straightened, prepared to pick up and clear out.

Quentin remained by Kendra's body. He stood with his head bowed and could very well have been paying his last respects, yet Edith wondered.

He wouldn't be *that* reckless, would he?

"Wait." Abandoning the satchel, she rushed back to insert herself between him and the platform. "You can't mean to."

He lifted his right hand. He had already removed his glove.

She felt a rush of terror. "It's not a good idea. Not after what you've already been—"

"You'll want to leave," he said, reaching past her to set his cane aside. It leaned on the platform, the draped silk helping to hold it in place. "If whatever is in the marks is triggered, I won't be able to protect you. Not while I'm . . . reading."

"No." She kept shaking her head. "No. What if you can't let go? Like what happened in Kendra's apartment?"

He was going to argue. It was clear in the rigid way he held himself. And he was angry. Angry enough to write her up for insubordination.

She could not have been more stunned when what he said was, "Fine. But don't touch me. Not at any point."

"Right," she promised, with unspoken addendums. In case of emergency, unless absolutely necessary, et cetera.

His silver-gray eyes narrowed skeptically. "Right."

"Right." She knew damn well she hadn't said anything aloud that she hadn't meant to.

He sighed, then, "Whatever happens, Edith, do not break the circle they're holding out there."

"I won't," she said, and reluctantly stepped aside. This was not a bad idea, it was a *terrible* one. "How dangerous is this?"

His bare hand reached for and then covered Kendra's.

Edith didn't have butterflies in her stomach, she had bees. "Maybe I should get—"

With what she would later remember as a yelp, he keeled over, straight as a board. Both votive stands trembled with the force of his impact on the room's sprung floor. His head made a sound like a dropped coconut.

She crouched at his shoulder. His eyes were open, staring, the irises glowing a silvery white. She waved a hand before them. "Quentin?"

No response.

"Quentin, please." Fear's grip tightened with each passing second. "Can you hear me?"

What could she do? She wasn't supposed to touch him. He hadn't explained why and she hadn't asked. She should have. She should have asked if opening the door would be enough to break the protective circle. What if someone else was to open it from the other side, if she called for help?

● ○ ●

Disorientation ruled Quentin's consciousness for a time as,

having joined with the remnants of Kendra Ross's memories, he found himself running down a set of stairs.

"Wait here."

Kendra knew the voice, even if he did not. It belonged to Neil Amundsen, her lover.

But Neil Amundsen did not belong in Founders Hall. Nor should he sound so malevolent. She had heard him, moments before, being cruel. Ruthless.

The stairs began to move, pulling and folding in on themselves, and she leapt over the deep, widening hole between the disappearing treads and the doorway ahead. Quentin put his attention toward the blackness beneath and immediately regretted it.

Death. Cruelty and pain and bone-chilling cold. He jerked his focus away, back to Kendra as she recovered her balance after landing and scrambled outside.

Get away. Take cover.

The timeline became erratic, skipping, repeating. Moments faded in and out. Images and sensations overlapped. Others were altogether absent.

Such was the problem with this method. It relied on what essences happened to remain—in amounts strong enough for Quentin's talent to detect and interpret.

Yet as the disjointedness and disorientation worsened, he had to suspect some of that had to do with the workings of Kendra's mind. The memories themselves were malformed. The spell embedded in the blue dye had affected her perception as well as her thoughts.

Flashes of shrubbery. The Landmark in the distance. Neil smiling over coffee. Kendra understood she was not thinking clearly. Stains on her fingers. The crosswalk on Main. She held her mobile phone to her ear.

"Kendra, sweetheart."

She went cold all over. Quentin ached with it.

"Do you have a moment?" The words went round and round in his head—Kendra's head—on a dizzying loop. She stared at her feet, the asphalt around them shimmered and blurred while the world spun.

"There's a good girl." New words to cycle round and round. A good girl. A good girl. A good girl.

A new voice calmed everything. "*Obliviscere.*"

Kendra knew this voice, too. It belonged to a good person. She wouldn't hurt Kendra. Alma wouldn't hurt anyone.

Quentin felt no such reassurance—quite the contrary, as he began to feel direct effects of the spell Alma was working. *Had* worked, past tense. Present. When he would have ended the connection he was yanked onward, the moments of Kendra's remaining moments playing like a mistimed slide show. He picked a spot near the end.

Kendra, looking straight at him.

No. At herself, in a mirror. Water running in the sink. Pale, drawn skin. Haunted eyes.

Her image became that of another. Neil Amundsen. Staring out of the mirror. Staring at Kendra, but at Quentin too.

«Hurry. You're running out of time.»

He was, yes. He accompanied Kendra. Lobby. Corridor. He should pull out. If he experienced the moment of her death, what would happen? Nothing good, he could guess. And no help to the investigation.

Yet there was curiosity, wasn't there? And a heavy calm, like being under a weighted blanket. Only a little while more.

Kendra pushed open the door and they went into the alley. Her killer left his position by the tree and walked toward her. When the young man pulled the metal bar from beneath his jacket, a distant part of Quentin knew he had overstayed. His mind was as blank as Kendra's; his willpower, as absent.

The young man lunged, swinging the metal bar. It struck the side of Kendra's head, sending Quentin's vision to white in an excruciating flash.

He awoke, if that was the word for it, to nothing. A black void, utterly silent. Was this it, then? The end?

At the time of his Great Mistake, there had been sights and sounds. There had been the Coachman.

Perhaps he was merely drifting, untethered—although the use of *merely* understated the situation rather a lot. He really ought to get back to himself.

Abruptly, he was.

As if a switch had been tripped, Quentin went from seeing nothing at all to seeing Edith's face—out of focus for being so near. Her nose bumped his. Her mouth shaped words he couldn't hear. She gripped his head, her hands on either side. Her fingertips were points of discomfort, he noted as feeling began to return.

He lay on his back, which meant he had dropped at some point. The floor was hard. He'd have a monster of a headache.

"Wake up!"

Ah, brilliant, his hearing returned.

"Quentin, please, I can't—"

"I'm here," he managed to croak, blinking for what felt like the first time in an age. Had his eyes been open throughout? That was odd.

Edith pulled her hands away, drew back a few inches. He could see her better. She knelt at his side. Every part of him felt leaden. Not yet in his control.

"You have freckles," he said, fascinated. How had he missed them before this? Her glasses frames, he supposed. But up close, they were obvious. A faint smattering across the crest of her cheekbones and bridge of her nose.

"You bloody bastard," she swore, dropping to sit. She wiped her freckled nose with the back of a trembling hand.

Her face was wet, he realized with some puzzlement. Funny that he had noticed the freckles before the—his gaze shifted.

Tears overflowed her eyes.

Lovely brown eyes that were staring at him in horror.

He tried to sit up, but rolled over instead, thinking to do this in stages. "Sweetheart, what—"

"I thought you were dead," she choked out.

Because he now lay on his front, he saw only the floor his forehead currently rested upon. Try as he might, he couldn't rush the feeling back into his body. "No," he insisted, "that's not what happens when—"

"I thought you were *dead*," she repeated with emphasis. She must have gotten to her feet because they moved into view. The tips of her sensible boots, about an inch from his left eye.

"I was about to get help." Her voice was raw. "One second more and I would have. I'd have broken the circle—I didn't know what the consequences might be and I didn't care. *I didn't care!* Bloody, *bloody* hell, Quentin. I could kill you myself. You could have goddamned warned me." She pivoted deftly and took several quick strides away.

Distance brought more of her into Quentin's limited view. Her back was to him. She had her arms wrapped around her middle. Her shoulders shook.

"You knew that's what would happen." She sniffled. "Didn't you? You knew and you didn't think to warn me."

"It isn't always—I've never read from a—" From a corpse. Images and sensations threatened to return. He took a slow breath, forced his mind, his memory to clear. His hip was not screaming, which was something. He pushed onto hands and knees.

"I can't keep doing this," Edith said, but so quietly that she must be speaking to herself. For herself. "I can't. I'm not cut out for—Are you going to be sick again?"

"No." Quentin swallowed. "Maybe."

CHAPTER 22

Thia was not much of a day drinker, but when Quentin went behind the unattended bar to fix himself a gin and tonic, she was tempted. But, since alcohol had never been much help when it came to her decision-making, she joined the others at the largest table to await the arrival of their lunch order. The taproom's kitchen wouldn't open until later, but staff would be bringing down food prepared by the upstairs restaurant.

"Is your partner all right?" Fiona Ross asked Edith, seated along with Thia and Abby on the table's gently curved booth seat. Because of the deal Jack Ross had made with Abby, the usual—unusual—group had expanded from six to eight.

There was such a pressured atmosphere in the otherwise empty room that Thia expected to see cracks develop in the window glass.

Fiona and Jack obviously hated Murphy. Cormac obviously didn't want to be a part of this. And obviously something had happened in the Ogham Room that had the two Brigantium agents barely able to look at one another.

"Quentin, you mean?" Edith responded tightly. She glanced over at the bar and her expression went from stiff to hostile. "Better than he was."

"What the hell happened in there?" asked Jack, across the table along with Cormac and Murphy, where there were separate chairs. Because of a lack of privacy until now, the analysis of the blue marks had not yet been discussed.

Edith removed her glasses and began polishing the lenses with a napkin. "My scanner was an unmitigated failure. The readings were too unstable. I need to get into the log file to try to diagnose the cause—find out whether it was on my end or to do with the substance itself."

"But you neutralized them, right?" Jack spoke with urgency. "My parents went back in with her."

"There's no danger," Quentin said, arriving to set his drink on the table. With the help of his cane, he lowered himself into the closest of two available chairs. "They're a tracking device, primarily, which was then used as a conduit. To have an effect, the medium must be absorbed. There's no chance of that now, not even when direct contact is made."

"You *didn't* neutralize the spells?" Jack was braced as if to rush off. "You left them operational?"

Quentin took a large drink. Instead of a traditional highball glass, his was a pint. "What harm they were capable of doing has been done," he said after he'd swallowed. "At this point, there's far more risk involved in trying to break them than in leaving them alone." He drank again.

"If the scanner failed," Thia asked, already anticipating his reply, "how do you know that?"

"He read them directly, that's how," Edith said, glaring.

"*Jaysus,*" Murphy said. "So that's what that was."

Attention turned his way.

"The energy surge."

Both Cormac and, more surprisingly, Fiona nodded.

"And of course there was the thump," Murphy added. "The room is soundproofed, but something of that nature does get through. That was you, I take it?"

"I did fall, yes." Quentin set down his glass. It looked as if only ice remained.

"Psychometry, is that it?" Fiona pointed to his gloved hands. "You're touch psychic?"

He made a noncommittal noise.

"What did you see?"

"Not much that wasn't already known. But I know who was in the building when she received the marks, and who was on the call she took in the middle of the street."

"Amundsen?" Murphy asked, intent.

"Yes, and—"

Loud, rapid tapping on the front window glass made several people, including Thia, startle.

Outside, almost up against it, Madame Demetka gestured and mouthed words while she sidled rightward, out of sight.

Destined for the door, presumably. The Alchemy had two ways in, one from the lobby and one from the sidewalk. Both led to the same antechamber, not visible from the main area, and both were currently locked.

"I'll go," Abby volunteered. Since she sat at the closest end of the booth, it was most convenient. "I don't need a key or anything, do I?"

"No," said Murphy.

Jack had yet to recover from astonishment. "Who is that?"

Edith fielded that one. "A local psychic. Of sorts."

By the sound of things, Abby had gotten a door open.

"Never do you call me." Madame Demetka's accented voice carried easily. "Always, my Guides must be the ones to alert me to these doings. Ah!" She hurried in. "Man with Limp, you are not scathed? There was much concern."

"I need another," that same man muttered, taking his glass to the bar.

"Excellent," she told him, "I will have Sazerac, please and

thanks." As she pulled the remaining chair around to the end of the table, she asked Edith, "He does know how, yes? Oh, but maybe not. He is English, and the drink, it is from—" She waggled her hand at Quentin, already pouring amber liquid from a fancy bottle. "Never the mind, please. Instead I will have Sidecar." With a dramatic sweep of her garments, she sat. "What have I missed?"

"He was telling us about what he learned from reading the marks on Kendra's skin," Abby said, retaking her place beside Thia. "But now he's bartending."

"No wonder my Guides were very much alarmed. Yes." She waved to get his attention. The multitude of bracelets around her wrist jangled. "Very dangerous to attempt such a thing," she told him loudly. "But you share with us now. Room is not big. We can hear."

He secured the cocktail shaker's lid with an overly hard tap. "The second voice on the call belonged to that woman who runs the Retreat." Ice cubes rattled as he agitated the drink.

"Alma?" Abby's voice echoed Thia's surprise. "*Alma* was on the phone with Kendra?"

"Indeed." He tipped the shaker over a coupe glass. Bright orange liquid poured out. "She helped Amundsen influence Kendra and affected her memory of events. Erased it, essentially." Cane in one hand, small tray of two drinks in the other, he returned to the table.

"Alma must have good reason to do such a thing," Madame Demetka said as he took his place. She reached past Jack to claim her cocktail. "Or is forced by bad reason. Oh, this is nice," she said after a quick sip. She toasted Quentin. "Very nice."

He grunted as he sat.

Thia studied him. The toll this was taking was obvious. He should be resting or, better yet, staying out of this altogether. Maybe they all should.

Overwhelmed, she rubbed her hands over her closed eyes. It was too late, wasn't it, to stop. Maybe there had never been a choice, not if there was to be justice for Kendra and the young man who had been used as nothing more than a tool. There was evil at work. Maybe good people—and she did not question that everyone at this table was (or had the potential to be) good—had no choice but to stand against it.

But . . . at what cost? What was Thia prepared to lose?

"You okay?" Abby asked.

"Yeah." She opened her eyes—and was relieved to see she was not the center of attention. Madame Demetka still was, as she had continued to opine on possible reasons for Alma's behavior. Only Abby and, apparently, Cormac noticed Thia's existential crisis.

He turned to Madame Demetka. "What was that you said about trees?"

"Oh, yes, yes," Madame Demetka said with another excited jangle of bracelets. "Alma. I have come to know her through our mutual work for the trees. To stop the slaughter. I felt a kinship, pleasant after many years of thinking she did not approve of my work with my Guides, so—"

"So she shares your concern for trees." His words slowed, as if to invite correction or elaboration. "To . . . save them? Particular trees? From . . . removal?"

"Yes, yes, all trees are important but Alma, she focuses on the oldest. Fundamental, she calls them."

"Such as the black cottonwood tree on Potters Street?"

"Behind the fence, yes! She encouraged much action there."

"Action against the city?"

Thia began to see where this was headed.

"Yes, the city. Some 'expert' told them of 'dangerous' trees. City government has been all too happy to listen." Madame Demetka's pointed, fuchsia nails made her air quotes especially threatening.

"Government," Cormac offered, "such as the city manager?"

"And council. And mayor. Pallister was the one who tricked us about the library cedar and—"

"Leverage," Murphy said over her. "He got to Alma through the trees."

"He, who?" Madame Demetka demanded. "Again I am out of circle."

Fiona raised her hand. "I'm afraid Jack and I are too."

The ice in Quentin's glass clinked when he knocked back his second drink. The sound almost covered that of Cormac's sigh.

"We're either in this with you," Jack threatened, "or we're in this on our own. And I think you'd rather we didn't inadvertently get in your way."

"We are all in this together," Madame Demetka said. "We here, and many more. Those who care about the trees. About Kendra. About right and wrong. And look, here is food." Sure enough, the first of two waitstaff came in bearing the meals. "There will be sitting and talking anyway while you eat. May I place a late order?" she asked as the waiter arrived at the table. "The portobello burger is favorite."

● ○ ●

"We need to approach this strategically," Murphy said to Jack Ross, who was having none of it.

Understandably so, Cormac thought. The Ross family was obviously close knit, and both the brother and surviving sister were determined to avenge Kendra's death.

"Bullshit." Jack tossed his crumpled serviette onto his plate of unfinished sandwich and crisps. "We know who is responsible. We go to the police—"

"With a potentially corrupted chief and officers," Murphy pointed out, gesturing with a fork. He hadn't been using it to eat; his meal was largely untouched. He had been toying with it, like a culinary version of a fidget spinner.

"Then we handle this ourselves. Between us, your organization, and the Brigantium, we've got more than enough to deal with this *huldrekall* if we—"

"Hold on," Edith interrupted with both hands raised. "The Society of Brigantium is not some vigilante force. Even if the director or the assistant director sends more agents"— she sent a questioning look to Quentin, who answered her with a shrug—"they couldn't—we aren't trained to—"

Murphy set down his fork. "Some are, of course. But there's the problem of time. We can ask, but don't count on their getting here when we need them."

"Justice," Jack Ross said. "Justice for my sister."

"She would not want us to cross that line, Jack," his living sister said quietly.

"No? *She* crossed it." He narrowed his eyes at Murphy. "She crossed it all the time, didn't she, working for you?"

The once hot-tempered Irishman did not so much as blink.

"Better to move quickly," Cormac put in, "than to wait until the party is underway." Ignoring Thia's questioning frown, he asked Murphy, "How many people can you get?"

"Enough."

"Wait," Thia said, a frown drawing down the fine arches of her brows, while Murphy began to text. "What are we doing? We can't just—"

"I have people." Madame Demetka took a flip phone from inside her sleeve. Glued-on beads and repair tape decorated the exterior. "Citizen's brigade. Tonight is a protest outside Pallister's home. The tree cutting, the Plaza nonsense. Some will already be there. I will ask what they see." Phone at her ear, she walked some distance away.

"I can ask the coven," said Abby. "I won't put members in danger. I can't do that. But Marge, for one, has contacts at the Retreat. She supplies some of their herbs. Maybe she can find out what ritual they're supposed to do."

"What are we doing?" Thia tried again, tapping her water glass with a spoon for attention. "I get that Amundsen needs to be stopped, but what are we talking about—going to the mayor's house and doing . . . what?"

Murphy tucked his smartphone away. "Whatever is necessary. Can you do recon?" he asked Cormac.

"Naturally." So much for the rest of his meal. And it was a very nice roasted vegetable with romesco. He stood. "What's the address?"

Murphy gave it, adding, "Northeast of town, near the base of the bluff."

Cormac put the address into his mobile. He would study the maps before setting off, give himself an idea of what to expect. "I'll be in touch."

He reached the antechamber before Thia caught up, stopping him with a hand on his upper arm. He let her turn him around, away from the door to the street.

"What are you going to do?" Her face was pale; her lovely hazel eyes, fearful.

What was he meant to do with that? He was ill-equipped to give comfort. "A flyover, that's all."

Instead of letting go, her hold tightened. The expression in her eyes held him even more firmly than that.

"What is it all leading to?" she asked. "What are we talking about—making some sort of attack? On the mayor's house? On Amundsen?" She withdrew her hand. "I feel like I got you into this. I'm sorry. I'm so sorry."

He could relieve her of that, at least. The O'Shannon's red book was a secret burning a figurative hole in his pocket. He hadn't come here for her. Not entirely. But he couldn't bring himself to say the words.

"*Muileach,* this life isn't for you. Keep yourself out of it."

"But I'm in it. I'm already in it. And I did help save the town last time."

"By nearly blowing it up."

"Okay, yeah, that was not great." Her aspect was part rue, part jest. "But it did work out in the end."

"So it did." He found himself smiling. Briefly. "But please, Thia, stay out of this. Stay safe."

"Kendra was my friend. Abby *is* my friend. The Brigantium wouldn't be here if not for me. And you, Cormac, you're—" Her lips pressed tight.

"I am . . . ?" he prompted before he could stop himself. That he wanted to hear her say it shocked and alarmed him. If he had needed more evidence of the threat she presented, here it was. He wanted too much.

She took a step back, out of reach. "Some other time. Or not." Her face could be so expressive. "Just . . . be careful, all right?"

"Always," he said, although they both knew that to be a lie.

● ○ ●

Remembrance Bluff

Twenty minutes later, he was crouched in a bramble thicket a mile from the mayor's rural property. He had entered it as a raven and would exit the same way. He would have avoided transformation at all if he hadn't needed to use his phone.

"This could get messy," he said into it. From the sound of things, Murphy had put him on speaker. "We will be outnumbered six to one, at the least, and that's assuming the Retreat won't work in opposition." He shifted his weight and thorns pricked into his scalp. The sooner he could leave, the better.

"No assault," came Abby's voice. "No violence if we can help it. There are too many bystanders. *Innocent* bystanders," she said over Murphy's objection.

Cormac had already relayed what he'd seen in his flyover. The mayor's property was relatively isolated, being in mostly undeveloped grassland with only an occasional upscale development. A few small wineries, an equestrian facility, and puffy modern homes set on expansive, fenced-in grounds.

Roads were few and far between, as were trees or other safe cover—hence his hiding at such a prickly distance.

As he had neared the rocky outcropping known as Remembrance Bluff, the mayor's house had been easy to identify by the crowd amassing along the road out front.

The Citizen's Brigade exuded New Age eccentricity. Not as flamboyantly as Madame Demetka, but the connection was unmistakable. A patchwork coat here, a tie-dye scarf there. They waved placards adorned with hand-done depictions of trees, peace signs, crossed-out chainsaws, and the like. Multi-colored lettering demanded an end to "The Desecration."

Thia's voice came on the line. "If the main thing is to stop Amundsen from doing *huldrekall* stuff at the party, why don't we make sure he doesn't get there—or if he's there already, take him out? Out as in 'away,' not 'take him out.'"

Try as they might, they had been unable to locate him. No sightings since yesterday.

"There's a spell or a charm for that, isn't there?" she asked. "I had it done to me. Cormac, you remember. Do you know how that was done?"

He did indeed, or a version of it. That was how he planned to empty Cassandra's storage unit once he gained access.

"Yes," was all he said.

"So what do we need—a silver charm, like what Matt gave me to wear, or would any object do for—"

"Thia," Abby interrupted with pronounced dismay. "What are you talking about? What charm? What was 'done' to you? And why didn't you tell me?"

How intriguing. Apparently, Thia had not told her friend about that rather memorable event, when she had materialized at Fiend's Fell, in Idris's private chamber.

"Oh." She sounded uncomfortable, and had reason to be. "I was transported, that's all. "

Cormac waited for what details might follow. She had been *transported* out of a bath. She had arrived dripping wet and naked.

There were aspects of that event which would be uncomfortable for him, too, if mentioned.

"I had been in a—been in a Brigantium safe house, and the next thing I knew, I was in a room where Idris Cathmor was. Nothing happened," she said. "To me, anyway. I don't believe Idris knew I was there before Cormac sent me away. It was you, right, who did that?"

"For fuckssake, Thia," Abby swore before he could answer. "You didn't tell me any of that."

"It kind of got lost in all the other things."

He doubted that. But it was interesting that she had kept it private. And it was interesting what she left out of this telling, which went more to *his* shame than any embarrassment she might have for being in the nude.

"The Inverness Airport attack was the next day," she said. "But my point in mentioning this was the method. Could we do that to Amundsen?"

"A relocation charm." That was Murphy. "Plant the object on him somehow, then trigger it. But that'll leave whoever did the planting behind."

"Not necessarily," Cormac said with regret. But if he worked the charm himself, he might be able to keep its secrets. He wasn't in the habit of giving his hard-earned magics for free. "There's one where it's enough for the person carrying the object to be in physical contact with the target. They'll be transported together."

"That's it, then," Murphy said to general murmurs of assent from the others. "I'll carry the charmed object into the party, take hold of Amundsen, and off we go—to where?"

"How about Founders Hall?" suggested Edith, and Cormac shut his eyes on a deep, silent sigh. "Inside it, if at all possible, and then you could open it to the rest of us?"

Damn, damn, and *damn*. But it was the most logical place.

This time, his sigh was audible. "If I'm the one to trigger it, yes." After getting inside the building himself.

What a personal disaster this was shaping up to be.

CHAPTER 23

Remembrance Drive
Granite Springs, Oregon
01 February

"I take it we're off again," Declan said, breaking a ten minute stretch of silence. He gave Abigail a sidelong glance, gauged her temper as he tried to check his own. "You and I."

"We were never on," she said tightly.

"Were we not?" Declan took the Maserati into a sweeping curve. Ah, he loved this car. The feel of it. Power and control, dressed up in a sleek, luxurious package. The feel of it on an open country road with a gorgeous woman beside him—he accelerated, toyed with the idea of opening her up.

"No," she said, and continued to stare straight ahead. "We weren't."

"Ah, well. You're right, of course." He kept his tone casual. Dishonesty, all of it. She knew that as well as he. Better, given her talent for picking up emotional cues.

He was adept at concealing such things—particularly from himself, which was half the trick. But around Abigail he had slipped up on occasion, and intentionally dropped his guard a time or two besides.

"Tonight, everyone has to believe otherwise," he reminded her. "People of your acquaintance. People who frequent your shop. You're able to do that?."

"I'll manage."

"You have to be sure, *mo rúnsearc*. It won't be too difficult?" He was prepared to turn around. "Amundsen will be suspicious. We have to be convincing."

"I already said I can do this." The leather of the bucket seat squelched as she repositioned herself to face him. "It would go a lot better if you left off nagging and sniping."

His grip on the wheel tightened momentarily. "At least I'm not wielding silence like a damned weapon."

"That's rich, coming from you, Mr. Strong and Silent Type. Maybe I simply have nothing to say. Maybe I'm looking ahead and worrying about what might happen. Maybe I'm thinking about Amundsen and how much I'd like to strangle him, but instead I'm going to have to act as if I don't know that he had my friend murdered. Not everything is about you, you insufferable, condescending ass of a—"

"*A mhuirnín,*" he warned as the car's frame took on an otherwise inexplicable tremor.

Abigail undoubtedly felt it too. She turned away from him to stare out the windscreen.

After a time, the vibration settled.

"We can't risk that at Pallister's," he advised.

"Don't lecture," she snapped. But a sigh followed a moment later. "I know. That's part of what I'm worried about."

Buildings had become scarce within an alternating mix of tended and untended land. Declan took the car into another curve. It wouldn't be long now. "I should've come alone."

"No." She sounded resigned rather than convinced. "None of this should be done alone."

Yet again Declan felt his temper threaten. "You don't trust me."

"Obviously. But that's not what I meant. No one should face Amundsen alone."

"You think to protect me?" He was genuinely stunned. Lest she pick up on that, when she looked over, he grinned condescendingly. "How sweet."

"Fuck you."

He laughed, halfway to genuine pleasure. "Would that you would, *a rúnsearc*. Would that you would."

With a squeal, the Maserati's wipers commenced scraping across the dry windshield while the overhead and instrument lights strobed.

That mad, was Abigail Collins.

And more fool Declan Murphy for deliberately provoking her inside an enclosed, moving vehicle. Rather than apologize (even if it were in his nature to do such a thing, she was liable to take it wrong and they'd end up overturned in a ditch) he held his tongue.

Gradually, the car's electrics calmed.

"You're such an ass."

He smiled. "I'll not argue with you."

"Now, you mean. You'll not argue with me *now*."

"While going fifty miles an hour? No. An ass I may be, but never a fool." The wipers made one last juddering pass before coming to rest. "But this is exactly why I shouldn't have let you come along."

"*Let* me." Abigail growled. "Maybe you could just not talk so we can get there in one piece." She proceeded to mutter too low for him to make out.

He didn't need to hear to take her meaning. This was, after all, how they were with one another: volatile.

It hadn't been his intention, this time, to provoke her. He'd stated a plain truth. He was letting her come along. He could have refused.

He should have.

To be sure, someone needed to approach Alma and make an

appeal, convince her to not assist Amundsen with whatever he intended; and there were good reasons why that someone should not be Declan. Namely, Amundsen and easily aroused suspicions if he saw Declan speaking to Alma. And it would be easier to have someone else be responsible for the group communications so he wouldn't be seen to be rudely texting while with Amundsen.

Since contact was needed for the transport charm to work, Declan would engage him in conversation and keep him from noticing Abigail with Alma. Meanwhile, she would send the group text to cue Cormac's break-in at Founders Hall. Upon receiving a reply—presuming success—she would make her way over to Declan and text to request the transport spell. It was a lot to ask of a novice.

Kendra Ross would have been perfect. High enough on his employment roster so as to be a sensible companion at such a networking event, with more than enough beauty, charm, and intelligence to make her a welcome addition in her own right. And with her training and experience, he could have counted on her to get herself out of trouble—so that he wouldn't be distracted by concern for her.

No one else ticked all those right boxes. Granite Springs was an insular community. He could arrive with an outsider and no one would think much of it, but should he arrive with any other of his known employees or associates, they would wonder why now, why here, when usually he never brought a "plus one." He was not known for having friends, but at least with Kendra they had been known to be *friendly*.

He had considered Thia for it. He had been seen to socialize with her previously—including two nights ago—and it would be easy enough to use her business as why he had invited her tonight. Hell, if she weren't so new to ownership, she would have been included on the guest list.

But she *was* new, not just to Granite Springs but to magic. Her lack of knowledge and control were liabilities.

Besides, Abigail never would have stood for it. Complain as she might about Declan's high-handed "let," there was no way she would have "let" her friend take such a risk. Her protectiveness of those she cared about was as admirable as it was problematic.

Much like the woman herself.

For a man not given to reflection, Declan had been forced to do a fair amount of late. It would be better if, after this, he avoided her. He should have never "let" himself entertain what amounted to a doomed fantasy.

He could see why he had—he did enjoy a challenge. But the risks to them both were too great, no matter what his feelings might be in the matter.

Feelings? What rot. He didn't do feelings. Not anymore.

"That's a bigger crowd than I thought," Abigail said as the car approached Remembrance Butte. The Citizens Brigade had gathered at its base, directly across the road from Pallister's puffed-up ranch-style manse.

With the butte's flat top and two-thousand foot height, it would offer a commanding view, but Cormac had assured him that no one had been up there when he'd flown over earlier, and Madame Demetka had tasked some of the brigade with making sure that remained the case.

Whereas the bluff hemmed in the whole northerly side of the road, the southerly was entirely open but for the house. The land's slope meant that it had expansive views all the way down to a wooded creek, miles distant, and Granite Springs to the southwest. Too exposed for Declan's taste, but favorable in this situation, offering multiple points of escape.

"Loretta is here," Abigail said. She was peering past him at the protesters and their enthusiastically waving signage as he guided the Maserati into the driveway. "Sonya and Luis, too."

"Your coven?" He glanced at her as he eased to a stop by a uniformed valet. Her face had tensed considerably.

"Yes. I hope they—" She blew out a breath as she rolled her shoulders. "I hope no one gets hurt."

"I'll do my best." Leaving the engine running, he put the car in park and set the hand brake. "Showtime," he said, and opened his door to get out.

The fob and key in the ignition was a spare. His regular set was in his left trouser pocket. He accepted the claim check from the valet, then went to meet Abigail as she closed her door.

Before she could start up the short walkway to the house, he took light hold of her elbow. The wool of her coat retained warmth from the car. "A moment," he instructed quietly, and watched as it was driven away.

At the drive's exit, it took a right. Presumably it would go to the end of the line of vehicles parked on the roadside berm, but Declan needed to be sure. It soon pulled over. The brake lights went out. Not the most ideal spot in terms of distance and quick access, but not terrible if one cut across the lawn and field. He checked Abigail's feet.

"Lovely," he said, torn between disapproval and eroticism.

The red velvet stilettos *were* lovely, but not fit for purpose, should that purpose involve running across rough terrain. Or running at all, he should think. He let his gaze travel back up the length of her—to land on her newly pinched expression. The heels' impractical inches put her near his height.

"I couldn't very well wear sneakers with formal dress," she said, annoyance sparking. Such a fascinating shade, her eyes. Declan itched to paint them. He had seen them as ultramarine violet at times; Prussian blue, at others. It depended on lighting and what colors surrounded her and on her mood. Currently, they were a tempestuous gray.

"No matter." He released his hold on her arm in order to slide his hand to her lower back. He began guiding her up the walk. Her slender frame held a brittle tension. He needed to remember that she was not a trained operative. He leaned in, catching the subtle lavender and angelica of her scent. "It'll be fine."

"Oh, are you psychic?" She strode ahead.

Wary of appearing all sorts of foolish, Declan let her go and adopted the loose stroll of a man who couldn't be bothered. If the staff and guests involved in the bottleneck at the entry assumed he and Abigail were in the midst of a lover's spat, it might make things easier.

This close, sounds from within the house began to compete with the protesters' shouts and disorganized drumming. Faint strains of piped-in music. The hum of massed conversations. The buzz of energy, too, and not all of a pleasant nature. There was a sharper element. If Declan had not arrived expectant of danger, that feeling would make him so.

All the window shades were drawn. Nothing beyond a faint, illuminated glow showed through. Protection and privacy.

Within the covered entry stood two men in ill-fitting dress suits. Each played the role of bouncer but had the ominous mien of an armed guard and the build of a rugby forward.

This had all the marks of walking into a trap, and Declan felt the absence of his weapons keenly. A scanner had been put in place, ill-concealed on the pole of a patio heater, else he'd be tempted to fetch his Ruger from the Maserati's lockbox.

By the time he caught up with Abigail, the bottleneck had cleared. He carefully pulled the invitation from his inner coat pocket, held it out for inspection. The nearer of the guards, a clean-shaven blond who topped Declan by a foot, inspected the card without making contact. At his curt nod, the other guard moved to open the door. "Welcome."

One thickly accented word was not enough to pinpoint the speaker's country of origin, but it did suggest the region and go a long way toward confirming suspicions.

Light, heat, and sound hit with surprising force after Declan crossed the threshold. There must be a dampening spell at work. Quickly, he absorbed and observed. It helped that he had been a guest here several times before.

"Allow me," he said, stepping behind Abigail as she began to remove her coat. With the way her hair had been gathered into a sleek twist and held by a rhinestone-studded comb, it left the nape of her neck exposed. Tempting. He breathed in, allowing himself the pleasure while he took hold of her coat at the artificial-fur collar. She stepped forward, allowing him to draw it away.

The revelation of her bare, smooth back made his breath catch.

Then she turned around and his vision telescoped, blurring all else but this lithe, glorious woman sheathed in crimson.

The body-tight dress ended a touch below her knees, show-casing long, shapely calves within some sort of glossy, sheer material that made him wonder what choice had been made—practical elastic or something more elaborate. Her shoulders, arms, and a deep, plunging vee of her chest were bare. He did his utmost to not stare at the bosom which featured in some of his best memories. His fingers clenched on the coat's fabric when it was her they wanted. Her waist. Her hips. Any and everything.

"Ah, Collins." Amazing that his voice worked at all. He felt winded. "You're like to stop a man's heart, you are."

Her lush mouth thinned as her brilliant eyes narrowed. She clearly wanted to tell him to go hang, but they had a hulking coat check attendant for an audience. She said nothing.

Declan laughed, and had a true smile on his face when he turned back to finish with the checks—hers and his. By the time he was tucking the claim into one of his formal jacket's two jetted pockets, he had himself back under control.

He found her waiting at the foyer's edge. She was surveying the milling crowd beyond.

Taking advantage of their agreed-upon roles, he stood close and again placed his hand on the small of her back. The velvet was as soft as it looked. He took care to stay within bounds, neither touching the available skin of her back nor landing too much below her waist, where the cloth clung to an ideal curve. The need to paint her was an ache.

She tensed but didn't shy away. "I hadn't expected so many people."

"High attendance, to be sure." With regret, he shifted his focus from the warm woman at his hand to the task.

The grand, vaulted room ahead was bustling with a winter-season who's-who of the most notable people the region had to offer. Unlike prior years, there were numerous unfamiliar faces, and the feeling of walking into a trap persisted.

There was power here, palpable despite skillful cloaking by those who possessed it. The larger the gathering, the higher the concentration. Slight leaks here and there added up.

"High number of staff, as well," Abigail said while, together, they continued to observe. She was correct. An abundance of workers—waitstaff in polyester tuxedos, caterers in white—threaded through the glamorous crowd to replenish drinks in hand and hors d'oeuvre stations located throughout.

Behind it all, stretched like a cinematic backdrop, was the distant view of Granite Springs, nestled into the shadowed foothills of the Siskiyou Mountains. The blinds had been left open along the panoramic windows, source of a great deal of mayoral pride. The sunset splashed the broken clouds with vermilion and gold.

"We need only concern ourselves with two," he said toward Abigail's ear as his thumb moved of its own accord, stroking the line between fabric and flesh. He was only human. "In and out. We should split up." Much as he would rather not.

Sighting a passing waiter, he stepped to the side, smoothly took a pair of champagne flutes from the carried tray. After a quick scan of the contents, he handed one to Abigail.

"Clean." He clinked his glass to hers before taking a sip. "It'd be suspicious not to imbibe, but do so sparingly. Socialize but don't linger. *Ádh mór.* Good luck," he translated brusquely as he moved off. He could ill afford the distraction of worrying about her, but he was going to do it anyway. When it came to Abigail Collins, it seemed he couldn't help himself.

Casually but with purpose—greetings exchanged with a city official here, quick banter with a business contact there—he worked his way into the crowd.

● ○ ●

First Street Parking Lot

"Shouldn't there be more of us?" Thia asked Edith. They were seated in the Brigantium SUV's middle row. Quentin was in the front passenger seat. He and the driver, Paul, were going over a detailed map of the block. From the back row, behind Thia, Agent Talbot was keeping watch out the rear window.

Almost a half hour had gone by since they had pulled into the public lot adjacent to Founders Hall. So far, nothing had happened—a good thing, but waiting had never been one of her strengths, especially when she had little idea of what she was waiting *for* other than it was dangerous and she was out of her depth. Maybe they all were, along with being woefully outnumbered. What were they thinking? There had to be a different, better—

"There *are* more of us here," Edith said in belated answer. "That we can't see them is a good thing." She paused in her scanner-tinkering to give Thia a smile that should have been reassuring.

Thia was beyond being able to find it so.

How could they be sure that Murphy's people were where he said they would be, positioned inside and on top of nearby buildings? Oh, she had no doubt that they would have *taken* those positions. But anything could have happened after.

She had seen them in action, both on Brodgar and during the holiday parade attack. They were obviously highly trained and skilled. But she had also seen the Rekkrs in action.

Add to that, there was the unknown of the so-called catering company. Murphy's people might have already been injured or lured away or killed.

Their plan—not very carefully laid out, it felt to her—could have been turned into a trap and the rest of them would not know until it was too late.

She looked past Edith and out the right side windows. They were parked by the bushes Kendra had used to hide. Were there people hiding in them now?

Whose people?

The rear of Founders Hall was yards distant across the all but empty lot. There had been six vehicles parked when they had arrived. Since then, people had come out of the ramen place, gotten into a Subaru and a Honda, and driven off. Were the remaining four as empty as they appeared?

Outside the lot and her line of sight was Jack and Fiona's rental car. She had noted them on the way in, parked by the Post Office. It would be in Agent Talbot's view, so that was one thing, at least, not on Thia's list of worries.

Which left the only other known participant in the area: Cormac. Although, as she kept reminding herself, he was not all that known. Not to her and, she suspected, not to anyone.

Across the lot, he stood in the shadow of the independent pharmacy. Its stretched-out, single-story building formed the opposite side of Founders Way, where otherwise there would be only parking spaces.

Despite the cold and general situation, he leaned with enviable casualness against a wooden electric pole. The setting sun was beginning to color the clouds in the sky and cast bronze highlights onto his wind-ruffled hair. What she wouldn't give to be so calm, so confident.

When this was over (assuming her survival), she would need to think long and hard about her feelings. She could get over simple, magnetic attraction. If she wanted. Probably. She did not need to act on it, anyway. Nor did she need to act on love, really. Particularly if it was an unhealthy sort.

Emotions didn't require action. Rage, for one. It was best to not act on that, wasn't it?

She already knew she was overlooking a number of serious faults and flaws in order to attempt a connection. She had also been quick to forgive, or at least overlook, past harms.

What if he didn't care that he had done them—like when he had terrified her at the fence before they "met" the next day? What if he didn't see himself as having any faults or flaws? As difficult as it was to comprehend, he had been alive for over two centuries. What if he didn't want to change?

What might that suggest about Cormac—or about Thia if she disregarded her own sense of right and wrong in order to justify an attraction? Could she be so malleable? So amoral?

She did not truly know him. She knew only what she had witnessed directly, and to a lesser validity what she had been told. Whatever else she thought she knew might have been fantasy, a fabrication made up of physical desire and her mind erroneously filling in the blanks.

He was *leanan sidhe,* of a whole Other world and time. He was disinclined to share anything of his past with her. Hell, he was disinclined to share his present. Likely, there was no place for her in his future, either, and no matter her feelings, she needed to accept that and move on.

She had enough problems. Talk about not knowing him or his world or what hers had become. Since last October, she didn't know *herself.* She needed to concentrate on that. On herself, alone.

That might be a bit ironic, given that she was sitting here despite serious misgivings because she felt safer in a group.

But she figured she'd be in no less danger of losing control of her power if she isolated herself, and there would be no one to help, to stop the power from overtaking her and doing untold damage for who knows how many miles around. She couldn't separate herself from what threatened her control— emotions like anger and fear. So, here she was, feeling those emotions and more, but perhaps able to do a little good. And not worry so terribly about the people she could see.

These thoughts were the opposite of calming. But there was nothing for her to do, currently, but stew in them. The others in the SUV were all involved in preparation work. Edith with her scanner adjustments; Quentin with his quiet discussion with Paul in the driver's seat. Thia wasn't familiar with Agent Talbot, but even if he was the type to engage in idle chitchat, she didn't want to distract him from his task.

She looked out at Cormac again. He wasn't the type for chit-chat either, but he could take her mind off these damn rumi-nations. But he had chosen to stand out in the cold instead of sitting inside the SUV with her and the others, part of the group until it was time for him to break into Founders Hall. There was no reason for his isolation. No reason that had to do with their plan, anyway.

But as Cormac took out his phone, it dawned on Thia that he might have his own reasons. His own plan.

After a frowning glance at the screen, he held it to his ear.

"That wouldn't be from Abby, would it?" Thia asked at large. "The call Cormac is taking."

"Shouldn't be," Quentin replied. They were supposed to get a group text before Abby and Murphy set the next phase in motion.

● ○ ●

"What is it you're waiting for?"

"O'Shannon," Cormac turned around, tilted his head up— so he looked directly at the vision crystal near the top of the pole. "Nice of you to get back to me." Far, far too late.

The O'Shannon laughed.

Cormac turned away. He had shown that he knew the crystal's location. No need to give the O'Shannon the ability to read his face during the rest of this. "What do you know?"

"The price of that would be more than you could pay. But I'll give you one for nine."

"You will give it *gratis,*" Cormac countered. "Getting these *huldrefolk* out the region benefits you as much as anyone."

"True enough, true enough. So here it is. After Yule, when the one you know as Amundsen returned, four of his Rekkrs entered through that door, and we've yet to see them again. After the Landmark's woman got inside, the same can be said of another Rekkr. He went in that morning. He has not come back out."

"There's another access?" Cormac had looked for any signs of one, including with his Sight. Nothing had come up. Not even the sealed-over entry under the neon arrow. It was no illusion. It truly was sealed.

"To be sure there is," said the O'Shannon. "But more to the point here, the *huldrekall* has a vicious temper and that can get him into trouble. Evidence, boy. I'm suggesting there might be evidence inside. Things he would be unable to defend even to those he has influenced or purchased. So once more, I'll be asking—what are you waiting for?"

The call disconnected.

What indeed, Cormac asked himself as he tucked his smartphone away. What indeed except for something that should not matter as much as it did: Thia's good opinion.

After what he was about to do, the truth would be revealed, or at least one piece of the truth, that he had come to Granite Springs out of his own interest.

That was the truth, wasn't it? He was here for what was his. But it was also true that his being here was to Thia's benefit.

His hands surprisingly tense, he rummaged in his pockets, located the pouch holding the doppelgänger discs.

She would see this as a betrayal. It was, of a sort. But he had made her no promises, no declarations, and in time she would come to understand. Hers was a forgiving nature.

Unlike his.

And if this led to justice for her friend? Forgiveness would be guaranteed. Not that any of that should matter. He should not care what she thought. He should not care if she decided to hate him forever. He had a life, and it would be better for them both if she was not a part of it. What should be a part of it was Idris's damned collection.

But, first things first. Cormac focused his intention on the O'Shannon's device and, holding a spell in his mind, spoke the trigger: "*Bloighich.*"

The magnesite crystal shattered into a puff of ineffectual dust. Having Brigantium witnesses would be bad enough; for the O'Shannon to watch could prove deadly.

From inside the SUV, Thia's view would be excellent.

Cormac didn't bother to hope that she might be looking in some other direction.

He took a hazel disc from the pouch and then, with it held between his thumb and outer two fingers, he snapped. "*Cruth atharraich.*"

The disc immolated in a flash.

He hadn't a mirror in which to check his face, but what he could see—hands, body—no longer resembled his own.

A quick glamour dealt with the appearance of his clothing, which hung far too loose at the waist and shoulders, and too tight over breasts and arse. Since clothes didn't matter to a security system, the illusion didn't take Cassandra's personal taste into consideration. It was simply a better fitting version of Cormac's current outfit.

"Here goes nothing." Or everything.

He walked across the Way. The alcove kept out most of the light cast by the pole's lamp. The fixture mounted above the doorframe was missing a bulb.

A kind of red-tinted laser beamed from a point on the door while a mesh of wards, visible in his Sight, wrapped net-like around his form. He could feel it, both as a constriction and an increasingly warm prickle upon—and then through—his skin as it scanned not only the surface of him but all the way within, through to the marrow of his bones.

If he matched what was on file, the net would release. If he did not, it would razor him out of existence.

It would try, at any rate. And it might succeed. He could heal from a lot, but to come back from being literal mincemeat would be quite a feat.

● ○ ●

"What the—"

Thia was out of the SUV before she realized she had flung open the door. She heard her name called—by Edith—when she was already cutting across the parking lot at a jog that she undoubtedly failed to make appear innocuous. Her heart was pounding.

Cormac had turned into Cassie and blithely walked up to Founders Hall.

As she continued to not-run, she saw him—as Cassie—open what should have been a locked door and, easy-peasy, enter a building that was supposedly so secure that no one could get inside, which was why they had been sitting outside for . . . how long? When apparently he could have just done *that*.

All this time, from the moment Cormac had arrived back in town, he could have *done that*.

When Jack and Fiona Ross passed Thia in a full-out sprint, she abandoned all pretense and ran.

What the hell had she seen? Cormac, now Cassie.

"Oh, God," she rasped in the icy air. Had he been Cassie all along? Had she escaped and somehow taken Cormac's form? Had Cassie done something to him? Thia's mind raced faster than her body and was taking her to terrifying and nauseating places. Surely she would have known? Last night. She would have noticed if the man she had done those things with was *not* that man?

Cormac was a stranger in so many ways, but she did know *him,* didn't she? She would not have felt that same attraction to anyone who looked exactly like him. The kaleidescope of colors when they kissed, that was special, wasn't it? Unique?

But what the *hell?* All this time, if he had a way to get inside Founders Hall, he would have said, wouldn't he?

"Apparently not," she heard herself wheeze. She came to a winded stop in the alcove. The door was ajar.

She couldn't see much through the crack except checkered linoleum and a glimpse of stairs. Jack and Fiona had already gone in. They hadn't waited for her (and why should they) or anyone else.

Should she wait? She looked back. Edith was running full out with about forty, fifty feet to cover. Quentin was some length beyond that.

Wary of touching anything directly, Thia stuck her foot into the opening, used it to swing the red metal door outward. It bumped against an overturned coffee can, sending it rocking. A scattering of sand and cigarette butts on the cement told what purpose that had served.

She tentatively crossed the threshold.

There was a dog-legged stairway ahead, a closed door on her left. The exterior wall was to her right, with a row of narrow casement windows high above to let in the alley pole's golden light. A bulb on a cord suspended from the ceiling made a minimal contribution. The air smelled musty despite a sharp chemical-pine scent, and had the density of a building prone to damp.

She hoped the footsteps above were Cormac's, Jack's, and Fiona's. She would like to believe the building was otherwise empty.

She shouldn't be here.

She knew that with absolute certainty even as she ascended the stairs. She was too worked up. The Cailleach's power was too present, roused by the onslaught of emotions. Everything from before, intensified and with the addition of . . . betrayal? And maybe rage.

Hadn't she just been warning herself about that? About how rage should not be acted upon?

She felt like a skier at the stop of a steep run; the slightest push would set the power off, sending her racing down in an inevitable, disastrous loss of control. She did not ski any more than she could wield the Cailleach's magic.

When her feet hit the top landing, she barely registered her surroundings. Her hand, thrust into her coat pocket moments before, cramped from gripping the wand so tightly.

It wasn't helping. All that stood between her and oblivion was nothing. Nothing at all.

CHAPTER 24

Remembrance Drive
Granite Springs, Oregon
Imbolc

Abby was reminded of a solar system. Small, conversational clusters of people slowly circled the room like planets caught in an orbital hierarchy. Their proximity to the sun—a central, X-shaped altar set up to correspond with the cardinal directions—was determined by level of influence in Granite Springs. When she moved through the outer rings, the ones which corresponded with her own status, progress was slow for having to exchange greetings and make excuses for moving on. The closer she got to the center, the fewer people there were for her to acknowledge, and if any even recognized her, they were not interested. She received barely a passing glance.

The power structure must be maintained, even at an event traditionally meant to celebrate seasonal rebirth and renewal. Its origins were agricultural; she supposed for a society more based on commerce, business deals were its version of crop sowing. Murphy, she noted in glimpses, received much more attention the closer he got to center.

The slower his progress, the more time Abby might have with Alma before she needed to send the initial group text, but also, the more time in which Amundsen might notice and react.

Weaving her way through the final orbit, she approached the Retreat's altar so that, for the two women there, she was obscured by the supply crates they were unloading.

Alma and her ancillary, Jeanette, were working unassisted in the juncture of the north and west altar branches. The other Retreat members were likely preparing themselves elsewhere in the house. Meditation and prayer were common pre-rituals with Abby's coven, but the ways of the Retreat were largely unknown. A certain amount of secrecy was to be expected with any spiritual group, but in light of all this, Abby worried it might have crossed the line into being a cult without anyone around them noticing.

Alma and Jeanette were dressed in silk robes of violet and gold. Matching beads adorned Alma's upswept braids, while Jeanette's usual orange-red spikes were entirely covered by a striped headscarf.

"What is all this?" There was such dismay in latter's voice that Abby decided to eavesdrop. Keeping herself aligned with the crates, she sidled close enough to a pedestal holding hors d'oeuvres that she might seem to be considering the labeled choices. Goat cheese and spinach fried wontons. Vegan pigs-in-blankets. Lingonberry-orange chutney on rye crackers.

"These are not for our Imbolc ritual," Jeanette was saying. "Why do we have a tincture of hops? And this—this shouldn't be out of the lockbox, let alone here with so many people and easy access. And the mugwort? *Mater,* these are all for—"

"Hush, please." Alma's rough whisper was hard to hear over all the surrounding noise. "I'm sorry. But after tonight, that'll be the end of it. The trees will be safe."

"But these ingredients, *Mater.* What are you saying? You've made an agreement on our behalf—without telling us? To do the memory rite?"

"Hush! Please. We must."

"On whom?"

"Everyone. I know, I know"—Alma's voice cracked as if she were near tears—"but we have no choice."

"Bullshit." Leaving her glass with the hors d'oeuvres, Abby came out from behind the altar crates. One on the floor kept her from getting right up in Alma's shocked face as she and Jeanette turned in surprise. "There is *always* a choice."

She worked to keep her voice low. Amundsen, as a member of the top social tier, stood a few feet from the other side of the altar's X, directly across from her. It was crucial that she maintain a pleasant expression. Unfortunately, skills mastered over decades in the service industry had deserted her. She was so upset she felt incendiary.

"*You* told me that," Abby said, "and not so long ago, either, that you could've forgotten. 'There is always choice. What is lacking is perspective.' Did you not mean it? Why did you not seek help? From the police, from your—"

"What would I have said? That the city manager was going to cut down mystically important trees unless I helped him do mind control? Half the force already thinks I'm a kook after I was caught sky clad at the upper reservoir. Best case, they'd laugh me out of the station. Worst would be a psych hold." Misery was in Alma's voice, her face, her every gesture. "And when word of that got to *him*, the trees would be down within the hour and I'd be put away."

Good points, all, and valid threats, yet, "Why not *me?* You could have come to me, or Thia—even Murphy, if you didn't trust us to—"

"Because of Kendra." Alma's brown eyes were mournful. "I had seen her and him together, out on the town like a couple. She was connected to all of you. I couldn't risk it."

"She wouldn't have betrayed you. She *wouldn't* have."

"No, but he might have picked up on something from her, if I'd told her what he was doing to me." A tear tracked down the rich umber of her cheek. "I'm sorry I didn't come to you.

More sorry than you'll ever know, if it would have prevented all of this."

"He had her *killed,* Alma. If we had known not to trust him, if we'd known what he truly was and how he was pressuring you, Kendra would not have been at Founders Hall that day. She might still be alive."

"Yes." Alma blotted her tears with a cloth taken from inside her robe's sleeve. "And I will carry that with me forever. But you must understand, the Great Trees are the heart and soul of Granite Springs. They must come before all. I couldn't—I *can't*—do anything that might jeopardize their existence."

"Alma," said her ancillary. "You should not have been bearing this burden alone. It is not our way."

"Forgive me." She wiped a tear. "I did not want anyone to come to harm."

As much as Abby could empathize, her fury remained. To take on a crisis single-handedly, to want to keep others safe— these were noble intentions, weren't they? Self-sacrificial. Yet the result in this case went to selfishness.

The danger had been present, regardless, and they had been unaware. Alma left them open to the danger, not safe from it.

"But harm came," Abby said, and did not care that Alma flinched. The truth of it hurt. It would *always* hurt. "Kendra is dead, and you're helping the man responsible. What memory does he want wiped from everyone's minds? Do you have any idea? It's not going to be for their benefit, I can guarantee that. Not like with Zoe."

After the kidnapping, Alma had performed a ritual that had wiped specific memories and planted false ones. It had been done for Zoe's protection. Some of those specifics would have endangered her. She now happily managed a popular cafe up in Portland and was in the process of buying her own home. There would be no such positive outcome here.

"He's not even human," Abby said. "Are you aware of that?

He's a *huldrekall.*" And what was their greatest talent, she realized in a terrifying, clarifying flash: influence. "Oh, Hecate," she exclaimed, bowling over whatever Alma was about to say. "City council. Police chief. Fire. Attorneys, judges. Chamber of Commerce. County clerk. And you're going to help him cover it up. No one will remember what happened. They'll think everything is fine when, in reality, they'll be under his control."

The particulars of the altar items suddenly registered. The malachite tower. The specific herbs and potions. The rosewood-handled athame.

"This is black magic." Abby tapped her index finger on the lid of the wooden chest. Hemlock. "As foul as it gets."

● ○ ●

Founders Hall

"That's a neat trick," Thia said from behind Cormac. If her voice had been a knife, it would have stabbed, hard and sharp.

He hadn't heard her approach. He'd been too intent on the door to the storage unit. Finding the correct one had taken a frustrating amount of time.

"*Muileach,*" he said to the door. He didn't turn. Shame was not something he often felt, and it was paired with another unfamiliar sensation: regret. From the start, he had known he was in the wrong. Known that he would get caught out. He ought to have prepared better for the moment. Now that it had come, the words to deny the undeniable would not.

And he looked like an enemy.

Though it would mean using another precious disc later, he quickly broke the illusion. Still, he could not bring himself to turn around. He spoke to the door. So close, he was. So close to getting what he needed. "*Muileach,* I'm—"

"This is why you're really here, isn't it? Not for Kendra. Not for me. You're here for *you.*"

The back of his neck prickled in warning. Power.

Slowly, he raised his hands—open fingers, palms front—in what he hoped was unnecessary caution before he turned to face her. "Thia, truly, I'm—"

"Don't." Her voice was a slap. And her eyes, he saw now, were luminous, the hazel burning like molten gold.

He kept his hands raised. Not an unnecessary caution at all, unfortunately. He opened his mouth to try again. "Th—"

"Don't." Her pointed finger jabbed toward him. "Don't you fucking dare." Fine, barbed lines of energy skittered over the skin of her hand. She seemed oblivious.

"Thia." He ignored her order, tried to direct her attention with his gaze. The power was making its way to the tip of her pointed finger, dangerously close.

"It's always lies with you. Lies or, at best, half truths and omissions. You didn't come here to help. All of this, all of us— we're cover for whatever it is you really want." Eyes flashing, she took a step forward and thrust her finger at him. Energy crackled, sparking blue between them.

They both startled and sprang apart. He couldn't go far, and bumped against the door.

"What was—oh God." She held out her hand, not in threat this time but in a plea. "What is this? What's it doing?"

The tendrils were coalescing, beginning to form a sphere of *wælfýr* above her fingers. Too small as yet, presumably, to be lethal but he would rather not test that.

"I didn't mean—I don't want it." Her eyes continued to glow but the ferocity was gone from her expression, supplanted by fear. "How do I make it go away?"

In her place, he'd simply take the power back into himself. "How much training have you had in *bæl*craft?" At her blank look, a leaden weight settled in his stomach. "None? None at all?"

"I can rarely light candles or levitate objects without losing control. Why would I risk *this?*" She stepped back, putting more distance between them. "It's growing."

"I can see that."

The sphere was roughly the size of a dunnock's egg, and as such was probably closer to *wanfýr* in terms of potential harm. As power continued to flow, size and strength would continue to increase. In someone who didn't hold much, this would not be such an issue, but in Thia? He didn't know how much she had received from the Stone of Shadows. No one did. And it was not just any power. It was ancient. Unpredictable.

"Please." Thia showed him her other hand, where a second sphere was forming. "Do something, or tell me what to do. Anything."

● ○ ●

When Edith arrived at the Hall's entrance, there was no one in the vestibule beyond. They must have all gone up the staircase. Should she call out? She tried to recall her training exercises, the protocols she had memorized for exams—but that was years ago and there had been little need for them since. She was not that sort of field agent. Her work was to observe and report. She was an analyst, not a participant.

"Christ," Quentin swore, coming up behind her. He was out of breath and sweating despite the cold. He limped past her and into the building. "Gone up, have they?" At the stairs' base, he leaned heavily on his cane. She heard him grumble "of course," and "it figures," before he adjusted his grip on his cane.

She felt a pang of sympathy. "Do you need—"

His head whipped to the left like a hunting dog locking on prey. The point of his fixation appeared to be a closed wooden door. It was painted the same beige as the walls.

She had assumed it was a closet, but by the way his face had so rapidly lost its flush, she had assumed wrong. "What is it?"

He took several seconds to respond. "Something."

Ridiculously vague, but the way it was said gave her a chill unrelated to the winter air she continued to stand in.

Floorboards creaked overhead.

She stepped over the threshold. "We should join the others, I think. Shouldn't we?"

"Go ahead," he said abstractly and went to the closed door. He held his cane up by the shaft and traced patterns in the air.

"It's warded?" She opened her satchel. "I'll take readings so we can—"

"*Aperi.*"

With the click of a lock disengaging, the door eased open a fraction. Quentin stuck the tip of his cane into the gap, used it to open the door wide.

From where Edith stood, the space beyond was a black void.

"Hm," was all he said before going into it.

Going, she realized, down stairs. He planted his cane ahead of him, lower, then took a careful step to join it. He did not take another until he had placed both feet on the same level.

"Stay there, Agent Wilkinson. Or go join the others. That's an order."

Before that, she would have told him she had no intention of going in there. But two things happened with his order: Edith remembered she was supposed to keep an eye on him, and she got extremely annoyed. Her father claimed it was in her nature to be contrary.

She managed to suppress it, mostly, except for the odd time once in a while. Apparently, she was due one of those times.

Quentin was already out of sight, and grumbling again. If she kept quiet, he might not notice her right away. She followed.

The dank chill increased. So did a stench. Musky yet sweet in the way of spoiled dough.

The vestibule's light only illuminated the first several steps. They were of cement, chipped from rough and long-term use. There was no rail. At the top, there was bare wall on either side. The one on the right soon terminated, leaving that side open. Open to what, Edith had no idea. The blackness was absolute.

She continued to hear Quentin, grumbling about "bloody damn stairs" and "nonsense."

The cloying dank continued to intensify. By the time she was down where there was no ambient light whatsoever, the air was so foul that she nearly gagged. Years ago, a rodent had died within a wall at her family's yoga studio. Not even the extreme use of Nag Champa had masked that awful odor, and they'd had to cancel classes for a week. This reminded her of that—minus the incense—multiplied by a factor of ten. By the time she reached the bottom, her eyes were watering and she was holding her scarf over nose and mouth.

Quentin no longer muttered, but she could hear his foot-steps and the metallic tapping of his cane on what sounded like more cement. She took careful steps forward while her eyes struggled. She knew she hadn't gone blind because when she turned and looked up, she could see, in the light from the vestibule, the doorway and those few top steps. But at her level, it was pitch black.

Light flared directly ahead.

She flinched, then blinked—first to help her eyes adapt and then because what she saw was so odd.

A man was on the wall. And there was a lot of blood. *A lot* of blood. The man's blond hair was almost fully red with it. His head had dropped forward, obscuring his face, but what was visible of his skin was red, too. Quentin stood to one side, his cane held aloft. Light emanated from the silver knob.

Behind her scarf, Edith's mouth opened but she had nothing to say. Her mind had blanked; her body had frozen.

The man was not several inches taller than Quentin; it was that his feet did not rest on the floor. He was literally on the wall, held by mounted shackles around his wrists and ankles, and also pinned in place by a multitude of spikes in his torso. The metal glinted in the cane's eerie light.

His clothes were too dark to show color, but they did show wet. There was a pool of blood beneath him. Quentin stood in it. As Edith's stomach lurched, she looked down at her own feet. The light didn't extend that far. "Is he—" Her throat was tight. "Dead?"

There was a pause. "Not quite."

"R-right. Okay." Unwinding her scarf, she forced herself to walk forward. There likely was not much she could do about the bleeding around the spikes, but she could try to staunch the flow from his head. "Here, we can use my scarf to—"

"No." Quentin moved to block her way.

She held out the scarf. "*You* can use this, then, and I'll call an ambulance."

"Not necessary," he said, turning away, went to lean his cane against the wall. With a soft word, the light from it increased.

"You've already called?"

He couldn't have. She would have heard him, and seen the light of his mobile.

"I need you to record this," he told her. "Will you be able to handle that?"

"Record?" Ah, of course. This was a crime scene. "Certainly, but doesn't the—the victim take priority?"

"Indeed." He stood close to the tortured man. "The perpetrator as well."

His hands were ungloved.

"No." Edith rushed forward, grabbed his arm. Beneath the plush, Bond Street layers of his overcoat and suit jacket, his muscles were rigid. She squeezed, pulling until he turned to her. "Don't do this."

His gray eyes were dull. "It's the easiest way."

"Not for you. I-I'll get the others down here and record the scene." Her head felt light. "We'll get him medical help, and he can give evidence against—"

"We have but minutes. You should have a clear shot from there." He indicated a spot to the right. "Stay out of reach, but no further back than there. For the microphone pickup. I'm not sure how much voice will be produced."

"This isn't—"

"I'll record on my mobile, if need be." He tugged against her hold until she let go. "It would be better done by you."

"Quentin."

"Shall I be more clear, Agent Wilkinson? Or do you truly believe continued insubordination will be tolerated?"

"No. Of course not." With shaking hands, she took out her mobile. She was thinking of the risks.

Dammit, she was thinking of *him,* and he was pulling rank? Threatening her future at the Society? A charge of insubordination would mean the end of her research and development privileges. Given Quentin's ties, it could mean her demotion. She went to stand as directed and unlocked her smartphone's home screen. "At least give me a moment to tell the others. You shouldn't—"

"After showing the full view, go in on his face and keep it there. Make sure his lips are in frame at all times, in case they need to be read. You're wrong, you know," he said, suddenly wry. "This is rather easy for me. That's the trouble." He eyed her phone. "Ready?"

To record, almost. For what might lay ahead? Not likely. No amount of training could prepare her for this. She rushed off a two-word text to Thia before going into the camera app and pressing record. "Go ahead."

"Agents Reynolds and Wilkinson," he announced, pitching his voice for the video. "In the basement of Founders Hall, we came upon the subject." A brusque description of the man's condition followed.

Edith did her best to keep her hands steady, but the longer this went on, the more they shook. When Quentin took the man's head between both hands and lifted it for the camera lens, her grip faltered and she lost the framing altogether.

"What is your name," he asked as she got it back, checked the autofocus. "And how did you come to be here?"

The man's face was a ruined horror. Red was all Edith could see at first. A good deal of skin was missing or burned. She couldn't fathom what had happened to the nose. Thankfully, the man's eyelids were shut. She suspected she wouldn't want to see what they might—or might not—cover.

What was left of his lips opened, roughly shaping words in a voice like a rusty hinge. "I was called Kjeld," the man said as fresh blood ran out his mouth. "I left the door unsecured. This was my punishment."

"Your present condition, the torture and wounds—who is responsible?"

"Skati."

"Skati gave the order?"

"Yes."

"Who performed the tasks?"

"Skati."

"Alone?"

"Yes. Others . . . watched."

Edith zoomed in as Quentin altered his grip, bringing his hands forward to bracket the man's face. Blood had smeared across them and the tension in his fingers was notable. She looked up from the camera's display. Quentin's complexion was naturally pale; in the odd light, she couldn't tell if it was alarmingly so.

She couldn't get a good read of his eyes, either. They were glowing blue. That was a positive indicator—or so she hoped, from what the assistant director had advised. Edith was to watch out for loss of saturation, as she had seen earlier in the

Ogham Room. The more intense the power in use, the less color his irises would give off.

"Who were the others?" Quentin demanded. "Names."

"Rekkrs . . . who work here." Seven names were given. The man's voice was losing what slight volume it had.

● ○ ●

If Thia could back further away from her hands, she would. As it was, she could only hold her arms out and beg for help. The power would keep flowing anyway, she supposed, with or without them. It would find some other exit point to feed the expanding *fýr*.

"Please," she begged, hearing the tremors in her voice. She couldn't stop those, either. "What do I do? It's getting worse. I can feel it getting worse." She could feel it in her bones. The Cailleach's power was well and truly on its way to waking.

"I can try to siphon it off," Cormac said. He seemed more thoughtful than alarmed, but she couldn't trust that. He was a masterful liar. "It worked before," he reminded her, which was true. "Although, you weren't calling *wælfýr* at the time."

"I'm not calling it *now*," she protested. "It's doing this on its own. Do you think I want—Oh, God, this is *wælfýr?*" The word had been slow to register. But of course it was. It was blue. "*Wælfýr* is lethal."

When she would have put more distance between them, he lunged forward, grabbed her by the wrists.

Thia had come in contact with an electric fence as a child. She had gotten bored while her parents played a round of golf at a course booked as part of their annual family vacation. She had wandered away from the green and, in her enthusiasm for a horse near enough to pet over a boundary fence, had overlooked the posted warning.

First there had been an immobilizing, full body numbness. Next had come the release, a kind of forceful push—because with such fences, the electrical charge was sent in pulses. Off and on. Off and on.

This contact with Cormac was almost like that.

There was an initial numbness, as if sensation had dropped away. But this current was continuous. There was no forceful push to follow, and after it adjusted to Cormac's intrusion into the circuit, full feeling returned. She almost wished it hadn't. Where his hands encircled them, her wrists began to heat.

The two *wælfýr* spheres flared to the size of racquetballs.

Cormac sucked in a breath, then muttered under it.

"I'm not sure this is working," she said while trying not to panic. "It feels . . . more." As if she were speeding along on a freeway and standing rigidly immobile at the same time. "I should go outside, away from people. Away from as much of everything as possible. What if I explode?"

"You are not going to explode." He sounded annoyed, and Thia looked away from the *wælfýr*, away from their hands. His eyes were glowing. Were hers? With so much else going on she hadn't picked up on the subtle pressure.

"Are you sure?" she challenged. "It feels as if I could." To stay still was impossible. She tugged against his hold.

"Don't," he said through clenched teeth.

That his tension was so obvious only increased her fear.

"I need to *go*." If she had not been so scared, she would be embarrassed by how pitiful she sounded.

He squeezed her wrists to the point of pain. "Focus."

"I am. That's all I'm doing, focusing, and that's making it worse!"

"Focus on something else." Without warning, he closed the distance, using his body to shove her backward, pinning her against the wall.

"What—"

He forced her arms out, splayed, and held them there. His chest pressed hard against hers. *Wælfýr* glowed at the edges of her vision.

"Focus," he ordered, inches away, his eyes a brilliant blue. His mouth covered hers, muffling the sound of her surprise, and then she was kissing him back, lost to color and light and overwhelming sensation.

It was as if a match had been dropped into a pool of kerosene—*whoosh*—and every disparate sensation, every thought coalesced into one all-consuming blaze. Energy and feeling, anger and fear and need. Whether her eyes had closed or if they remained open, she couldn't say. She felt Cormac, the shape and weight of him, pressing against her fully and yet not enough.

Never enough.

His knee went between her legs. She might have made a sound, or maybe he did. Maybe they both did. The angles of their heads changed and his tongue entered her mouth. She met it with her own as his thigh pushed upward in invitation. He released his painful grip on her wrists and she took hold of his shoulders, anchoring herself as she adjusted her hips and wrapped one leg around his. This was what she wanted. Uncomplicated. Instinctive.

The rush of power was glorious, not terrifying. With it she could—

She heard Cormac's voice, a word unknown to her, and then he was gone. There was a roar like a violent, approaching gust of wind followed by a sudden, pulling absence, as if she had lost a tug-of-war she had not known she played. The energy that had been so close to overwhelming her was no longer there.

Off balance and dazed, she would have fallen if not for the wall at her back. Her arms remained lifted, her hands shaped as if they still held onto Cormac's shoulders. She felt stupefied. Vacant. The Cailleach's power seemed to be back under control. The color show in her vision was dissipating. *Wælfýr* no longer hovered at her hands. Instead, the spheres were at

Cormac's hands—

Cormac, who stood on the other side of the corridor. How had he moved so fast? He closed his fingers and the spheres vanished.

"Were those mine?" she asked stupidly.

Turning away, he began to walk toward the main hallway. This short corridor was lined with numbered doors. Storage units.

Thia was too stunned to immediately follow. She had gone from sheer terror to—to *that,* with him. Her heart no longer pounded in panic but it continued to race.

What had happened to the Cailleach's power? There had been so much. All she felt now was a confused sort of buzz along her nerves, like when she sat too long in meditation and her feet started to fall asleep.

Much as she might like to take at least a few minutes to try to get herself together she could not, would not stay here. She caught up with Cormac at the stairs.

"What was that?" she demanded, following him down.

"Distraction."

Feeling a return of her anger, she glared at his back. "Was that all it was?" Had he used her attraction in order to help her regain control of the power, or had he used it against her, for himself? "Did you take the power?"

"Of course." His tone was infuriatingly bland. They reached the bottom of the stairs. The outside door was open. So was the door to the right. "I said as much."

He had, when he had offered to siphon it off.

Thia had understood that, and had accepted it . . . or had been about to, probably, when he had gone ahead and done it.

"Right"—she stayed close on his heels through the interior doorway, down steps—"but did you have to do it that way?"

She concentrated on keeping her balance as it became more and more difficult to see. And, good lord, what a smell.

Cormac's voice came to her out of the black. "It worked, didn't it?"

CHAPTER 25

Two steps down the stairs and Thia couldn't see a thing ahead. Light from the vestibule should penetrate further than this. She should take that as a warning.

Or a metaphor—for staring into her own future. What did she know of anything? She couldn't even control her own self. She took the wand out of her pocket. It hadn't been enough to simply have it with her. If she had been able to grab hold before the energy had begun to gather, would she have been able to regain control? Never had she felt like such a failure— and the real challenge had yet to begin.

Running footsteps on the other set of stairs, above, pulled her attention. She carefully turned to look. Jack and Fiona were coming down from the second floor.

"The offices are locked and warded," Fiona said, catching sight of Thia through the doorway. She came over. "Where's Cormac? We need help to get in. When we passed him on our way in he said he'd join us."

"Yeah, well, you can't really trust him. He went down there." She pressed herself against the wall as Fiona and Jack brushed past.

No hesitation; into the foul-smelling darkness they went.

How were they able to see? Did they, like Cormac, have a version of the Sight? Or were they simply, blindly charging into the unknown?

Thia considered using her Sight but while ignorance in this case was not bliss, she suspected that knowledge would send her running back the way she'd come.

As she descended, she trailed her left hand along the rough wall in case she needed to catch her balance. There was no railing and the space to her right was open. No telling how far the drop to the bottom might be. The smell defied description. She tucked her wand away, lifted her sweater up to hold it over her mouth and nose. The air was thick. Oppressive.

She could just make out the shapes of Fiona and Jack ahead, walking toward a faint, glowing light. Her own feet touched level floor and she hurried to catch up.

"Holy shit," exclaimed Jack, and both he and Fiona stopped short. Past them, illuminated by the strange light from Quentin's cane at the wall, there was—there was a—

Thia's left hand joined her right to double-cover her mouth. Instead of a scream, all that emerged was a stifled squeak.

There was a man on the wall. *Spiked* to the wall. Quentin stood by him and his hands were on the mess that had been made of the face. "Who is Skati here?" Quentin's voice was harsh with strain. "What guise does he use?"

Gagging, Thia looked anywhere else. At Edith, recording. At Cormac, standing at the light's edge. He made eye contact as he lifted his phone to his ear. His mouth moved, speaking too quietly for her to hear.

She could hear the man on the wall, though, much as she would regret it. The eerie, moaning rush—like wind through a leaky window frame—would haunt her.

"Am."

If mummies could talk, Thia thought, they would sound like this.

"Am . . . und . . . sen."

"Neil Amundsen?" Quentin did not sound much better.

Shaking, Thia took one hand away from her mouth to grab onto her wand inside her pocket.

"Yessss."

"—no time to text," came Murphy's voice. Cormac had put his phone on speaker. "He's chatting up the mayor and Chief Nash but he's noticed Abigail with Alma and I need to grab him."

"Fine," Cormac replied. "Bring the chief."

He must have ended the call, because his next remark was to Edith. "Agent Wilkinson, you'll want to stop him now." He nodded toward Quentin.

● ○ ●

Remembrance Drive

"We cannot risk the Great Trees," Alma insisted, her voice rising despite the danger. Amundsen had gone from glancing over to outright staring, and Abby could see him calculating. Soon, she feared, he would realize that his plan was in jeopardy. Murphy had not yet reached Amundsen's group. Minutes earlier, he had been waylaid by Pallister himself, closer to the east altar branch than Amundsen's south.

"We cannot do this." Jeanette snatched the hemlock off the table. "It is *wrong.*"

Alma held out her hand, palm up. Expectantly. "That can be dealt with later. We can reverse it."

"Even if you *can* give everyone back their memories," Abby said, "the real damage would remain. Amundsen would still have control."

There was a disturbance on the other side of the altar. It was Murphy, and Abby felt a jolt of dismay. He had broken away from Pallister's conversation and was cutting a bold, intent path toward Amundsen. If he had abandoned discretion, the plan had changed.

Because of her? Despite her best intentions, she had utterly failed at *not* arousing Amundsen's suspicions.

"We have a way to stop this," Abby said hurriedly, dividing her gaze between Alma and Murphy. She needed to text and get over there for transport. "That's why I'm here. You're not in this alone. Not anymore. You don't have to do anything—just don't perform the spell he asked for. Keep this a genuine Imbolc celebration while we—" She broke off when Murphy, nearly at Amundsen's group, locked eyes with her.

"Run," he mouthed as his arm went up. He pitched something at her. Something small.

"What?" Too slow, too confused, she felt it hit her chest. She smashed both hands there, trapping whatever—a set of keys. The Maserati emblem was on the fob.

He had told her to run and thrown her his keys. She looked up from them on her palm, saw him lunge. There was a scuffle around Amundsen, people shifting, blocking her view—and also her way when she began to skirt the altar toward them.

She had nearly made it when Murphy grabbed Amundsen's shoulder and, next to him, Chief Nash's arm. All three men vanished. She stopped, as did anyone who had seen the same. Astonishment and apprehension spread outward through the crowd like ripples from a tossed stone in a pond.

"Oh my," she heard Alma say. "We'll need to do the memory spell after all."

Shouts and jostling at the periphery made Abby realize why Murphy had told her to run. Her hand clenched painfully on the keys. "Damn him." She would kill him. She really would.

Over her shoulder, she told Alma and Jeanette, "I've got to go." She didn't wait for a response. Amundsen's people were forcing their way through to where he had been.

Hopefully no one connected her with his vanishing, but it was only a matter of minutes, maybe seconds, until that was connected to Murphy, and soon after to her by association.

Going wide, she wove her way outward, then laterally.

It was impossible not to bump into people. She kept her expression neutral, but her whole body was tense with a mix of rage and fear. How dare he? He had *left* her. She assumed he had stuck to the plan as far as where he had gone, which meant Founders Hall, and Abby was miles away.

She did not stop at the coat check. Murphy had the damn claim ticket. There wasn't time to spend on excuses.

"I left something in my car," she said, striding toward the door. Instead of moving aside, the man there moved to block. "My asthma medication," she lied. "I need it. Please let me by. I'll come right back, so—" He froze.

Where hostility had been, there was only disinterest—and Alma's voice carrying from some way behind Abby: "It won't hold for long."

"Thank you," she called back, darting past the motionless man and out the door.

Despite the patio heater, the air was freezing and the shock temporarily robbed her of breath. The two men outside were statue-still. What kind of spell had Alma used? And did Abby have time to get her coat? No, better not try.

She set off at a jog—the best she could do in her shoes and icy conditions. She was halfway down the driveway when the first motorcycle fired up. The sound came from behind the house. A second and third followed soon after.

"*Miri mora!*"

Abby looked toward the familiar voice, ahead. The Citizens Brigade had stretched themselves into a single line along the road's opposite side.

Some had stuck their signs into the ground so that, standing behind them, they could shine flashlights down to illuminate. Others continued to hold theirs up, having fitted them with ribbon lights.

Abby caught sight of Madame Demetka as she handed her placard off and began to hurry across. "What is happening? Is crisis?"

Abby held her hands out, flapped what she hoped was a *stay there* gesture. She had no intention of stopping. She couldn't. More and more motorcycles were revving. There were shouts as well, the Rekkrs psyching themselves up.

"He left me behind," she shouted, as if that was explanation enough. "I have to go."

Madame Demetka's cloak, made up of enough material for a parachute, billowed as she came to a stop, waiting, in the road. In this part of the valley, sundown often brought strong wind from the mountains to the north. The Citizens Brigade stood silent and attentive. How much had they been told?

Abby should have thought about that earlier. Reaching the drive's end, she swept one arm out, pointed behind herself. "Hold them back . . . if you can."

Her breath was choppy. She had been doing cardio, yes, but there was enough adrenaline coursing through her to launch her into space.

"But don't risk yourselves," she stressed as she turned onto the road. She was leaving them, like Murphy had left her. "Be careful!"

The cold air burned in her throat and chest as she increased speed down the slope to where the valet had put Murphy's car. She cursed that young man along with her choice of shoe, and then returned to imagining how it would feel to throttle Murphy—if she didn't slip and crack her skull. The road had become too steep and too slick; she either had to slow back down or go onto the unpaved shoulder where she could trip instead and end up in the ditch she knew was there but was having trouble seeing. The moon was not out yet.

Her phone was in her evening bag, bouncing against her hip. She was fumbling one-handed with the latch when she heard raised voices—unison chants overlaid with angry bellows as motorcycles revved and backfired.

She chanced a look. Most of the Brigade was blocking the mayor's driveway but some had formed a circle in the road. She couldn't tell, but she knew those were coven members.

Her hand closed on her phone but she no longer needed it. She was almost at the car. She let go and, with her other hand, pressed the button on the key fob to disengage the locks. The rear lights flashed and the internal ones came on.

More backfires—or were those gunshots?

She wrenched open the driver's side door, flung herself into the seat. She got the key into the ignition on the third try. She was shaking.

The engine fired immediately, a powerful rumble that at any other time would have thrilled her. She had never admitted how much she had wanted to get her hands on this car. But not like this. *Hecate,* not like this.

The insulation was so good, she couldn't hear anything from back at the house. If there had been more shots, she would have heard those, wouldn't she? She prayed that the ones she *had* heard had gone into the air.

She could not dwell on that. Could not go back. Could not help. Lights—motorcycle lights—danced in the rear and side mirrors. She was out of time.

The headlight control was not on the steering wheel.

"What kind of—" There was an array of recognizable icons on the central screen in the dash.

She poked the obvious one. The headlights came on, illuminating roadway and parked cars alike. A beacon. She released the hand brake, shifted into drive, and stomped on the gas.

Declan's Maserati leapt forward, straight for the back of the pickup parked close ahead. She wrenched the wheel, clipped the bumper and, with a crunch and the crash of glass, jounced onto the road. The rightmost headlight was out.

She worked the steering wheel madly, going from over-steer to over-correction and nearly taking off the side mirror of a car further down the parked line.

"Shit, shit, shit," was a whispered mantra until she eased off the gas, felt the car settle. Her Mini Cooper was classed as a sports car but no, *this* was a sports car.

And she was a good driver, she reminded herself. A damn good driver when she wasn't panicking.

She eased more weight onto the gas. And then more.

Murphy's pride and joy hugged the deep curves as if they were mere suggestions.

If she could see better, she could push it to go even faster, but minus that headlight, she would have to wait until the road was better illuminated.

Granite Springs felt terribly distant, a cluster of minuscule, sparkling dots in an almost entirely black expanse. Along the road, the lights of homes and other buildings were too few and far between. Distance was impossible to judge.

There weren't any headlights in the mirrors but that would not last long.

She prayed that Madame Demetka and the others had not tried anything foolish.

● ○ ●

Founders Hall

Murphy's people and the other Brigantium agents had not yet arrived when he, the chief of police, and the *huldrekall* materialized in the basement. Five to one, where the one was of unknown strength. Cormac called two spheres to hand—one of *wanfÿr,* one of *wæl*—before Amundsen realized what had happened. His eyes were wide, struggling to adjust.

Murphy released his hold and pulled the police chief some distance away. The latter would have a fine view of the wall's morbid tableau once he, too, had recovered enough to process it. With them, the Ross siblings to either side, Quentin at the wall, and Cormac blocking the way to the stairs, Amundsen was surrounded.

At least Thia was at a safe enough remove. For the moment. She had argued at first, but good sense—and a reminder that she could have combusted the entire building a few minutes prior—had prevailed. Edith, after some threats from Quentin regarding agent status, had left the basement with her.

That had been an exaggeration, the bit about combusting the entire building. But Thia *had* raised a troubling amount of power. What Cormac had been able to take continued to hum, a volatile energy that didn't easily meld with his own. It would take days, he knew, and even then would retain its distinction.

"Don't try it," he warned, playing with the ball of *wælfýr,* when Amundsen's left hand began to shape a spell.

"Or do," said Jack Ross from his place in their impromptu circle. He held a gun.

A foolish move, no matter that he held the weapon expertly enough. This kind of nonsense was why Cormac would always prefer to work alone.

"What's that to one such as I?" Amundsen sneered. "You have no idea what—"

"I dipped the bullets in salt water and angelica," Jack said, displaying a surprising grasp of the lore. But, then, everyone had internet access via smartphones these days. "We know what you are."

"And what you've done," Fiona Ross said, and Cormac felt the tentative control of the situation slip further. She, too, held a gun.

"Stand down!" The police chief tried to join Amundsen but Murphy interrupted his phone call in order to block. "All of you. What in the hell is going—" His breath wheezed out and he stilled, his eyes bugging. He had noticed the wall. "Who," he rasped, "in the everlasting hell is that?"

"He was Kjeld." Quentin held the light of his cane closer to the remains. "We have his last words on video. That's why you're here, I believe. Apologies for the rushed nature. This was, as you may imagine, rather unexpected."

"Yes, well. I'll have to call this in."

"We thought you might," Quentin said amiably, "so we took the liberty. Officers should be here shortly."

"Everything by the book," Murphy said. "As I'm sure you agree. Such a monstrous act. Indicative of psychopathy, and presenting an obvious threat to the public."

The chief was slow to agree, likely trying to scheme his way out of a bad situation. He settled on nervous deference—to Amundsen. "I-I'll need to take you into custody, sir. While I review the video and . . . get this straightened out."

"Of course, Chief." Amundsen smiled like someone facing a mild inconvenience. "I understand perfectly."

So did everyone. Whether the chief gave it willingly or out of prior compulsion, his allegiance was clear.

Cormac contemplated the *wælfýr* at hand. The target was a *huldrekall,* but if struck in the right location the blow should be lethal. It would be the work of a moment.

But then he would be the one on the hook for homicide.

"I'm sure we can all be civilized about this," the chief said, watching him. Then he expanded his interest to include the Ross siblings and their firearms. "Let's put those things away. Now."

Because the *wanfýr* would have little effect, anyway, Cormac banked it. The *wælfýr,* he kept ready, and shrugged when the chief glared. The Rosses hadn't put their weapons away, either.

Sounds of a stampede heralded numerous arrivals. A voice called from the top of the stairs, "Do you need us down there, boss?"

"Not as of yet," Murphy answered. "See about setting up

a perimeter. We're expecting police and some less welcome arrivals in search of their *skati*."

● ○ ●

Trying to keep out of everyone's way on the dirty, linoleum stairs, Thia sat as squished up against the outer wall as possible. Edith had gone with the other Brigantium agents to the second floor as soon as they'd arrived. She had obviously been upset at being ordered out of the basement, and much as Thia might have appreciated her company, she needed calm more.

Unfortunately, she wasn't getting much of that here, either, while Murphy's people—some familiar, some not—rushed up and down the stairs in their haste to . . . She wasn't sure what. Secure the building? Gather evidence?

She really could not think about that right now. She needed a damn moment. Her brain was running a one-minute mile, her body felt as if it was too, and her emotions were nothing short of a mess.

And of course the Cailleach's power was still present, ready to turn her into a bomb.

She couldn't tell how much Cormac had taken into himself. Did the amount even matter? The power seemed to replenish over time.

"You could've combusted the entire building," she muttered in a mockery of his voice. How dare he?

Unless he was right. Which he probably was. She had been crafting *wælfýr* when she certainly had not wanted to.

Or had she? She had been so angry. Subconsciously, had she wanted that?

She was still so angry.

And she was afraid. Afraid of what might be happening in the basement. Afraid of herself.

Sirens wailed in the distance. No question that an immense law enforcement response was coming. She only had a bit of time in which to settle herself.

Elbows braced on her knees, she pressed her face onto her palms and squeezed her eyes shut.

At least they weren't glowing anymore. Her eyes. Probably. She felt the lids with her fingertips. Could she tell that way?

"I don't even know *that*."

She was useless—No, she was *worse* than useless: She was dangerous. If she got through this, she would talk to Beatrice about going into training with the Brigantium. She couldn't keep—

The deep roar of a car engine, squealing brakes, a slamming car door, and Abby's furious voice: "Where the hell is he? I'm going to kill him, I swear I will!"

Thia sprang to her feet when the outside door opened and Abby, pushing past two members of the Landmark's security team, stormed in.

"Abby," Thia called, hurrying down.

"He *left* me," her friend exclaimed. Her hair was escaping the sophisticated twist it had been styled into for the party. She wore no coat over the siren-red dress she had been given by the Landmark concierge. Her face was a distressed mix of pallor and flush. "He *threw* his *keys* at me and *left* me there."

Thia attempted to steer her to the stairs. They could sit, keep out of the way, and both try to find some calm.

But Abby refused to budge. "Where is he? He *is* here, right?"

"Where is he?" Abby refused to budge. Thia wasn't sure she even knew

"Probably. In the basement with Amundsen. And Quentin. Cormac. Edith went upstairs."

"Probably?"

"That's what we were expecting when they told me to leave. Cormac and Quentin did. For my safety."

"Isn't that just like them," Abby snapped. Rather than giving reassurance, somehow Thia's words had added to her upset. "Like an exclusive club. A men's club."

"Sure, but it was for my own good." And didn't that sound clichéd. Yet it was true. And they hadn't needed her to potentially wreck things. "Fiona is down there," she added. So it wasn't necessarily a patriarchy thing.

"But you don't know for sure that Murphy got here? I saw him vanish with Amundsen and Chief Nash. What if—what if they ended up somewhere else?"

The distant sirens were no longer distant. Colored, flashing light shone through a bank of dirty upper windows.

"I'm sure they made it," Thia said, although she couldn't be. But she didn't want Abby to go charging down there to find out. "There's a body. It's awful. That's why the plan changed. Amundsen killed him, and we can prove it. Quentin got the dying declaration on video, so—Is that the Rekkrs?"

The rumble of their motorcycles, tuned to be antagonistically loud, was unmistakable even with all the sirens.

"Ah, shit," Abby said, and then the shooting started.

"Basement!" Thia pulled her toward it as footsteps pounded overhead. Murphy's people would run toward danger—several were already coming down the stairs—while she would prefer to run *from* it. Except there was danger in the basement too. And the danger she carried within herself.

But to stay here meant gunfire.

"Go, go, go," she repeated, prodding at Abby's back as they hurried to the basement door.

There were more shots and the sound of a crash, metal into metal.

Abby pulled the door open, started down. "Don't push," she snapped as Thia followed her down. "I can't see my feet."

"It's just stairs. You'll be fine." Had the smell gotten worse? It seemed worse. "The left wall is there the whole time. There isn't anything on the right." She looked. The group was some distance down and over, arranged around Amundsen. There was what sounded like a stampede up in the vestibule. "Come on, Abby. Just go."

"I can't. Cormac's right here."

"Oh."

"Thia," he said, and she peered over Abby's shoulder.

She could barely make out the shadowy shape of him, but his eyes—those, she could see unnaturally well. They held a faint glow, reminiscent of moonlight on cobalt glass.

"There's gunfire," he said. As if she didn't know.

"Yes. We're coming down. If that's okay now," she griped. "I thought it would be safer."

"I was coming to check if—"

"What's the holdup?" Murphy asked from a near distance behind Cormac.

"You utter jackass," Abby said. "You *threw* your *keys* at me and *left* me there to—"

"Excuse me," said Cormac, and there was a shuffling on the stairs as he and Abby exchanged places. He began to ease past Thia. "I'll just—" Whatever he read on her face, in her eyes when their gazes met, shut him up.

She wondered what that might have been. She couldn't tell, anymore, what her feelings for him were.

"You do that," she told him. She didn't care if that made no sense with his unfinished sentence. *Go to hell* would have been a better match for tone, but people outside were shooting. She wanted to hurt him—payback—but she didn't want him *hurt.*

With a flash of what might have been anger, he broke eye contact and finished climbing the stairs.

Out of sight if not out of mind.

"Collins," Murphy said to Abby, moving up several steps to bring himself almost level.

"I don't want to hear it." She slammed a hand flat against his chest as she barged past him. He startled but caught whatever she had pressed on him before it dropped.

A set of keys, Thia saw, before his hand closed around it.

"Thia," he said as he brushed past her.

"Murphy." She moved to catch up with Abby.

● ○ ●

Outside was chaos.

Declan crouched in the alcove, out of sight thanks to his bloody car parked cross-wise before it. He flinched as bullets strafed the side exposed to Founders Way and the lot beyond, where thirty-odd Rekkrs roared around on nineteen motorbikes. Two of the Maserati's side windows exploded—a bullet going in one and out another—and showered him with safety glass pellets.

He shook his head, shook himself, but experience told him he'd not be rid of the damn things so easily.

He might curse Abigail for leaving his car where she had, but it was convenient for what was currently in its lockbox. And she had returned his keys. He pressed a button on the fob.

With a click barely audible amidst the engines and gunfire and shouts—his people, police, Rekkrs—the boot popped up an inch. Unlocked and unlatched. To access it would put him in the indiscriminate line of fire. He didn't believe any of the Rekkrs had seen him. They were firing at his car—*his car*—simply because it was there.

On the rooftop of the pharmacy across the way, Timmons and Miranda were maintaining a good position. He managed to catch their attention and gesture his intent, then waited while Miranda relayed that through her headset. Police and sheriff's cruisers, lights flashing, doors open, lined the perimeter streets, their officers occupied with taking and returning fire.

He hoped they had been patched into communications, but even if they mistook him for a threat, the chances of anything reaching him from their distances were slim.

When Miranda gave the all-clear, Declan gave the nod and, as they provided cover with flash-bangs and smoke grenades, he scampered to the car boot and flung it up. He made quick work of the safe's security code, grabbed the double shoulder holster with his two Rugers, three loaded clips—and because his temper was up—his battle axe.

He didn't anticipate anyone getting close enough for hand-to-hand, but he'd relish the opportunity.

Two weeks. He grabbed a tactical headset before slamming the boot shut. Only two bleeding weeks since he'd had the Maserati back from the shop. Moving at speed, he returned to crouch behind it, set the weaponry down, then put on the sleek little headset.

Thanks to the shenanigans at the solstice parade, he'd had to replace the windscreen, fenders, hood—

He slipped out of his dinner jacket in order to shrug into the double holster.

—both outside mirrors along with every lamp and indicator. Not to mention the tires. He'd be looking at all that again and then some. Engine shot up. Interior shot up. Fucking hell.

He put his dinner jacket back on and angrily shot the cuffs before picking up the axe. Nothing fancy, this one. Not like the ones his brothers had favored. He was adjusting the lay of its strap across his back when, behind him, the door opened. Lopez, Smitty, and Fran emerged. They crowded in, hunkered down.

"You're out of position," he reprimanded as he picked up his extra clips. One for each besom hip pocket; one for inside.

"The half-*Sidhe* is up there," Lopez said. He'd taken a more exposed spot to Declan's right. "Shame about your car, boss," he added as more bullets thunked into the far-side panels.

Declan felt his teeth grit.

"Incoming," warned a voice through the headset. And, sure enough, a van swerved through the police-cruiser barricade to jump the curb and enter at the car park's southeast corner.

The catering van.

Doors were flung open and an impressive number of men and women, tactical vests over their white catering uniforms, rushed out—firing full automatics and lobbing *wælfýr.*

Not messing around, this lot.

They quickly placed four tripods around the van, then set a perforated metal orb on each.

Some kind of shield, Declan assumed, as the orbs began to emit a milky vapor. In a matter of seconds it coalesced into snaky wisps that wove themselves into a basket-like dome. It flashed a brilliant cadmium red and then faded into a faint, glowing translucence.

"Protection wards?" asked Fran. "Since when can those be object-emitted?"

"Since now," Declan said dryly, more taken aback than he cared to reveal.

"Is it blocking bullets?" Lopez asked, but the answer was self-evident.

"I'm after getting that for my car," Declan remarked, torn between shock and envy. "*Jaysus.*"

"Who the hell are they?" That was from Timmons, via the headset. Within the protective circle, a rocket launcher was being assembled with professional efficiency along with, by the look of things, a spell fire. One of the catering crew held a metal staff. Iron, that would be. "What happened to 'if you cut off the head of the snake,' and all that?"

The body dies, went the rest of the saying—meaning, none of this should be happening. Amundsen had been removed.

"There's more than one snake," Declan said, and tried to identify who might be its head.

With an unholy roar, dense clouds rolled in, obscuring the stars and slivered moon on their way to filling the entire sky.

"Who in the hell *are* these people?" Timmons' exclamation was distorted by static as wind with the force of an Irish gale blasted in from the north.

"Not sure that's theirs," Declan said as the frame for the spell fire toppled, sending the metal basin to the ground. The flaming oil spread, setting nearby "caterers" alight. Activity within the warded dome became frenzied.

The temperature had plummeted twenty degrees Celsius in the past minute, not counting wind chill. None of them—not his people, not the Rekkrs, not the people at the van—were prepared for that. Soon even Declan would feel the effects. The network of charms and spells that for the most part kept him from noticing such things would not be enough.

His gloves were in the pocket of his coat, left at Pallister's coat check. That was a problem. His guns wouldn't be much use if his hands were too cold to function.

Yet, they might not be necessary. As the Rekkrs' struggles to maneuver increased, there was a pronounced decrease in gunfire.

"What's going on, boss?" Miranda asked in his ear. "What do we do?"

Before Declan could answer, the snow came. It was as if a paintbrush, loaded with white, dragged across the canvas of the parking lot, and his vision went from clear to obscured in the blink of a near-frozen eye. He had always admired later Turner paintings for their impressionistic forms and violent, sweeping strokes—but he had never wanted to be in one.

Police cruisers were visible only for the strobing splotches of their red and blue lights. The white catering van, while half as distant, blended almost entirely but for its two front lights. The caterers must have succeeded in dousing the spell fire. Declan could see no hint of that anymore. The snow might have helped them with that—unintentionally, to be sure. This storm was not theirs. They were as vulnerable to it as anyone.

The Rekkrs—stubborn fools to the last—continued to ride around but most of their threat was gone. They were fighting to stay upright in the wind, and as more and more snow blew in, icing the tarmac, they were rapidly losing traction as well. Two narrowly avoided one another as a third, ridden double, went over into a leg-crushing slide.

Declan got his hands to work well enough to retrieve his mobile from his jacket. He used voice commands to place a call to the most likely suspect.

Cormac picked up on the third ring. "Bit busy here."

"Thought you might be." He would have been impressed if he wasn't so annoyed. And cold. "A warning would have been nice. How are my people supposed to do anything while—"

"I didn't exactly expect all this. But you're welcome."

"I'll not be thanking you for this, you absolute—"

In front of him, the Maserati rocked on its tires, a Rekkr's motorbike having slammed into its side. Metal crunched and buckled and any remaining glass shattered.

CHAPTER 26

Founders Hall
Granite Springs, Oregon
Imbolc

After he disconnected the call, Cormac assured himself that it had been right to call the storm. He tucked his mobile back into his jacket, flipped up his collar. It *was* right; it had worked too well, that's all. He'd been honest when he said he hadn't expected so much. He hadn't. But he didn't have time to reflect on that now. He stuffed his hands into his pockets, hunched his shoulders as he protectively ducked his head. On exposed skin, the wind-driven snow felt like needles.

From his vantage point at the roof's edge, it was obvious that the car park melée was as good as over. Around the van was chaos, with the wards unable to keep out the elements, and the "caterers" struggling to pack up their equipment and flee. Some *wælfýr* was launched as law enforcement and what must have been some of Murphy's crew attempted to close in, but distance and the fierce wind made those little more than performative. Around them, Rekkrs were attempting a slip-sliding exodus—now or never, as snow and ice accumulation would soon force them all off their bikes. Several already had been and were trying to flag down their compatriots.

Police vehicles around the car park's perimeter had begun to move. No doubt the intention was pursuit, but traction (lack thereof) was an issue. Aside from that, really, this was a brilliant result—but Cormac had to work fast. Once everyone realized the state of things, he would lose his advantage.

He turned away and, with a thought, unraveled the warming spell he had put on himself. Shortly, he wouldn't have need of it, and he redirected that energy to strengthening the identical spells he had put around the three sleep-charmed men slumped against the HVAC unit. Murphy's people held him in distrust—not that he blamed them, but it meant he'd had to subdue these three when he began to call down the storm. They should wake soon, and as they were warm enough, no harm done.

It would be another mark against him, though. Along with the storm itself.

He hurried through the access door, shut it firmly behind him. The wind's roar was reduced to a faint hum.

He retraced his earlier route past a glass-fronted section of separate offices and open-plan desks. The Brigantium agents within paid him no notice this time, either. He turned, strode along a corridor of door after door of locked storage units, down a central flight of stairs to another maze of corridors and more units. When he was back at the one he wanted, he closed his eyes, took a steadying breath.

After so much, he was about to have a taste of triumph. Dare he hope for the Achill Bell? Whatever the contents, they were about to be his, well and truly. Years of Idris's orders. Idris's cruelties. At last, here was reward.

When Thia had found him, he had just finished disengaging the security protections. Now, the regular locks presented no trouble.

Inside, he closed and relocked the door. He didn't bother to search for a light switch. His Sight and *wanfýr* would serve. He formed a sphere, kept it floating above his upturned palm as he went further in. The room was largely empty.

Two wooden crates and seven cardboard boxes—the latter the size one might choose for storing books or other small to middling goods. He refused to be disappointed.

Given the challenges ahead, he might consider this a best-case scenario.

He set about placing tracking tags and, with hexing chalk, crafted the transport marks. He would trigger the spells when he was at Thia's car. Good thing she was already furious with him, or he might feel *some* remorse for his planned use of that. Not theft—an uninvited borrowing.

He tucked his supplies back into their slim case, pocketed that, and envisioned the glass unicorn he had bespelled in her kitchen.

A snap of his fingers sent him on his way.

● ○ ●

On the bright side, the basement's nauseating odor probably kept Thia from fear-induced hyperventilation which, in turn, could be helping to keep the Cailleach's powers in check. The careful, measured breaths she took while seated on the third-from-the-bottom stair tread were akin to a stress reduction exercise.

That was about it, though, for bright sides. Oh, and they had not yet been overrun with Rekkrs. That was another.

The deep dark was a third, although it seemed odd to call that a bright side. But what she was able to see, smell, and feel was traumatizing enough. She didn't need to see more.

The muffled sounds of gunfire were less frequent. That was good, right? As was the fact that no one had come rushing inside in a panic. There had been no calls to anyone's phone to tell them to run like hell, or to barricade the doors.

And there she had been thinking there weren't many positives. She'd get a full gratitude journal entry out of this yet.

Abby was over with Kendra's siblings. They'd been deep in conversation for what felt like too long—but uncertainty and stress made Thia a poor judge of time. Elbows resting on her thighs, she gripped the crystal-tipped wand with both hands.

Incredible, now, to think that a stressful situation used to be a drive past the Hollywood Bowl minutes before a concert start, or having to check out dozens of Eclectica's customers before their Festival matinée, or doing her own tax returns as an independent contractor.

She had been trying in vain to blank her mind. Instead, she kept having more thoughts.

She tried again, staring at the wand even as Quentin made a slow approach, his cane tapping. Since its knob was one of the *wanfýr* sources, the area around her brightened as what he moved away from dimmed.

Her wand gleamed; the crystal's facets glinted.

The light went out and, on an audible exhale, he lowered himself to sit beside her. He laid his cane down and carefully stretched out his legs.

"You're not out fighting," she said, still studying her wand. He had given it to her. He had told her it would help.

"No," he said. "In case he should attempt anything."

He clearly referred to Amundsen, currently shackled to the wall some distance from the dead man. The whole basement might be set up in that way.

"Aren't his powers bound?" There had been mention of that. A brief ritual performed.

"Temporary version. Subpar." Quentin shifted, seeming to take weight off his right hip. "Best we could do with what we had, but I've concerns about potency and duration."

She nodded. Maybe if she acted as if any of this made sense, it eventually would. Magic. Violence. Lies.

"What if people are getting killed outside?" she asked. "Was this a huge mistake?"

There was a heavy pause. "No dead. So far."

"You can tell that?" With only the one light source, distant, it was difficult to see him despite his nearness. It reminded her of when they had first met—in an elevator with a broken light, all those weeks ago. London. It felt like so much longer.

"I have an acquaintance with death," he said with a kind of bitter amusement. "Of sorts."

Voices were raised. The discussion between Abby and the Rosses was growing heated. "Tell me why we should not just end him," Jack said. "Here and now."

"Try it," Amundsen called out, sounding cocky for someone whose wrists and ankles were fastened to a wall.

Jack spun, moved toward him before Fiona stepped in. She set both hands against his chest. "It is not our way, brother. Think of Mom and Da."

"That's what you said to keep me from going out there." Jack swept his arm rightward, toward top of the stairs. "You can't use that for everything you don't want me to do."

"I can if it applies."

Quentin levered himself up to stand, "He has information we want."

"Then let's go about getting it," Abby said. Heartbreak and rage strained her voice. She sidestepped Fiona to put herself too close to Amundsen. "You killed my friend. Why?"

"Abby." Thia followed Quentin as he limped over.

Her arms were crossed over her chest. Holding herself in. Or holding herself back. "What could she have possibly—"

"She became a threat," Amundsen said. "Obviously."

"How? A threat to what?"

"Oh, sure, of course I'll tell you," he sneered. At the ends of his outstretched arms, his fingers made repeated air quotes. "I'll tell you all of my *nefarious plans* because *you've got me* and *it's over.*" He laughed. "You may have noticed, I'm not nice. It pleases me to deny you closure of any kind, and whatever you may believe, this is not *over.*"

"Looks like it from where I'm standing," Jack said.

"Does it?" Amundsen's pale eyes narrowed as his voice took on a silky malevolence. "You seem to know *what* I am, but do you know *who?* We will destroy you."

"Then I'll have to make sure you're not around to—"

"*I* don't need you to talk," Quentin said. "I don't even need you alive." Slowly, he lifted his right hand. He was not wearing his gloves. And he had not cleaned his hands from when he'd touched the dead man. Blood was crusted on his skin.

"Wait." Thia reached out, intending to grab his arm. Whatever was meant by his oblique threat, he was in no condition to follow it through.

But before she made contact, footsteps sounded overhead. The stair door opened with a bang. She spun around, ready to be terrified.

Police officers rushed in and down. Flashlights clicked on, beaming this way and that. She moved well out of the way. So did everyone but Quentin.

"All clear," the chief said from above. "Clear of everything but snow, that is. We'll take custody of the city manager now. I've called for the coroner and crime scene techs for the—for the other guy. But with the storm, there's no ETA."

Quentin pulled a ring of long, old-fashioned keys from his coat, handed them to the nearest arriving officer. "We're not done, you and I," he told Amundsen. "Count on it."

Suddenly, the basement was too much. Too much activity, too many people. The body on the wall. Amundsen and the menacing atmosphere. The stench. Her emotions. Thia was at the limit of rage and grief.

As officers prepared to unshackle Amundsen and take him away, she realized she didn't need to stay. All clear, the chief had said. She made eye contact with Abby and then went up the stairs.

"Excuse me, thanks," she said, darting past the chief at the top. She had shove her shoulder into the outside door to get it to budge. When it did, wind whipped it wide, pulling the handle out of her grasp. The cold was a slap in the face and an almost immediate chill against her body. Before the door could get wind-blown back against her, she pushed out into a blizzard that had definitely not been in the forecast.

She was pelted with snow that was more like shards of ice, stinging skin that was already burning with cold as she fought to button her coat.

Visibility through all the white was ten, twenty feet at best. She could make out Murphy and a few others who were with him, their hair and clothing frosted, at the far side of his car. By their gestures, they were deep in discussion. It was impossible to hear over the wind.

She tried to see beyond them, out into the parking lot, but it was no good. Red, blue, and white lights flashed in the far distance; the vehicles they belonged to were no more than blurry shapes.

"This is crazy," she said for her own benefit, and felt like she risked freezing her lips to her teeth. She turned around, prepared to wrestle with the door—and had to step quickly back when it whipped open, crashed against the wall.

Abby burst out, missed running into Thia by inches thanks to quick reflexes and an abrupt stop. "What the—"

Thia pulled her out of the door's path as it swung back to slam closed. "It's crazy out here. And it's too cold." Especially for Abby, in that red party dress and no coat. "Let's go in. I need to check upstairs."

"Sure, in a minute." Abby's hair was already collecting snow. She was watching Murphy—who, Thia noticed, was watching back. Neither of their expressions boded well.

"In one minute. *One.*" She dodged, got the door open. "Be careful."

"Aren't I always?"

Was that a joke? Thia decided it was best not to answer.

Inside, she moved quickly, feeling inexplicably pressed. The danger had passed—for now. Amundsen was in police custody. Whatever had happened outside with the Rekkrs was over. For now, anyway, with a storm like that going on.

She hurried along the narrow second-floor hallway. Closed, numbered door after closed, numbered door.

How could there even be such a storm?

Not only had nothing been predicted, not only was it late in the season, but this elevation rarely got more than a few inches of snow. Up in the mountains, sure, but this far down the foothills? No. The city didn't have a single, proper snow-plow—just pickup trucks with plow attachments and gravel sprayers.

Thia went down an offshoot hallway she had taken earlier. One of its doors stood open. She reached in, flicked on the overhead light.

Vacant.

She stared. There was no reason to go inside.

She hadn't understood why she had been pursuing Cormac until now, when faced with proof of his absence.

First came sorrow. She would have expected anger, picking up where it had been left off—but it didn't come until a few instances later.

Sorrow, then bewilderment, then hurt, and then anger.

And this time, it came to stay.

● ○ ●

Abby was primed for a fight. She was also freezing. The dress she had been given was amazing but there was not much to it. Her coat probably would not have done much for her, either, in these conditions—but it would have been *something*.

Murphy stomped over from his car. He also didn't have his coat. His dinner suit was encrusted with snow. So was his hair.

"Aren't you cold?" she demanded, furious. The goatee that

she should find pretentious instead of sexy was flecked with ice.

"I'm bloody freezing," he bitched, and before she could take another verbal shot he brushed past her, fought the door, and went into the building.

She quickly followed. The door slammed, either his doing or the storm's. The noise dropped considerably. Her temper did not.

Murphy was brushing snow from himself and his clothes. Icy clumps and droplets flew every which way.

"You *left* me there," she accused. His head came up and he paused mid-shake, his hands on his lapels.

"There wasn't time," he said. "Not after you got Alma so worked up. I had to get him out before he went at you." His eyes, dark by nature, went darker still with a fury to match her own. "Did you *see* my car? The state of it?"

She hadn't. Not really. Only the side facing her, which had looked fine aside from all the broken glass. "You're blaming me?"

His brows went up. "Did someone else park it there?"

"Where did you expect me to go, Declan—after you *threw* your *keys* at me? Where the hell else would I have parked to come here with the Rekkrs following?"

"The Landmark would have seen you safe." In anyone else, she would have said he sounded overwrought. He dragged a hand through his hair, making it stand up in wet points. "I didn't expect you to put yourself at risk by coming anywhere *near* here, not knowing what the situation was."

"Oh, right." She flung up her hands. "I should've led a bunch of Rekkrs, armed and ready to do violence on behalf of their vanished leader—I should have led them to a hotel filled with innocent guests while most or maybe all 'security' was here. Yeah, that's what I should have done. Definitely." She went and poked him in the chest. "Maybe you could have shouted that at me, right after you told me to *run*"—poke—"and you *threw*"—poke—"your *keys*"—poke—"at"—poke—"me." Poke.

Poke.

He grabbed her hand in a crushing grip. Wouldn't release it when she tugged.

"Collins." He inclined his head to put his face scant inches from hers. There was fury in his gaze, all right, but something else, besides. Something which had her frowning.

"Abigail." His voice had changed. Softened. She closed her eyes. "I'm sorry for—"

"Don't." Her voice had softened, too. She could smell him, the cologne or aftershave he had put on ahead of the mayor's party. The damp, luxurious wool and silk of his suit. "I want to stay angry. I need to stay angry."

"Then stay," he murmured, his breath warm on her face. It contrasted with the chill coming off him from being so long out in the cold. "Stay angry. I do."

Sudden noises had them immediately springing apart. Abby blinked, disoriented. Murphy used his hand on her shoulder to guide her to the base of the main-floor stairs, away from the parade of law enforcement officers out of the basement.

Neil Amundsen was in the middle of it, his arms cuffed at his back. He glared past her, first, at Murphy. She was second. She glared back, but felt shaken as his gaze continued to hold.

This isn't over, his eyes promised. He didn't believe this was over.

And then he was gone, taken away . . . to jail? For what had been done in the basement, not for Kendra's murder or the death of the young man. Would that change? Would proof be found of more crimes? There would be a trial for this one, at least—or would he be able to use his power and influence to get out of that, to get out of everything?

"This was too easy," Murphy said, and Abby stepped away, out of his protective hold.

She felt shaken to the core, but he seemed impervious.

"And it isn't finished," he said. "At the least, the Rekkrs will try to get him out. And they'll want to punish us for this. All of them will—Rekkrs, 'caterers,' family."

Quentin emerged from the basement stairway. "We win for now. Take it. Deal with the future when it comes."

"Fine for you to say," Murphy grumbled, "when you'll be in London."

"True enough." Quentin looked past, out one of the upper windows. "What's with that storm?"

Abby's evening bag vibrated against her hip, startling her. "Phone," she said by way of explanation, and got it out. She felt a rush of surprised relief at the name on the screen. Was it awful that she had forgotten about Madame Demetka and the Citizens Brigade? And the Retreat, and Alma? She answered. "Are you all right? What's been—"

"All is well." Madame Demetka's accented voice was broken and fuzzed by static. "We are all inside with Mayor and his party. We await the storm's passing. He needs to stop it."

"The Mayor?"

"Ha! You joke but is not the time. No, Cormac, of course. Always with the storms. This one is too much. Effective, we understand from minutes ago call from chief, but too much. We will be here for days unless this stops soon. Tell Cormac, please."

Madame Demetka had to be mistaken. Hadn't she? Cormac had called a storm down on Orkney. But this one was so much bigger.

Abby had been frightened for Thia before, the way she was tangled up with him. She ought to have been *terrified*.

"Okay." Her voice was unsteady. "Of course. I'll tell him."

"Speaker," Murphy griped.

Grimacing, she switched the setting. "The mayor got a call from the chief?" she prompted.

"He did, yes. To inform him of arrest and say all is under control. Here, too, is good. Only party guests and the Retreat remain. And the Mayor invites us to stay if roads close. We'll have a proper Imbolc feast. Is big success, your plan."

"Is it?" Abby wasn't so sure. Murphy was right with his talk of jailbreak attempts and revenge. "Do your Guides confirm that?"

"*Pah,*" Madame Demetka scoffed. "Is complicated."

"Yeah, that tracks. Listen, Madame Demetka, I need to—"

"I am sorry to miss the mission debrief. You call my cell—or set up a Zoom on computer when it is to start."

"I don't—I mean, I'm not sure—"

Quentin, reluctance in his every aspect, spoke up. "To be frank, Madame Demetka, we hadn't planned that far ahead. But you're perfectly correct. And Murphy will set that up."

"I bloody will not."

"Excellent, excellent. Alma is telling me the blessing ritual is ready. We begin now. Ah—she says to tell you it is the real one. I do not understand this, but you must, What is—*aha,* she also says that the memories are all fixed. Of the moments before you left. She saw to that." What she said next was inaudible. Meant for Alma, presumably, then, "Okay, you explain to me all this in debrief. Much to say. Many questions."

"Later," Abby said as pleasantly as she could while Murphy was making hostile sorts of "wrap it up" circles with his hand. Quentin had his eyes closed and was pinching the bridge of his nose.

"Yes, later," Madame Demetka agreed. "Later we will—"

Wincing, Abby hung up on her.

"She is correct, though," Quentin said after a moment of blessed silence. "We need to go over what happened. For the most part," he amended somewhat cryptically. "And discuss next steps."

Abby had hoped that her next steps would be to her bed

for a long, long sleep. She read the time on her phone. Early evening. It was official.

"Happy Imbolc, everybody."

● ○ ●

The handcuffs were standard issue: stainless steel and absent any charms or hexes. Skati could have been out of them in less time than it took to blink. Two uniformed officers, one on either side, led him through the blizzard toward a police car parked to block the Way's ingress on First Street. He could break the officers' one-handed holds, shift forms despite the binding spell and be across the parking lot and away in only slightly more time than with the cuffs. Even with so many potential pursuers, he could get away.

He always did.

He considered what to say in such a moment. What would most intimidate his escort and, with their retelling, instill the most fear in those he would destroy for what they had done. He decided upon silence. Let his posture speak for itself.

Head unbowed and shoulders back despite the fierce wind and the cuff that kept his hands in front and the officers that gripped his upper arms. Let them see his determination, his pride. Let any witnesses wonder and be afraid.

The blowing snow muted the lights of the official vehicles crowding the intersecting streets. There was to have been a fireworks display at the Imbolc feast. He had arranged it to coincide with the finish of the Retreat's memory spell. The more overwhelmed people's senses were, the easier they were to influence, and the less they were able to remember what had come before. Not a necessary component, the fireworks, but an extra layer to his meticulously crafted plan.

Wasted, now. So much time and effort—*years* of work—for nothing. Oh, he would destroy these people, all right. Every single one. With Granite Springs no longer of use, he would raze it to the ground.

As Skati neared the cruiser, the driver's silhouette became visible through the closed windows. An officer moved in from the sidewalk to open the rear door. His two escorts released his arms to guide him inside.

He went easily. The bench seat was not uncomfortable. The door closed with a secure click. One of the men got in the front passenger seat; the other went around the rear to come in from Skati's left and sit beside him. The metal cuffs clinked as Skati calmly interlaced his fingers.

The driver shifted the cruiser into gear. Not until they had turned onto Conker Way, headed west out of town, did the officers drop their guises. Their faces were instantly familiar.

"You have made a hash of things, brother," Agnar said with a dangerous edge. "Yet again."

The cruiser accelerated as it passed beneath an old railroad bridge. Skati's hands clenched.

● ○ ●

The Pass

Outside Granite Springs

As snowflakes pelted the windscreen, Cormac downshifted awkwardly with his right hand and chastised himself for not having taken—borrowed—a vehicle with an automatic transmission. The controls would still be on the wrong side, but at least he would have avoided a shifter and clutch.

But Thia's car had been such a natural part of his plan, with the spare key on a hook in the kitchen. Plus it was a hatchback, able to accommodate what had been in the storage unit along with his own bag from the hotel.

He deftly skirted a spun-out truck—the third such vehicle on the approach to the high mountain pass before the California border. Hazards flashing, it was stopped on the Interstate's shoulder at an angle, jutting into the lanes and facing the wrong way. He sped up. He needed to get over the summit before snow and ice accumulation forced a closure.

He hadn't intended to leave such a mess.

His initial suspicion as to the storm's surprising magnitude was that the Cailleach's powers were unstable. Also, the old goddess had been associated with storms—winter storms in particular. Her powers might work especially well there.

That his abilities had changed was an unsettling concern. And one that he could not address until he was able to make a proper study. They were stronger, obviously, but that wasn't necessarily a good thing. Not when that strength was paired with instability.

He was going to be *persona non grata* throughout the region, if word got out about the storm's origin. He was undoubtedly already that to Thia and her circle of friends.

None of that should matter since a return to Granite Springs was unlikely. He would hire someone to drive the car back. He had said as much in the note left on the kitchen counter.

He was under no illusion that Thia would appreciate either effort. Rationally, there was no call for regret. He had done what he'd needed while making himself useful—*ifrinn,* he had brought what could have been a nasty, prolonged battle to a quick, victorious end.

How many times did he have to prove his good intentions? He was entitled to his own business without explanation or justification.

He had hurt no one, despite Thia's feelings on that. And he had put himself in harm's way for her sake and for people of no interest to him whatsoever. He and the Brigantium had been adversaries for decades. His life at the moment would be made instantly better without Murphy in it. Murphy and their cursed bargain. Yet he had helped them. He had helped them all.

Blowing snow obscured all but the tallest and most reflective signage. It was thanks to his Sight that he was able to see the lane markings.

This was the last time he put himself at risk for anyone else. He was done. Done with expectations and feelings. He had his own business to mind.

Adding more power to the traction charm, he sped past a sign advising of the steep grade ahead. The sooner he left the mountains and the storm behind, the better. The sooner he left Thia behind . . . Well. He would convince himself that was better, too.

After he arranged for the transport of the items in the car and then for the car's return, the transatlantic flight out of San Francisco would give him some time to work on that.

EPILOGUE

Pine Meadow
Near Granite Springs, Oregon
04 February

When the officiant handed the Ross family the brands to set the pyre alight, Thia had worried about how she would react. Such an intense, emotional event overall, and she was afraid she would become overwhelmed and lose her hold on the Cailleach's power. She could not anticipate her reaction to watching a body, even one shrouded beyond recognition, catch fire.

The pyre was now engulfed—and had been for several long minutes. Kendra's form was a vague silhouette within a crackling, dancing blaze of brilliant oranges and reds and yellows. Beautiful, entrancing fire. Elemental, and difficult not to see it as having a life of its own. The more it consumed, the more it wanted. Needed. With fire, there was before and there was after. There was no in between, and certainly no going back.

Smoke rose skyward, blending with the gray of the twilight clouds. Gentle, puffy flakes of snow drifted down to spot the jackets and hats of the mourners with white. What landed on Thia's face melted quickly and mixed with her freely flowing tears. Never had she experienced anything so profound, so sacred.

Here was the visual, physical proof of the end of the human

life known as Kendra Ross. Of a friendship barely begun.

Thia had assumed there would be more time with her and with Lettie, too. More time spent finding the ideal work-life balance thanks to Eclectica and this quaint, lovely town. Even after so much of that had fallen away, she had believed the ground was steadying beneath her feet and she would be able to find her way to a simple, comfortable life here—only to have the ground drop out from under her again.

She had misjudged Cormac when she ought to have known better. No, she *had* known better; she had ignored it.

She had known that he operated solely from a place of self interest. She had allowed herself to believe otherwise—willfully deluded herself—because she wanted him to be other than he was.

She had not known herself to be so driven by feelings and fantasy. But he was *leanan sidhe,* and they excelled at exploiting those.

Who was to blame or in what proportion, though, was not the point. Thia had misjudged. Thia had fooled herself. How many other mistakes had she made?

As the pyre's flames burned bright and fierce in the deepening twilight, she felt some of her own confusion burn away. Whatever hopes and intentions she had held onto from her life before the Stone of Shadows were gone. She truly understood that now, and felt herself letting go of what, for months, had been mere remnants. Illusions. She released them to drift with the smoke into the sky.

● ○ ●

"It's my fault," she told Abby when they emerged from the woods. Most of the cars that had parked along the road were gone. Of those still there, most had engines idling, warming, while their people sat inside or stood nearby to talk. Only the Ross family and the officiant remained in the meadow for the private service that would continue for hours yet, until only ashes were left.

"Kendra's death," Thia specified, in case that had not been clear. She had given this a lot of thought. Too much thought, possibly, but that didn't make it any less true. "It's my fault."

"Nonsense." Abby turned on her with a fierce frown. "It was all Amundsen, afraid that Kendra had gotten too close to his corruption."

"Right, because she was looking into the property records for—"

"For Murphy."

"Sure, because so many owners want to sell due to damage from Cassie's revenge attempt—on *me,* because I killed her brother, helped kill her father, and ruined their scheme with the Stone of Shadows. From the moment I opened that box from Lettie, my decisions led to today. My misjudgments. My mistakes. If not for me, there would've been no damage to Main Street. There would have been no reason for Kendra to be researching Founders Hall and making connections to the Rekkrs and triggering alarms—figurative and literal."

With mittened hands, she swiped at the tears running down her cheeks, patted her coat pockets. She had tissues, some-where. "It's me. This all traces back to me."

"To Lettie, you mean," Abby said pointedly as she held out a travel pack from her own pocket. "She sent you the Stone. You might as well assign blame all the way back to where it started."

Thia removed a mitten so she could pull out a single tissue. "Yeah, well, I'm not happy with her about that, if I'm being completely honest." She blew her nose. "But I didn't have to do what I did, after. I should've given the Stone to Arthur and Beatrice and gone the fuck home."

"Who's to say that wouldn't have been worse?"

"Oh, come on."

"No, I mean it. You're blaming yourself all the way back to

the Stone—when the Brigantium had been unaware of their loyalty problem. What if you had given the Stone to them and Cassie had given it to Idris? What if Cormac had been able to take it from you first and done the same? What if the ritual at Brodgar had been successful?" She took a tissue for herself.

"Hecate knows I loved my friend, and I'll miss her for the rest of my life," Abby continued after blotting her eyes. "And I'll always regret that I hadn't known to do more for her that night in the restaurant. But I didn't know. None of us did, and we thought she was going to go get checked by a healer." She tucked the tissue away. "I can't let myself get eaten up by might have beens, and neither should you, Thia. Yes, things in your life and choices you made set off a chain of events that affected us all—but that's life. Each and every day, each and every one of us makes choices that affect other people. That's the deal."

"Okay. So maybe I'm not responsible for everything," Thia said—while a large part of her remained unconvinced. "But there's no denying that I'm a danger."

"Just because you lost control of your powers—"

"Again."

"—doesn't mean you're a *danger.*"

"Yes it does." She had hoped she wouldn't have to argue a decision that gave her so much anxiety even though she knew it to be right. "And that's not all. I'm a magnet for trouble. I shouldn't have come back here after Brodgar. I should have taken the Brigantium up on their offer."

"Of training? But we've been doing so well with it, you and I and . . . Kendra." Abby's expression fell. "Oh."

"Right."

The reality of that settled around them. Headlights blazed on a Subaru pulling onto the road. The final group had broken up.

"The Brigantium is my best hope for getting control of the

powers," Thia said gently. "And of myself. In London they can protect against whatever threats I might attract. They have safe houses. They have security agents."

"So does Murphy, but obviously I'm not promoting that as an alternative. Damn it. Goddess damn it, Thia. I don't want you to go."

"I don't want to either." She used to take pride in her adaptability and resilience. She wasn't sure she had any left. "But I don't see another way. Not one that won't keep endangering everyone around me."

"It's not forever," Abby said quickly and with an endearing amount of conviction. "And there's Facetime or Zoom, and hell, I didn't do so bad traveling the lines to Orkney. Granted, I had a lot of help, but with a bit more practice I'm sure—"

"Abby, good grief, no," Thia said, aghast. From what she had been told, the physical form was atomized or put into some equally unimaginable state. "Please, don't. Not leylines."

"With an experienced escort I could be in London in a few hours. Anyway, you're a fast learner, Thia, really you are. You'll be back here in no time."

Would she, though? Trying to see her future was like trying to see through Druid Fog. She could barely make out a few steps ahead, and the more she tried, the more disoriented she got.

"Sure," she said, expending a lot of effort toward sounding confident. Toward *being* confident. Fear could be contagious, and Abby had enough to deal with. Better for Thia to pretend she could read the map of her own life than to let her fear of being lost infect her friend too. "I'm sorry for the added burden this will be, with Eclectica. I can do a lot online, and we can hire a new clerk to fill in on site, and—"

Abby laid a hand on Thia's shoulder, gave it a squeeze before letting go. "Eclectica will be fine. It always is. Besides, I ran things before you came, when Lettie would be off on one of her extended trips." She smiled, but it was shaky.

"Okay." Thia used the crumpled tissue to blot a fresh run of tears. "Anyway, I'm not leaving yet. I haven't even mentioned this to anyone from the Brigantium."

Abby nodded, but they both knew that as soon as Thia said anything, the Brigantium would push to get her on a plane. Or would they have her travel the leylines? The knot in her stomach tightened.

Had it been wrong not to train with them from the start? She felt as if she had made a long, wild series of bad decisions, as if her judgment had been off wandering within her own, internalized fog.

Was she at last seeing clearly?

GLOSSARY OF TERMS

A mhuirnín: (Irish) my sweetheart

A rúnsearc: (Irish) my secret love

Ádrúwe: (Old English; imperative) Dry up

Bloighich: (Gaelic) Break into pieces; shatter

Buggane: shape shifter native to the Isle of Man

Cáeptha: (Old Irish) fool

Cailleach: (from Old Irish, *caillech* "veiled one") a
    goddess from Celtic mythology

Claimsech: (Old Irish) bitch

Cruth atharraich: (Gaelic) transform; change appearance;
    shapeshift

Glamour: spell used to disguise/alter appearance

Fjolmenni: (Old Norse) many people; crowd

Fýr: (Old English) magical energy/power in visible form
        Wanfýr: non-lethal; white
        Wælfýr: lethal; blue

Ifrinn: (Gaelic) Hell

Inns Orc: (Old Irish) Orkney Islands

Kite m 'pou kont li: (Haitian Creole) Let me alone

Lethsíd: (Old Irish) half-Sidhe

Mac conlón: (Old Irish) son of canine excrement

Maw!: (Romany) an exclamation

Miri mora: (Romany) my friend

Muileach: (Gaelic) beloved

Rekkr: (Old Norse) warrior

Seidr: (anglicized from Old Norse, *seiðr*) form of Norse magic related to divination and shaping the future

Sidhe: (Old Irish; also *sídhe, sí, síth*) supernatural race of Irish and Scottish mythology

Sláinte: (Gaelic and Irish; drinking toast) Health

Vánagandr: (Old Norse) a monstrous wolf also known as Fenrir, son of Loki

Vitae et requies: (Latin) Vitality and rest

Wafti: (Romany) bad

Wheel of the Year

    Samhain: 31 October - 1 November
    Midwinter: 21 - 22 December
    Imbolc: 31 January - 1 February
    Vernal Equinox: 20 March
    Beltane: 30 April - 1 May
    Midsummer: 20 - 21 June
    Lughnasadh: 31 July - 1 August
    Autumnal Equinox: 22 - 23 September

Abby's Circle Casting

    Bless this circle formed today
    To keep all trouble far away
    While safe within its unseen light
    We do our work for good and right
    As above, so below
    Lady of Silence, please hear these words
    And make it so

Cormac's Disguise Spell

    Exs koutino, kele kom welo.
    Tre moi waito.
    Out of hair, conceal with deceit.
    Through my blood.

Cormac's Spell to Summon Cassandra
Akor kei waito lergo. Nadske kwe fyera.
Turete.
Open this blood path. Bind and bring forward.
Come.

Cormac's Spell in the SUV
Quiesce et accipe hoc donum.
Dormi pacifice usque aurora.
Quiet and accept this gift.
Sleep peacefully until the dawn.

ACKNOWLEDGMENTS

As always, my heartfelt thanks to those who encouraged and supported the making of this book and its predecessors.

This took many forms, from hunting for goofs and plot holes in the final draft to reaching out to say how entertaining the other books were and ask: "Where is the next one and why is it taking so long?" Whether large or seemingly small, all had an influence on the result.

My thanks, too, for those who took a chance on a relatively unknown author and purchased her work. There are a lot of books to choose from, and many demands on your time (and money). Thank you for spending a bit of both on this.

ABOUT THE AUTHOR

R. A. Finley is the author of three published novels (so far); a former 3D-animator of technical gizmos and systems which she can't share due to nondisclosure agreements; an aspiring artist and photographer; a hobbyist knitter; and a graduate of the London Film School, Gnomon School of Visual Effects, and Southern Oregon University (not in that order).

A self-described middling adventurer, terminal eccentric, and gardening enthusiast, she is surprised to (now) reside in the Midwest. She may be found searching for a coffee shop to favorite, familiarizing herself with the local parks, and (sometimes) posting on www.rafinleybooks.com and various social media (as @rafinley).

Expected in 2025

The Achill Bell

The Wheel of the Year: Book 4

For news and updates: www.rafinleybooks.com